D0779311

ACCOLADES FOR
THE ANGEL KNIGHT

"A magnificent romance of medieval Scotland, richly textured with passion, history—and a touch of magic."
—Mary Jo Putney, *NY Times* bestselling author
of *A Distant Magic*

"Susan King is a charmer. She cast spells like a sorcerer—her books always enchant."
—Patricia Gaffney, *NY Times* bestselling author
of *Saving Graces and Mad Dash*

"Susan King, a visual writer extraordinaire, has blended a mystical and historical tale so precise that the reader will be drawn in and won't ever want to leave."
—*Romantic Times Book Club* (4 ½ stars)

"A romance of tremendous beauty and heart. Readers will not be able to put this one down. King's books will stand the test of time."
—*Affaire de Coeur* (5 stars)

MEET BEST-SELLING AUTHOR
SUSAN KING

Susan King is a multi-published, bestselling, award-winning author with, at last count, sixteen historical romances, two novellas, and a mainstream novel to her credit. A former art history lecturer and a mom to three sons, she has a bachelors degree in art and did her postgraduate work in medieval studies. Her keen eye for historical detail and her lyrical writing style have helped create award-winning, national bestselling stories. She has won multiple honors and awards, including a career achievement award from Romantic Times Book Club and two starred reviews from Publishers Weekly. Susan visits Scotland as often as possible for research and inspiration, and lives in Maryland with her family. Her latest releases include To Wed A Highland Bride, Avon 2007, and Lady Macbeth: A Novel, Crown Publishing, 2008.

THE
ANGEL
KNIGHT

Susan King

QuestMark
HISTORICAL
ROMANCE

Questmark Inc.
Published by the QuestMark Book Group
Questmark Inc., 15 Paradise Plaza, #351, Sarasota, FL 34239
www.questmarkinc.com

THE ANGEL KNIGHT

A QuestMark Romance / Published by arrangement with the author.

Copyright © 1996, 2008 by Susan King.

Cover design and interior text design by Jeanie James | Shorebird Media.

Cover photos: © Darren Turner | Fotolia.com

ISBN: 978-0-9798856-5-5

PRINTED IN THE UNITED STATES OF AMERICA.

10 9 8 7 6 5 4 3 2

Dear Reader,

I am delighted to introduce to you my third novel, *THE ANGEL KNIGHT!* Among all the books I have written since, this remains one of my personal favorites.

The novel began when I first read about the iron cages that King Edward I of England ordered for two captive Scottish noblewomen in 1306. The women were held for years with little dignity or comfort. Appalled and fascinated, I began to write.

Just before her capture by the English, Lady Christian MacGillean burns her own Scottish castle to prevent the enemy from taking it, knowing they want the gold hidden in its ruins. But weeks in an iron cage bring her to the brink of death, and she sees a vision of an archangel—but he is a mortal English knight.

Sir Gavin Faulkener objects to the cruel treatment of the beautiful Scottish rebel. Demanding her release, he is given custody of the lady and her castle—but he must find the treasure hidden there. He has secrets of his own—an ancient bloodline gives him a mystical healing power that brought only tragedy before. Yet the ailing Scottish rebel mysteriously recovers in his care.

He finds that the lady's castle is a smoking ruin, inhabited by rebels . . . and the lady herself once again takes up her rebellious cause. Soon old secrets are exposed, love blooms—and the deepest wounds begin to heal.

I sincerely hope you enjoy *THE ANGEL KNIGHT!*

Best regards, Susan

For my father, with love

ACKNOWLEDGMENTS

I owe thanks to: Deborah Barnhart, Jo-Ann Power, and Eileen Charbonneau, wise, humorous, and wonderful friends and writers; Mary and Ed Furgol, Ph.D.s *(non angli sed angeli)*; my sister Paula Longhi for insights beyond the norm; and David for being the basic model for the Angel Knight.

Thanks, too, to Dr. Ted Wells-Green and Dr. Lisa Edinger for diagnosing the heroine and offering sound medical advice, although I opted for a miracle in lieu of antibiotics.

And thanks to Ann Heymann and Sue Richards for beautiful harp music when I really needed it most.

PROLOGUE

SUMMER 1306
GALLOWAY, SCOTLAND

SHE STOOD ON A GREEN HILL AT DAWN and watched her
home burn. Thick charcoal clouds billowed up from the castle
walls to darken the pale sky, and acrid smoke stung her eyes. But
Christian refused to allow tears to form. Glancing down at her
fair-haired daughter, she gently squeezed her hand.

"Màthair," the child said. "Your *clàrsach*—"

"My harp is safe," Christian murmured in Gaelic. "I have hidden her away. As I will hide you, my sweet girl." She tightened her
grip for an instant. "The English shall have nothing of value from
Kinglassie Castle."

She was the widow of an English knight, yet Lady Christian
had been declared a traitor and an outlaw by King Edward of
England, who had dispossessed her of her Scottish lands. As if he
had any claim to the land himself, she thought bitterly. Now her
survival, and her daughter's safety, depended on hiding from the
English soldiers who sought her. She could not stay here.

But her last act as owner had been to set the castle's interior ablaze. Setting the torch to a pile of straw just before dawn
had taken all the courage she possessed. Profound sadness twisted through her now, though she reminded herself that she had
obeyed the orders of her king and cousin, Robert Bruce.

Her daughter glanced up again. "But what will become of the legend of Kinglassie?" she asked.

"The legend is safe from the fire," Christian said. But she closed her eyes briefly to hide her doubt and her fear.

Pushing back her thick, dark braid, Christian laid a hand on her chest, swathed in the blue and purple plaid draped over her gown. She slid her hand beneath the wool to touch the golden pendant that hung on a leather thong around her neck. Her sensitive fingers traced the inlaid garnet, surrounded by swirls of gold wire embedded in a golden disk.

This was all that remained, now, of Kinglassie's legend.

She had been able to save her harp and a few other things. But the fire that raged ferociously through the castle would surely destroy the ancient treasure—not yet discovered—that lay hidden somewhere inside Kinglassie. Buried, turned molten, it would surely disappear forever, spirited away by the flames.

Christian lifted her head to stare at the dark smoke. Her fingers tightened around the golden disk at her throat.

She knew that the burning of Kinglassie was an act of defiance against the hated English, and a necessary measure to protect Scotland. When the English soldiers arrived, there would be no Scottish castle to conquer and hold, no prisoners to take.

But Christian felt more like a traitor to Scotland than a loyal rebel. The fire she had begun would consume more than this stronghold in central Galloway: it would also destroy an ancient legend that foretold hope for Scotland.

Collapsing timbers crashed and roared inside the thick walls, sending up hot, bright sparks. Kinglassie's four towers were great belching chimneys now, blackened shells inside a curtain wall that enclosed only fire and smoke and ruined stone.

Set on a promontory overlooking a loch, the castle backed up to dense forests and the high, wild slopes of Galloway. From those high crests, on a good, clear day, the hills of Ireland across the sea seemed very close. On a bad day, the fires of the English armies sullied the sky like Kinglassie's smoke.

"Christian!" She glanced toward her cousin Thomas Bruce, who tapped one foot impatiently, holding the reins of two restive horses. He looks like a wild, proud prince, she thought, truly the brother of a king. "We must hurry!" he called.

"Aye, Thomas," she said, answering in northern English, the language that her husband had taught her. She sighed and turned away from the dark clouds that spiraled into the early light.

"King Robert's message to you was urgent," Thomas continued. "Now that you, too, are outlawed, my brother wants you to meet him in Strathfillan. You are to travel with his queen and family to safety at Kildrummy Castle. My brother Neil will guard all of you there. But I beg you to hurry."

"Spare me another moment to speak to my daughter," she said.

"Only hurry," her cousin said. "We are all renegades in the heather now, along with our king. The English are looking for us even now. We have little time."

She nodded quickly, frowning. Her life had been thrown into turmoil when Robert Bruce had made his bold move to take the throne of Scotland. He had stabbed his key rival within the sanctified confines of a church and had had himself crowned King of Scots. Following the disastrous battle in June at Methven, where the Scots had been soundly defeated by the English, Robert Bruce had taken to the hills with only a few followers. All of his supporters had been declared outlaws by the English king.

Each event in these past few months had deeply affected Christian's life. As a cousin to the Bruces through the shared blood of her maternal great-grandmother, Christian had offered what help she could: men, arms, some coin. But like a stone dropped into a pool, her decision to help had created rippling waves in her life. Her English husband had died in battle but a month ago, and the considerable fury of the English king had been directed toward her.

And now her home was burning.

Pulling gently on her daughter's hand, she walked toward her friend Moira. Because Thomas Bruce had said that bringing the child along would be far too dangerous, Christian had asked Moira and her husband to keep Michaelmas until she could return. As soon as possible, Christian intended to flee with her daughter into the western Highlands, to Clan MacGillean and her father's people. She hoped that the English presence, the English nightmare, would be less obvious there.

Looking down at her adopted daughter, she smoothed the girl's pale hair, as fine and thin as cream-colored silk. The child tilted up her delicately shaped face, her light blue eyes far more serious than nine years should have allowed.

"Moira and her husband have a fine croft in which to keep you, and their children are your friends," Christian said softly in Gaelic, the language she most often used with her child, though both of them understood the northern English that so many Lowland Scots spoke. "I promise to send for you as soon as I can." The girl nodded, but Christian sensed her fear. "You are safe, *milis*, sweet one," she said. "Believe me."

Wrapping her arms around Michaelmas, she laid her cheek against the pale hair, her own thick dark braid sliding down in deep contrast.

"Christian," Thomas called, nearly pleading.

"Mother," Michaelmas said. "Thomas Bruce looks very angry now, as if he will ride without you."

"The five Bruce brothers are known for bravery and handsomeness and cleverness," she replied, "but not for patience. Shall we try him further?" The girl's sweet giggle made Christian smile.

She pulled the pendant and its thong over her head and handed it to Michaelmas. The ancient golden disk, no larger than the child's palm, was decorated with golden wire twisted in a graceful interlace design, surrounding a center garnet. Michaelmas touched the pendant delicately and looked up.

"Why do you give this to me?" she whispered in awe.

"I trust you to keep it safe," Christian said. "The women of my mother's family have always been the keepers of the legend. This piece is all that we have left of the treasure that is said to lie at the heart of Kinglassie." She slipped it over her daughter's head. "Wear it and protect it. The English already know that Kinglassie holds some secret important to the Scottish throne. They must never find this, or they will have a fever to tear even these ruins apart until they find our gold."

"But I do not have your mother's blood in me, to be the hereditary keeper of such a thing," Michaelmas said. "Moira says I am a child of the fairy folk, a changeling."

"Hush. You are no changeling, but an orphan," Christian said. She sighed, touching the pale head gently. "I wish that I knew who your mother was. But I am certain that she must have been a beautiful lady, for you are a lovely child. And you were born on Saint Michael's feast day, so your name brings you the protection of the angels. Remember that always."

"I hope the angels will be with you, too, *Màthair,* when you leave here," Michaelmas said.

"Christian, hurry!" Thomas called. "Do you want to see the English lances coming over those hills?"

Christian tucked the pendant inside the neck of her daughter's gown. "Keep all our secrets safe until I send for you, *milis,*" she whispered, hugging her again. Then they walked toward Moira.

Embracing her tall friend, Christian thanked Moira for her kindness and turned away. The tears that she had been willing back now suddenly pooled in her eyes as she ran to join Thomas.

Her cousin boosted her into the saddle of the tall English charger and turned to mount his own horse. Settling into her seat, Christian wiped her hand hastily over her eyes before she picked up the reins, ready to ride.

Thomas smiled at her, his brown eyes twinkling. "Lady Christian MacGillean," he said. "Christian of Kinglassie, who has burned her own castle, kissed her child farewell, and now rides as an outlaw to join a fugitive king." He bowed his head. "I am in awe of your courage—and your beauty, my lady."

Christian laughed reluctantly. "Thomas Bruce, you have a silver tongue and a bold heart, and you are far more beautiful than I. And I dinna feel brave at all." She stared at the dark smoke drifting overhead. "I feel frightened."

Thomas nodded and urged his horse forward. "I know. But when the English leave Scotland at last, we will all gain back some measure of peace in our lives."

"I crave solitude and peace more than you can know," she murmured as she guided her horse alongside his. Soft mist wrapped around the horses' legs. "I was wed for eight years to an English knight, with an English garrison in my castle. Never again," she said vehemently. "Never again do I want to be near the Sasunnach knights who take our castles and land, and murder our people in the name of their king."

"Robert will succeed in defeating King Edward, although he will need far more support from the Scottish people than he has now. But in time, we will have Scotland back."

Christian sighed and nodded. "All that I had was Kinglassie, Thomas. The English allowed me to keep it only because I did homage to King Edward for the land."

"You were very young then," he reminded her.

"Fifteen, and not yet wed, and I knew little what to do. My uncle forced me to sign the oath of fealty for my own protection, and then he pushed me into a marriage with a Sasunnach knight to further keep me safe."

"Was that a disservice? Not all English knights are bad."

"Hah," she answered simply.

"Your husband was called a fair man."

"And I am called his murderer now," she said quietly.

"You had no direct hand in Henry Faulkener's death."

"No direct hand," she said. "Tell that to the English." She glanced back. Still and slight, Michaelmas stood on the hill beside Moira, watching them. Anguish, keen and deep, pulled in Christian's chest. She looked away.

"Your husband gave a home to an orphaned babe," Thomas said. "I heard that he was a good enough man."

"He was—to all but his wife." Snapping the reins suddenly, she urged her horse forward.

As she rode, her nostrils filled with the rank odor of black smoke lingering in the wind. The English who now trampled Scotland so freely had destroyed the life she had known. Her husband, her home, her daughter's future were all gone.

Suddenly she wished she were in the western Highlands, where her father's castle had once overlooked the wild gray sea. When she had been very small, her father's Highland rivals had skirted around his tower in mute fear of the laird, and of his wife, a fierce and beautiful woman from Galloway. But the English had changed that.

They had taken his castle, and killed her father and her mother both. And her brothers had died, years later, fighting the English knights.

And Christian had wed the English knight whose garrison had crowded Kinglassie's towers. Until it had been captured by the English, Kinglassie Castle had always belonged to her mother's people, descendants of Celtic royalty. Upon the great rock that overlooked Loch Kinglassie, a succession of fortresses had been built, each one guardian to the old legend.

But Christian had made Kinglassie into a ruin. She had destroyed the heritage that she had been taught to preserve.

Resisting the urge to look back at the churning tower of smoke behind her, Christian rode on.

SEPTEMBER 1306
THE HIGHLANDS

THE STONE CHAPEL, bathed in autumn sunlight and tucked in a shallow valley, was filled with screams, its stone portal doused in blood. Christian lay hidden behind a stand of nearby trees, shivering and crying, helpless to interfere.

She felt as if she was suspended in a nightmare. While she had watched from behind the trees, Robert's queen, Elizabeth, and their young daughter, Marjorie, along with Bruce's sisters and a young Scottish countess, had been hauled, screaming, out of the chapel by English soldiers. And the Scottish knights who had tried to protect them had been slain, or captured and led away.

During the long weeks since Christian had joined the queen at Kildrummy, she had come to know all of those men and women.

They had been riding north to escape to the Orkneys when they had stopped to pray at this Highland chapel. English soldiers had ambushed the Scottish knights who stood guard outside the chapel. Although the Scots had fought valiantly, they had been far outnumbered.

Now, breathing in hard, tight little gasps, stretched flat on her belly among the bright autumn leaves, Christian watched, and prayed, and hid, weaponless and defenseless. She, too, was one of the women that these Sasunnach knights sought with such ferocity.

Christian had prayed in the chapel earlier, but had gone outside for a brief walk, stiff from long hours on horseback. Returning, she had heard the screams, and had dropped to the ground in horror.

But now the chapel was quiet, surrounded by the blazing golds of the forested hills. At the heart of that peaceful setting lay the still, silent bodies of the Scottish knights whose bright blood mingled with the autumn leaves.

Trembling, she rose to her feet. Determined to tell the loyal Scots who lived nearby that the queen had been seized, she ran through the birchwood.

Her stride was strong and swift, her legs nimble as she leaped over fallen branches and skimmed over leaves. Her breath and pounding feet created the only rhythm she heard until too late. Four horses closed in behind her, their heavy hoofbeats muffled by the dense leaf cover. English soldiers shouted for her to stop, but she ran on.

A thick arm swathed in chain mail reached out but missed her. She darted sideways. The man swore, spurred his horse, and trapped her between his mount and a second charger. Someone grabbed her plaid and wrenched upward; the twisted cloth choked her. She stumbled and fell, then managed to scramble to her feet again, trapped by the plaid.

One of the men dismounted and threw himself on her, slamming her into the ground. The massive weight of his body, clothed in padding and chain mail armor, threatened to crush her. She could not move, could barely breathe, though she bucked and cried out desperately beneath him.

"Let her up." The voice above her head cut like cold steel.

The soldier came off of her, grunting, and she was jerked to her feet. Her head hung forward and her loosened hair slid down in wild dark ropes. Tossing back her head defiantly, she looked up to face a tall knight in chain mail and a red surcoat.

Dhia, she thought; God, not this man. Fear turned heavily in her belly. Of all the English commanders who had met with her husband at Kinglassie, this man, Oliver Hastings, was known for vicious acts exceeded only by Edward Plantagenet himself. The priest of Kinglassie had once told his parish that when King Edward had turned his wrath toward Scotland, the devil had sent Oliver Hastings to carry out the king's word to the letter.

"Lady Christian." Hastings stared at her intently, his dark eyes narrowed, his mouth grim. The neat black beard edging his jaw gave his face a lean precision. "I am not surprised to find you here with Bruce's other women. I have seen Kinglassie Castle. No wonder you run from the English. Were those Bruce's orders? He favors scorching Scottish earth, I hear."

"We will prevent the English however we can from taking our land and our lives," she said, raising her chin haughtily. "King Edward has no cause to invade Scotland. But we have just cause to resist."

"Nicely said. You will soon have a chance to tell the king your pretty speech. But he will see beyond your fair words and fair face, and recognize you for a traitor." He drew off his leather gloves, slapping them against his right palm. His eyes were flat and dark. "King Edward has declared that the women supporters of Robert Bruce are to be treated as outlaws. No mercy need be shown you. Any man may rob, violate, or murder you without reprisal."

Christian's heart thundered in her chest; her breathing came fast and shallow. "No reprisal here on earth, that is," she said between her teeth.

He tipped his head in acknowledgment. "That may be. But you are without protection now, my lady. Know that you will be safe in my care—if I can rely on your compliance."

Her mouth went dry with panic, but she stood silently while

Hastings tapped his gloves against his palm.

"I have seen the damage you did at Kinglassie," he said. " 'Tis not far from Loch Doon Castle, my newest holding. We took Loch Doon from Bruce sympathizers several weeks ago, you know."

"I hadna heard," she said. Loch Doon was but a few miles north of Kinglassie. She drew in her breath, wondering what had become of Michaelmas, yet unable to ask. She did not want Hastings to know that her child had remained near Kinglassie.

"Kinglassie Castle is an empty shell," Hastings said. "Before you set the first torch, I assume you moved whatever was of value. Scots are not as stupid as they might seem, I have learned." He looked at her expectantly.

"What do you want?" she asked.

"Kinglassie holds a treasure that supports the throne of Scotland. King Edward wants that hoard."

Her heart began a furious beat, more in anger than in fear. "My own husband searched and couldna find it," she snapped.

"Then he was a fool. I am not. And I am concerned for your life, my lady. Once the king discovers that you have burned that castle, he will be furious. He will demand that you deliver the gold to him. Remember," he added softly, "you need my protection just now. Tell me where it is hidden."

She raised her chin slightly. "I can only tell you that the treasure of Kinglassie has not been seen for generations."

"I said I am no fool, my lady."

"And I am no liar."

He smiled as he pulled on his gloves. "A rebel who does not lie? A wonder, indeed. That treasure exists somewhere, and you hold the truth to it. King Edward lays claim to whatever relics support the throne of Scotland."

"Robert Bruce has the only true claim to the throne, and thus has the right to Kinglassie's gold."

He sighed. "Very well, lady. Keep your secret for now. But remember that rebellion earns its due." He held out his left hand to her. "Come with me, then."

Christian's breath caught in her throat, pinioned there by a cold, piercing blade of fear. "What will King Edward do?"

Hastings paused, a stiff smile on his lips, his hand outstretched. "My lady," he said. "Have you ever imagined hell?"

CHAPTER ONE

JANUARY 1307
CARLISLE CASTLE, ENGLAND

"A BIRD," GAVIN SAID THOUGHTFULLY. He looked over the edge of the parapet. "A small bird in a cage."

Cold fog drifted through the latticed boards of a timber and iron enclosure, a square cage, which had been attached to the outside wall of the parapet. The mist passed over the form of the woman, wrapped in a purple and blue plaid, who lay huddled on the wooden floor.

She lay still as a statue, reminding Gavin Faulkener of some gruesome portrayal of death or the plague. When her slight form shifted beneath the wool, he saw a tangle of dark hair, long, thin fingers, and a small foot in a worn leather boot. He heard a deep, stifled cough.

"God's very bones. Caging a woman," he said in dismay. Shaking his head, he glanced at his uncle. "What in God's name prompted King Edward to do this? In the eight years that I have been ambassador to the Parisian court, I have never heard of a Christian sovereign who dared to treat a woman in such a manner."

"'Tis similar to a barbaric device I once saw in the Holy Land, thirty years ago," John MacKerras said. "But from the man called the flower o' chivalry, 'tis a muckle savage thing."

Gavin nodded grimly. "The king's hatred of the Scots cuts deep. I can well understand why you, Uncle, as a Scotsman, are horrified by this."

"Aye," John said. " 'Tis part o' the reason I wanted you to meet me up here."

Gavin stretched an arm out to tug on the small door of the cage. Locked. Scanning the unusual structure, he noted that it was barely six feet in length and width, lashed and nailed into place on the outer side of the castle wall. The planked base was nailed to the jutting wooden beams that normally supported hoardings, the timber constructions that protected soldiers during battle. The door had been placed in the opening in the crenellated wall.

The girl coughed again, long and deep, and turned her head. A tangled mass of dark hair slid away from her face. Exhaustion and illness tarnished her pale skin, and shadows purpled her closed eyes.

"Jesu," Gavin muttered. "She is ill. How long has she been exposed like this?"

"Since September," the guard said.

Gavin swore softly. " 'Tis past Yuletide. She looks but a child, to learn such a lesson of English chivalry. What in God's name is her crime?"

John laughed, flat and dry. "Her crime is that she is a cousin to the Bruce, captured wi' his womenfolk in the Highlands. King Edward has declared those Scotswomen rebels and traitors."

"But Edward has read the treatises of proper conduct in war. Noncombatants, especially women, merit protection by simple Christian charity."

"*Ach*, Edward ignores the rules o' chivalric conduct when it suits him. He claims the Scots are rebels under English jurisdiction, and nae a separate sovereign country." John looked at Gavin. "Edward has had similar cages made at Roxburgh and Berwick for Bruce's sister and the young countess of Buchan."

Gavin set his mouth in a grim line. *Berwick*. The very name of the town sent a chill down his spine. Within Berwick's walls, ten years ago, he had witnessed enough savagery to change him from an idealistic young knight to an outspoken traitor in the space of one day. His actions that day had cost him much; too much. He had spent years redeeming his reputation in order to gain back what he had lost.

Now, looking at this Scotswoman, he wondered if he even cared to have the esteem or the generosity of a king who would do such a thing to a woman.

He glanced at his uncle. "We only arrived at Carlisle this morning, and yet you've learned all this, and have been up here most of the day, from what the sentry told me."

"I saw the wee lass like this, and couldna leave, somehow," John said quietly. "I thought you'd want to see her, too, but you were at Lanercost Abbey, in audience wi' the king and that pack o' French bishops we brought here. Truth be told, I couldna bear another moment wi' those mitre-heads complaining like spoiled bairnies all the way from Paris."

Gavin chuckled. "I misdoubt I have had a more tedious journey as ambassador. You were clever to ride away from our traveling party and wait with the king's host here at Carlisle, while we rode on to Lanercost."

"Edward wouldna wish to see a Scot in your entourage, even your own uncle and man at arms. 'Twill be a relief to return to France, where they welcome Scots."

Gavin loosened the leather thongs at his throat and shoved back his chain mail hood. Dark golden hair blew across his eyes, and he shoved that back, too, impatiently. "We will not return for a while yet. I've decided to stay through the winter at least. The king owes me good English land for my services to the crown. I mean to ask payment now."

"Aye, lad, I know you do." John sighed, heavy and deep. "But seeing this lass, some part o' me regrets the years I've spent in English service. I wouldna be part o' this."

"Does your old Scottish soul yearn to fight in support of Robert Bruce?" Gavin asked softly.

John shrugged. "You're half Scots, lad, by my own sister. Can you trust a king who would do this to a lass?"

Gavin sighed as he looked into the cage. The Scottish girl

reached out a thin, fine-boned hand to pull her woolen covering closer. Cold wind stirred her hair. The tips of her fingers were reddened from the chill.

Layers of warm wool and quilted linen beneath his chain mail and surcoat shielded him from the cold. His thick dark blue mantle, lined with fur, whipped around his legs. Suddenly Gavin wanted to tear off his cloak and lay it over the Scottish girl.

"Edward sets her out here like some bit of flesh bait," he said. "Is she a lure for the king of Scots?"

"Robert Bruce is in hiding, a renegade since last spring. Edward cages this lass out of spite. She hasna been formally accused of any crime."

"What more do you know of her?"

"She's widow to an English knight. Her father and brothers are dead, all of them rebels who ran wi' William Wallace and later wi' the Bruce. The lass inherited a castle in Galloway that Edward sorely wanted. Still does, I hear."

"Does she have a name, then, or is the unfortunate marker of cousin to the Bruce enough?"

"Lady Christian MacGillean."

"MacGillean is a clan name. You said her husband was an English knight."

"Many Scotswomen dinna take their husbands' names."

"Ah. And who was this English knight she wed?"
"Henry Faulkener."

Gavin swore. He pushed his fingers roughly through his hair. He swore again. "My father's cousin?"

John looked at him grimly beneath thick gray brows. "Aye. The lass is your cousin's widow."

"Jesu," Gavin said, stunned. "Henry was older than my father. I hardly remember the man. In ten years I have had word from him but twice. When did he die?"

"Last summer, fighting the Scots. He wed this girl several years ago when he took possession of her castle. 'Tis all I've learned of it."

"So that is why you had me meet you up here."

"Aye, that," John said, "and because I think someone should

speak to the king on her behalf."

"Edward will not pardon a Scot easily."

"He would listen to your appeal. You were once one o' his most favored knights."

" 'Twas long ago. I lost that favor, and it has been a sore challenge to win it back. Now he owes me but one promise, land and a castle, which I mean to collect."

"But you've successfully negotiated the marriage of his heir to the wee French princess. You're well in his graces now."

"And I intend to claim what is owed me."

"You're a skilled ambassador, lad. Convince the king—"

"John," Gavin said curtly, "the only matters I plan to negotiate after I claim that land are the sale prices of my own wool and grain at next season's harvest fair."

"Ach," John growled. "He values your diplomatic opinion."

Gavin frowned, gazing through the timber slats of the cage. The drifting fog blurred the coarse woolen bundle of Henry's little widow, then lifted again. He watched as the girl raised up on an elbow, coughed harshly, and sank back down to the rough wooden floor.

"She is your cousin by marriage, lad. Speak to the king."

"She is a little dying bird in a cage," Gavin said softly. "Look at her. She has no time to spare while I intervene on her behalf." He sighed heavily. "But she should be removed to a convent and allowed to die in peace."

"I did hope you'd see that," John said.

FOG DRIFTED BETWEEN THE WOODEN BARS like shapeless ghostly souls. Christian wondered if her own soul would drift out of the cage soon, like a fragile wisp of fog. She drew another slow and heavy breath, feeling the deep drag of the illness in her lungs. Her feet were cold, and she pulled them under her plaid for better warmth.

The English king would never let her leave this place. Only her death would free her from here. The thought made her angry, which stirred the will inside her, and roused her a little. Her daughter waited for her, and as long as Michaelmas needed her, she could not die. Pray God she would not.

Curled on the damp floor of the cage, she rested her head on her folded arms and stifled another cough. The coughs were frequent now, so painful and deep that she had begun to resist them, though she knew that thick, poisonous matter was collecting inside. She had been exceedingly tired of late, too exhausted to fight the cough and the chill and the hunger much longer.

Beyond the door of the cage, she could hear the deep murmur of male voices. Guards were sometimes there, talking among themselves, though by king's order none of them ever directed a word to her. She had grown accustomed to the devastating loneliness of their silence, just as she had become used to the constant chilly touch of the air.

Turning her head, Christian looked at the bold, cruel design of timber struts, dark against the amorphous fog. Sun and rain, cold wind and frost entered her prison freely. The woolen undergown and tunic and the thick plaid she wore were not enough protection from the bitter winter air. The blankets that had been there yesterday had been taken away again, but she was not surprised. She was rarely allowed to keep blankets for long. She shivered and coughed.

The men outside the cage continued speaking softly, although she could not hear the details of their murmured conversation. One had a gruff, older voice, in a lilting Scots English. The other spoke northern English in a deep, mellow voice, as soothing and warm as the lowest strings of her harp.

With an effort, she turned her head. Two men stood by the cage door, watching her intently, clearly discussing her. She frowned. The older man was Scottish—were they both, then? Her heart beat a little more rapidly, fed by hope. Perhaps they were loyal Scotsmen sent by Robert Bruce to ransom her. She raised her head to peer at them through the dark matted curtain of her hair.

And caught her breath in a startled gasp. The younger knight, taller than his gray-haired companion, looked like a warrior saint, shining and glorious. He could even be Saint Michael himself, she thought suddenly, sent down to guard the last moments of the dying. She blinked, wondering if he truly stood there, or if he was a vision or dream of some kind.

His armor shimmered like silver, and his white surcoat was embroidered with a pattern of golden wings. Free of a helmet, his hair touched his wide shoulders and caught a golden light. He gazed at her silently, his expression fierce, yet wholly compassionate.

He seemed made of shining steel and gold and heavenly peace. Surely, she thought, he was no mortal man, but a vision. An archangel sent to comfort her. Fascinated, she tried to raise up on her hands. She wanted him to take her from this place; she knew, somehow, that he thought of it, too.

Then a chilling fear plunged through her. If heaven had sent her a savior—if an archangel truly stood there—then she was indeed dying. She would not see her daughter again.

As she cried out against this, she folded into the soft blackness that seemed to have replaced the floor.

GAVIN FELT AS IF HE HAD BEEN STRUCK to his very soul.

Lady Christian had lifted her head, straggling tendrils of hair hanging loose over her face, and had looked directly at him. Only the space of a breath or two, and her eyes had lowered again. That flash of deep, glorious green was a startling burst of color and life in her shadowed face. Her steady gaze had shown strength and pride and had asked no pity from him.

But her lustrous eyes had held something else, a spark of recognition, a look of adoration that had wrenched his heart into sudden pounding life. And had reached deeper still, as if her fragile soul had touched his own, carefully guarded as it was.

He drew a breath, exhaled, and glanced at his uncle.

"She's fainted, I think," John said. "God save us, lad, she looked at you as if you were saint, standing there. As if you were—" He stopped suddenly. "What was it Queen Eleanor called you, years ago? Aye—the Angel Knight. This lass looked at you as if she believed that. I swear she did."

Gavin cringed at the embarrassing memory of that youthful name. Thank God, he thought, age had creased and hardened the soft angelic looks he had inherited from his beautiful Celtic mother. He had changed much in the years since Queen Eleanor had first called him her Angel Knight. He had triumphed on the tourney fields through skill, and he had charmed the ladies of the court with his looks and his manners. He had enjoyed splendor and favor. But those days had been long ago, before the queen's death, and before Berwick. And before he had wed Jehanne.

He had changed immeasurably in the two years since Jehanne's death. Until then, the adoration of so many had created a hint of arrogance in his character. He was glad to be rid of it, though the price of humility had come high.

After years of having what he pleased from women, he had finally married, expecting a comfortable life with a kind and delicately pretty woman. But he had soon found himself having to watch helplessly as his sweet young wife began to waste away under the relentless, insidious grip of a lung ailment. The experience had been both humbling and devastating for him.

Jehanne had needed his help, just as this Scottish girl did now. But his wife had died. He had been no savior for her, despite what he had wanted to believe of himself at the time.

His soul had grown hard, had retreated into shadow. No one should call him angel now. Least of all this small, dying girl.

No matter what he might attempt diplomatically, the Scotswoman could not ultimately be saved. He knew the signs too well: rapid, shallow, noisy breaths; pale skin and bluish lips; heavy coughing and extreme weakness. There was no doubt that the lung illness had taken a fierce hold over her.

Gavin had a sudden impulse to tear open her cage and carry her away to safety. He might have done just that ten years earlier. Now he knew it for a foolish notion best left to a *roman de chevalerie*. He was wiser now, more cynical, far more guarded than when he had been younger. Lessons learned hard and well.

"King Edward has little mercy where the Scots are concerned. He will not listen to me in this matter," he said, turning away.

John laid a hand on his sleeve. "We canna leave Carlisle without seeing her free first."

"What would you have me do? Steal her away? I can speak to the king, but I have no assurances for you. Or for her."

"The sentry told me that Oliver Hastings brought her here last September," John said as Gavin turned away.

Gavin stopped. "So the king's demon still rides for England," he said bitterly.

"Aye. He acts as Edward's sword arm in Scotland."

"No doubt he relishes every stroke."

"I hear, too, that Hastings visits this girl whenever he is in Carlisle. Withholds her food, orders her blankets removed. The guards say he questions her mercilessly."

Gavin's fingernails bit into his palms. "He has always had a taste for cruelty to women. What does he want from her?"

John shrugged. "The sentry didna ken the issue between them. She willna talk to Hastings, though he has beaten her, they say, and held a blade to her throat."

"Jesu," Gavin growled. "Must you tell me this?"

"Aye, lad," John said quietly. "I must."

Gavin sighed, glancing back toward the girl. Though his heart seemed to twist in his chest, though he wanted to reach through the bars of the cage and grab her up, he turned away abruptly and began to stride along the wall walk. "She will likely die before the king even grants me an interview."

"You'll help her. You're nae that hard," John said as he walked with him.

Gavin laughed flatly. "Eight years in the French court. A man emerges from that jaded, glittering kiln a cynic or a sinner. Never a saint. She is dying, and a Scot, and I doubt the king will even listen."

"You'll ken well what to say when the moment comes."

"As well as I knew what to say when I saw what Edward ordered done at Berwick years ago? I earned myself charges of treason and exile with my remarks there. The king thought too kindly of me at the time to have me hanged." He shook his head wearily. "I am scant hope as that girl's savior. Do not forget, John—how could you—that King Edward hates the Scots with a poisonous fury." He stalked ahead, then saw a sentry nearby. "Bring a coal brazier and blankets to the prisoner," he snapped.

The guard blinked. "My lord—"

"Do it now, man!" Gavin roared. The man nodded and ran along the wall walk.

"Ah. Nae so hardened," John said, as they walked on.

Gavin scowled. "Little enough to do for the girl."

"That, and asking permission o' the king to remove her to a convent, is little enough well done."

"You are a dedicated and stubborn man when you decide to place your loyalty and declare your cause. And think you must be suffering from a lack of a good adventure. These years in France have been exceedingly dull for you."

John grinned. "Well, that may be. The day your father and I rescued that Saracen princess near Acre is a day I havena forgotten. And you may need a fine adventure as well, lad."

Seeing the quick gleam in John's brown eyes, Gavin smiled ruefully, shaking his head. "What is it about this girl that has captured your tough old Scottish heart? Henry Faulkener was no favorite marriage-relative of yours."

John shrugged. "Lady Christian reminds me some o' wee Jehanne, I think. I canna watch another lass wither like that."

Gavin looked away, fisting one had to control the burst of grief and frustration that rolled inside his gut. "If we get her free from here, John, she will only die in your arms for your trouble. I, for one do not want to go through that again."

"I dinna ask that of you," John murmured. "I only ask that you get permission to take her out o' there. Your own mother was Scottish."

"Aye, and my lady mother might have laid hands on her in that strange Celtic way she had and healed this girl. But my mother is dead now, and this Scottish girl has not the rarest hope of a miracle. Edward's cage has determined her fate."

"*Ach,* once they called you the Angel Knight. You were a hero. Where is your compassion now, Gavin?"

Gavin wanted to reply that he still had it, tucked away inside. That wasted bit of womanhood had tugged firmly on his heart. He sighed deeply. " 'Twill take a miracle to convince King Edward."

"You'll do it," John said firmly.

"But I no longer believe in any sort of miracle," Gavin said abruptly, and strode away, leaving John standing in a drift of cold fog.

HE MUST HAVE BEEN A FEVER-DREAM. Christian raised her head, her thoughts clearing, and looked toward the bare wooden bars of the cage door. No one stood there now. No guards, and no angels.

What weak folly, to have seen a shining and powerful angel in the midst of a gray, dank mist. She forced herself to a seated position and leaned back against the bars, coughing harshly. Shivering, she pulled the worn plaid up over her shoulders. The illness had surely begun to affect her mind.

She wondered if the hour neared the time when Dominy would come again. The English servant woman tended to her two or three times each day, bringing soup or bread and wine, and escorting her to the privy in the tower. Christian had come to look forward to those moments in the day, as if they were sunlit beams in black darkness.

Dominy's hands were warm and gentle, giving Christian scraps of comfort, for Dominy would often hug her, or warm her hands with her own plump ones, even feed her when she was too tired to eat. And Dominy had a vein of courage lacking in the guards, for she always spoke to her, in spite of the king's orders.

But Dominy had not yet come, and Christian had already guessed that Oliver Hastings was back at Carlisle again. She knew that because her blankets had been removed and her food that morn had been delivered by a guard who brought bitter wine and stale bread: Hastings's usual orders for her.

She hoped that he would be too busy with the king to visit her this time. She could hardly bear to hear his voice. He spoke in a low, acidic tone, sounding like a brass harpstring buzzing out of tune, about to break.

She did not think that he would hit her again, or press his dagger point to her throat, frightening her and hurting her, as he had done in the first weeks that she had been in the cage. Her sentries would not tolerate Hastings's brutality toward her while they stood nearby. There, she thought, was true irony.

The king's guards would not allow Hastings to abuse her, but they had obeyed King Edward's orders to cage and deprive her, to expose her to cold and wet until she had grown ill. She closed her eyes and leaned her head back, pulling in a few raw breaths.

Hastings wanted Kinglassie's gold, but she could not help him. She had even considered fabricating some tale of its location when Hastings had tempted her with a full pardon; but that day she had been starving, and freezing rain had cut through the bars of her cage. In truth, she did not know where Kinglassie's treasure lay hidden. And now she was certain that it was gone.

Thinking of Kinglassie the way it once had been she settled into a familiar daydream. She pictured herself in its vast great hall, seated at her harp. The fire-basket in the center of the room radiated heat from glowing peat bricks. Her gown was soft and thick, lined with fur. Her belly was full. She would sleep that night in a soft enclosed bed.

As she imagined this, she could almost feel the cool, polished willow wood harp in her hands, could sense the tightly drawn brass wires beneath her fingertips. She imagined the delicate sounds as she touched the strings, and heard the familiar tones, pure and round and true, as she thought through the plucking pattern of a melody.

The memory of the music, all these months, had helped to save her. She had learned to play the wire-strung harp as a child, and knew, with a harper's finely detailed memory, a great many of the Scottish and Irish songs that had been played by generations of Celtic harpers. Those melodies had always brought her joy, or a sense of healing, or a sense of peace.

And she had found those feelings again, even in this brutal place. She often closed her eyes and listened to the music in her mind, listened endlessly, strumming her fingers in familiar patterns. She had hummed the songs, too, but her voice had grown hoarse from coughing, and so she had stopped.

Whenever she listened to her inner music, she did not feel

the keen bite of the cold, or the painful weakness in her lungs. She heard the songs floating on the air, light and lyrical and soothing. She imagined them shining in the darkness like drops of gold and silver, a design made of stars.

She closed her eyes, and moved her fingers in a complicated rhythm, and gave herself up to the music. Soon the bars of her cage disappeared from her mind. Though she imagined herself playing the harp in her home, she tried never to recall the smoldering ruin of Kinglassie Castle as she had last seen it.

Such thoughts surely had the power to kill her.

CHAPTER TWO

"WE SHALL FIND A NEW MISSION for you now that you have returned, Gavin." Edward Plantagenet tipped back his golden goblet to down the contents gustily.

"I misdoubt that any ambassador can convince Robert Bruce to give up his crown to you, sire," Gavin replied wryly.

"He has no rightful crown," Edward growled. "The young craven has turned traitor. I once trusted him as one of my finest knights. Now he calls himself King of Scots. Hah. King Hob, my soldiers call him." He gestured impatiently. "I will see him captured and drawn through the streets of London before he is hanged and quartered, like William Wallace. I will display his head at London Tower and his arms and legs throughout Scotland." He smiled, a feral-toothed, humorless grimace. "I have made a solemn vow to be avenged on Robert Bruce and all of Scotland for this rebellion. I will not rest until 'tis done."

Gavin made no reply. He poured wine into the king's golden goblet and then filled his own silver cup. The red liquid glowed like melted rubies in the generous light of the hearth fire. The roaring blaze made him think of Henry's little widow, in her cold, dank, open cage. He wondered how best to remind the king of his obligation as a merciful sovereign.

He downed his wine quickly. Edward did the same, and clapped the goblet to the table. Gavin had been surprised, at first, to learn that Edward stayed at Lanercost Abbey and held his royal audiences in a small abbey chamber, instead of within the garrisoned castle at Carlisle. But once he had been with the king for a while, Gavin understood why.

Edward was clearly ill. He had suffered for years from bouts of fever acquired in the Holy Land, and now that illness was taking its toll. The king had aged since Gavin had seen him last: his broad shoulders were bowed lower, his graying leonine head had turned a striking white, his skin had become thick and pallid. Even his voice, always commanding despite a lisp, was strained and tired.

The quiet of the abbey would be beneficial for an old, sick man, and the monks were clearly tending to him medically. Gavin saw the bruised cuts from recent bleedings on Edward's long forearm, where his velvet sleeve had fallen back.

Edward rubbed his wide hand over his chest and shifted in his chair, his long legs angled out awkwardly. The X-shaped design of the abbey chairs was unsuited to tall men, Gavin thought, seated in one himself, his own long legs stretched out before him. Edward Longshanks, who towered above most men, was likely quite uncomfortable.

"Have you plans to return to France?" Edward asked.

"Not as yet, sire. My castle at Fontevras runs smoothly with or without me. I thought to stay in England through the winter."

The king nodded. "Fontevras remains yours through the tradition of *curtesie,* I understand."

"Aye, your grace. When I die, 'twill revert back to my wife's family, since Jehanne and I had no children."

"How long has it been since Jehanne died?"

"Two years, sire. She was but nineteen."

"Ah. So young. A sad thing, her long illness. I recall that Eleanor loved little Jehanne dearly. She would have been pleased to know that her niece grew to womanhood and married you. My first queen loved you well, Gavin. She even gave you that name of yours. Angel Knight."

"I was devoted to Queen Eleanor, my liege."

"Aye." Edward frowned into his cup, his jowls deepening. "You were barely eighteen when Eleanor died, though you were already a worthy knight. And I do not forget how you rode by the side of her coffin all the way from Lincoln to London. When I wanted stone crosses erected at each place we stopped for the night, you saw that 'twas done." Edward was silent for a moment. "Sixteen years have passed, and I love her still."

"She was a gracious lady, sire."

"I am forever indebted to you for that journey, in spite of what you did later." Gavin watched the king down another long draught of wine, saw it dribble from the corner of his mouth. "You betrayed me at Berwick, just as Robert Bruce has betrayed me," Edward added in a soft, low growl. Gavin saw that the king was more than halfway toward sodden drunk.

"Sire," he said. "I but spoke my honest mind to you at Berwick."

"Only the fact that you showed such devotion to Queen Eleanor saved you from a hanging then."

"I endured exile and dispossession for my words to you. 'Tis past and paid for."

Edward grinned slyly. "Well, I made you pay at the French court. An unpleasant nest of vipers, eh? I needed a clever and intelligent man there to help arrange truces and marriages. And you have done well."

"I did what I could, sire."

"Aye. And now you have brought the French bishops here to convey the pope's approval for my son's marriage. But so far the bishops only want to discuss the situation with the Scots. The pope has sent several messages along with them. Not all of his letters are to my liking." Edward sighed heavily and glanced at Gavin. "Do you mean to stay in England now?"

"I will stay for a while." He looked meaningfully at the king.

"And where will you live?" When Gavin said nothing, the king grinned. "Men shall never say of me that my memory was lacking. I dispossessed you, and now I owe you lands for your capable services to me since then. I might give your disinherited lands back one day, but first I mean to grant you some other holding within the English realm."

Gavin narrowed his eyes. "The English realm?"

"Scotland," Edward said. "You will take over the castle of Kinglassie in Galloway. Your cousin Henry had a garrison there. Now I grant those lands to you."

Gavin was stunned. "My liege, I—"

"Go there, and help bend those stubborn Scottish rebels in Galloway to English will. I assume you have learned the proper attitude since your youthful outburst at Berwick." Edward slid him a sharp, fast glance. "Perhaps we shall call this return to Scotland a test of your loyalty."

Gavin straightened in the hard curve of the chair. He had not anticipated Scottish lands. And he surely did not crave involvement in the morass of problems between Scotland and England. "I still do not care for your policies in Scotland, sire," he said, distinctly, softly. "I never will."

"Have a care how you speak to your sovereign," Edward warned. "You have been in France too long. They are overly sympathetic to the Scots. Surely you have greater wisdom."

"I have not changed my opinions, sire, in that regard."

"See that you do. You owe your fealty to me. My opinions in this matter are therefore yours." Edward glared at him. "Hold Kinglassie and garrison it. Robert Bruce may well hide in Carrick or Galloway, and Kinglassie sits in the mountains between those lands. I want Bruce found. You are one of the few knights who can match his superb skills with weapons. Hunt him down and bring him to me. Act as my arm in that part of Galloway."

"Sire." Clenching a fist beneath the table, Gavin bowed his head in reluctant acceptance, knowing he had little choice in the matter. Necks, unfortunately, were fragile in nature.

Kinglassie in Galloway had been Henry's holding. How ironic that he should come to this meeting on behalf of his cousin's widow, and end up bestowed with her widow's dower lands.

"Pass this test, Gavin, and I will reward you very well," Edward said, his voice blurred with wine.

Gavin opened his mouth to speak—in protest or question, he was not certain, for he was still astonished—but a loud rap sounded at the door.

"Ah," the king said. "That will be my commander in that part of Galloway. I sent for him to join us, since he is in Carlisle. Let him in."

Frowning, Gavin went to the oak door and pulled it open. A tall knight stood in the corridor, his red surcoat vibrant in the shadows. He stepped quickly past Gavin without a greeting and advanced toward the king, dropping to one knee and bowing his head.

Even after ten years, Gavin easily recognized Oliver Hastings. He had heard that the knight had attained a post as one of Edward's most trusted commanders in Scotland. But then, Hastings had always had a ruthless taste for the Scottish war.

"Hastings. You remember Sir Gavin Faulkener. He's just come from Paris with those bishops sent by the pope," the king said.

"Oliver," Gavin said. He did not hold out his hand when Hastings rose and turned.

Narrowing his dark eyes, Hastings slowly removed his gauntlets. "Faulkener. Much time has passed since we last saw each other. Berwick, was it not?" He turned abruptly away and bent toward the king to murmur something.

Leaning against the wall, Gavin waited while the king and Hastings spoke in low tones. He remembered John's remark about Hastings's mistreatment of the Scottish female prisoner. Gavin wondered what was truly at stake. He knew Hastings well enough to realize that the man would not bother with Henry's little widow unless he wanted something very specific.

Gavin was aware that Hastings had brutalized women in the past; he had witnessed his deeds in Berwick himself. And Gavin had heard a horrifying report of his other actions on behalf of Edward's war against Scotland.

Gavin summoned control, revealing no expression, no clue to the old rage still simmering within him. Doubtless Oliver Hastings had forgotten one Scottish nunnery among the many towns and religious houses sacked in Scotland. But Gavin's mother had been among the women who had died when Hastings's patrol had sacked that convent eight years ago.

He knew that the ultimate blame for that raid rested on King Edward, who had ordered the Scottish nunneries closed. At the time, Gavin had known that Hastings rarely acted on his own. Oliver Hastings had always been a very efficient sword arm, never questioning the order, and never considering the destruction he caused.

Gavin had tried, these past eight years, to accept his mother's death as a tragic casualty of war, a war that he, as one of Edward's knights, was obligated to support. The raid on the convent had happened while he was in France; he had received an official apology from King Edward regarding her death, for his mother had been the Scottish widow of an English baron. The king had prayed, and made brief penance and had appointed Gavin ambassador as reparation. Gavin was told that Hastings had been fined and punished for his brutality.

'Tis in the past, Gavin told himself. Such a loss was pointless to avenge. Naught could be recovered. He sighed heavily and shifted his feet, feeling the tension of long-held bitterness, as well as the keen weariness of his journey. The chain mail that he had donned for his arrival in Carlisle today suddenly hung very heavily on his shoulders.

Folding his arms over his chest, he scowled, turning his thoughts to the king's grant of the obscure Gallovidian castle. For whatever reason, Edward was determined to pull Gavin back into the Scottish dispute. Gavin was sorely tempted to refuse the grant and the order, but he knew Edward would regard that as a treasonous act.

Still, before the night was done, Gavin intended to flirt with treason once more. He relaxed his shoulders against the wall and waited for a moment to speak to the king about releasing the Scotswoman.

"COME WITH ME, my lady." Stirred from a heavy sleep, Christian felt a hand shake her shoulder lightly.

"Dominy," she whispered, and opened her eyes to focus on a young face, round and pleasant, and a pair of deep brown eyes framed by dark braids and a linen head kerchief.

"Aye, my lady," Dominy murmured. "Get up, now, dear."

"Do not speak to the prisoner," a guard snapped.

Uttering a soft groan, Christian turned on the cold, hard floor and tried to sit up, but failed. The timber slats leaked cold air and light, and the cage swayed gently as she fell back down. She drew a raspy breath and tried again to sit, though her head spun and her limbs felt as wobbly as aspen branches.

She was alive; that much was true, but the golden warrior angel who had stood by her cage door had been a dream. She sat up when Dominy slid a supporting arm around her back.

Christian frowned at an unaccustomed sensation: her feet were quite warm. She raised her eyebrows in surprise when she saw that a small iron brazier, filled with glowing coals, had been placed in one corner of the cage.

"Aye," Dominy murmured. "Someone brought ye a brazier. I asked several times to have one put in here for ye, but the captain of the guard always said me nay. Who gave ye this gift, d' ye think? And more blankets? By the saints, mayhap the Scots have sent coin to the king for yer comfort."

"Do not speak to the prisoner," the guard barked out again.

Dominy turned, her hand resting on Christian's shoulder. "And how am I to wake her, Thomas, d' ye suggest?"

"Well, you're not to speak to her."

The servant woman snorted in disdain and turned back to Christian. "Can ye get up, sweet? I've brought broth and fresh bread. Thick with onions, the soup is, and hot."

"Dominy," Thomas said sternly. "The woman is to be tended to in silence, by king's command. I have told you often enough these weeks, but you blabber on each day. 'Tis treason to disobey the king's orders."

"Then arrest me, too, and throw me in with her," Dominy said. "She might get better care then. How can ye stand there each day and watch her grow ill and weak? My husband, bless his departed soul, was a king's guard too, but he would never have let this happen beneath his very nose."

"I only follow king's orders," Thomas grumbled.

"Hmmph. Who ordered the brazier and the blankets?"

"A lord, newly arrived today. I know not who he is."

Christian glanced up in surprise. The image of the warrior angel with the steady gaze and deep blue eyes came into her mind. Not Saint Michael come to take her after all, but a mortal man—a knight who had stood outside her cage a few hours ago. The concern she had seen in his eyes had been real.

"Well, it's a good man who ordered that done, and brave, too, for going against king's orders," Dominy said as she turned to hoist Christian under the arms, helping her to stand.

Grunting with the effort of lifting Christian, she thrust out an ample hip to support her. "Get in here and help me, man," Dominy huffed out. "She's too weak to stand alone. And she's slippery as a buttered eel in this damp plaid, though she must weigh no more just now than my own little son."

Christian tried to straighten her legs, but they felt leaden and not entirely hers to command. Thomas opened the door wider and reached in toward them, grunting as he leaned forward and scraped his heavy mail-clad torso over the stone battlement.

The small door of the cage, hardly bigger than the hatch of a bread oven, opened into the space between two merlon blocks on the crenellated wall. Thomas gestured impatiently. "Bring her here, then, and I'll lift her out."

Dominy dragged Christian toward him, and the guard closed his big hands around Christian's waist. He flopped her over his shoulder and slid backward through the door. Dominy clambered out after them.

"Carry her to the tower. She cannot walk far. And remember she is a lady, and no sack of barley grain!"

Thomas shifted Christian in his arms. She leaned her head on his shoulder and looked up at the wide, beautiful twilight sky as he carried her toward the tower door.

They went down a torchlit staircase, while Dominy followed. When Thomas set Christian down by an interior door, she stood upright, although her legs trembled.

"Wait here, Thomas," Dominy said, and led Christian through the door, along a narrow dark corridor, withdrawing when Christian used the small privy area. A few minutes later, Dominy returned.

"Now we can talk without that man to hear us," Dominy whispered loudly. "Can ye believe I ever thought him handsome? He has a nose like a Paschal loaf beneath that helmet, and a belly like a boar's. Breath like one, too."

Christian laughed, and the soft sound felt good. She leaned against the wall and relished the musty, close air in the corridor, enjoying the warmth and the torchlight, and the solid enclosure of stone walls. She was so heartily tired of wind and mist and cold. Her legs were feeble and uncertain from months of planked boards and open air beneath her feet. These brief moments in the tower, allowed a few times each day, were havens of peace and comfort to her.

"Curse old King Edward," Dominy grumbled. "Will the Scots not ransom ye from here, my lady? I fear for yer health, I truly do, if ye stay in that foul cage longer."

Christian began to answer, but gave in to the insistent cough that burst viciously from her raw throat.

Dominy frowned and rested a hand on Christian's brow. "Yer cough grows worse, and ye feel a bit feverish. The broth may help. I asked the cook to add more onions and garlic to it." She sighed. "By the saints, I wish I could help ye more."

"You have done much for me these weeks." Christian's voice was strained with illness and disuse. The broth would help both her throat and her cough, she thought. She had forgotten what true appetite was, but she would force herself to eat, because now she had a small wellspring of hope inside of her. The golden knight had shown her kindness; she prayed that he was a Scot, sent by her cousin Robert Bruce to ransom her freedom.

"Dominy!" Thomas called. "Bring her out!"

"A moment more! Wretched man," Dominy added beneath her breath. "Wantin' to take ye back there so soon." She put an arm around Christian's waist. "Dear saints, yer but bones and skin now. And ye must be so cold there at night, though that brazier is a blessing from heaven itself. Can I bring ye aught else, then?"

Christian shook her head in refusal. She had asked nothing of the English so far, and would not do so now.

"Nay? Then I'll bring ye an extra bowl of broth this evening,"

Dominy said, and wrapped Christian in a hug.

The embrace was so deeply comforting that tears sprang into Christian's eyes. But for this one friend, she had not been touched or held or loved in so very, very long.

"Then where in God's name has he gone?" The king shouted. "The last word my commanders sent me was that Bruce was in Ireland!" Leaning against the wall, his thoughts wandering, Gavin stood straighter, more attentive now.

"Robert Bruce has surely gone west," Hastings answered. "I think he has been hiding these last few weeks in the western isles. Clan Donald there supports him loyally. I suspect that he will try to cross into Carrick and Galloway—perhaps from the Isle of Arran—at the first chance he gets."

"Now?" Edward barked. "In winter?"

"Aye, sire. The weather in that part of Scotland, near the Irish sea, is not so harsh as here along the border. A crossing and a campaign would be quite possible."

The king nodded. "Bruce's lands in Carrick—which we have rightfully taken—may contain supporters loyal to him. But if you and the rest of my host have done as I ordered, Robert Bruce will find no support wherever he goes."

"Exactly, my liege," Hastings said. "We hold nearly every castle in Galloway and Ayrshire now. And I have just now taken Loch Doon. When Bruce lands, he will be quickly captured."

"Nearly every castle, you say."

"We had Kinglassie, as you know, sire, but—"

"Aye," Edward muttered. "I know. And I have given Kinglassie to Faulkener to hold." Edward beckoned to Gavin.

"Kinglassie? To this man?" Oliver asked in astonishment.

"The castle was held by his cousin," Edward said. "Gavin, I want you to assess the situation at Kinglassie. Then request your men and supplies through Hastings at Loch Doon Castle."

"My liege," Oliver said, "Loch Doon is not far from Loch Kinglassie. I can easily take command of both castles."

Edward turned a flat glare on Oliver. "Do you question my

orders?"

"Sire, that castle is not yet ready to house a garrison."

"Then Faulkener will take the responsibility of preparing it to do so. Then he will join you and the rest of my host in quelling this Scottish rebellion. The more Scottish castles we hold, the better the Scots will remember just who their overlord is." The king stood, pushing back the chair to look down at them from his full and considerable height. His face suffused with deep red to the roots of his hair. "Until my health returns and I am strong enough to ride at the head of an army once again, I must rely on my commanders to deal with the Scots as I would deal with them. You are all my sword arms in Scotland."

"I am always that, your grace," Hastings answered.

"I have sworn upon my own soul that Scotland will be conquered!" The king slammed a heavy hand to the table. "I will not rest until 'tis done. I want you to raise the dragon. Raise the dragon for every patrol, for every skirmish and every battle, until Robert Bruce is defeated, and Scotland falls to our might!"

"Sire," Gavin said, "asking your garrison commanders to raise the banner of death each time they ride out is a declaration of no mercy. There is no political advantage to using the *guerre mortelle* in this war."

"That approach is exactly what is needed here," Hastings said. "The Scots are a rebellious lot and need a fierce hand."

"They will resist more strongly than before," Gavin said.

"Resistance only whets our appetite. Raise the dragon banner when you ride through Scotland," Edward said. "I want it done."

"Aye, my liege," Hastings said. His face was a cold, stony mask. Gavin realized that Hastings, along with so many English nobles and knights, had become a merciless extension of Edward Plantagenet's vengeance, as eager and determined as the king to conquer and destroy the Scots.

And Christian MacGillean was simply a prize in that war. Gavin sighed. This was hardly the best moment to ask the king for leniency regarding the girl. He wanted to attend to it before Edward ended the audience and dismissed them, but he would have to go about it tactfully.

"Sire," Gavin said, "Pope Clement is very concerned about your actions toward the Scots. He has instructed the French bishops to make a private report to him."

Edward tipped a brow. "I know. He sent me a letter on that subject. But he has also directed the bishops to excommunicate Robert Bruce and his supporters, so his holiness is not entirely against me in this. The rites will be performed on the morrow."

Gavin nodded. "The pope wrote me as well, sire, and bid me remind you that he will excommunicate you as well if you do not ease your harsh policies toward the Scots."

"I will not pull back. I leave it to my ambassadors to smooth the way with the Holy Church of Rome."

"Then, sire, as one of those advisers, allow me to suggest a small gesture that may reassure Rome."

"What is that?"

"Sire, you hold Henry Faulkener's Scottish widow prisoner at Carlisle—"

"Aye. She has committed treasonous acts. She did fealty to me for that land years ago, but one day last summer she captured the damned tower from her own husband when he rode out. Henry had to siege his own place just to get back in for his supper! Hah! Killed him, she did," Edward said more soberly. "And so I have placed her where she will serve as an example of how Scotland falls to the English."

Gavin leaned forward to speak in a quieter tone. "Sire, I suggest that you reconsider her situation. The woman is seriously ill. 'Tis one matter to confine a noblewoman to a convent as a political prisoner. 'Tis another matter to allow such a woman to die of mistreatment in a cage, witnessed by the public." He paused. "And by the French bishops."

"Christ's blood. You have a point," Edward muttered.

"A virtuous prince tempers his anger with clemency, sire," Gavin said. "She is dying. Let me remove her to a convent."

"If deaths weighed heavy on my conscience, I would scarce be able to lift my head from my pillow," Edward said. "Still, the bishops are here—" He frowned and scratched his silvery beard thoughtfully.

"One other point, sire," Gavin said. "Remember her name."

"Eh? Christian? Oh." Edward frowned. "The pope will hardly overlook the death of a captive woman called Christian, just after Yuletide, and in one of my castles."

"Exactly, sire," Gavin said.

"Sire," Hastings interrupted. "You proclaimed that these Scotswomen were to be punished in accordance with the crimes of their male relatives. I captured her myself, on your order."

"Oliver," Edward barked out. "Did you get the truth from her regarding that gold, as I asked?"

Gavin frowned. "Gold? What is this about?"

"An old tradition holds that there is treasure hidden in Kinglassie Castle," Edward replied. "Including some object that supports the ceremonial reign of Scottish kings."

"Ah," Gavin said, and suddenly understood why Kinglassie had more than ordinary importance to Edward.

"The girl has refused to say where she has hidden it," Hastings said to the king, ignoring Gavin. "I had food withheld from her for days and did what I could to coerce her myself. If she is indeed near death, I must question her again."

"Find out the damned truth of it," Edward muttered.

"Your grace, I remind you again that Kinglassie is near Loch Doon. Let me act as commander there. I will search the place thoroughly, every stone," Hastings said.

"Faulkener will have that search made," the king said. "Gavin, my chamberlain will draw up a charter of ownership for the castle and its environs. As for the Scots wench—" He frowned. "You are certain she is dying?"

"She is exceedingly ill and weak, sire. A lung disease."

Edward rubbed a hand over his face. "I would hate to have to endure another barrage of letters from Rome, and more penances." He nodded. "Remove her from the cage and bring her to a convent. Tomorrow I will sign the order for her release. She remains a prisoner until she dies. However—" the king paused.

Gavin raised his eyebrows politely, hardly daring to speak.

"I want the truth of that hidden gold before she dies. I have captured the Stone of Scone and the Scottish royal regalia and brought them to London. Whatever else the Scots have hidden away in Kinglassie, 'tis mine by right. Find it."

Gavin frowned. "I will do what I can, sire."

"Do more than that. You may tell her that if the gold is found and sent to me, I will pardon her."

"I told her that myself," Hastings interrupted. "She refused and spat in my face. The woman is a shrew."

"You should have used more force," the king snapped. "Or better yet, charm. Women are susceptible to sweet words."

"She would not tell her own husband," Hastings said.

"Henry was a good soldier, but he had no talent with women. Neither do you," Edward said bluntly. "Unlike Gavin, who has caused countless ladies to do his bidding," Edward slammed the table triumphantly. "By God! Hah!"

"Sire?" Gavin asked apprehensively.

"Gavin, you will win her trust. Charm her and then press her for the truth of that gold. Marry her if you must."

"Sire, she is dying," Gavin said between his teeth.

"Then hurry! You will be a wealthy widower." Edward grinned. "Convince her that she must tell her beloved husband where the gold is kept."

"Sire, I will let the girl know she will die untried and excommunicated if she refuses to speak," Hastings said. "The threat of hell should loosen her tongue."

"She'd die to spite you, I think," the king said. "Gavin will wed her and secure the truth with honey." He grinned.

Listening, Gavin clamped his back teeth together until his jaw ached. Edward was unconcerned that the girl was dying because of his treatment of her, and he did not care that his order would render Gavin a widower again within the week. The king cared only about his war, his bottomless greed for land, power, and gold, and his consuming need to defeat the Scots.

Gavin sensed the truly frightening depth of the king's wild obsession. Edward would twist and destroy any life, English or Scots, to see his desires met in Scotland.

Gavin saw, too, as he watched the king sit down again, heavily, that Edward was thoroughly, soddenly drunk. The validity of the king's promises and orders suddenly became very shaky indeed.

"Gavin." Edward looked at him warily. "You trod perilously close to treason once. Do not betray me again."

"My liege," Gavin bit out, and bowed his head curtly. He shot one piercing look at Hastings that vented only a fraction of his anger, then turned on his heel and left the chamber.

CHAPTER THREE

GAVIN CLIMBED THE COURTYARD STEPS to the para-pet, taking them two at a time. He had not found John MacKerras during a quick search through Carlisle Castle. The hour was well past matins, and his uncle should have been asleep on a pallet in the great hall, where so many others, soldiers and barons alike, had found space to rest within the crowded castle.

Suspecting where his uncle was, Gavin hurried forward. He had been delayed at Lanercost waiting for the king's chamberlain to prepare the necessary documents and explain the location of Kinglassie. Then he had ridden the five miles back to Carlisle in a fury of speed and tumultuous thought.

Reaching the parapet, he strode out across the dark wall walk, which was lit only by a few torches. His quick steps echoed loudly and brought one of the guards forward to stop him. Gavin explained his identity and why he was there, casting surreptitious looks around through the darkness as he spoke.

"We've had no orders to release the prisoner, my lord," the guard said doubtfully. "Comte de Fontevras, you say, my lord? And an ambassador to the French court?"

"Aye, and now Baron of Kinglassie. I bring you the order for Christian MacGillean's release directly from King Edward. Here is the signed document." Gavin displayed a parchment with a dangling seal.

The guard peered at Edward Plantagenet's signature, and nodded. Gavin tucked the charter for Kinglassie away inside the lining of his cloak, relieved that his hunch had been correct: the guard could not read. He could not take that chance again, though; sooner rather than later, he would find a guard who knew his letters. Edward had given him no document of release for Lady Christian, promising it on the morrow. For now, he had only the king's word. Experience told him that was not enough.

He moved quickly around the perimeter of the walk toward the front wall, where the cage was attached. Near it, he saw the shadow of a tall, broad-shouldered man. Glancing behind him, he noted that the closest sentry was a hundred paces away. Swearing beneath his breath, Gavin strode forward.

John turned and placed a hand on the hilt of his broadsword with a curt nod. A steel mace swung at his belt, and the blade of his dirk, grasped in his mailed fist, caught a glint of moonlight. He looked invincible, brutal, and somehow, Gavin thought with an inner groan, delighted.

"You've come to help, then?" John's wide gray mustache twitched, and his brown eyes were lit with an eager gleam.

"Help with what?" Gavin dreaded the answer.

John threw back his shoulders proudly. "I mean to rescue the wee lassie. And this is the verra surcoat I wore when I rescued the Saracen princess years ago, wi' your father." Gavin recognized John's embroidered blue surcoat as one that his uncle had kept folded and unworn among his gear; it barely stretched to cover the width of his shoulders and the breadth of his middle.

"How is it the king's guard even let you onto the wall walk, fully armed and ready for war? You're a Scotsman!"

"Ach, I spoke French to 'em. They think I'm the bodyguard for the king's ambassador to France. Which I am," John added.

"You are fortunate you were not arrested. And you are enjoying this far too much," Gavin muttered. "Surely we must be the most conspicuous pair on the wall walk. What is your plan? Do we flatten the guards and tear open the cage? We could swing down the castle walls on ropes and gallop away to safety, if our horses were waiting below," he added sarcastically.

John frowned, considering that. "At Acre, when I brought the Saracen princess out o' her bower, I killed the harem guard wi' a fast blade to the belly, lifted the princess over my shoulder, and went out the window on a rope to meet your father. But such a plan willna do here."

"You are a full thirty years older, for one thing."

"I was about to twist open the lock when you came," John whispered, unperturbed. "I mean to take her to some abbey."

"Lanercost is closest," Gavin growled. "I hate to ruin your plan, but I have the king's permission to remove her to a convent."

John let out a long breath. "I'm glad to hear that, lad."

"I will wager that. I have no written order as yet. Tomorrow I am to remove her to a convent. But the girl should be gone from Carlisle tonight, before Edward can change his mind."

"So we still make a rescue," John murmured.

"Well, we must be quick and clever." Gavin paused, and sighed. "Edward has granted me the castle of Kinglassie for my trouble. I am to garrison it and join the search for Bruce."

John gaped at him. "Henry's Scottish castle? Has the king finally forgiven you for Berwick, then? He sends you up there as one o' his commanders. But you dinna want this, I think."

Gavin shook his head. " 'Tis one of his tests, John. If I cannot comply, he will have his rope around my neck this time."

"But you dinna have a taste for his Scottish war."

"No taste at all," Gavin said. "I have too much respect for the Scots to take part in this war against them. These years in France have kept me out of this dispute. But I cannot refuse this grant. Edward has a murderous streak of late with regard to refusals. So I will take over the castle. But if Robert Bruce is to be captured, 'twill not be by me," he added low.

John glanced toward the cage, its latticed top visible over the parapet wall. "If you have possession o' this Kinglassie, what then for Henry's widow? 'Tis her property by right."

"She has no rights, according to King Edward," Gavin said. "And I doubt she will live out the week." He glanced at his uncle. "The king has decided that I should marry her."

"Wha' is the use o' that?" John asked incredulously.

Gavin shrugged. "There is some secret of hidden gold, I know not what. He wants me to charm it out of the girl."

"Holy Jesu," John muttered. "Charm a dying lass. We're rescuing her from a madman, I think."

"Pardon, my lords," said a soft voice nearby.

Startled, they turned. From the dark wedge of shadow beneath the tower, the rotund form of a woman stepped forward. She carried blankets in her arms.

"Do ye mean to help the Scottish lady?" she whispered.

"Who are you?" Gavin demanded. He noticed that she was young, and wore the sturdy, plain garments of a servant.

"If ye mean to make a rescue, let me help, my lord. Please. I am Dominy of Averoe, widow to a knight. Nearly a half year, I've waited for the king to decide on my petition for my widow's dower land. I've been working in the king's household for my meals and bed, and I've been caring for the Scottish lady. She is ill, and needs help."

Gavin glanced at his uncle. John frowned sourly, clearly unwilling to involve a woman in their venture.

"We need to remove her tonight," Gavin murmured.

Dominy nodded. "I can help, my lord. D' ye have somewhere to take her? She needs to be tended at a hospital."

"We'll take her to a convent," John said. "Be gone from here, lassie."

"There are no convents within two days' ride of here," she said. "The English lords have closed them. But I know of a monastery a few hours' ride into Scotland, which has a good infirmary. They are sympathetic to both Scots and English there." She looked over her shoulder. "I have an idea, my lords, if ye'll wait but a moment while I speak to the guard." Without waiting for their approval, she hurried along the wall walk. Gavin exchanged a glance with John.

"A decisive woman," Gavin drawled. "Let us hope she has good judgment along with boldness." John rolled his eyes.

"Thomas," the girl called. "Let me in to see her, then."

The guard turned and strolled toward her. "Dominy! Back again? You just fed her some soup! Why not tend to me this time?" He grinned.

"Mayhap later, do ye let me in there. I brought the lady some blankets against the cold."

"Blankets and a roaring brazier. Wish I had such comfort at night," Thomas said as he unlocked the door. "Now, you're not to speak to her."

"I know," Dominy said. Thomas stepped back, and Dominy climbed in with her stack of blankets.

A few moments of silence passed. Then Dominy let out a shriek. "Thomas!" she cried. "Oh, dear saints!"

"What is it?"

"God help us all! The lady is dead!"

"Dead!" Thomas paused. "What was in that soup?"

"Oh God! Lady Christian! My lady!"

"You're not to speak to her!" Thomas leaned into the cage.

"Idiot! She is dead!" Dominy retorted. "Oh God above!"

"Sweet Christ," Gavin muttered. He and John walked toward the cage. "Is there a problem here, Sergeant?" he asked.

Thomas, who had wedged his upper body into the cage opening, turned awkwardly. "My lord," he said. "The lady has died!"

"Aye!" Dominy called, peering around Thomas's wide shoulder and looking toward them. She stretched out an arm and beckoned to them in agitation. "Most surely dead!" She shoved Thomas roughly. "Get back, man. Could be a pestilence!"

As the guard stepped back in a panic, Gavin came forward to lean into the narrow opening. He looked at the still, slight girl who lay on the bottom of the cage. Hesitating, uncertain, he hoped that Dominy only attempted to create a ruse. But he knew that the girl could well have died.

"She surely looks, er—" he began.

"She's dead, my lord," Dominy said. "Certain dead." She quickly wrapped a blanket around the girl, swaddling her like a babe. "Mayhap your man there, my lord, should come in and carry her away."

"Let me see her." Gavin swung a leg up to climb inside.

"A pestilence, say you?" John asked, peering over Gavin's shoulder. "Then the body must be removed quick! We'll get her out, eh, my lord?"

"I thought you spoke only French," Gavin hissed.

"I'm a muckle versatile man," John muttered.

"Then lose that lilt," Gavin said.

"If 'tis a foul disease, no one should touch her," Thomas said.

"You'd best stay well away," John said, turning to the guard. "My lord and I, we survived a pestilence in the Holy Land. Devil of a thing, and people rottin' in the streets like—"

"John," Gavin said between his teeth.

"I thought you were in France," the guard said.

"Aye, that, too. But we dinna fear disease," John answered smoothly, ignoring Gavin's glare. "Just get out o' the way and let my lord tend to the body! Stand back, now!" John placed a hand on Thomas's shoulder to lead him firmly away. "We'll take care o' this."

Gavin entered the cage. As Dominy wrung her hands expressively, he knelt beside the Scotswoman, who lay on the floor like a discarded cloth doll. He peeled back the blanket that covered the girl's face, unsure what he would find.

She lay still in the moonlight, her face as pale and perfect as a marble tomb effigy. He noticed the delicate oval shape of her face, the slender dark brows, the lashes like black crescents over hollowed cheeks. He touched the side of her face, and felt her sigh beneath his hand. Her skin, feathery soft, was warm, even feverish. She seemed to grow warmer beneath his touch.

But he had to admire her quick wit; as ill as she was, she seemed to have caught on to Dominy's scheme with ease. She was still as death, yet she was breathing and seemed to be awake. His hand lingered as he stroked gently along her slender jaw, wanting to reassure her that he meant her no harm.

As he touched her, a sudden shiver went through him, a surprising rush like lust, plunging to his loins and swelling there. He pulled his hand away as if he had been burned.

Not lust, but a spontaneous, elemental urge to act. For one wild instant, he wanted to sweep her into his arms and carry her away. His hand clenched as if he were ready to slice his sword at anyone who dared to bar his way.

He wanted her to live. The conviction was strong and sudden. Gavin knew that he would do whatever he could to make certain that the girl at least had the chance to survive.

King Edward's orders echoed again in his mind, and he sighed, rubbing his hand over his eyes. The king had placed him in a difficult position. Gavin had no interest in a hoard of Scottish gold, and less interest in pursuing Robert Bruce.

Berwick, ten years ago, had turned him finally and utterly against the English cause in Scotland. His mother had been Scottish, and he had spent part of his childhood in the Lowlands. As a young English knight, he had felt uneasy and disloyal acting against the Scots. He still did.

But he had wanted land and a castle. He had waited years for a grant from King Edward, who was notoriously ungenerous to his lords. Gavin had no doubt that a marriage to this Scottish girl would strengthen his claim to the property.

If Robert Bruce prevailed over the English, Gavin's claim to Kinglassie would be based on his marriage to Lady Christian. As her widowed husband, he would possess Kinglassie under Scottish or English law. He was not by nature a manipulative man, but his years as ambassador had taught him to be cautious and never to overlook small details.

Glancing down at the girl, he sighed deeply and rubbed his jaw. King's demands aside, he knew, quite simply, that she would die if he did not get her out of this cage. And his conscience would not let him sleep well in that distant Gallovidian castle if he left her here like this.

"Is she dead, my lord?" the guard asked.

He glanced up. John, crammed between two sentries now, peered at him through the doorway. Dominy watched him warily.

He had naught but the king's inconstant, cupshot word that he could remove the girl on the morrow. And Gavin knew better than to trust Edward's promise where it concerned a Scot. A keen sense in his gut told him to act on Edward's orders immediately.

"She is alive," he said at last. "But she is close to death. I am taking her out of this cage."

"My lord," Thomas said. "The captain of the guard will have to decide—"

"I have the king's permission to remove her to a convent. Your companion has seen the king's signature on it." The other guard nodded. "She is too ill to delay. We go tonight," Gavin said.

He lifted the girl in his arms and stood. She was a limp, slight weight, an easy burden. John reached into the cage, and Gavin handed her out to him. Assisting Dominy, who needed a moment to squeeze her ample bottom through the opening, he then climbed out.

"The captain will have my head unless we have direct orders from the king on this," Thomas said.

"He has a signed order," the other guard said.

Gavin nodded. "I saw the king at Lanercost this evening. He gave me the order and bid me tend to it." He glanced toward John, who stood holding the girl in his arms, looking anxious.

"Is it a pestilence?" Thomas asked. "I carried her in my arms today. She coughed when I held her. The priests say such diseases can be spread by touch, by unclean sputum and blood and evil humors." He shivered.

" 'Tis not a foul illness," Gavin said. "But she has caught a lung disease from being exposed to the cold and wet here." He turned to John. "Go on. Tell the stableman that we need our horses readied, and that we will need a cart for the girl."

John nodded and strode away, carrying Christian, while Dominy hurried along behind them.

"What should we tell the captain of the guard, my lord?" Thomas asked as Gavin turned to leave.

Gavin looked over his shoulder. "Tell him," he said, "that the lady is done with English hospitality."

"REMOVED THE LADY in the dead o' the night, like thieves, we did," John said, grinning widely as he sat on the cross bench of the two-wheeled cart in which Christian lay. He chuckled with pride and looked over at Gavin. "D' you think the king's host will hunt us down for what we hastened past them?"

Riding alongside the cart, Gavin glanced at the silent girl huddled beneath blankets in the back of the cart. The ride out of Carlisle had been rough and fast and cold, over deeply rutted roads slick with icy patches, but Gavin had heard barely a sound from her beyond an occasional cough. "They will surely pursue us if they discover that we had no signed order to take her as we did," he told John. Turning, he scanned the dark, rolling terrain, which was lit only by a thin slip of a moon. "All seems quiet. We have not been followed."

John grunted, and gave the cart reins an unenthusiastic snap. "I canna believe I agreed to drive this thing. A knight o' my experience. 'Tis a disgrace."

"We surely had no time to find ourselves a driver. And 'tis only until we reach a religious house. Your own horse is tied to the back."

"Aye, a fine destrier, and now he's a packhorse," John muttered. He glanced at his bay charger, which carried, across its empty saddle, a few hastily rolled packs of gear that contained items of clothing, weaponry, armor, and several bags of silver coins, mostly English pennies and French *deniers*.

Gavin stilled his own black destrier, and glanced at the sky. A deep gray-blue tint spread over the horizon, and the air felt cold, heavy, waiting. " 'Tis nearing dawn."

"We should continue north as quick as we can," John said.

"First we'd best see to the girl. Stop just under those trees, John." Walking his horse off the roughly cut road, Gavin waited beneath the bare, spreading branches of a pair of oak trees. As his uncle drew the cart to a stop, Gavin dismounted to look at the girl.

In the faint light, Christian lay curled in the flat cart bed, swathed in blankets and still as death, her delicate face almost ethereal. Gavin reached out to touch her apprehensively, his heart thudding, knowing she could have died in the last hour. But her small, bony shoulder shifted beneath his touch, and she began to cough, a deep congested barking.

She was having difficulty breathing; alarmed, he slid an arm beneath her shoulders to lift her a little. Her head fell against his chest, and she looked up at him, her eyes like great dark smudges in the starlight.

Balancing the girl against him, he shoved another blanket beneath her head to incline her torso. "Can you go on, Lady Christian?" he asked her. "The way will be just as hard as it has been. Harder, in fact."

She nodded, coughing. Gavin adjusted the folded blankets beneath her. "There—you'll breathe better now, my lady."

She laid her hand on his mailed sleeve; he could hardly feel the weight of her light touch. "You took me from the cage," she said, her voice a dry rasp of sound. "You rescued me. Thank you." He detected a gentle accent to her English, a musical and enchanting lilt that told him her native tongue was Gaelic.

"You are safe now, my lady," he said.

"Who are you?"

"Gavin."

"Gavin," she repeated in her gentle accent. "Has my cousin paid a ransom? Did the English king—"

Gavin placed a fingertip to his lips. "Hush now, and rest."

"I thought your name was Saint Michael, when I first saw you," she said.

He leaned closer. "Did you?" he asked gently, well aware that lung fevers could cause a person's mind to wander.

"I did." Christian closed her eyes and turned her head away. Still frowning, Gavin mounted his horse, then glanced at the sky. A thin rinse of rose and gold had begun just above the dark hills.

"How is the lass?" John asked.

"Alive," Gavin murmured.

"I see you still have that gentle hand wi' the sick, lad."

Gavin shrugged. "Once learned, never forgotten."

"She'll soon adore you, do you continue to minister to her like a saint."

"Well, pray that we can escort her to a religious house before the saints come to escort her to heaven."

"Will she need last rites so soon?"

"Aye," Gavin said softly. He was about to urge his horse forward when a cluster of moving shadows along the road caught his attention. "Hold," he warned John. "Look there." They watched as a single destrier drew closer.

"What in the name o'—" John said. " 'Tis a woman!"

Gavin kneed his horse to surge forward out of the sheltering trees. He rode swiftly to interrupt the rapid progress of the woman's horse.

"Dominy!" he called, pulling up on the reins. "What are you doing here? Go back!"

She halted her horse. "My lord! I am so glad to have found ye! Is the lady well?"

"Well enough," he answered curtly. Behind him, John rumbled the cart toward them. "Has aught happened? Have you come to warn us?" Gavin asked Dominy.

"Nay," she answered, adjusting the rather bulky front of her cloak and patting its folds. "I've come to join ye."

"What!" John said. "Whose charger is that? 'Tis a fine knight's animal."

"He's mine," Dominy answered, smoothing her hand over the dappled charger's broad neck. "He belonged to my husband, and has been stabled at Carlisle. But now we will come with ye."

"We?" Gavin asked, eyeing the front of her cloak. It was shifting. He frowned.

"And why should we have a woman along, then?" John grumbled.

"Ye've a woman there in yer cart," Dominy pointed out. "And how will ye take proper care of the lady, without me?"

"Sir Gavin will watch after her," John said. "He doesna fear a wee sick lass."

Gavin, scowling, stepped his horse closer to Dominy. He reached out to flick open her cloak.

A slight, dark-haired boy blinked up at him, his head nestled against Dominy's comfortable bosom.

"And who's this bairnie?" John growled.

"This is William. My son. He is six years old."

"William." Gavin nodded gravely to the boy, who blinked uncertainly at him. "Dominy, we cannot allow you to—"

"Please, my lord," she said. "We've been living at the castle, Will and I, since my husband died at Turnberry—in Ayshire, 'tis, in Carrick lands. He was fightin' the Scots. I do not want to stay at Carlisle any longer. I beg you, sir, let us come."

"We've nae use for women and bairns—" John began.

"Ye'll want to take the lady to an infirmary," Dominy said quickly. "I know the best place to take her. And I can show ye how to cross into Scotland. Due north of here, the land is too boggy this time of year for travel. We should head northwest, and ford the firth at low tide, where it runs shallowest, and cross to the Galloway coast. I'll show ye just where."

"She could be useful," Gavin said to John, who spitted in frustration.

"And I can stay with the lady wherever you leave her. Please, my lord," Dominy said. "My son will be better off away from knights."

"*Ach*, and wha' are we?" John said. "Wet nurses?"

Dominy scowled at him. "Two knights are better than two thousand." She looked at Gavin. "My lord, ye cannot take Lady Christian to a Scottish convent. The English burned most of them years ago, and the rest are too far away for her to travel."

"What d' you suggest, lass?" John drawled sarcastically.

"Well, we must avoid the first monastery we come to, just north of here, for that hospital tends lepers. And we must ride past Caerlaverock Castle. 'Tis garrisoned to the brim with English, who ye might wish to avoid just now, with the Lady Christian in yer care."

Gavin glanced at John. "I think we'll need her. Very well, then, Dominy. Come with us until we reach the monastery. Then we will decide where you would be safest."

"My thanks, sir," she said. "William, thank the baron."

"I thank you, sirrah," the boy said in a light, clear voice. "You are a fine man, and no part of a whoreson." He smiled innocently. Gavin blinked in mute surprise, and John gave a startled laugh.

Dominy shushed her son and looked at Gavin. "He means to compliment you, my lord. But he's spent too much time in the garrison quarters, y' see. He hardly knows how to speak as a child should."

"Aye, well," Gavin said in dismay, looking at the boy. Will's wide grin, and sweet little face showed more than a hint of mischief. "See that he is careful of his speech in the monastery." Dominy and William nodded vigorously.

"Hmmph," John said. "If they must come, then, the lass should drive the cart."

"We'll do well to have her with us, John," Gavin said, trying to placate his uncle.

"Bah," John muttered. "We'd do better to have her horse."

Gavin held up his hand. "What is that?"

"Bells!" John said. "Is this a feast day?"

"No feast day," Dominy answered. "As I was leaving the castle, some bishops rode through the town, with their cloth-of-gold and their mitres. The bells are ringing in the cathedral. I know not what they celebrate so early, at dawn. But surely it must be important."

A realization hit Gavin like a punch. " 'Tis no celebration. And 'tis very important to King Edward. Dominy, is there a priest near here?"

"There's a village church a mile that way. A priest lives beside it. Oh, sir," she breathed out. "Is the lady worsening, then? Must the last rites be spoken over her so quick?"

"The bishops have ridden into Carlisle to excommunicate Robert Bruce and his supporters," he said curtly. " 'Twill take them an hour or so, no more. We must hurry. A mile, you say?"

John frowned. "What d' you mean to do?"

Gavin tugged at the reins to turn his charger's head. "I mean to marry the lady, as the king ordered. When the ritual is complete, Lady Christian will be cast out from the Holy Church. Her name is on the bishop's list. A wedding must be performed now, before the bells cease to ring, or it cannot be done at all. Come ahead!"

CHAPTER FOUR

A HAND, LEAN AND STRONG, gripped hers. Christian held on with what little strength she had, afraid to let go. She was surrounded by dark and cold and filled with discomfort, but the hand held her safe.

Her chest hurt with each breath, and her head ached so badly that she kept her eyes closed much of the time. Gavin's hand, warm and steady, remained over hers. She listened as he spoke quietly, his voice deep and calm. But her muddle, fevered mind could make little sense of his words.

He had carried her inside a building, a church, dimly lit by candles. She could smell stale incense, and sensed the deep peace there. Others were in the church—she heard Dominy and two men murmuring softly. One man spoke Scots English; the other spoke in a quick blur of Latin. A priest, she thought foggily.

The priest asked her a question, and another. She said aye, aye, holding fiercely to Gavin's strong hand, thinking that the priest asked her if she repented her sins. She desperately wanted absolution. She was afraid that she might die of this heavy weakness that filled her body.

But mostly the voices spoke English, too low and fast for her to follow. She drifted in and out of a bleary, dark fog, hearing without understanding. Gavin's hand held hers firmly, an anchor for her awareness.

The priest asked her another question, and she nodded,

exhausted. She heard him speak to Gavin, who answered softly.

Then Gavin leaned over and touched his lips to her brow in a dry, quick kiss. Surprised, she drew in a breath to speak, but began to cough, deep and congested, fighting for breath until the fit passed. She clung to his hand. He did not let go.

Then he picked her up and carried her out of the church. "Easy, my lady," he said. "You are safe now, with me."

SHE DREAMED OF COMFORT AND WARMTH, of soothing touches on her body and music like heaven. But she woke to painful, racking cough, cold air, and the bumping cart. The dream vanished like a candle flame blown out in the dark.

But she heard Gavin's deep voice somewhere over her head, and knew that he rode his horse beside the cart. Closing her eyes, feeling safe, she slept again, this time an exhausted, black, dreamless sleep.

Some time later, she was aware that she was being lifted and carried, but she slid away from the vague words and the comforting hands, and sank into the darkness again.

CHRISTIAN OPENED HER EYES to soft daylight and a quiet that was almost tangible. She was in a small, simply furnished room. Thick blankets and linen sheets covered her, and she lay on a deep straw mattress with pillows that supported her like a cloud. She felt clean and warm, but exceedingly weak.

She did not know if hours or whole days had passed since Gavin had lifted her from the cart. The weakness that filled her limbs was profound. Her head ached, her chest hurt with each indrawn breath, and she scarcely had enough strength to lift her own hand.

The door creaked open, and quiet footsteps padded across the floor. Christian looked up as Dominy entered the little room, followed by a thin man clothed in a brown robe.

"How does the lady now?" the man asked Dominy softly.

"Very weak, Brother Richard," Dominy laid a hand on

Christian's brow. "Still fevered."

Christian peered up at them. "Where am I?" she managed to croak, though her voice was weak and dry.

The monk looked down at her. "You are at Sweetheart Abbey, my lady," he said. "I am Brother Richard, the infirmarer."

She nodded. The monk was English—she recognized his round tonsure as of the Roman Church—but she knew that Sweetheart Abbey was located in southern Galloway. Many religious houses in Scotland were filled with English priests, just as many Scottish castles were garrisoned with English soldiers.

And Sweetheart was only a few days' ride from her daughter at Kinglassie. She sent up a prayer of thanks.

The two men who had rescued her from Carlisle—how many days ago? she wondered—were surely Scottish knights loyal to the cause. No Englishmen would have removed her from that foul cage to bring her here. And she had heard the older knight speak Scots English.

The tall golden-haired knight, the one she had once thought was the archangel Michael, had spoken both northern English and Norman French. But language was no definite marker of political loyalties. Her cousins Robert Bruce and his brothers commonly used French, English, and some Gaelic.

But she was certain now that her rescuers were Scots, because they had taken her back to Galloway. Relief and hope filled her like a fresh breath. But she lacked the strength to ask the many questions that tumbled through her mind.

She recalled little of her escape, though she remembered Dominy urging her to lie still, and recalled the gruff-voiced Scotsman carrying her away from the cage. She remembered, too, a rough, cold ride in an uncomfortable cart. And a visit to a church—or had she dreamed that part?

But her clearest memories were of the beautiful golden knight: his hand over hers, his deep, soothing voice, his dry, gentle kiss. She remembered asking his name. *Gavin,* he had said. *Hush,* he had said; *you are safe.*

The monk laid a hand on her head and looked at Dominy. "She is still feverish," he said. "Continue to bathe her face and feed her broth and watered wine if she will take it. I will prepare a fresh poultice for her chest."

"Aye, Brother Richard."

He turned to leave, but halted. "Dominy—the abbot has had a talk with your son. We hope for no more such incidents as happened in the brothers' dining hall last even."

Dominy sighed. "Aye, Brother. I am sorry. The bowl overturned, and William just spoke out too quickly."

"Well, his choice of words horrified the abbot. Swearing by any part of our Savior's blessed body is a serious sin for anyone, but for a child to swear by the—er, backside of our Lord is not fitting, although some of the brothers found it amusing." Brother Richard tried to hide his own chuckle as he left the room.

Dominy lifted the blankets and removed the heavy, soggy poultice, which smelled strongly of garlic, from Christian's chest. Coughing, Christian felt as if the lung congestion had loosened some. But every breath she drew, every fitful cough, was tinged with pain, and she ached with a cloying, heavy need for sleep. She coughed again, and shivered.

"Yer awake, and that's good," Dominy said, as she drew the blankets higher.

"You have a son?" Christian asked hoarsely.

"Aye. William," she said. "Six years old, he is, and thinks he's a full-grown knight. The men at Carlisle treated him like a soldier. Even taught him to roll dies. Now, will ye take some broth?" She rested a wide hip on the bedside, raised Christian's head up and brought a wooden spoon to her lips.

Sipping obediently, Christian grimaced as the warm, salty liquid went down. She swallowed a little more, then shook her head. She had little appetite. What she wanted, above all else, was to sleep.

"Tired," she croaked in a raspy voice. "So tired."

Dominy stepped away and sat on a wooden bench. "Sleep then. I will be just here, do ye need me. And Sir Gavin has promised to come back again. He sat through the night with ye, and most of the day. But ye likely did not know that, my lady, as weak as ye've been these two days."

Dominy chattered on softly, but Christian heard no more beyond the mention of Gavin. Why would he sit with her? she wanted to ask. But her eyes drifted shut.

"SHE'LL LAST THE NEXT DAY or two only, I fear."

Lying awake in the darkness, hours later, Christian heard Brother Richard speaking softly, just outside the door that was close to the end of her bed. His ominous words jarred her to greater alertness. Opening her eyes, she saw only heavy shadows.

"What can you do for her?" Gavin asked. She felt a curious thrill run through her at the deep, velvety sound of his voice.

"I have given her poultices, and have offered her broths. I have mixed healing herbs with her wine. But she has taken little. Few treatments are successful against such lung ailments. She is young, and I presume healthy before this struck her. That is in her favor, but she is still in danger."

"Dominy says the fever lingers."

"Aye. I have told Dominy to bathe the lady's head and face with mint water to cool her. In a day or two I may begin bloodletting to drain the thick humors from her. But naught we do may matter," the monk said. "Her lungs are filled, and her breathing is fast and poor. The devil enters with such illnesses, and drags upon the soul until it can no longer defend itself. Then the angels of heaven enter the battle and fight the demons. Only if the girl is without sin can she hope to survive the struggle."

"I have heard such medical philosophies before," Gavin said. His tone seemed wry, even bitter, Christian thought as she listened.

"Then you understand why our herbs often do little against these lung fevers." The monk paused. "I know you are concerned for her, Sir Gavin."

"I am very concerned." Their steps echoed along the stone floor as they moved away.

Tears filled Christian's eyes. She feared that her body was succumbing to this constant, draining weakness. Had the devil truly entered her soul, as the monk had said? She did not think that was true. English clergy were always such doomsayers.

Her mother, had she been alive, would have said that the disease had come from being in the cage for weeks in poor weather with little food or warmth. Surely rest, nourishment, time, and the proper herbs would cure her. She had always been healthy and strong before this, and she was determined to gain that back.

But both the priest and the knight fully expected her to die. She squeezed her eyes shut in anguish. Her will to live was strong. Did they not see that?

Her only choice was survival. She sent up a prayer to the angels and saints, asking that she might recover, and asking them to watch over her daughter until then. Whispering the words, she floated into a heavy sleep.

GAVIN WOKE WITH A START, surrounded by darkness, and sat upright on his narrow bed. Soft rain pattered against the outer walls. Across the small chamber, on a floor pallet, John snored deeply.

Vivid dreams had rolled through Gavin's mind, the last one jarring him awake. He had climbed a steep slope in moonlight to a castle gate. Inside, the castle was dark and deserted. But he moved toward one chamber that glowed with light from hundreds of candles. White doves flew overhead, settling on the rafters, cooing.

At the center of the room, Christian waited for him. With a little glad cry she ran into his arms. He wrapped her into his embrace and kissed her, and a sense of relief flooded through him when he realized that she was well and healed. He felt as if he knew her and this place well, and truly belonged here with her.

Never, in life or in dreams, had Gavin experienced such profound joy and such loving warmth as existed in that dream. Abiding love, sustaining and utterly real, had filled him when he had held Christian.

Now, awake in the cold darkness, he clenched his empty fists. He would give anything, his very soul, to have that kind of devotion in his life. But such passion, the strength of bonded hearts, was rare. Certainly it had eluded him.

A few hours earlier, he had sat with Christian in her chamber, smoothing a wet cloth over her fevered face and holding her hand. She had not awoken, had not known he was there. He remembered doing the same for Jehanne, endless days and nights of tending to her, sitting by her bed. He never thought he would find himself in a similar situation.

Yet the tableau had repeated itself. Rather than leave the girl here in the monastery for the monks to perform their deathwatch and burial, Gavin had decided to stay. Somehow he needed to be with her, though he did not understand why. And he wanted desperately to see her again before she died.

Rising to his feet, shivering, he snatched up his tunic and yanked it over his head. Then he pulled on soft leather boots and left the room.

DOMINY ANSWERED THE DOOR at his soft knock. Her eyes were foggy with sleep. "Go to your room and rest," Gavin whispered. "I will stay with Lady Christian." She nodded sleepily, and he stood aside as she left. Then he closed the door gently and turned toward the bed.

In the flickering glow of a single candle, Christian slept, her face fragile and serene. Her long, gleaming hair spread over the pillow like a midnight shadow. He sat on the edge of the bed and touched her brow gently.

Her skin still felt fevered. He touched her upper chest. Through the blanket, he could feel the shallow, labored rise of each breath. Leaning forward, drawing the blanket down a little, he put his ear to her chest. Her skin was soft and warm against his cheek. A Saracen physician, whose fee had been exorbitant but whose knowledge had been invaluable, had taught him how to do the listening technique—among other treatments—when Jehanne had been ill.

He heard a soft, distant bubbling in her lungs. A subtle, insidious, dangerous sound.

She moaned softly, murmuring a few words in Gaelic, airy,

gentle sounds, like breathing out music. She turned her head back and forth on the pillow.

Soothing his hand over her brow, Gavin felt the intense yearning that he had experienced in his dream. Here in the cool stillness before dawn, where reality and dreams blended without effort, he was aware of a pure, vibrant love for this woman.

He closed his eyes, but the enduring web of the dream still held him: a simple flood of joy, touched with an undercurrent of yearning, flowed through him. In that moment, somehow, she was an essential part of his very soul.

And he would do anything to help her. He wrapped his hands around hers, and felt the soft, sudden press of her returned touch. She turned her head and gave out a blurred little cry.

"Christian," he whispered, "I am here."

He had health and vital life, an abundance of it, yet hers was slipping away, and he could not stop it. The sight of her so pale and weak, the rasping sound of her breathing, pressed upon that old wound. The pain was still there, deeper than he had imagined. He did not want to witness this again. Yet he could not leave.

Sighing, he released Christian's hands and touched his fingers to her upper chest. The breaths that lifted her breastbone were too rapid, too shallow. The elusive magic of his dream faded as the hard edges of reality took precedence. Unless the fever subsided, unless her lungs cleared, she would die.

A way existed to help her, but he was not the one to do it. He had tried that method once, a long time ago, with devastating results. He felt more cursed than blessed by the potential that ran through his blood from generations of healers. Because he lacked the gift.

He wished, suddenly, that his mother still lived. She had had such a fine, sweet hand for miracles.

CHAPTER FIVE

"**H**OW DOES THE LADY?" Dominy asked. She knocked on the door of the chamber and stuck in her head. "I thought ye would send for me if she grew more ill."

"She has been coughing, but now she sleeps, and seems a bit more comfortable," Gavin answered softly. He sat on the edge of the bed, his hand on Christian's bare shoulder. She lay half turned on her side. He could hear the whine of each breath.

Dominy came into the room. "Still fevered?" she whispered.

He felt Christian's head. "Aye."

Christian coughed, and Gavin leaned forward, lifting the silky, warm mass of her hair. Lowering his head, he placed his ear against her bare back. A sound like the crackle of a low fire, or like the rustling of parchment sheets, accompanied each shallow, rapid breath and filled the silences in between.

Frowning, he looked at Dominy. "We must clear her breathing as best we can," he said. "We will need hot water and clean linen. The hour is late, but there will be monks awakening in shifts to pray in the chapel. Find someone to show you to the kitchens. Tell them 'tis urgent. Tell them I sent you, and that my wife needs hot water and linens."

"But my lord, 'tis not proper for me to—"

"Go! And bring another candle back with you, for God's sake. That one has burned down. 'Tis black as the devil's soul in here."

"Aye." Dominy padded away quickly.

He rested a hand on Christian's slight shoulder, and slid his hand down her arm to encircle her wrist. He swore softly. The girl was naught but bones and skin. She had been near starved to death in the cage. He marveled that she was alive at all. She must be very strong of will, for her body must not have much physical strength left.

A spasm of coughing grabbed her. Gavin slid his fingers under her thick, curling hair and began to rub her back. His fingers moved gently over her ribs. He could have counted each one. Her body felt frail, small, and hot beneath his hands.

When her breathing calmed again, he reached over to the wooden chest beside the bed and picked up a damp cloth that lay there. Holding it to her cheek, he drew it along her jaw and throat. But when the cloth, soaked in mint water, became overly warm itself, he laid it aside.

Sighing, Gavin wished again that he had inherited his mother's ability. The mysterious Celtic gift ran like a vein of rare gold through his mother's family. Her side was descended from a sainted healer, generations back, and the gift of the healing touch had come down, eventually, to Gavin's mother.

But the day that Jehanne had died in his arms, Gavin was certain that he had no rare magic in his hands, no blessing from his Celtic blood. Although the resembled his mother strongly, he did not share her natural talent.

Christian was severely ill, yet he could do little but apply common sense and comfort. He had made a husband's promise to her in the sanctity of a church, fully expecting her to die within a day or two. But his commitment had deepened while he had watched her spirit struggle.

Christian had a strong will, but her body was fragile just now. He would do what he could to give her the best chance at recovery; the years with Jehanne had taught him some practical ways to ease discomfort. But even if all efforts to treat her failed, Gavin would stay for as long as she needed him.

He HAD DOZED LIGHTLY while seated on the foot of Christian's narrow bed, leaning back against the wall. When she stirred and began to cough, Gavin awoke immediately, and shifted to sit beside her. He picked up a wooden cup of water from the chest beside the bed, and brought the cup to her lips.

"Drink slowly," he murmured. She sipped at it thirstily. Her eyes were bright and she shivered, her teeth chattering, as if her fever had risen.

Gavin pulled the blankets higher over her shoulders. Dipping his fingers into the cup of water, he touched her forehead. A drop slid over her temple and disappeared into the heavy mass of her hair.

"We must cool your body down," he murmured. He moved his damp fingers along her neck and slid them gently through the warm tangle of ringlets. Then he picked up the damp cloth that lay on the chest and stroked it across her brow. "The priests here know much of heaven and hell, but perhaps not enough practical treatment. Mint water will do little to bring down such a fever."

She coughed again, trembling. He frowned, knowing that the fever must be lowered or she would weaken further. Immersion in a tepid bath might help, but he doubted that a tub was readily available here at the monastery. And the January winds that whined through the cracks in the window shutters made a severe body chill too risky.

"Ah," he said softly, after a moment. She blinked up at him silently, still awake. "There is something else that can be done to help you."

He wrapped the woolen blankets snugly around her, then lifted her onto his lap. She leaned against his shoulder, her weight slight and limp against him. He slid her hand down to free the ivory-handled dagger that was sheathed at his belt. Christian squeaked hoarsely when he brought the gleaming blade near her.

As she tensed her arm, he realized that she expected a bloodletting. Gavin ran his fingers slowly through her hair and gathered its curling thickness into one hand.

"Hold," he said softly. "Be still, now." He tugged, and the blade rasped faintly as it sliced into her hair.

Long tresses fell like spirals of black silk in the moonlight, drifting over her shoulders and the tops of her breasts, sliding to the bed. She cried out in dismay as he cut, and reached up a hand. He gently pushed her hand away.

Soft, short locks soon cushioned his fingers. Gavin squinted at his handiwork critically. He had bobbed her hair like a man's, the only way he knew how to manage it, shorn straight and simple just below the level of her slender jaw. She cried out again, wordlessly, and turned to stare at him.

He brushed the drifts of hair off the bed. His own hair, longer than hers now, swung down and caught a glimmer of moonlight. He shoved it back and looked at her. "I am sorry, my lady," he said. "That hair was like a thick blanket, overheating you. Your body will have a better chance to cool, now."

"But I am cold," she rasped.

He tucked the blanket more securely around her. "Those are fever chills. What I have done will help."

She huffed and turned away. Gavin smiled a little. "Well," he said, "if naught else, the hair-shearing has given you a bit more spirit. And a rise of pride or temper is sometimes as good as a noxious potion for bringing round a patient."

Christian tilted her head in haughty anger.

"But do not overtax yourself." Chuckling, Gavin placed a hand on her shoulder, drawing her back toward his chest. "Rest, now," he told her. "Lean against me. You will breathe more easily if you sit up, like this."

Beneath his fingers, her skin felt a little cooler. He dipped his fingers into the water again and soothed them over her brow, over the fine bones of her face, down her throat to her sharp little collarbones. A few drops ran under the edge of the blanket, into the shadowed valley between her firm, rounded breasts.

She tried to pull away, but had little strength to do more than twist a little. He smiled and touched wet fingertips to the back of her neck, newly bared. "Hush now, and do not struggle so. I have put my knife away. I am a defenseless man."

Christian shrugged one shoulder in an eloquent display of disdain, but relaxed against him. Her silence, however, was icy.

"At the risk of displeasing you once again," he said, "I will insist that on the morrow, you swallow Brother Richard's herbal infusions and whatever food Dominy brings. You need medicines and nourishment. I will feed you myself if you refuse to eat again." He lifted the water cup. "Drink this."

She tipped her jaw indignantly, displaying the slender, graceful line of her throat, showing that she cared little for his opinion. But she sipped the water like a thirsty babe when he held it to her lips.

Footsteps sounded outside, and Dominy came into the room holding a fat, blazing candle and a stack of white cloths. The monk who entered behind her carried a kettle of steaming water.

"Set the kettle just there," Gavin directed, pointing to the chest beside the bed. The monk set down the iron pot, glanced nervously toward the bed, where Gavin sat holding a naked woman who was covered only by a blanket, and hastily left the chamber.

Dominy turned, holding the candle high, and shrieked as the light fell over Christian's bed. She looked accusingly at Gavin. Glancing down at the thick carpet of dark hair on the floor, she shrieked again.

" 'Twas a necessary thing," Gavin said. He looked at the floor. "She did have a great deal of hair," he admitted.

"She looks like a skinny boy!" Dominy said. Christian made a small, unhappy squeak. "Did it all have to go?" Dominy asked. "Such beautiful curls—"

"Those curls would have adorned her dead body, laid out on a bier," Gavin said bluntly. "She is fevered, and is better off without that mantle of black sheep's wool." Dominy turned away to set down the candle, and muttered to herself as she bent to sweep away the lengths of shorn hair. Then she straightened and looked at him. "Why did ye want the steaming water? A bath? They've no tub here."

"Not a bath," Gavin answered. "Bring the kettle closer to the edge of the chest—aye. And drape the linens here. Just so." Seated at the end of the bed, he gathered the blankets around Christian and lifted her more directly onto his lap.

"Have you ever had a steaming bath under a tent?" he asked Christian. " 'Tis helpful for coughs and chest ailments. Since we have no tub, this will do. Lean forward over the kettle." Holding her around the waist, he pushed her head and shoulders forward gently. Dominy draped a linen sheet over Christian's head to catch the whorls of steam.

"Now breathe," Gavin said.

His hands were wrapped around her inside the tent, and he could feel the hot, moist air beneath the covering. Christian inhaled, swathed in blankets, and rested her arms over his. She settled her hips on his thighs, her thin buttocks pressing against his groin.

The blanket slipped, and his fingers touched the smooth, bare skin of her hip, his other hand grasping her rib cage just below the soft, globed underside of one breast. Suddenly he was keenly aware that a thin woolen blanket was all that separated them. Holding her steadily, he drew in a deep breath.

Rocking her hips, Christian leaned forward a little to breathe in the steam. The blanket slipped further. Candlelight flowed over the pale contours of her back, forming delicate shadows along her ribs.

Hot mist, warm, soft flesh beneath his hands, and shared body heat produced a mellow, relaxing blend of sensations. But that enjoyable warmth soon edged toward something more dangerous. Gavin realized that his body had begun to respond to hers. Clearing his throat, he shifted her hips slightly away from what stirred to stubborn life within the pool of his lap.

Glancing up, he saw Dominy looking at him oddly. He could feel a blush begin to heat his cheeks. Lifting the linen cloth, Gavin felt a refreshing draft of cool air enter the snug tent.

"Enough, my lady," he said. " 'Twill help. You should not get overheated." Nor should I, he told himself grimly.

He lifted her from his lap, and helped her to lie back on the pillows again. Dominy reached over to tuck the blankets around her.

Christian looked at him in the candle's glow. Gavin saw a curious reflection in her eyes, as if he could see through the clear green irises to the pool of her soul. A bright, strong will burned there. He felt a sudden ripple in his chest, like a small burst of hope.

Smiling, he reached out to touch her hair. Short, moistened curls spiraled around his fingers. "Better," he murmured. "Not the image of death that you were earlier. Your cheeks are pink. And your hair looks fine like this."

"You like sheep's wool," she said, her husky voice edged with annoyance.

He laughed softly. "I apologize, my lady, for that remark. Though not for the shearing I gave you."

Christian scowled, then coughed again. Gavin could hear greater looseness in her chest.

"Sounds a bit better," Dominy said.

He nodded. "But she is still fevered and weak. The steam will not cure the lung ailment, but 'twill ease her breathing. We will repeat the treatment often tomorrow. I will ask Brother Richard to add some helpful herbs to the water."

Dominy took the linen cloth from his hand. "My lord, how is it ye know treatments that the monks do not? Ye know herbs, too, it seems. Are you a physician?"

"Nay," he answered. "I am not trained as such. But I dealt with physicians often enough in France."

"Were ye ill then, my lord?"

"Nay. "I was someone else. But I learned that good plain sense often serves better than talk of demons and bloodletting."

Dominy nodded. "Aye. And the rest we must leave to God." Leaning forward, she offered Christian another sip of water, and plumped the pillows.

"Aye," Gavin murmured, watching. "The rest is for God."

DEEP IN THE NIGHT, CHRISTIAN AWOKE to a long spasm of coughing, which racked her body and sucked the air from her lungs. She fought to regain her breath.

"Here," Gavin said, "sip some water. Go easy."

He was still there, though Dominy had left again. Seated behind her on the bed, he lifted her into his lap and pulled her back against his wide chest, supporting her in the cradle of his arms.

He held a cup to her lips. Cool water wet her mouth and slipped down easily. She swallowed more and rested against him.

The texture of his woolen tunic was thick and soft against her back; beneath it, his body was warm and solid and vastly comforting. As he held her, gently and silently, she felt grateful for his kindness, for his patience with her through the long night, but was too weak to utter the words.

She coughed again, bringing up a small amount of pinkish blood, which Gavin wiped away with a cloth. Afterwards she could hardly get her breath. Clawing at Gavin's arms, she began to thrash, trying to suck in the air that she needed.

"Hush, my lady," Gavin murmured, soothing a hand over her brow. "Jesu, you are fevered still, but it seems less. Be calm, now." His words reassured her in the midst of fear. She relaxed slightly and closed her eyes, resting her head on his chest.

The draining weakness seemed to take her over, as if the last of her strength had finally slipped away. She could no longer resist the floating sensation in her head and body. Like a boat moored on a loose rope, her awareness drifted away and came back again. Frightened, she gripped his forearms.

"I dinna want to die," she whispered.

"Hush," he said. "Hush. You will not. I will not let you." She clung to his arms, believing what he said.

His hand felt hot, so hot and good on her skin, comforting her, enfolding her. He placed a hand on her upper chest, and one on her back. Heat seemed to kindle in his palms and radiate throughout her body, sinking into her lungs, easing her breath. She tried to breathe it in, as if she could absorb the strength and support his hands offered her.

Though her head spun, she desperately tried to fasten her awareness to his sustaining hands. But she was tired and weak, and could no longer focus her thoughts.

Floating away again, this time she seemed to cross a misty threshold, as if she entered a dream. A soft golden blur of light surrounded her. She stood within its splendid, radiant center, suddenly aware that the draining weakness had subsided. She felt stronger, lighter, more whole.

Turning, she saw an angel, winged and tall, wearing pale, flowing robes. His luminous, beautiful face was somehow familiar. He seemed to be made of shining light, of strength, perfection, and power. And his wide, soft wings beat in a slow cadence, holding back the darkness, holding back the fear.

As he smiled at her and held out his hands, she felt an overwhelming flood of peace. She knew that he offered her safety and respite, and rescue from her illness. She moved forward, and he wrapped her in an embrace that was profoundly loving, as if the angel were mother, father, friend, and lover all at once.

The warm, tangible love he offered her filled her like water flowing into a vessel, like sunshine pouring into a room. She closed her eyes and felt its soothing current flow through her body. Inhaling deeply, she took in the nourishment of comfort and peace.

And felt healed. Truly, completely healed.

She wondered, in that moment, if she had died.

Glancing up at the angel, she wanted to ask where she was, who he was. As he smiled down at her, she saw again that he looked familiar. And then she recognized Gavin's face.

I am dreaming, she thought; *surely I am dreaming.* Only in a dream could a man have the wings and countenance of an angel, and the heavenly power of healing in his hands.

But she was healed. She knew it to be true, utterly and wholly. The disease had vanished.

She reached up to touch his face, and her lifted hand seemed to take on the glow of the misty brightness that surrounded him. She opened her mouth to ask him who he was, and if she dreamed.

Then the light faded as if a thousand candle flames were extinguished at once. And she sat once again in the shadowed abbey chamber.

But Gavin still held her, and she felt the afterglow of the angel's touch in his hands.

AS SOON AS SHE OPENED HER EYES, the brief, beautiful dream became a lost echo. She gasped and shut her eyes again, wanting that shining tranquility to return. But she could recapture only a beautiful shadow, and not its substance. She recalled a brilliant light, already fading as it swirled through her memory, and a deep sense of peace that had flooded through her to wash away her illness, leaving her with a calmness when she awoke.

And she remembered an angel who had somehow been Gavin, in the inexplicable way of dreams. She looked up and saw the same face, now lit only by the poor yellow light of a flickering candle flame.

"Christian," Gavin whispered. "Ah, God. I thought you had ceased to breathe. I thought, for a moment, that you had died." He laid his cheek against her head, and touched his lips to her hair.

She sat silently in his arms and rested her head on his shoulder. As Gavin held her, she sensed a steady, strong rhythm, like the beat of the angel's wings. But it was the deep throb of his heart at her back. She felt a radiating power that recalled the gentle, shimmering touch of an angel. But it was Gavin's hand on her shoulder.

Turning her head, she looked up at him in sudden wonder. In the faint glow of the candlelight, she saw the strength and grace and power in him: the muted gold of his hair, the masculine beauty of his features, his wide shoulders, all matching those of the angel. And his eyes had a similar sparkling depth, dark blue shadows gathered from the night sky.

But Gavin was simply a man, large and powerful and handsome, with the ability to gentle his strength. Looking down, she saw the hard, muscled contour of his long thigh fitted firmly beside hers. Sitting naked in his arms, covered only by blankets, she felt no threat or shame. His body shielded her and supported her. Her bare back was pressed against the soft, thick wool of his tunic. She felt the heat and hard strength of his body beneath it, and sensed the vital life that ran through him.

Just as before, a fevered delirium had led her to believe that he was an archangel. She had not passed over some heavenly threshold. She had sat in his arms in the depth of illness.

And had dreamed a replenishing, vibrant, miraculous healing.

Sighing, she turned her cheek against his shoulder. Like sunlight dispelling cold fog, her body now seemed to surge with bright, newborn energy. She had forgotten the simple joy of feeling healthy. She drew another breath: the deep, clear inhalation surprised and delighted her.

She felt as if she had awoken after a long illness. Perhaps the lung ailment had not been as serious as everyone had thought; perhaps she had just passed through a crisis.

Could a dream, however magical, have healed her? She could not comprehend it, but she knew that the dream had been like a prayer answered. A miracle, but a private one. She did not want to speak of the beautiful dream, as if doing so might diminish its power and its joy. She did not want to tell Gavin, this man she barely knew, how he had held her and loved her in the guise of an angel.

Gavin shifted and wrapped an arm more securely around her. Christian pulled at the blanket that had slipped down, and shivered a little, longing to feel the soothing, hot touch of his hands again.

"Are you cold?" Gavin asked. His deep voice was like a spark of welcome flame in cold darkness, sending an indefinable thrill coursing through her.

She nodded, and he tucked the blankets higher around her. Then he laid his unshaven cheek to her forehead for a moment.

"How do you feel?" he murmured against her hair. "You seem a bit stronger."

She hesitated. "I am tired," she whispered. "Only tired."

"Rest, then, Christian," he said.

"You are good to me." She glanced up at him. "Why have you stayed here with me?"

"I want you to live," he whispered. "Just that."

I *will*, she wanted to say, but slept even before the words could come.

CHAPTER SIX

"By my faith, Lady Christian," Dominy said, "ye've beaten two bowls of that broth, and near a whole loaf of bread."

Intently sopping thick salted broth with a heel of fresh bread, Christian scooped up the last of it, licked her fingers, and sat back against the pillows. "Dominy," she said, "that was delicious. Can you bring more, with some meat in it this time?"

"My lady, Brother Richard said ye were to have broth and bread only. He will be amazed at how much ye've tucked away." Blinking in amazement herself, Dominy picked up the bowl.

"But I'm still hungry," Christian said. "And I feel much stronger." She coughed, a deep and congested sound, but did not worry over it; she knew the coughs were cleansing now, bringing up the last of the illness. She drew a strong breath afterward. The feeling was wonderful, like the fresh, clear sense of energy that she had felt the night that Gavin had sat with her, almost two full days ago.

Dominy had told her that she had slept through an entire day and nearly half of another. They had worried greatly about her, Dominy said, until Gavin had listened to her breathing, pronouncing it much clearer. He had reasonably pointed out that the heavy, peaceful sleep was healing, replenishing her strength. But he and the others had been amazed at the pace of the recovery.

When she had awoken late this morning to golden sunlight

pouring into the little whitewashed room, the burgeoning sense of well-being that she had felt in the dream was still with her. She felt weak but peaceful, calm and cleansed, like the watery glow of dawn after a ferocious storm.

And now she was so hungry that she could not seem to fill her stomach for long enough to satisfy it. She smiled now in response to Dominy's concerned frown.

"Ye still have the cough," Dominy said, "though we cannot expect miracles. Barely six days have passed since we brought ye here, and so weak I swear I saw the shadow of the angel of death at yer side. But between the poultices and herbs, and Sir Gavin's hot steam tents, ye're recovering very nicely. None of us would have thought it possible, my lady."

" 'Tis a blessing from heaven, Dominy," she said softly, remembering the angel of her strange dream, who had embraced her in a blazing light and surrounded her with love and peace and protection.

She was certain the dream must have been a fevered illusion, but one that had brought with it some kind of miracle, one that she could not explain. She felt as if she had glided easily past the worst of the illness, and had only to regain her strength.

Giving a quick, silent prayer of thanks, she added a word of thanks for the savior sent to help her. Gavin had been there with sure, steady strength and kindness. And he surely looked like an angel, tall and strong, with golden beauty, and power tempered by gentleness.

Smiling, she watched dust motes dance on a sunbeam, and shivered pleasantly. She wanted to see Gavin again, wanted to thank him for staying with her when she was ill. She hoped, too, that he would touch her again, even just to hold her hand before he left. His touch had been wonderfully soothing; beyond the dream, the warmth and strength in his hands remained the most vivid memory she had of the worst part of her illness.

Melodic and peaceful, the chanting of the monks in the chapel, which she had been hearing all morning, drifted into her thoughts. She sat up further and moved her legs to the side of the bed. "I want to dress and go to the chapel," she told Dominy.

"That plainsong is beautiful."

"Aye, 'tis, and listen to it from yer bed," Dominy said, coming over to shove Christian's legs beneath the covers. "Now that ye've had a good meal, ye think to get up? Hah! Ye recovery may be heaven's blessing, but ye'll need to go slower, my lady, or be ill again. Ye may feel stronger, but ye're still weak as a newborn kitten." Dominy handed Christian a comb. "Here. This will help ye feel better. And I hope ye know how difficult this was to find in a monastery." She grinned.

Christian laughed appreciatively as she took the comb and began to draw it through her hair, still damp from the washing Dominy had given it earlier. She pulled the comb through too quickly, scraping the teeth over the bare nape of her neck, and then raised exploring fingers to the blunt cut ends of her hair. A bit of rough linen toweling had nearly dried it already. With the weight gone, it curled freely, and her head felt light and unburdened.

Tugging at the strands, she smiled. A tingling rush swept through her as she remembered that Gavin had cut her hair out of concern for her.

She might see him if she went to the chapel, or to the dining hall. The soup that Dominy had given her had not filled her for long; her stomach was rumbling again. "Dominy, I want to get dressed," she insisted.

"I cleaned yer gown and plaid as best I could," Dominy said. She took the gray dress off a wall peg and helped Christian slip it on. "Near rags, yer clothing is, but ye will feel more comfortable dressed. But I say ye will keep to yer bed."

"I want to go to the chapel, and to the dining hall. I am hungry." Christian felt surly enough to pout; her stomach was not satisfied with thin soups and bread. She shoved back the covers, and shifted her legs over the side of the bed. A wave of dizziness swamped her, and she sat still.

"My lady! Ye cannot mean to leave this room!" Dominy took her arm. "If I fetch more food, will ye promise to stay in bed?"

Christian sighed and nodded, drawing her legs back up under the woolen blankets. "Ask the cook for some roast chicken," she said hopefully, and closed her eyes to rest.

SHE DOZED UNTIL A SOFT SOUND brought her to awareness. Thinking that Dominy had returned with the food, she shifted her head and opened her eyes.

Just inside the doorway of the chamber, Gavin stood taller than the lintel, his broad shoulders filling the opening as he extended one arm to lean against the jamb. He wore a black tunic beneath the white surcoat embroidered with golden wings. His hair glinted with similar touches of gold; his beard, increasing daily, was darker than she had thought. Smiling to see him, she sat up.

"God's blessing, my lady," he said in greeting. His voice was more compelling than the chants that floated so peacefully on the air. Seeing him, she recalled again his strong, warm, gentle hands on her that night, supporting and soothing her. A delicate, wonderful shiver coursed through her. His kindnesses when she had been so ill, and his rescue of her from Carlisle, deserved her sincere thanks. In her magnanimous mood, she even felt inclined to forgive him the dreadful hair shearing.

"God's greetings," she said, and smiled.

"You look well," he said. His eyes sparkled, and he returned a little smile that made her feel distinctly odd and wonderful all at once.

"I am fine," she said, suddenly aware of her ragged dress and gaunt appearance. She raised a hand self-consciously to her cropped hair and thin neck.

"I expected to find you in much the same state as yesterday. I came early this morn, but you still slept." He smiled softly. "But now I am amazed, my lady. You look wonderful."

She grimaced. "I heard Dominy say that I looked like a skinny lad."

He grinned. "She did say that, but she was wrong. I have never seen a lady more beautiful."

Christian blushed fiercely, though she knew full well that she was thinner than a lake-weed in winter. Certainly she must look frightful with shorn hair and pale, sunken cheeks.

"You had me worried," he said softly.

She felt more heat rise into her face. His deep voice and the tender meaning in his words thrilled her. "I am much stronger now," she said.

"I see that. Tell me," Gavin said, leaning casually against the doorframe, "are you still fevered? And have you been breathing in the hot steam?"

"My fever is gone, Dominy says. My cough is better—see, the kettle of hot water is just there, and I've sat under the tent already, just as you said to do. And I've eaten my fill of broth and bread. Almost. I am very hungry."

Gavin smiled. But then he looked as if a grim thought occurred to him. His brows drew together. "I am glad to hear that you are better. If so, then there are matters we must discuss."

"I would thank you for your help," she said. "For rescuing me, and for seeing me through the crises of my illness. 'Twas kind of you."

He nodded a silent acknowledgment, gazing at her steadily. She noticed that his eyes were a deep, rich blue in the muted sunlight. Then he lowered his brows further. The frown shadowed the brilliant color in his eyes.

Sensing the tension in him, realizing that something troubled him, she wished that she could ease it for him somehow. She owed him so much.

More than steam had helped her recover, of that she was certain. Gavin's warm, compassionate touch had given her some strength, as if he had worked with the angel of her dream to infuse healing into her.

But she would not speak her thoughts. She would cherish the dream as her secret joy.

"Lady Christian," Gavin said, still frowning, "there are some matters we must discuss when you are strong enough."

"I am well enough now," she said. "Speak."

He cleared his throat, but then looked around and stepped back. Dominy breezed past him, a bowl in her hands. Behind her, a small boy entered the room, carrying a large loaf of bread. He had torn off the end to munch on it, trailing crumbs as he walked.

"Broth, with chicken this time," Dominy announced, setting the bowl on the table. "And more bread, fresh from the monastery kitchen—oh, William! Ye've eaten some of the lady's bread." She turned to Christian. "My lady, this is my son, William. Ye've not met rightly, since ye've been so ill."

William bowed solemnly, handing her the loaf, while Christian smiled and nodded her thanks. "My lady," he said, "my sword is yours. I am your knight."

Christian smiled. "Thank you, sirrah," she said.

"If you like, my lady, I'll roll bones with you," William offered. Dominy gasped, and Gavin stepped toward the bed to lay a hand on the boy's shoulder.

" 'Tis not the best game to play in a monastery, Will," Gavin said, sounding amused. "And I am sure that when the lady is stronger, she would rather play chess than gamble at dice."

"Thank you for bringing the bread, William," Christian said. "And I'd be delighted to play chess with you." Nodding happily, William turned away. Dominy murmured her leave of Christian, and left the chamber with her son.

Christian closed her eyes for a moment, hearing again the sweet, low chant that wafted through the air. "Plainsong," she said. " 'Tis so beautiful. I havena heard it for so long. I would like to go to mass, and take communion. Can you escort me there?"

He frowned. "I suppose 'twould do no harm to take you into the chapel when you are strong enough for a short walk. But—"

"Do the monks object to having a woman share communion with them?"

"My lady—" he hesitated, then came toward the bed to sit on its edge, his weight sinking the straw-filled mattress. Her thigh rolled toward his. He looked at her somberly. "There is much I must explain to you."

She looked up at him, waiting, and decided that his eyes were the dark, frosted blue of juniper berries. This Scottish knight had rescued her from a vile prison, carried her back into Galloway, and seen her through a serious illness. Gentle, he was, brave and kind. And handsome.

She realized that she was besotted, totally infatuated with him. Perhaps even in love, though she had never been in that state before.

The thought sent tiny shivers up her spine.

"What would you tell me?" she asked.

"My lady, just after we left Carlisle, the supporters of Robert Bruce were excommunicated."

She stared at him. "All?"

"The women as well," he said, "by order of Pope Clement."

"Then I canna receive communion." She bit her lip.

"I hardly think God would disapprove if you just visited the chapel," he said. "You were not cast out because of your sins, only because of your political opinions. But there is more—"

"Tell me," she said, seeing the glint of gold in his hair as he turned his head. She was surely besotted. Excommunication should have struck terror into her very being. But somehow she felt no danger, no threat, physical or spiritual, while this man was with her.

Truly the angels had sent him to her. She almost giggled. A little health and a little fancy of love had gone to her head as quick as new wine.

"Lady," he said solemnly. "In a little church just outside Carlisle, I made certain that the last rites were said over you before the excommunication was done."

"Thank you. You have been very kind to me."

"And then the priest wed us, my lady."

She blinked. What had he said? Her brows drew together, a match to his frown, for he surely did not look pleased. Married? Should she thank him for that, too?

"Wed?" she echoed, confused. He looked so grim. She reminded herself sternly that, as perfect as he might appear, she knew nothing of him. "You are my husband now?"

He nodded. " 'Twas by king's orders," he said. "I was not certain that you remembered taking the vows."

She frowned more deeply. "I dinna recall—"

"You were very ill at the time," he said. "But the king commanded that vows be said between us."

She nodded. "My cousin has been concerned for my welfare. But I dinna even know your full name. Or your clan."

"Clan?" he repeated. "Cousin?"

"My cousin is Robert Bruce. But you know that—his orders brought you to Carlisle to rescue me."

Gavin let out a fast breath and shoved his fingers through his hair. He stood quickly, and the rope bed shifted beneath her.

"I wed you on orders from King Edward," he said.

A cold sensation crawled through her. "King Edward?"

"I am English."

She sat up slowly, her eyes never leaving his. He frowned, had been frowning all along, and now she knew why. He had been forced to wed a hated Scotswoman. She was still in the hands of the enemy. She was still in danger.

"English. You are English," she repeated, almost stupidly. "But I heard your companion speak Scots English. You rescued me from that cage! No Englishman would have done that. You canna be—" she dimly heard herself babbling, her voice low and rasping. Her heart was beating too rapidly, and her quick breaths took on a wheezing sound.

"You heard my uncle speak. He is a Scotsman."

"What is your full name?" she demanded. "Who are you?"

"Gavin Faulkener. Ambassador to Edward of England."

"O Dhia," she said. "Oh God. Faulkener. Oh God."

"Christian—"

Her breath came in tight little gasps. His words thundered through her mind. Sasunnach. An English knight. A Faulkener. Perhaps a brother or a cousin to Henry. Whoever Gavin Faulkener was, he had no loyalty to Scotland or to the Bruce. He had no thoughts of kindness toward her.

She had been wrong. So wrong. She felt as if King Edward had reached out once again to choke her and her family. She felt as if the health and joy she had found had begun to drain away.

"Why did you take me out of Carlisle and wed me?" she asked.

"I now hold the charter for Kinglassie Castle." His voice was soft and deep, so gentle. She hated him for that gentleness.

Squeezing her eyes shut, she leaned her forehead against her updrawn knees. Her whole body trembled with shock. "What else do you have to tell me?" A sob tore at her throat, and she swallowed it. Her hands shook violently. "What else?"

"Christian," Gavin said. "God knows I did not mean to upset you with this. But I am English, and I am your husband now. 'Twas necessary to explain it to you. There was no easy way. But I mean you no harm."

"No harm? You are the new laird of Kinglassie. But you English say baron, not laird." Her voice rose higher, cracking in its hoarseness. "Did you make the rescue at your king's orders?"

"He gave permission for your release," he answered.

"He condemned me to stay in that cage. Why would he agree to let me go?" She swung her trembling legs over the side of the bed, sitting up straighter to face him. Her entire body seemed to shake with the effort.

"He had reasons of his own," Gavin said simply.

"I know well what the English king's reasons are," she muttered. Her hand closed over the bread load left on the bedcovers, and she picked it up. Then she threw it wildly. Gavin caught it and laid it aside.

Next she reached out and shoved the bowl of soup off the chest beside her, wanting, in some uncontrolled part of her mind, to fling it full in his face. He stepped back, and the hot liquid spread across the rushes.

"Get out!" she shouted. She shoved back the bed covers and stood, the ragged gown hanging on her thin frame. Through her legs faltered beneath her, she stepped toward him. Straightening her back, lifting her head, she drew strength from her rage. Each step was an act of pure, seething will as she crossed toward him. She shoved at his chest. "Get out!"

He grabbed her wrist. "Stop this," he said firmly. " 'Tis not so bad as you might think. Stop, now, or you will make yourself more ill." His eyes were dark as night, grim and hard, as he frowned down at her.

She fisted her hand, caught in his, and glared up at him. Why had she not noticed that stony look before, an expression she had seen in the eyes of so many English knights? How could she have thought him so compassionate, so caring? So perfect?

"Sasunnach!" she rasped out. "Damned Sasunnach knight!" She struggled, flailing at him with her fist. Trapped by his grip, twisting against him, she began to sob, great angry bursts that ripped, raw and hurting, from her.

"I know why you took me from the cage!" Her breath heaved painfully in her throat, but anger hurtled the words out in a rapid stream. "You and your greedy king want Kinglassie's gold. The king has sent others to take it from us. But I didna tell them, and I willna tell you. I would die first."

"You nearly did," he snapped. "Christian, enough of this."

"Enough!" Her chest burned with each heavy breath. " 'Tis enough, what the English have done in Scotland. And now they want our treasures as well!"

Her knees gave way, and she half fell, stumbling against his chest. She twisted in futile protest when he lifted her into his arms and crossed the room to lay her on the bed. She struggled, and he sat beside her, pushing her back against the pillows.

"Let me go!"

"Hush," he said. "Be calm."

"Dinna touch me. You have betrayed me. Let me go!"

She pushed at him, but his hands on her shoulders felt like broad bands of iron, fixed and unyielding. "No one has betrayed you," he growled.

"I thought I was safe with you!"

"You are."

With the next choking, angry sob, her constricted breath seemed to freeze in her throat. She gasped for air, then caught her breath again as she twisted within his grip.

"Be calm, now," he said. "For the love of God, be calm." His thumbs rubbed her shoulders. The tenderness in his touch brought fresh tears to her eyes.

She turned her head away. *"Aladh oirbh,"* she muttered.

"I do not understand Gaelic," he said.

"A plague on your head," she translated. "Now leave me alone. Dinna touch me again." She twisted away.

He sighed and lifted his hands. She kept her head turned away, and felt him rise from the bed. She heard the door close.

Turning over, she laid her head in her arms and sobbed, releasing angry tears long held, and new, sad tears of loss.

"WILL YOU DO AS THE KING ordered, then, and put her in a convent?" John asked.

Gavin shook his head and twirled his wine cup in his fingers. "I would not put her in any convent left to Edward's protection, and you know well why not." He glanced up at his uncle, who sat across from him in a chair. A brazier at their feet glowed hot and red, providing the only light in the small chamber that they shared for sleeping.

"Aye, I know why. But living wi' such a virago as a wife would scare even me," John said. "The monks heard her shouts when they were in their chapel. The abbot wasna pleased."

Gavin lifted a brow sardonically. "I was not overpleased myself. But what am I to do with her? I will not consign her to a nunnery, though Edward ordered it. She is my wife. The king did not think through the details of his plans for my future."

"The king expected her to die."

"We all expected her to die."

"But now she lives and grows stronger. And Edward didna say wha' to do if she lived. You've no direct orders in that event."

Gavin raised his brows. " 'Tis true. Aye, true." He sat forward, his attention caught, his thoughts quickening. "If the king hears of this, he could lay a charge of treason on my head if I do not confine her somewhere, or bring her back to Carlisle. He will forget fast enough that I married her on his whim."

"And part your own whim, lad. For the land. And for the sight o' her, near death like that. But now 'twill be a miracle if the king doesna hae us both drawn and hanged for removing her from the cage as we did."

"Aye," Gavin agreed ruefully. "He is overfond of drawing, hanging, and quartering of late. We are surely doomed if he finds this out. At least I am."

John grunted and sipped at his wine. "What o' the other orders King Edward gave you?"

"The gold is unimportant to me. I do not care if 'tis ever found. The king ordered me to hold Kinglassie for the English and join the search for Robert Bruce immediately. I have little interest in that search, but I will go to Kinglassie and claim the castle and land."

"The abbot made it clear that Christian canna be left here at Sweetheart Abbey," John said.

"I know." Gavin looked evenly at him. "She will go with us. In spite of the risks."

John nodded grimly. "What o' Dominy and the wee lad?"

"They'll come as well, I will decide what is best for them later, when the king sends his garrison."

"Lady Christian may be of some help to you. She kens the land and the people. She was wed to an English soldier once before, and was lady in that castle when 'twas garrisoned."

Gavin smiled, flat and bitter. "I misdoubt the lady will ever speak to me again, let alone help me."

John nodded. " 'Tis a muddle, this."

Gavin sighed. "I am concerned, John. Finding out about the marriage has been a great shock to her. She could still fail and die of this illness."

"Ach. She isna like Jehanne. This Scottish lassie has the will of ten men. Lady Christian doesna ken how to die, lad, or she would hae done it long ago in that cage."

"You may be right. But I had to tell her the truth."

"Aye, you did."

"And now I have no choice but to take her with me. Edward has finally granted me land and a castle, and I will not give them up easily."

John grunted. "Even though he gave you land that might sit in the middle of a Scottish battleground?"

"Even then. And if Edward decides to declare me a traitor over this muddle with Christian, he will have to siege that castle to get to me."

"Angel Knight, is it. There's too much o' the rebel in you for that name. You've a devil's way o' reasoning matters out when you need it."

Gavin shrugged. "Mayhap I do, when it serves."

CHAPTER SEVEN

ER TENACITY AMAZED HIM. Gavin shifted in his saddle and glanced once again at the curtain-enclosed litter that swayed on poles balanced between his and John's horses. The girl who lay behind those curtains had survived the final crisis of a lung fever that might have taken a toughened man in a matter of hours.

She had remarkable will. He had never seen anyone heal so fast, or with such determination. And throughout this journey, he had heard little more than an occasional cough from her. Despite blankets and furs and hot stones, he knew that the ride, which had taken three days, must be jostling, chilly, and uncomfortable for her. Yet Lady Christian had uttered no word of complaint.

She had barely spoken to him.

He sighed. Dominy's small son had created more of a concern due to natural restlessness, his boredom alleviated only when he rode with John or Gavin. Tired now from his earlier stint on John's horse, William had fallen asleep riding in his mother's lap, while she guided her gray charger ahead of the others along the side of the burn.

Traveling slowly because of the litter, they had left the abbey to head northwest toward the soaring round-tipped hills of central Galloway. Following along a river and then a wide burn, they had ridden past land as diverse and beautiful as the Highlands. Wide bare moors and glassy blue lochs alternated with rocky slopes, pine and leaf forests, and cold tumbling burns. The air was clear and crisp, and the dark mountains held a fascinating power.

Now, on the third day of the journey, they road through biting winds and wet, spitting snow. Gavin scanned, once again, the craggy hills and the pine forest that edged the wide stream nearby. He watched warily for Scots ready to attack a party of English.

Glancing again at the swaying litter, he thought about the woman inside. She would probably welcome an attack by Scots. She had let Gavin know, through gesture and expression, that she was furious with him. When he had lifted her into the litter the first day, her tight-lipped cold-eyed stare had bitten like a bee's sting.

He had never seen a green like ice. She had chilled him with that gaze, and had pierced him with it again just an hour ago, when he had handed her a flask of water.

Only a few nights ago, her condition had been severe, and he had not held much hope for her survival. But he was greatly relieved that she lived, for he had begun to care deeply about her. This intensity of feeling made him uneasy. He admired her spirit and willpower, but he had no logical understanding for the depth of his feelings toward her.

Lady Christian was different from Jehanne, who had been gentle, quiet, and shy, and who had never shown anger, or even expressed a strong opinion, in the three years they had been wed. She had been a sweet, fetching beauty when he had met her, but ill health had drained her steadily despite the prayers and efforts of many. Jehanne had been like a fading blossom, withering to a shadow as he had watched.

He had watched Christian fade, too. And then suddenly, like a miracle rose bursting on a dry midwinter vine, she had revived. He could hardly comprehend it, though he thought, wryly, that her growing health need only be attributed to sheer stubborn will. And temper.

He was relieved, yet baffled by the entire situation. The current of his life of late seemed to be plotted with twists as unexpected as those that turned the course of the burbling, icy stream that lay to his left.

Less than a fortnight ago, he had obeyed his own conscience and the order of King Edward, and had wed a dying Scottish rebel. Now he would have to make some kind of peace with his wife, who was no longer dying, and apparently despised English knights. A diplomatic crisis would have had more appeal.

Gavin sighed again. Surely King Edward would not enjoy this turn of events. He might condemn the lot of them once he learned of her survival and, even worse, her freedom.

If Gavin had been entirely faithful to the king's orders, Christian would have been in an English convent by now. But he had chosen to take her to Kinglassie, acting independently as he had so often in the past. His ability to solve difficult situations had always been an asset at court.

Now he simply courted danger.

He was taking his wife north without explicit permission from the king. His sympathy for her had earned him not only the lady's unrelenting fury, but the risk of treason.

He hoped that Kinglassie Castle was worth all this trouble. He had already decided that the lady was worth any challenge.

THEY FOLLOWED THE STREAM STEADILY northward, John silent and weary beside Gavin, Dominy ahead, her child asleep across her lap. Glancing at the gray, cold sky, Gavin scanned the steep hills that rose on all sides; wild, impenetrable tangles of forest and bramble and rock, winter-bleak and formidable enough to depress him. He was more tired than he had guessed.

In the distance, the broad burn flowed into and through two small pools. Exhaustion dulling his mind, Gavin needed a moment to grasp that he gazed at the landmark that the king's chamberlain had described to him, weeks ago in Carlisle when Gavin had asked directions to Kinglassie.

"The castle is northwest of here, less than a league from those two pools," Gavin told John. "Somewhere nearby there must be a bridge to cross the water."

"I dinna think so. Most of Scotland wants for good stone bridges," John said. "We'll have to ford the water, but getting across willna be easy with a litter. Lady Christian can share your horse, if need be."

Gavin nodded in agreement and rode slowly onward, looking among the winding course of the burn for a suitable fording place. He blew out a little frosted cloud of breath as he listened to the quiet bubble of the water and the slow crunch of horses' hooves over icy ground.

A mournful sound, long and sad, startled him. He glanced up and saw a dark flash, and another, between the bare trees that fringed the base of a near hill. Gavin instinctively touched the hilt of the sword sheathed in his wide belt.

"Arrows and bows would do us well in this place," he said to John. "I will mention that to Hastings when I meet with him. We may have to defend ourselves from the local population in more ways than we had thought." He gestured toward the hilltop.

John glanced up. "Aye. Wolves dinna care if we be Scots or English. Fleshmeat is fleshmeat." He reached out a hand to soothe his destrier.

"Dominy does not seem to have noticed our hillside companions," Gavin remarked quietly. The girl rode ahead of them on her gray charger, William asleep across her lap, his thin legs, clad in woolen hosen, dangling from beneath the cover of her cloak.

John glanced around. "Wild as the Highlands, these hills are. I will be glad for sturdy castle walls and a hearth fire when we reach Kinglassie."

In the hovering gray dusk, the twin pools shone like dull silver in the low light. Gavin noticed an area of shallows just before the first pool, where slabs of rocks were scattered through the sluicing water.

"There is our fording place," he said to John. They slowed their horses in tandem, careful not to disturb the angle of the litter. Dismounting, they turned to lift the cloth-draped framework to the ground. While John walked away to speak to Dominy, Gavin took a flask from his saddle, walked to the burn to fill it with fresh, cold water, and returned to the litter. Dropping to his haunches, he opened the curtains.

Christian opened her eyes and turned to look at him. Her

face was pale in the shadows, but her eyes were clear and alert, twin shards of green ice once she saw him.

"You have a good deal of stamina, my lady," Gavin said. "Have you more? We must cross a stream and ride on for a league or so."

"I have the strength. I willna die just to please you." Her voice was a hoarse scrape of sound, the soft Gaelic accent a sweet lilt in spite of her bitter tone.

Gavin huffed a flat laugh. "Weak as you are, you have a sharp tongue. And a keen memory for a grudge."

"I do." The dark centers of her eyes snapped with anger. "And I canna forget that you are a Sasunnach with no loyalty to the Bruce."

He sighed, and offered the flask to her. "Are you thirsty?"

At her curt nod, Gavin reached into the litter to slide a hand beneath her shoulders, and helped her sit up. She did not protest at his touch, but only swallowed the water when he held the flask, and lay back. As he replaced the rolled leather plug, she laid a hand on his arm.

"What stream do we ford?"

"One not far from Kinglassie."

"Kinglassie—" She looked at him, her eyes forest green smudges, lush and beautiful in the shadows. The ice had melted out of her glance at the mention of her home. "You take me there?"

"Aye. 'Tis your home. And mine, now."

She lifted her hand from his arm. "You have the castle. You have no reason to be kind to me. Why do you help me, Gavin Faulkener?"

He had wondered that himself, more than once. Perhaps, he wanted to say, he had seen a fine strong spirit locked in misery, and had wanted to set it free.

This slight, dark, valiant girl had compelled and fascinated him from the first. Fragile in appearance, she was nevertheless truly strong: he had already seen the fine quality of her will. And he had felt the keen sting of her temper.

"Why do you help me?" she repeated. "Is it for the gold of

Kinglassie?"

He shook his head. "I did not like the cage at Carlisle. So I made a change."

"You mean to imprison me elsewhere." Her eyes held his.

"Nay."

She lowered her gaze. "When I first saw you, I was fevered. I thought you were an angel come to take me to heaven."

"I would not call myself an angel."

She nodded. "Unless 'twere one of the fallen ones."

He nearly smiled. "You seem to have the angels waiting on your whim."

"But I willna go with them."

He nodded slowly, watching her. Behind him, he heard John approach. "Come, my lady," Gavin said, reaching toward her. "Can you sit my horse with me? We must cross the burn." Without waiting for a reply, he tucked the blanket around her and slid his arms beneath her to draw her out of the enclosure. She felt light and easy, no burden, as he stood.

He walked toward his horse, and John and Dominy came forward to dismantle the litter. They rolled it up and began to tie it behind the saddle of Dominy's charger. William sat in the high saddle, calling out battle cries until John hushed him sharply.

"Let me down," Christian said while Gavin held her, waiting. "I can stand while you mount your horse."

Gavin lifted his brows in surprise. "As you wish," he said, releasing her. She straightened and stood tentatively, leaning against him. He could feel the tremors that ran through her body. But she gave a little laugh of triumph, and looked up at him as if proud to show him that she was strong enough to stand.

The small spark of happiness brought a glow to her eyes and an appealing roundness to her thin face, a transformation that hinted at true beauty. He blinked, distracted by what he saw.

Feeling her tremble against him, he squeezed her shoulder gently. "Do not faint on me, now," he said.

"I willna," she said, frowning. "I am much stronger."

"You are," he murmured, holding her steady. "You are."

Dominy approached them, grinning, and Christian turned to

step forward into a warm hug. Releasing her, Gavin felt a strange twinge of regret when she readily turned away from him.

SEATED CROSSWISE WITH THE HIGH SADDLE pushing uncomfortably against her hip, Christian leaned against Gavin's broad shoulder. His left arm held her tightly, and his thighs, astride the black horse, were strong and steady beneath hers. His unshaven chin brushed against her forehead as he turned his head, and his voice, when he spoke to John, thrummed deep in her ear. Those sensations were oddly and undeniably pleasant.

She had not felt so safe, so secure, since she had been a child lifted into her father's arms. But she frowned, reminding herself that Gavin was an English knight. He may be her husband, but he could not be trusted. He was no source of safety. She straightened her spine to move her weight away from him.

Though he took her back to Kinglassie, she wondered what he truly planned for her. She knew that he meant to hunt the Bruce, as Henry and the other English soldiers had done. There would be war at Kinglassie again.

Kinglassie. She pressed her eyes shut against the image of its walls ablaze, and drew a deep, shuddering breath.

Looking around, she saw John and Dominy riding behind them. She glanced down at the swirling water as Gavin eased his black charger into the shallows. She knew this burn well, had crossed here many times.

She knew those silvery pools, too, and the dark forest and the surrounding mountains. She breathed in, relishing the crisp, cold air after hours inside the stuffy litter. But the cold tickled her throat and caused her to cough.

Gavin glanced sharply at her, his eyes a searing, deep blue. Then he returned his concentration to the task of guiding his destrier carefully over the rocks and into the deeper water. As the horse surged through the rushing burn, Christian listened to the loud rush of the water and shivered.

"Hold, Englishmen!" The cry sounded over the churn of the stream. Gavin and Christian looked up at the same moment.

"Jesu," Gavin muttered, just above her ear.

Two men stood on the bank, legs apart, faces glowering. They held iron-tipped lances twice their height, and looked eager to use them.

"Hold where you be!" one of the men shouted.

Christian frowned, and sat straighter. She knew these men; they were brothers, younger than she was, sons of her dear friends. She knew that they supported the Bruce's cause, and would not let an English escort pass unchallenged.

Gavin swore softly and pulled on the reins. One arm gripped Christian fiercely. She could sense the strength and the tension that ran through him.

"Who are you? English?" the taller one shouted. He tipped his long lance toward them menacingly.

"I am Sir Gavin Faulkener. There are women and a child in our party."

"I can see that. And since you're English, we'll hae your weapons and armor afore we let you go." Both men stepped down into the shallow water and advanced toward them.

"If we let you go," the other one called.

Gavin shifted his right arm as if to reach for his sword, scabbarded at the wide belt around his hips. But he held Christian in his left arm, and the reins in his right hand. Encumbered, he only stepped the horse sideways cautiously.

"This woman is ill," he called. "I ask that you leave us in peace."

Christian knew the brothers had not yet recognized her; she had changed in these past months because of illness and weight loss. She would have called to them, but her voice was weak and hoarse. Pushing back the plaid that hooded her head, she looked straight at them and lifted a hand.

The taller one, wearing a leather tunic with furs wrapped around his legs and a belted plaid draped over him, looked suddenly astonished. "Holy Mother of God! Lady Christian!" he called.

She lifted a hand. "Greetings, Iain Macnab, and Donal."

"How is it you are with a Sasunnach?" Iain asked in Gaelic.

"Are you hurt? We will have his heart for our supper!" He shifted his lance and pointed it at Gavin, calling out in Scots English. "Get down from your horse and let her go!"

"Lady Christian is my wife," Gavin called back. His arm tightened around her. "And she is ill. Let us pass. I am taking her to Kinglassie Castle."

"Kinglassie!" the other man said. " 'Tis no place for—"

"Let us pass!" John roared suddenly, charging past them through the water, his broadsword held high. "Clear the way and let us pass!"

Faced with the formidable prospect of an armored knight on a huge destrier, waving a broadsword with relish, Iain and his brother exchanged quick glances, then turned and ran to the bank.

John rushed after them, bellowing threats. They disappeared into the trees. After a moment, John sheathed his sword and turned to grin at Gavin.

"They willna trouble us now!" he called.

"Jesu," Gavin muttered, shaking his head. "He does love a victory." He urged his horse forward, and glanced down at Christian. "Those men are friends of yours, my lady?"

"They are," she answered. She craned her head to look toward the bank, anxious to catch another glimpse of the Macnab brothers, knowing that where there were two, there might be more, since there were eight brothers all together.

"Hold, now," Gavin said, grabbing her more tightly with his left arm as he pulled at the reins with his other hand. "Be still. Fording this stream is a hard enough task without a squirming girl. Easy, now. Hush," he said distractedly, looking down at the water.

She was not sure if he spoke to her or to his horse. They rode through the rest of the stream in silence.

Reaching the bank, Gavin cantered over to John.

"Have they gone for certain?" he asked.

John nodded. "Aye."

"Likely they have many friends in those woods. We had best ride swift for Kinglassie. 'Tis a league or so, no more, from here."

"It grows dark quickly," Dominy said, riding up behind them. "John, will they return?"

"Nay, lass, they're gone. Ride by me, now." She nodded and moved her horse into place beside him.

William, riding in front of his mother, shook a small fist and grinned up at John. "Harrow! Those beggary old shrews are gone!"

"Aye, lad," John said, grinning. "You've a way wi' an insult, but remember what the abbot told you."

"God loves our sweet words," the boy chirped.

"Aye. Now hush." John turned away to look at Gavin.

Gavin snapped his reins. " 'Tis no place to tarry. Come ahead." He leaned sharply as his horse launched forward. Curled against him, her legs dangling over the charger's side, Christian leaned, too, compressed and uncomfortable. She wrapped her arms tightly around Gavin's waist to hold on.

They rode rapidly, moving abreast over a wide stretch of rocky, rough moor edged by dense pine forest. In the gathering twilight, the hills and forests were soon black against the murky sky.

Reining in his horse, Gavin looked around. "The castle is due west from here," he said to John. "It cannot be far." He glanced down at Christian. "Am I right, lady?"

Her impulse was to offer him no help. But fatigue swamped her anger. She needed rest. And she had to see her home, as much as she dreaded the moment. Scanning the dark contours of the hills, she searched for a familiar gleam of smooth water.

"There," she said, lifting a hand to point. Her fingers shook with exhaustion. "Through those trees. A loch."

Gavin spurred his mount and followed where she gestured.

Beyond the stand of trees, Gavin drew the horse to a halt at the top of a slope. A long, wide loch lay at its base, its dark, silky surface rippled with soft light.

Stark and silent, a castle rose up from a huge promontory of rock that jutted out into the loch. No welcoming light warmed the bare windows of the castle. Silhouetted against the twilight sky, four corner towers rose broken and roofless, their thick walls shattered at the top.

Gavin stared for a long time. " 'Tis a ruin," he finally said.

Christian forced herself to sit straighter, resisting the profound weakness that made her limbs tremble, biting her lip against the tears that gathered in her eyes. She gazed upon the dark, unwelcoming walls of her home.

"Burned out. Destroyed," she said. "Last summer."

He looked at her. "You knew?"

Her head spun. She could feel herself slipping into cloying exhaustion. She had to grip Gavin's arm to hold steady in the midst of the dizziness.

"I knew," she whispered. "I knew. I burned it myself."

CHAPTER EIGHT

I N THE COLD, WINDY HOUR BEFORE DAWN, Gavin climbed the stone steps that led to the parapet. Standing on the wall walk in the faint gray light, her surveyed the ruin of Kinglassie. Though the others still slept inside the shelter of the largest tower, he had awoken restless, and had gone outside. Now, high above the courtyard, looking out across the devastation, he felt an overwhelming sense of frustration.

Earlier, using torches made from cloths wrapped around resinous pine branches, he and John had explored the castle. The fire had gutted three of the four round towers and the massive gatehouse, rendering them roofless and without floors and ceilings. Two of the towers had wide cracks in the stone walls.

The courtyard was filled with haphazard piles of charred rubble, the remains of the wood and thatch buildings that had once clustered against the surrounding curtain wall. Everywhere the walls bore the blackened stains of ferocious heat and smoke.

They had found adequate shelter and stable space in the ground-floor level of the largest tower, which had sustained the least damage. The main entrance to that tower was on the second level, but the floors and ceilings inside had collapsed. The ground floor had a usable, if narrow, entrance, meant only for access to the storage area.

Kicking at a broken bit of stone, Gavin watched it skitter over the edge of the parapet and land in the courtyard below.

He sighed, leaned against the crenellated wall, and looked over its width. The loch stretched away in the distance, surrounded by high, dark forested hills, the whole blanketed in a chilly mist.

He peered straight down. The massive bare rock of the promontory thrust up from the loch to meet the base of the high, thick curtain wall, forming a sheer, dizzying drop at one corner, where the great tower was situated. A deep ditch, cut into the rock, surrounded the castle on three sides. Opposite the lochside, the gatehouse faced thick forest.

Water, rock, and forest had protected Kinglassie from enemies for centuries. The castle must have been a formidable place once, Gavin thought, resistant to almost any invasion but one: fire.

And now, because of the action of one spiteful Scottish rebel, Kinglassie Castle was a defenseless ruin. Gavin picked up a pebble, rolled it in his hand, and flung it violently. It clattered away, loud in the cold, silent darkness.

Anger rolled through him, heavy and bitter, as he realized the extent of the betrayal the king had handed him. Edward had promised him a castle and lands in return for years of service. But Gavin had always been wary of the king's word; even a signed charter could be a temporary agreement in Edward's eyes. This marriage to Christian had at least ensured that Kinglassie belonged to him legally.

He had waited years for a grant of an English castle. His French lands, acquired through his first marriage, had filled his coffers with gold, from grapes grown for wine, and from wool. He had coin enough to finance the building of any stronghold. All he had needed was good English land.

He gazed down toward the smooth dark loch. A chill breeze fanned through his hair. While he watched, dawn began to lighten the sky, just above the black shoulders of the mountains that edged the loch.

Somehow, though he had been here only hours, these charred walls, the loch, those craggy mountains, seemed more like home to him than his French castle ever had.

By one deft stroke of fate's sure hand, he had acquired a wife, and land, and crenellated walls.

Listening to the soft rush of the wind and the steady lap of the water far below, he knew, suddenly and decisively, that he would stay here. He would rebuild. No one, English or Scots, would take Kinglassie from him.

He had a home and a wife at last. He would remain. And he would do his best to protect both, and see that both grew stronger.

HEARING THE CRUNCH OF BOOTS on stone, he turned and looked through the shadows. John mounted the steps to the parapet level. Gavin nodded in mute greeting as his uncle sat beside him with a great huffing sigh.

"The others are sleeping still?" Gavin asked.

"Aye, all three snoring like bairns. I couldna sleep well. I've just gone to look around the gatehouse. I saw you up here, watching for invaders."

"Hah. A child could invade this place." Gavin threw down another pebble. "Look over there. The portcullis is stuck, the gatehouse is a ruin, the drawbridge is down. Anyone could walk into the enclosure. And we have no weapons to defend ourselves, beyond what we brought."

Gavin laughed, flat and hard. " 'Tis a cozy place for the few of us to sleep, but a garrison would crowd us some." He shoved his hair back. "Roofs and outbuildings can be replaced, but as long as the castle is gateless, we are open to attack." He glanced toward the gate, where the massive oak doors that should have sealed the inner courtyard hung loose and charred on their iron hinges.

"I went as far into the gatehouse as I dared," John said. "The portcullis is jammed in place, halfway down. That fire must hae roared like a blacksmith's forge. Inside the winch room above that entrance arch, the iron chains for the portcullis are melted to the pulleys. Melted!" John shook his silvery head in amazement. "The floor is collapsed there, and the winch for the drawbridge mechanism looks like a Yule log after Twelfth Day."

Gavin nodded. Beyond the outer gate, the huge drawbridge

was collapsed downward, its heavy chains trailing into the wide ditch on the side of the castle that faced the forest.

"The drawbridge canna be drawn up," John said. "The pulley chains for that are ruined."

"The king and Hastings must have known that Kinglassie was in this condition, and could not be garrisoned," Gavin said.

"I'd wager Edward Longshanks knew just wha' he did when he gave you Kinglassie. A sound betrayal, lad. A ruined castle in return for years o' service. And ye ken well why."

"Aye," Gavin said. "I know why. King Edward has a memory longer than most. Payment for my opinion at Berwick, ten years late."

"Likely Hastings hasna let the king forget it, either. And now that Edward's slapped your face, he expects you to clean this mess up for him so he can send his soldiers here."

"He ordered me to meet with Hastings to discuss provision. He must have had timber and nails in mind, rather than weapons and supplies for a garrison and fodder for their horses."

"Will ye stay, then? Or will ye return to France?"

"Edward would have my head if I left."

"Well," John drawled, "that threat hasna stopped ye afore." He looked around. "But 'tis a poor trick the king has played. He owes you good land."

"Aye." Gavin tossed another small stone into the darkness. "The debt does not bother him. Edward's blood feud with Scotland has precedence over any man's rights."

"Will you ask him to make good on his promise to grant you land and stout walls?"

"He would say the promise has been kept. These walls are stout enough. Look there." Gavin gestured toward the curtain wall. "Thick and high. And capable of withstanding a great fire," he added wryly.

"Well," John said, glancing around, "where there are strong walls of any kind, and land good enough for cattle and sheep, a man may find what he needs."

Gavin hesitated, then nodded slowly. "True." He stared at the tower that contained the small room where his new wife slept.

"Christian said she burned Kinglassie with her own hand."

John nodded. " 'Tis a Scots practice from generations back. Burn a stronghold so the enemy canna take it. The Scots return, sometimes years later, after the enemy have lost interest, and rebuild. I hear Robert Bruce believes in scorching good Scottish earth and Scottish walls to prevent the English from taking over. I will wager he ordered her to do this."

"Likely so," Gavin said. "But a woman would need a strong heart to set her own home ablaze." He remembered Christian's face when she had seen the castle again. She loved the place well, and no doubt of it. And when she had told him that she had burned the castle, she had sounded infinitely sad.

"Scotswomen are full o' courage and will. Whatever a man will do, a Scotswoman will try, and surely match him much o' the time."

"Well, she did her task well. There will be no English garrison based here for many months, if at all."

"There's a great deal o' work to be done here."

Gavin rubbed at his chin. "Well, then, you and I, dear uncle, have our task ahead."

"Hmmph," John said. "That Dominy looks strong enough for one or two men, herself."

Chuckling, Gavin glanced up as the dawn sky pearled through a gap in the largest tower. Through the early, cold mist, the first burnish of the sun warmed the stone and spread over the enclosing wall. A flock of white doves flew up from somewhere, catching a current of wind and drifting like pale smoke.

Washed in a moment of golden light, Kinglassie looked whole and strong, as it must have looked once, and could again.

"I'LL NOT LIFT ANYTHING," Dominy said firmly, folding her arms across her ample bosom.

"*Ach*, you're as strong as we are, lass," John said. "You've a fine great arm on you, and a broad back like a man."

Dominy gasped. Christian, watching from her pallet on the floor, blinked wide, and glanced at Gavin, who was seated on the floor near her. He said nothing, though his lips twitched. She felt a laugh bubble up, too, but held it back.

"John means to compliment you, dear," Christian said.

"Hmmph." Dominy tossed her head back. "For that flattery, he'll get as much help from me as milk from a sparrow." Beside her, William listened, his eyes wide.

"He only teases you because you get so angry at him," Gavin said. "He means to say that we need whatever help you could give us in making repairs."

"I'm strong as a bull," William offered. "I'll do the lifting." John patted him on the shoulder.

Dominy looked at Gavin. "I'll help where I can, then. My father was a mason. I learned something from watching him as a child. Do ye know aught of such skills?"

"Masonry?" John frowned, considering this. "I ken well how to undermine a castle wall wi' fat and fire."

William's face brightened and he leaned forward eagerly, but his mother made a sound of disgust and shook her head. "And what help is firing the walls in a ruined castle, man?"

John scowled and turned to Gavin. "Wha' are our most immediate needs?"

"A bath and food," Christian grumbled.

"My lady," Gavin said, his tone sharp enough to startle her, "we have all done the best we could with cloths and warm water. I assume your tubs have been burned. Until we build a new one, we will wash as we did this morning. And we will all have to sleep together in this chamber until we repair some rooms."

"The oats the abbot sent with us willna last long," John said. "Food is a priority. We will need to go out hunting."

"Aye. And beyond that, our most immediate need is to fix the gate and construct new floors in this tower, so that we can use some other rooms here," Gavin said. "I will ride to Loch Doon Castle to meet with Hastings soon, to request tools and materials, and enough laborers to make repairs here. If any of those are available."

"Oliver Hastings?" Christian asked.

Gavin looked at her. "Aye, my lady. Do you know him?"

"He captured me in the Highlands," she said softly. The mention of that name had conjured a dreadful unease and fear in her. Drawing the plaid up over her shoulders, she shivered.

She glanced at Gavin. He watched her, his eyes blue-black in the flickering light and shadow. If she had not known that he was an English knight like Hastings, like her husband Henry had been, she might have interpreted that silent, steady, frowning gaze as concern.

She lowered her eyes, blushing, and looked away.

"The winter weather will delay our repairs," John said.

"Winter in Galloway tends to the mild," Christian said. "We get cold winds and rain here, but scant ice and snow."

"If we can work out of doors through some of the winter, we may accomplish this faster than I thought," Gavin said.

"Mild, eh? As mild and balmy as this wee chamber?" John waved his hand around the small ground-level storage chamber, with its low, vaulted stone ceiling and thick walls.

"Not quite," Christian said, smiling a little. Gavin and John had found some iron kettles that morning and had filled them with water from the loch. Two kettles had been set to boil over the makeshift central hearth, built from a circle of stones, and Gavin had sealed the gaping entrance and one narrow side door with curtains taken from the litter. Smoke drifted upward through a gap in the roof, but the enclosed air was moist and warm, and her breathing was easier because of it.

"Feels like a summer rain in here," John said, standing. "I need some good chill air. Come, Will. I saw some pigeons and doves roosting in one o' the towers, and I've a taste for a pie. We'll do a little hunting, eh?" Will jumped up eagerly, and John turned to Dominy. "And I'll show you the castle. Mayhap we'll find some stones or beams for you to hoist." His brown eyes twinkled with mischief.

Dominy stood up. "I'll hoist a stone at his head soon enough," she hissed loudly to Christian, and then followed after John and her son.

Christian turned to see Gavin smiling slightly at Dominy's parting remark. He had made no move to rise to go with them, but watched the fire in the hearth, twirling a small stick idly in the long, nimble fingers of one hand.

"You seem stronger today," he said.

"I slept most of the day," she said. And now she felt both hungry and restless.

"I hear from Dominy that your appetite is good."

"I ate more than my share of the oatcakes that Dominy made," she admitted. "There isna much left in that bag of oats we brought from the abbey."

"You need the food more than we do, just now," he said. "My lady—there are matters we must discuss, if you are strong enough."

She nodded, watching the fire crackle inside a circle of stones, and waited for him to speak. But he let the silence linger, the only sounds the fire and the faint bubble of water in the steaming cauldron.

Gavin bent forward to toss a few more sticks into the low blaze, and she glanced at him. His hair flowed over his shoulders, glistening strands of gold and brown, like the grain in polished oak. Clean from a morning's scrubbing, his unshaven beard was thickening daily, blurring the strong line of his jaw. But his profile had the strong clarity of fine stone sculpture.

He did not wear chain mail or his golden surcoat. Yet even in the somber black of his woolen tunic and trews, he seemed to radiate a noble, controlled power.

She recalled his dazzling appearance in polished chain mail and the white tunic with its embroidered design of wings in golden thread; now she knew the meaning behind the design—falcon wings, for Faulkener. Not for angel; she almost laughed at her misinterpretation.

But no wonder, she thought, that she had once taken him to be an archangel, all gold and silver and strength. He had the earthly form of a warrior saint, and the beautiful chiseled face of an angel. But she knew, now, that he was none of those.

"I thought you were Saint Michael, once," she said softly.

He watched the flames. "So you have said. Am I to take that as a reproach?"

She shrugged. "If you like."

"Ah. Now that you know for me an Englishman, rather than some sainted Scots knight, you feel betrayed."

"I do," she said softly.

"I took you from that cage, and wed you."

"You took my castle on your king's order, and you mean to destroy my cousin Robert Bruce."

"*I* took your castle?" He waved a hand in abrupt anger. "Lady, look around you! You were the one who destroyed it!"

"I destroyed it to guard against such as you!"

"We would not be suffering now from lack of shelter and safety if you had had less of a hand with a torch!" he shouted.

She jumped slightly, startled by the depth of his sudden anger. But it kindled her own. "I never thought to come back here with another English husband!" she yelled. Her hoarse voice cracked on the last word.

He heaved an exasperated breath. "Do you forget that you are lady of this castle again, when you might have been in prison?" he asked between his teeth. She saw that he barely controlled his temper, but she did not care to back down.

"I am a prisoner still. You say you own Kinglassie now. You say we are wed, but I dinna recall that." She fisted and unfisted her hands. "How can I trust that you willna harm me or mine? I dinna know you! I surely dinna trust you!"

He broke a twig in his fingers and threw it down. "You are particular about your rescuers."

"Just my husbands," she snapped.

He nodded brusquely. "Very well. Then learn this: my father was an English knight who fought beside King Edward in the Holy Land. My mother was a Scotswoman. Both are dead. I have spent the last ten years in France, some of that time as royal ambassador to the French court. I came back to England to escort some French bishops to Carlisle. King Edward granted me Kinglassie and ordered me to come here immediately. Now you know what you need to know."

"King Edward also ordered you to marry me," she added, folding her arms decisively across her chest.

"He gave permission for me to take you from the cage and marry you before you . . . in case you died." He watched the fire again, while a muscle tightened and relaxed in his cheek.

"What were his orders to you about Kinglassie?" she asked.

"He wanted me to come here and set up a garrison, and to pursue the Bruce."

"And he wants you to find the treasure hidden here," she said, narrowing her eyes.

Gavin shrugged, still looking away. "He mentioned that. But he may have given me this place as a sort of family legacy. Henry Faulkener was my cousin."

"Cousin!" She drew in a sharp breath. "Then you have heard of his death."

He tossed another stick into the flames. "I heard you caused it."

"Ach! Now I see it!" She sat forward. "You took me from the cage and brought me here, meaning to take some horrible revenge for your cousin's death. Wasna the cage cruel enough for you? Do you mean to imprison me here for the Scots to see? Will you torture me to learn the secret of Kinglassie's legend? Hit me? Starve me? Watch me die?"

"Lady—" Gavin bit back a solid curse and looked at her. "You have a vile temper. Are all Englishmen but heartless brutes in your eyes?"

"I have received only brutality from the English!"

His gaze was unwavering. "Have you had only that from me?" he asked softly.

She hesitated, then shook her head miserably. Until now, he had shown her only gentleness; and betrayal, she reminded herself.

"I have no wish to quarrel with you, my lady. But you seem capable of naught else since you began to gain back your strength. You did not appear to be such a virago when I took you from the cage." He threw the twig, lancelike, into the fire.

She lifted her chin. "I am wed to another Sasunnach without my consent. 'Tis another of King Edward's schemes against the Scots."

He angled toward her, his eyes glittering and hard. "And what did you want? To be left undisturbed in your cage at Carlisle? Would you prefer that to marriage with me?"

She turned her face away at his bitter tone. Dark, foul memories of the cage suddenly pulled at her viciously. She sometimes felt as if they would suffocate her if she gave in to them. Tears leaked down her cheeks in warm rivulets, and she put up a shaking hand to hide them.

Gavin Faulkener had saved her from that horrible prison. She owed him gratitude, not anger and spite. But he was English. She could never trust him. Ever. She squeezed her eyes shut and tipped her head into her arms, folded on her updrawn knees.

He had not told her who he was, or why he had taken her, and she had believed him her savior. That was a betrayal of a sort, and surely felt like a deep loss and disappointment. She had trusted him once, implicitly, when he had rescued her, and when he had held her in his arms at the abbey.

He had shown her kindness and caring, even love. She had never thought to feel those again in her life. She desperately wanted that compassionate man to return.

But the hard sarcasm and anger that Gavin had just shown her reminded her too much of Henry. Cousins, they were, both pledged to a cruel king. Hiding her face, she caught back a sob.

"Christian—" Gavin said. She did not answer. She heard him stand, heard him walk across the slate floor and pick up his cloak. Be he did not go out.

He came back and held out two folded parchment pages. "One is the charter to Kinglassie. The other is a record of our marriage, which I had the priest write out. Look at them. I want you to have no doubts about my claim to either."

Sniffling, she opened the charter first, with its dangling blood-red royal seal. Scanning the French, she recognized only a few words. But the writ of marriage was in Latin, which she could understand.

A sudden memory came flooding back: candlelight and shadows, and Gavin's hand, warm and strong over hers. A man had droned on in Latin, a priest. And she had clung to Gavin's hand

and had answered aye, and aye again, thinking her sins absolved. But she had answered a vow.

And she remembered a gentle, dry kiss, still so compelling and poignant that the very memory tugged at her heart. Now she knew that it had been a marriage kiss.

"Do you recall the marriage?" he asked.

She nodded and laid the pages aside. "I am wife to another Sasunnach knight who intends to destroy the Scottish people. Who intends to find my cousin the Bruce and kill him."

"Think you I am so foul a villain, lady?" he growled.

"You come here on the orders of a king who has no right to invade Scotland. Henry and his garrison destroyed so much here. I canna watch that happen again." She touched trembling fingers to her brow.

Gavin laughed bitterly. She glanced up. "What could I destroy here?" he asked, waving his hand. "There is naught left here but some charred walls. No one near Kinglassie need fear this English knight. Without a garrison—and none can house here, lady, well you knew that when you torched the place—I can hardly scourge the countryside in search of Robert Bruce. I cannot even provide adequate food and shelter for the few of us. Our sack of oats from the abbey's larder is nearly gone. All we have to live on are those pigeons that roost everywhere here."

"Wild doves," she said. "They are wild doves. They have always been at Kinglassie."

"Well, I hope you like to eat them," he snapped, and walked away. Slamming a fist against the wall vehemently, startling her, he swore, viciously and crudely. Leaning a hand against the stone, he stared at the soot-blackened wall.

"We may starve here, Lady Christian, but for your doves. There is little enough game to be hunted in winter. We have no grain for our bellies beyond what little we brought from the abbey. There is no fodder for the horses. We do not even have a sound chamber to stay in through the winter."

She tipped her head, watching him. His tone surprised her. "You sound as if you feel responsible for us."

"Of course I do. Will you still fear me, or call me a Sasunnach villain for that?"

"I dinna fear you," she said softly. Sighing, she rose to her feet, knowing what she should do, what she should have done already. But she had been so tired that she had not thought clearly or wisely. She walked over to him, feeling dizzy, willing it to pass. "Gavin," she said. "Come with me. Bring the torch, and your cloak."

He gave her a frowning, puzzled look, then picked up his cloak and swirled it over his shoulders. Grabbing one of the flaming resinous torches, he waited while Christian wrapped her plaid over her worn gown.

She led him through the curtained doorway in the side wall into a tiny chamber, once used for storage but now empty, its walls and slate-covered floor blackened by smoke. The scent of charring was so strong that it irritated Christian's throat, and she coughed. Leaning against the wall, she rested for a moment.

In the far wall, a wide oak door, partially burned, hung crooked in its stone frame. She pushed against it.

"Here. Let me," Gavin said. Handing Christian the torch, he shoved his shoulder against the door; its planks split and fell. "What lies through here?" he asked.

"The bakery," she said.

"Ah. Perhaps a loaf or two escaped the conflagration," he said sarcastically as he passed through the doorway.

"More than that, I think," she said, smiling to herself.

CHAPTER NINE

"**B**E CAREFUL. There are burned timbers on the floor," Gavin said. He scanned the charred wreckage of the large room, and turned back to take the torch from Christian. The girl was clearly in need of more rest, yet she insisted on searching for a loaf of burned bread. Sighing at the futility of this venture, he waited while she came into the room.

Stepping past him, she looked around. At least, he thought, he would not have to endure her hysteria over the state of her castle. She seemed calm and sure of what she wanted here.

His first influx of anger had passed, and he now regretted shouting at her. She was weak still, and he should have been more careful of her fragile state. But her temper apparently did not suffer from weakness; her anger had been as strong as his.

"Those boards were once two great oak trestle tables," she said, gesturing. "Over there, the cupboards are burned as well." Raising her skirts, she picked her way carefully through the jumble of ragged planks. "This bakery lies just below the kitchen, next to the great hall above. A great deal of cooking was done here, in that great hearth." She indicated a spacious fireplace with baking ovens built into its side walls.

"Think you some bit of grain remains here for us to eat?" Gavin asked. "You will more likely have empty hands, and a thump on the head if that vaulted ceiling collapses. Go careful, there. What is that, a well? Careful!" He grabbed her elbow and pulled her back from the unprotected edge of a wide, dark hole in the floor. A thin black gleam of water was visible far below.

"I wouldna have fallen," she said. "I knew it was there."

"What in the name of sweet Christ is a well doing here?" he asked, peering into the depths of the hole, and holding Christian back from the collapsed stone wall.

"That draw-well has been here longer than the tower," she said. "Much of the castle is ancient. An ancestor of my mother grew weary of dragging buckets in from the yard, and built this tower around the well itself. 'Twas convenient to draw water directly into the bakery, and then up to the kitchen." She pointed to a gaping hatch in the ceiling above their heads.

"I am certain it was," Gavin said wryly. He kicked a stone over the edge; it rattled all the way down. "And now 'tis conveniently dry." Squatting down, he peered at the shadows and ripples at the bottom of the well. "Jammed by debris, I think. But John and I can clear it so that we will have a water supply, at least." He stood and looked around. "The walls of this tower are still sound, from what I have seen so far. The stone vaulted ceilings down here seem strong as well, though a skilled mason should look at the castle. Above these rooms, the floor beams can be replaced in the kitchen and the great hall. Was the kitchen floor all wood?"

"Nay," she said, glancing up. " 'Twas oak covered with slating."

He touched her arm briefly. "Christian—you know the design of the castle before the fire. Help me. Explain what you know of the structure."

She stared down into the well. "If I help you to rebuild Kinglassie, you will use its strength against my people."

"English or Scots, we must have a place to live. We need to work together if we are to survive the winter. And the work must begin now."

"I know," she said. " 'Tis why I brought you here. Will you move that burned cupboard away from the corner? Aye, just there, near that wee door." She took the torch from his hand.

"What is it, another storage place?" he asked, bending to shift the pieces of charred oak. Lost in shadow, a narrow niche was cut into the wall, its wooden door partially destroyed. He frowned. "No sack of meal could have escaped a thorough roasting, my lady. But we will look, if it pleases you." He grabbed hold of the scorched edge of the door and pushed it open easily. "A corridor?" He glanced at her.

She gave him a little smile, slow and secret, and stepped through. Intrigued, he followed.

The corridor was high, but barely large enough for a tall and broad-shouldered man to pass through. Walking between walls made of flat, stacked stones, Gavin looked around curiously.

"This looks like an ancient tomb. I hope you have no plans for me here," he drawled.

Christian gave him a scathing look, then glided ahead of him, holding the torch high. The snapping, brilliant light spilled over the dark cloud of her hair and illumined the plaid she clutched across her shoulders. She stopped at a heavy door, bound and studded with iron.

"This is the pit," she said. "The dungeon, with one wee window. A second pit below it was used only rarely, a black and awful place no bigger than a coffin."

He cocked an eyebrow at her. "Ah," he said. "And is that where you would have me sleep, my lady?"

"Perhaps later," she said, smiling.

Gavin chuckled softly as she turned away to descend a few broad, shallow steps. He followed. The floor sloped downward into shadow. His arm and hand brushed against the wall once or twice, bringing away sooty smudges.

"The blaze reached at least this far," he said.

"It did," she said. "But we go farther."

The passage ended at yet another door, its surface blackened but otherwise sound. Christian handed him the torch, then stood on her toes and reached into a crevice high in the wall. Withdrawing an iron key, she inserted it into the lock and turned, stubbornly pressing her slight weight into the heavy door until it gave. Then she stepped into the darkness beyond to enter another corridor.

This one was much larger, a long, sinuous tunnel that

stretched into darkness, its rough-cut walls and ceiling crudely rounded. The air was distinctly chilly, with the raw, earthy smell of stone and a hint of dampness and draft. Holding the crackling resinous torch high, Gavin walked beside Christian as they followed the gradual slope of the corridor.

Every sound they made—their breathing, their footsteps, the fluttering torch flame—echoed loudly in the vaulted space. Gavin took Christian's elbow when she stumbled on the rough stone underfoot, and then kept his hand on her arm, knowing that she was fatigued. Wondering how she found the strength to walk this far, he reminded himself that she was a strong, obstinate woman. Still, she did not refuse his support.

"This is cut directly into the rock that supports the castle," he said. He touched the gritty stone.

"Look how clean the walls are down here—the fire didna reach this far. Thanks be to God."

Her relieved tone told him that whatever was hidden down here was of great importance to her; this place had been built to house secrets. "If you intend to show me the treasure of Kinglassie, my lady, may I remind you that it will not feed us or warm us," he said.

"The treasure isna hidden down here."

"Is it not? What better place that a subterranean passageway behind locked doors?"

" 'Tisna here," she repeated, and stopped abruptly.

Sheer rock, the end of the tunnel, loomed in the torch's glow. Christian turned to the right and pushed her hands against a tall slab that angled out from the wall. It turned easily, canted on a hidden turning stone, to reveal a wide opening. She stepped through. Gavin followed her into a small stone chamber.

"Sweet Christ," he murmured, looking around. "This must be cut from the center of the promontory."

"The very heart of the rock," she agreed. The whispery echo of her voice seemed soft and intimate. She walked toward a door that was dark with age.

Watching her, Gavin was enchanted by the place, and by the graceful, quiet girl enclosed here with him far below the earth.

The deep silence and solitude held peace as well as mystery. Time seemed suspended, without expectation or demand.

He stepped forward to look at the decorative interlaced carving around the door, and the flat stone lintel. "This door is very ancient," he said.

"The Galloway princes who were my mother's ancestors cut the tunnel and the chamber," she answered. "Reach to the center of the lintel, please—a key is tucked in that crevice."

He found the heavy iron key and handed it to Christian. She looked up at him in the torch's glow, a delicate, dark-haired beauty washed in golden light.

"Gavin—before we open that door, I would ask something of you." Uncertainty, even fear, flashed in her eyes.

He frowned. "What you will, lady."

"Promise me that you are no Englishman in this place," she said. "Promise me that here you are just a man."

He narrowed his eyes. A thrill raced through him at her odd, earnest words, a sudden plunge that tingled and swelled through his loins. "Aye. Only a man," he murmured.

Nodding soberly, she put the key in the lock and turned it, grunting softly with the effort. "Here," he said, and leaned forward to help. Together they pushed the heavy door open.

HE HAD STEPPED IN BEHIND HER, holding the torch high. Astonished, then delighted, he turned in a slow circle.

"God save us," Gavin said, " 'tis a storage chamber."

The room was high, wide, and long, chiseled, like the corridor, from solid stone. But this space was far more vast, its walls set with iron sconces meant to hold torches, its ceiling pierced with smoke vents at either end. Translucent beams of light from the vents sliced down to illuminate an odd assortment of wooden chests and barrels, stacked against the walls and ranged haphazardly across the floor.

While Christian remained near the door, he walked through the room, shining the torch toward the various boxes, chests, sacks, and barrels.

"Holy Mother Mary," he said, running a hand along the top of a barrel. A few loose grains of barley swept to the floor. Beside that were piled several plump sacks. He looked down at some scattered oats near the toe of his boot.

Touching, next, a stack of thick, folded cloths, he found woolen blankets and heavy plaids; lifting the lid of a chest, he discovered a tangle of leather strapping and iron bits, horse collars and tools. The chest beside that held a jumble of items: kettles, candlesticks, spoons, tongs, wooden dishes.

He found a barrel of dried beans, another of dried peas, and a third with assorted herbs wrapped in cloths; a cask of pepper and one of cinnamon; and a barrel of salted fish. Another barrel, set on its side and sealed with pitch, sloshed when he tilted it.

"Wine?" he asked, turning to Christian.

"Imported from Gascony," she answered. "We purchased three casks of red wine at the market in Ayr last spring. There are two left."

Shaking his head in amazement, he continued the length of the chamber. Ropes of garlic bulbs and bunches of dried herbs hung from a wooden rack. Shriveled apples filled two barrels, onions another two. Stacked in a corner were the dismantled skeletons of bed frames, with plump feather beds tossed over them. Benches, chairs, trestle boards, and supports had been placed near the beds.

He stopped to examine the contents of several large wooden chests which contained pieces of mesh armor, spurs, a few maces and axes among other weapons. Three barrels were filled with arrow, and several longbows, their strings separately looped and hung on the wall, stood near a bundle of tall lances. He recognized the English design of the lances.

"These belonged to Henry's garrison, I presume," he said, looking at Christian, who waited by the door. She nodded.

He turned and came back, placing the torch in a bracket near the door. Christian watched him silently, her eyes huge and wary. He stood beside her, so close that his arm brushed her shoulder.

"An entire household is stored down here," he said.

"Near enough. 'Twas well protected from the fire," she said. "I hoped that these things would be safe."

"Down here, they would have been protected from even the fires of hell," he said. "This ancestor of yours was an ambitious architect. And a clever one."

"Long ago, he built a fortress on the promontory in the same spot that the castle stands now. There were many wars then— about the time of the first Christians in Scotland—and he had this hall cut so that his people could hide from the enemy. But for a very long time it has been used only for storage."

"These are your household goods," he said. "Things collected when Henry owned Kinglassie."

"Henry didna own Kinglassie," she snapped. "He took it, on the order of his king. As you have done."

He sighed, familiar with her temper now, and elected to pursue peace for the moment. "John and I will move what is most useful from down here—food and blankets, some tools, and such."

She nodded and picked at the worn fabric of her sleeve. "I will need to go through the clothing chests for a fresh gown. And I would ask you to carry this up for me," she said, turning toward a large object, covered in hide and shaped like a sturdy wing. Pulling at some thongs, she lifted off the covering. "My *clàrsach*."

"Your what? I do not understand Gaelic."

"My harp. I am a harper, but much time has passed since I last played." She streamed her fingertips across the strings, releasing a delicate swell of sound, a silvery enchantment in the stillness.

Gavin looked at the triangular frame, made of dark and light woods, polished and gleaming in the torchlight, and elaborately carved. Slender brass strings shimmered like dark gold. "I have heard that a Scottish harp makes the music of heaven," he said.

"Of heaven and earth, of the soul and the heart," she said reverently. She plucked at a string, releasing a soft golden sound into the air. "Have you ever heard one played?"

He shook his head. "But my mother told me how beautiful such music was. She would sing some of the melodies to me when I was small. I look forward to hearing you play your clarsa."

"*Clàrsach*," she corrected him, laughing. He smiled and repeated the word. "But I willna play well for a while yet," she said, looking at her hands critically. "The ancient punishment for a harper who displeased a chief was to cut his fingernails. Mine are already split and short."

He took her hands in his. "Your hands are graceful and strong. A harper's hands." She looked up at him quickly, as if his compliment startled her. "Now, as for the rest of your hoard here, my lady, I will not carry up the beds and tables until we have cleared out living space in the towers and made repairs. Then we will have better use for the furniture you have stored here." He glanced down at the dark, gleaming crown of her head. " 'Twas clever of you to put these things here for your return."

"The wine barrels and much of the grain were already here. The rest I had moved down here before I . . . left Kinglassie. I didna want it to go to waste."

Gavin cocked a brow. "Just the castle."

She pulled her hands away from his, and tilted her head in a haughty way that he recognized as a defense. "My cousin the Bruce ordered me to burn Kinglassie. 'Tis his policy to scorch the very earth to cinders rather than let the English take over Scotland. But I didna want to burn goods that could be useful to the people who live near the loch. I told the village priest about this place, but the room looks undisturbed. No one has been here."

"Mayhap he was waiting for you to return," Gavin said.

"That may be," she said. Then she shivered, and suddenly faltered where she stood. Gavin grabbed her arm.

"Sweet rood, you are exhausted," he said. He led her to a wooden chest placed against the stone wall, and when she sat on its lid, he sat beside her.

"My lady," he said, "you may have saved our lives with this hoard of yours."

"Now that you know of this place, what will you do?" she asked, glancing up at him. Fear flickered briefly in her eyes.

"I made you a promise," he said softly. "Think you I will not honor it?"

She shrugged, a hesitant lift of one shoulder. "You are a Sasunnach knight."

"Not here," he said. "Have you forgotten? Here, in this place,

I am but a man."

Silence. His heart began to pound; he was acutely aware that her shoulder was pressed against his arm, that her body was warm beside his own.

"Did you think that I would ride out and summon the nearest garrison to cart this stuff away?" he asked quietly.

"I wasna certain. But I knew that I had to show you this place, and take the chance that you wouldna betray me again."

"Christian—" he paused, and sighed. "I have not betrayed you. When I took you from Carlisle, I surely did not know that you thought me a warrior saint, or at the least a Scottish knight. Either one is exalted in your eyes."

She turned her head away. "I dinna exalt you. Neither do I trust you."

"You trust me some, I think," he said. "Else you would not have shown me this place at all. You might have sent Dominy and Will down here in secret to haul up your harp, and bags of oats and barley to appease that great appetite of yours."

Christian laughed reluctantly, then sobered. "I had to show this place to you, for all our well-being. But dinna let the English have what is here. Please."

Frowning, he took her chin in his fingers. "Have Henry and the English hurt you so deeply? Do you mistrust me because of their deeds?"

She jerked her head away and stood, folding her arms, turning her back. "You saw how gently the English kept me at Carlisle," she snapped. "And you have your king's orders."

He stood. "King Edward trusts me less than you do."

She looked up at him, her interest clearly caught. "He doubts you? Why?"

" 'Tis a tedious epic, my lady. Now, find whatever clothing you need. I will bring your *clàrsach*—is that the word?—into the tower. What do you wish to bring out of here for supper? Oats, or some beans?"

"Barley and beans, I think. And some onions. There is a wee cask of salt here as well. Dominy and I can make a thick soup."

He nodded, and she brushed past him. Reaching out, he laid

a hand on her arm. "Christian. I am not your enemy."

"I dinna know that for certain," she murmured. "But I know it." He raised his hand to touch the side of her face. She turned to look up at him, and his fingers sank into the cool, soft mass of her shortened hair, sliding along the nape of her slender neck, bared to his touch. "There is no need for war between us, lady."

She stared up at him silently, standing in the warm circle of light cast by the fluttering torch. He stroked the back of her neck, and moved his fingers down to her shoulder. She drew in a little breath, sharply, and closed her eyes for a moment.

Deep within his body, a steady pulsing rhythm urged him to draw her closer. When he did, she did not resist. He eased his fingers along her neck. Her head slanted back under his gentle touch and her eyes drifted shut.

"This bitter anger between us cuts deep," he said, "and 'tis wearing to both of us. I am tired, as are you, my lady." And he needed comfort. Aye, and more; he was a man, English or not.

Christian sighed wearily, and laid a hand on his chest. He knew that she should go back up to the tower and rest. But he wanted to stand here, lost in the small pleasures of touch, the soft texture of her skin, the cool weight of her hair. He wanted to follow the tide of desire that was edging him closer to her, urging him to pull her into his arms, to kiss her, to love her, his wife.

He sighed, and rubbed her shoulder gently, feeling her gradually give in to his touch. An infusion of warmth spread through his hands and throughout his body. He felt the keen heat of desire, yet something fine as well, a sense of peace and comfort born days ago in the abbey, and rediscovered in this chamber, hidden deep within the heart of the stone.

He moved his head lower, and felt her breath warm the corner of his mouth. "You asked me to be just a man, here in this place," he murmured.

"I did," she whispered. "I did." A sudden fire plummeted to his loins as she spoke. His heart pounded like a taut drum. He touched the side of her face and traced its shape.

"You are so finely made," he said, "like silk and velvet." He rested a hand at her back and glided her closer. "When you were ill at the abbey, I held you. You were not distrustful of me then."

"I felt safe then," she breathed.

"Then feel safe now," he whispered. His mouth hovered over hers, and he grazed over her lips, sending a lightning strike through his body. The gentle kiss he gave her was an aching, silent question. Her lips moved beneath his in acceptance, giving the answer he craved.

Drawing in a sharp breath, he pulled her closer and kissed her, breathless and deep, turning his head to fit his mouth over hers. Slanting her head back, he buried his fingers in the cool, thick, glossy silk of her hair.

He had been wanting to touch her like this, to kiss her and hold her. Sensing the life that flowed through her, he imagined how she would feel beneath his hands, how he might plunge into her sultry warmth, surrounded by the sweet salvation of her body.

She moaned softly against his lips, her body swaying with his. The soft globes of her breasts pressed against him. Her hands slipped up to his shoulders, and she pushed at him.

The shove brought him to awareness like a cold draft of air. He had been lost in a jumble of sweet touches and powerful urges. Tipping his forehead to hers, he blew out a slow breath, trying to clear the hot, moist fog that clouded his mind.

"I wish you were Scottish," she blurted.

"I am no English knight here in this place. You have had my oath on that."

"But up there, in the castle, you will remember it."

"Are you so certain?" he asked softly.

She lowered her head and did not answer.

CHAPTER TEN

"SOMEONE COMES," John called over his shoulder. Shielding his eyes, he peered out over the parapet. "Four or five, walkin' out o' the forest."

"Who are they?" Gavin called back, leaning his ax against a wall. Wiping an arm across his forehead, mingling dirt with sweat, he looked toward the open gate but saw no one approaching.

"I canna yet say," John called. "But they're coming."

Gavin walked across the courtyard, where he and John had spent most of the day clearing charred timbers and broken stone. With help from Dominy and Will, they had burned some of the wreckage, and had employed two of the destriers, equipped with makeshift panniers, in transporting the heavier pieces of stone to a mounting pile of rubble.

The smoke that rose now from a corner of the courtyard came from an open cooking fire, where Dominy bent over an iron kettle, stirring a stew of barley and dried, salted fish. William was close by his mother, wielding a broom taller than himself.

"They're closer now!" John called.

"Dominy—Will—into the tower!" Gavin said. Dominy nodded and grabbed Will, who protested only a little as his mother pulled him along toward the northwest tower to join Christian.

"How many? Are they rebels?" Gavin called to John. With the castle wide open to attack, he and John had maintained a steady vigil, keeping their weapons at hand. His sword lay nearby in its scabbard, and he stepped toward it.

"Rebels?" John glanced again. "They look wee."

"Wee? A good distance away, then?"

"Close now," John said. "And wee."

Frowning, Gavin grabbed up his sword and thrust it through his belt. He ran toward the gate and looked through the shadowed tunnel of the overhead arch, beneath the teeth of the portcullis grille that hung crooked and useless. Beyond the drawbridge lay the narrow track that led into the forest.

He blinked, and looked again. Three children walked out of the woods and came steadily toward the castle.

A girl walked ahead of two boys. She appeared to be the oldest of the group, no more than nine; Gavin assumed she was older only because she was taller than the boys. One of them, his red hair bright in the sun, appeared close to her age. The other looked younger than Will. They came resolutely across the soot-blackened drawbridge.

Gavin relaxed his hand from his sword hilt and watched as the children walked beneath the entrance arch and stepped carefully over some fallen stones.

The girl stopped just inside the courtyard and surveyed it for a moment. Then she turned to stare at Gavin, who stood a few yards away from the gate. She pushed back the plaid that covered her head, revealing a delicately shaped face and pale blond braids that glinted in the sunlight.

Gavin wondered if these children had made it a habit to play in the deserted castle. He expected them to run off once they discovered that it was held once again by English.

But the girl, who wore a simple green tunic beneath the plaid over her shoulders, did not seem alarmed by his presence. She walked into the yard. Behind her came the two boys, their thin, muscular legs bare but for deerskin boots. Bulky plaids and long linen shirts flapped to their knees, and small hunting bows were slung over their shoulders. The boys frowned fiercely at him, while the girl looked around calmly.

"This is no place for children to play," Gavin called out. "Go home now." He stepped toward them.

The boys suddenly grabbed their bows and straightened their arms. Two small, very sharp arrows were trained on him in tough, grimy little fists. Gavin's hand went instinctively to his sword hilt. Across the yard, at the edge of his vision, he saw John run down the stone steps from the parapet.

"Are you the English knight who holds Kinglassie?" the girl asked Gavin.

"I am," he said. "Go home, and stop this nonsense."

"You're our prisoner," the older boy called out. "Lay down your weapon, Sasunnach."

"By the saints," Gavin said. "Put those bows down now, or I will do it for you."

The bowstring was drawn and released so fast that Gavin barely had time to turn aside. The short arrow hit a rock near his foot and clattered away.

"Boy!" he roared toward the younger archer, who had shot at him. "Put that thing down!"

The child dropped his bow and stepped back. Gavin marched forward. The other boy lowered his weapon quickly and skittered away from his advance.

"Hold!" he yelled, stomping after them both. He managed to catch the smaller one by a handful of plaid, and swiped toward the other boy, but missed. The one he held glanced wildly toward the others.

"I'm taken!" he yelled. "Run, save yourselves!"

"Hush up," Gavin said, exasperated. John had reached them by then, and grabbed the other boy by the shoulder. Then he growled at the girl to stand still.

"Well, Gavin," John drawled, keeping his grip tight, "you did say a child could take this place."

Gavin shot him a wry look as he held onto his squirming, twisting bundle of plaid; the little boy had surprising strength. Gavin neatly avoided being kicked.

"English dogs, I see your tails," the boy rasped out.

"Let them go, please," the girl said. "They were only protecting me."

"Oh? From evil Sasunnachs?" Gavin asked, hanging on to his

frustrated captive.

She nodded vigorously. Beside her, John laughed. "Well, Sir Gavin may be a Sasunnach, but I am a Scotsman."

"Some Scots are friends to the English," the older boy said. "You'll be one o' those traitors."

John raised a brow as he looked down at his charge. "Call me a traitor, eh? And are you loyal to the Bruce?"

"Aye!" The youngest boy spoke up, straightening his shoulders proudly. "We're his eyes and ears—"

"Hush, Robbie!" the girl hissed.

"The Bruce's eyes and ears?" John asked. "*Ach*, then, Sir Gavin, we may hae caught some wee spies here."

"Mayhap so." Gripping his prisoner by the arm, Gavin sidestepped to collect the bows, then looked sternly at the children. All three eyed him nervously. "Sit down over there, and tell us your business at Kinglassie." He led them toward a cluster of stone blocks.

Walking beside him, the girl stopped and turned in a slow circle. Gavin thought her wide blue eyes looked deeply troubled for one so young. He watched her, increasingly perplexed. She was lovely, softly colored and perfectly formed. And she looked familiar to him, as if he had seen her before. But he knew that he had not.

"What is your name?" he asked. The girl looked up at him.

"Michaelmas," she said. "This was my home. 'Tis all burned now." Fat tears quivered in her eyes, and she set her chin stubbornly.

"I will rebuild it," he said. "Did your mother or father work here, as servant to the old lord?"

She shook her head. "My father was the laird here. I am Michaelmas Faulkener. Where is my mother?"

Gavin stared at her in astonishment. "Your mother?"

She had turned away. "*Ach! Màthair!*" She ran forward. "*Màthair!*"

Gavin watched the girl cross the courtyard. Beyond, framed in the doorway of the great tower, Christian leaned against the stone jamb. She opened her arms, her pale face bright and happy.

"Michaelmas!" she called.

Gavin watched in amazement as the girl ran straight into Christian's embrace.

SITTING IN THE COURTYARD, listening while John questioned the boys, Gavin kept glancing toward the tower into which Christian and her daughter had disappeared.

He was aware that Christian and Henry had been married for several years, but he had never considered that there might have been a child. She had not mentioned any children, and he simply had not thought about it. Realizing that he was stepfather to the little girl, he shook his head slightly. The concept was too much to ponder just now.

Sighing in chagrin, he turned his attention back to John and the boys, who, he now knew, were brothers. Between these two, his new stepdaughter, and William, his world was suddenly awash with children. Having never dealt much with the little creatures before, he was not sure he had the knack for it.

"And where did you say the Bruce is hiding?" John was asking.

"Nae hiding here," the youngest archer, called Robbie, said. As he shook his head adamantly, his prominent ears caught the sun like pink glass.

"Our da says Robert Bruce is beating the Sasunnach army at Ayr, north of here," the older one, called Patrick, said.

"He is nae here at Kinglassie," Robbie insisted. Patrick elbowed Robbie, and they shook their heads in rapid, intense denial, their eyes wide enough to make Gavin suspicious.

"You have never seen the Bruce?" he asked them. Again the heads shook vigorously, red and brown hair flying outward.

"And would you vow the truth on a holy relic? That you've never seen the Bruce near here?" John asked.

"On a sliver of the True Cross, perhaps?" Gavin added.

The boys looked at each other. Patrick gulped.

"Here, now!" a voice called. "Wha' are you lads doing?"

Gavin turned. A man walked under the half-lowered portcullis with barely a glance at it. "We must repair that gate," Gavin muttered to John.

His uncle nodded in agreement as the man crossed the courtyard. Short and broadly muscled, he wore a brown tunic beneath a bright plaid, the hem of both flapping around his powerful calves. He carried a cloth sack in one hand.

Gavin noticed that the man's brown hair was shaved clean over the front of his head. A priest, he realized with a start, though his tonsure was peculiar. The man fisted his hands on his hips and looked at Gavin. "Who are you, and wha' are you doing wi' my lads?"

"He's a Sasunnach, Da! And we're his prisoners, and you'll hae to pay a ransom!" Robbie yelled, bouncing up and down where he sat. Gavin noticed that the boy bore a strong resemblance to the priest, particularly in the prominent ears and brown hair.

"Did you bring coins, Da?" Patrick asked.

"As if we had any. Hush," the priest said. He turned to Gavin. "Wha' did they do? I hope they didna use fire arrows on you. They tried those the other day, but I put a stop to that quick."

"We were capturing the Sassunach!" Patrick said. He frowned. "But he caught us."

"Ach. Well, your mother is looking to capture both o' you. Get on home, now. Where is Michaelmas?"

"With Lady Christian, held prisoner in the tower! And we were being questioned by the English dogs!" Robbie yelled enthusiastically. Listening, Gavin groaned to himself and rubbed a hand over his face.

"Ach, go on, then. You dinna look like prisoners to me," the priest said. "Take your bows and snatch us something for supper. And dinna shoot at the hens again, they're nae game birds. Your mother wasna pleased wi' that trick." He leaned forward as if to smack their behinds, but the boys laughed as if they knew it was only a game. Grabbing up their bows with anxious looks at Gavin, they ran out of the courtyard as fast as they could.

The priest turned to Gavin and held out a hand. "I am Fergus Macnab, rector o' the church o' Saint Bride, a league from here over the moor. And you're sent by King Edward?"

"I am Sir Gavin Faulkener. We are sent by the king, aye."

"Faulkener!" Fergus Macnab exclaimed.

Gavin inclined his head. "Sir Henry's cousin, and husband to Lady Christian now. This is my uncle, John MacKerras."

The priest nodded slowly. "Well, then. Husband to Lady Christian, and cousin to Henry Faulkener? You've wed the widow, and intend to rebuild and garrison the castle for the English king?"

Gavin nodded. "You are a man of the Church. May I regard you as an ally?"

Fergus frowned. "I am nae more a friend to English than are my sons. But you are only two men here. And my sons told me that Lady Christian was ill, and so I came."

"Your sons?" Gavin asked.

"Aye. You met two o' them yesterday at the burn."

"We took them to be forest outlaws," John said.

"My sons are good lads, though the English call them outlaws. They were burned out o' their homes by that king's demon, Oliver Hastings." He raised his square chin proudly. "My wife and I hae eight sons, six grown. Our two youngest bairns you've just met."

"Those boys are yours? You have a wife?" Gavin stared at him. "Are you not a priest?"

"*Ach*, aye, a priest o' the old Celtic Church, whose traditions run strong in this part o' Galloway," Fergus said. "There are many parish priests, rectors o' small churches, wha' still follow the Celtic rules. I wear the Irish tonsure, as you see." He tipped his head obligingly.

John glanced at Gavin. "Priests o' the old Church are common enough in the Celtic areas of Scotland. The Roman Church frowns on them because they still marry, and hold farms and own cattle and sheep. And their sons inherit positions as priests in village churches."

"Nae many parishes abide by the old rules now," Fergus said. "My father was a priest, and his afore him—my name, Macnab, means son o' the abbot. But only one o' my eight lads wants to follow the Church, and he is wi' his brothers now, following the

Bruce. And the two wee laddies think only about joining their elder brothers." He turned to scan his gaze around the courtyard. *"Ach,* look at this. Kinglassie is a bit o' a ruin now, eh?"

Gavin nodded. " 'Twill take time, but repairs can be made."

"The damage would hae been much greater, but a fierce storm came up the day the fire began, and doused the blaze."

"You were here?" Gavin asked.

"I saw it. Lady Christian left her daughter wi' me and my wife." Fergus spun in a slow circle, his gaze narrowed critically. "You'll need to repair that yett straight away. Your castle is wide open. Melted chains, most like. You'll need a smith to make that right again." He clanked at Gavin. "Your garrison can do that— when does it arrive, did you say?"

Gavin paused. Priest or not, Fergus was likely as loyal to the Bruce as were his eight sons. "I do not know," he answered warily. "Sir Oliver Hastings will send the forces later."

Fergus's face darkened. He turned his head and spat. "Oliver Hastings! If you're sent by him, man, I willna be a friend to you."

"I am here by order of King Edward," Gavin said. "And I do what I deem best. Hastings is not my commander."

"Well, then. 'Tis good to hear that." Fergus frowned. "You'll find English allies here quick enough. A good many Galloway Scots favor the English over the Bruce. But my sons and I, we support Bruce's fight. I'll be honest about that, Gavin Faulkener."

"As is your right."

"But let there be peace atween us, man. I wouldna see harm come to Lady Christian."

"No harm will come to her," Gavin said. "You have my word on it. Now, sir priest, can you help me to find laborers to do the repairs here?"

Fergus peered at Gavin for a moment, his hazel eyes clear and forthright, and then scratched at his shaved brow. "Well then. As for labor—I can bring you a blacksmith, and men to lift your stones and cut your timbers, if you've grain or meat wi' which to pay them."

Gavin raised an eyebrow doubtfully, and cleared his throat.

"Cheese, perhaps?" Fergus ventured. "Ale?"

"Coin," Gavin said. "I will pay good laborers' wages. Six pence a day for carpenters, twelve for masons."

"Aye, well, coin," Fergus muttered. "They can use that at the fairs in the big towns, come spring. But food and livestock would be more welcome payment in the winter months. I'll spread the word, and men will come here to ask for work. Dinna shoot at them wi' your English longbows, thinking them to be enemy Scots."

Gavin hid a smile, feeling as if he had been scolded for thinking of shooting the yard-hens. "We shall have a truce in order to repair the castle."

"Well enough. Now I came to see Lady Christian," Fergus said as he lifted his sack. "My sons said she was ill, and my wife sent along some eggs and cheeses."

"She was ill, aye, near to death, but she is recovering."

"God save her. Moira and I heard nae word o' her since the day she left. How is it she has wed another Sasunnach?"

"A long epic, Father," John said. "Ask the lass herself."

Fergus eyed John for a moment. "You're Scots. MacKerras, was it? Fine blood, that clan. How is it you're wi' the English?"

"I've been wi' my nephew Gavin for ten years, while he was ambassador to the French court," John answered. "Before that, most o' my time was spent in the Holy Land."

Fergus looked at Gavin. "Nephew? Are you part Scots?"

"My mother was a MacKerras from Perthshire," Gavin said.

"*Ach!* You're only partly a Sasunnach, then." Fergus seemed pleased, and smiled at Gavin. "May I see your lady now?"

"Aye." Gavin walked with Fergus toward the tower. "Tell me, sir priest, what news you know of the Bruce."

"Only wha' all men know. He landed on Galloway shores a few weeks ago, and gathers a force o' men to rout the English. He and but a few men took Turnberry Castle from three hundred English soldiers. Henry Percy hid quivering inside the walls. Watch your towers well, Gavin Faulkener. If Bruce comes here he'll take Kinglassie quick. Your castle lacks a yett."

"Where is Bruce now?"

Fergus laughed. "Only those who are wi' him day and night

ken the whereabouts o' the king o' Scots. Even my own sons will-na tell me."

Gavin sighed and nodded. He had not really expected the priest to tell him where to find Robert Bruce. And he was not sure he wanted to know.

WHEN HE AND FERGUS entered the small, warm chamber Gavin saw that Christian sat on a floor pallet, her arm around Michael-mas, speaking quietly with Dominy and William.

Christian looked up as they entered the room. "Fergus!" she said, smiling. "Thank you for keeping her safe."

"God be with you, Lady Christian," Fergus said, hurrying over to her. "You're thin as a reed, though you look well, your hus-band, there, said you were near to death not long ago."

"I am well enough now," she said, and looked at Gavin, her eyes bright, her cheeks rosy. She wore a gown taken from one of the clothing chests in the underground storage chamber; the dark blue wool, simply cut, gave depth to the remarkable color of her eyes and heightened the translucency of her skin. A white veil of soft lightweight wool covered her short dark hair. She wore a cloak of a mulberry wool, lined with silky black fur that matched the deep gloss of her hair.

Gavin stared at her, thinking how well the deep colors enhanced her beauty. She looked as if she were wrapped in the rich colors of a twilight sky. Sucking in his breath sharply, he reminded himself that he had never been inclined to love poetry before and did not intend to start now.

"Here's eggs, and cheese." Fergus handed her the sack.

"Cheese!" Christian said, with obvious delight, peeking into the sack and sticking her hand inside.

"Moira sent them for you," Fergus said. "Iain and Donal came to tell us that they had seen you, and that you were ill."

"I am much better," she said, withdrawing a chunk of golden cheese.

"The Lord watched over you, and we're grateful," Fergus

said. She nodded, glancing briefly at Gavin. "*Ach*, but He didna keep you from the Sasunnachs," Fergus went on as he sat down beside her. Christian blushed deeply and sent Gavin another little glance. Leaning in the doorframe, Gavin gave her a little bow that only she could see.

She cleared her throat and touched Michaelmas's shoulder. "Gavin Faulkener, this is Michaelmas," Christian said. "My daughter."

Gavin nodded. "Aye, we have met."

Michaelmas looked at Gavin, and then turned to her mother. "This is your new husband?"

Christian nodded. "And your stepfather," she murmured. Michaelmas tilted her head and frowned speculatively at him. Again he saw something familiar about her face, but he could not place it. He smiled and nodded at the child, feeling suddenly awkward under her steady glance. After a moment she smiled, too.

"Will you have some cheese?" Michaelmas asked him.

"Thank you," Gavin said, and leaned forward to accept the small chunk that the girl broke off and held out to him. He chewed for a moment, standing there, while everyone watched him.

He cleared his throat. "I will leave you to your visit," he said, bowing his head, and left.

"ANOTHER SASUNNACH," FERGUS SAID, and shook his head.

"Fergus, if you repeat that one more time I may scream," Christian said. They spoke softly in Gaelic, leaning together near the fire. In a corner of the little chamber, Dominy murmured a story to Will and Michaelmas, who, after a supper of bean and barley stew, had stretched out on pallets made of thick blankets, and now looked ready to fall asleep.

"I am amazed, is all," Fergus said. "To think you rode away from here those months ago to escape the English, and came back wed to another—"

"I had no choice," Christian said, as she tore off another small piece of cheese. She felt as if she could not get enough of its creamy, salty taste. "Gavin wed me when I was ill, and he saved my life. He took me from Carlisle, as I told you."

"A cruel thing, that cage, and no surprise coming from Edward Longshanks." Fergus shook his head. "But Gavin Faulkener took you from there, so he must have a good heart. His mother was a MacKerras from Perthshire, so he has good Celtic blood in him."

"He told me that his mother was Scottish," she said. "But I know little of him."

"Would it not serve you to learn more?" Fergus asked gently.

"It might," she admitted. She looked up after a moment. "Tell me news of my cousins."

"King Robert and his brothers? *Ach.* Iain and Donal have seen the Bruce," he whispered, casting a glance toward Dominy.

"Dominy cannot understand Gaelic," Christian reminded him.

Fergus nodded and continued. "Robert Bruce was near these very hills but a week past, with the small band of men who have been with him since last summer. They live like the lowest outlaws in the heather, taking food and shelter where they can. He greatly needs more men, and food, and weapons. My eldest sons are with him. Iain and Donal will join his band soon. For now they guard the hills and forests until the Bruce returns here."

"What of Robert's brothers? Thomas, Edward, Alexander?" She frowned, biting her lip against the sudden tears that threatened. "Fergus—did you know that Neil Bruce was captured at Kildrummy, and hanged at Berwick?"

"I heard," Fergus said softly. "I heard. The eldest of his brothers, Edward Bruce, is with Robert still, as are James Douglas and Neil Campbell and the Earl of Lennox." He laid a hand gently on her arm. "But your cousins Thomas and Alexander Bruce were caught two weeks ago, when they landed in ships near Loch Ryan." He paused. "They had hundreds of men with them, Highlanders and Irish *gallòglach,* in many ships. Many of the men were killed on the shore, or drowned. Some were captured. Macdouells, it was, Galloway Scots, who headed the English ambush."

She watched him warily. "What happened to my cousins?"

Fergus sighed. "Thomas and Alexander were executed by the

English at Dumfries," he murmured. "I am sorry, Christian."

She lowered her head and squeezed back sudden tears. "Thomas Bruce helped me to escape the English here at Kinglassie. *O Dhia,* Fergus. Robert's own brothers. Three of the four are gone now, all lost to the English." She remembered playing with her Bruce cousins as a child, when her grandmother, who had been first cousin to Robert Bruce's mother, had brought her to visit them at Turnberry Castle. She shook her head sadly.

"My sons said King Robert was filled with a terrible grief when he heard the news of Loch Ryan. He even talked of giving up the cause of Scotland. He said the price of his brothers dying for him is far too dear. Christian, you must let him know that his queen and his daughter, and the rest of his womenfolk, are alive, if still held by the English. He has had no word since you were all captured last September."

She nodded. "The queen is in a private house, and his daughter and his sister Christian are in convents. His sister Mary, and Lady Isabel of Buchan, are at Roxburgh and Berwick, held in cages like my own. But the last I heard of them, they were well enough. Fergus—help me to meet with Robert. I will bring him this news myself. If he sees me well, he will be more assured of their safety."

Fergus frowned. "You may be able to do that, when he returns to the hills near Kinglassie, but—"

"A quick meeting in the forest would be safe enough. Ask Iain to arrange it for me, and bring me word of when and where."

"Perhaps you could bring the king some news of English plans," Fergus said. "Since you have an English husband."

Christian widened her eyes at the suggestion. "I only thought to warn Robert that the English are gathering their forces in this area, determined to find him. But spying—" she frowned. "I know nothing of English plans."

Fergus shrugged. "Keep your ears sharp. Gavin Faulkener will have visitors. You could do a great service for your king."

She hesitated. "I do not know if I could do that again."

Fergus sighed. *"Ach.* So you like this husband better than the last, eh?"

She blushed and looked away.

"He looks a reasonable man," Fergus said. "But he is a Sasunnach, and we must be cautious. Do what your heart tells you. But as I tell my parish flock, if fighting with Saracen devils in the Holy Land is not sinful, then neither is it sinful for the Scottish people to resist the English."

CHAPTER ELEVEN

A MELODY FLOATED on the night air, now cascading, now rising, a sparkle of sound like tiny silver bells. Gavin left the parapet where he had been watching as sentry, and approached the great tower. Leaning in the doorway of the small chamber, he watched and listened while Christian played the *clàrsach*.

In the amber light cast by the fire, she sat straight and still on a low stool, holding the harp between her knees. Its rounded upper corner was tipped back against her left shoulder. Rapid and graceful, her fingers struck the brass strings to bring forth a delicate, lovely melody.

Nearby, on pallets laid out on the floor, Michaelmas, Will, and Dominy lay sleeping. John snored gently in the corner nearest the door, in keeping with the arrangement that he and Gavin had worked out between them: while one slept for a few hours, the other watched out over the parapet at night.

Christian tilted her head as she played, her hair, without a veil, like a full, dark cloud. Clever and quick, her fingers created the decorative melody and its lower harmony. Beneath her skirt, one foot tapped a soft beat.

She began another song, floating tones soft as mist, a lyrical, haunting pattern of sound. Gavin closed his eyes and rested his head against the doorjamb, feeling the song flow through him and then draw him into its quiet, dark depths.

The music, magical, lilting, seemed to surround him, and

Gavin found himself caught within that exquisite, serene web of sound. He listened, soothed, and felt as if she played only for him.

Christian let the harp strings ring into silence.

Gavin opened his eyes. "You have the touch of an angel," he said softly. His words hovered in the air like the last low breath of the strings.

She looked up, her eyes large and dark in the shadows. "That was an ancient song," she said, "called a sleeping tune. 'Tis said the druids used such a melody to work enchantments."

He smiled slightly. " 'Twas no doubt successful for them."

She set the harp upright. "Michaelmas asked me to play for her while she went to sleep. In my father's castle, 'twas the task of the harper to play the whole household to sleep."

He chuckled, listening to the soft snores around them. "You have surely done that in this household. And now you should get some rest yourself. 'Tis well past compline. God keep you the night, my lady." He turned, then looked back. "Christian—thank you for the music."

He stepped out into the starlit courtyard.

AN HOUR OR SO LATER, Christian watched as Gavin, silhouetted against the deep color of the night, walked the parapet, unaware that she stood below in the shadow of the great tower. She had been unable to sleep, stimulated by the music, as she sometimes was when she played. She had grabbed up her cloak and had gone outside, hoping that the brisk night air would tire her. But now she was more alert than before.

And Gavin's soft words kept ringing in her thoughts. *You have the touch of an angel*, he had said; *thank you.*

Across the wide courtyard, high on the parapet, his shadowed figure was turned away from her. He stood at the battlement and stared out over the loch, his cloak billowed on the wind like dark wings.

If any had an angel's touch, he did. She smiled ruefully. Gavin Faulkener had shown her more kindness, compassion, and caring in a few weeks that Henry had shown her in years of marriage.

But she felt utterly confused. She had seen a hard soldier in him, too. He had been sent to Kinglassie as an oppressor rather than as a savior. That was the cold, real truth. She could not let herself forget it.

She sighed. Fergus wanted her to act against Gavin and help the Bruce by supplying information about the English. She had done that once before, when Henry had lived at Kinglassie, without much struggle of conscience over it. Her loyalty and obligation then had clearly belonged to her king and cousin, Robert Bruce, rather than with her English husband, who had shown her only coldness and disdain.

But if she did the same with this second English husband, Gavin Faulkener would never be more than her enemy. There were moments when she craved his touch, his kindness, his affection so much that it frightened her. She fervently wished that he was not an English knight. But wishing would not change it.

She sighed and peered up at a black sky pierced by countless glittering stars. Her fingers played with the leather thong that hung down inside the neck of her gown, and she pulled at it. The golden pendant tumbled into her palm, its filigree work gleaming in the starlight.

Michaelmas had returned the pendant to her last night, after Fergus had left. The child had worn it around her neck all the months that her mother had been gone. When Christian had tied the thong around her own neck, its familiar weight falling once again against her breastbone, she had been keenly reminded that the treasure of Kinglassie might never be found.

The gold was rumored to lie in the heart of the castle. But surely the fire had destroyed it, wherever it lay hidden. She could imagine molten gold seeping down between fitted blocks of stone like veining in a mine.

Without the treasure, Kinglassie's old legend had no substance. She was the keeper of nothing but a pretty pendant, golden wire and a garnet, linked to an empty legend.

GAVIN TURNED AROUND on the parapet and looked down into the courtyard. Among the jagged shadows of rubble, he saw a slight, slim figure, and recognized Christian. She moved gracefully across the center of the yard and stopped, looking up at the night sky. Dressed in the dark blue gown and mulberry cloak, she blended with the shadows. Then her hood slipped back to reveal the shape of her face, pale in the starlight.

Frowning, Gavin moved slowly down the steps, wondering why she stood so still. He crossed the courtyard toward her.

"Are you well?" she asked. "Why are you out here?"

She turned quickly, obviously startled. "I am well enough," she answered. "I was just walking."

"You should be asleep," he said. " 'Tis hours till dawn."

"I couldna sleep," she said. "I thought the night air would help me to relax." She began to walk across the courtyard. Gavin moved alongside her, slowing his long stride to match hers.

"You have made progress here," she said, glancing around at the shadowed piles of rubble.

He nodded. "We have done some clearing, John and I. But we are only laborers—we can lift and stack, break stone and saw wood. We cannot make the repairs that are needed here. Dominy has more masonry skills than we have," he said. He turned to her, glad of this chance to ask something that he had been thinking about recently. "Christian, I know something of castle design, but I have no ability to carry it out. Earlier I asked you to help me restore Kinglassie. I can make better decisions if I can understand the way it used to be. Show me each room, and explain what is missing and what is damaged."

She blinked up at him. "Now? 'Tis dark."

He smiled. "Not now. Meet me at first light outside the great hall. We shall begin there, if you will help." She tilted her head in thought. "I will do it," she finally said. "We need a roof over our heads quicker than you know. The winters are usually wet. We have been fortunate in the dry weather of late."

A strong draft of cold wind stirred their cloaks, and rippled through their hair. Taking her arm, he drew her into the shelter of the doorway of one of the ruined towers. He was keenly aware that she stood only a breath away, her shoulder brushing his arm. Behind them, in the blackness of the tower, he heard the occasional ruffling of the sleeping doves.

"We need to begin repairs," Gavin said. "The king expects me to go to Loch Doon and report to Hastings for whatever supplies are needed here."

"War comes first for King Edward," she said stiffly.

He could not deny that. "The king will want the necessary repairs made quickly so that he can house two or three hundred men here." He heard her draw in her breath sharply, but she did not speak. He continued. "Edward will expect me to see to those improvements only, and put off the rest of the work indefinitely. The gate needs repair soon, but in this winter weather, the next step is to fix the roof and floors in the great tower first, for our own comfort and safety."

"You will need coin for any repairs, and your king is not generous with funds. Henry always had difficulty acquiring the means and the supplies he needed."

"I know that. I plan to hire the laborers and pay them myself. Is there a town within a day's ride of here?"

"Ayr is closest, but the English have the castle and town."

"I am English, my lady, as you love to remind me. Is there a market there?"

"They hold a weekly market every Saturday. The great fair is twice a year."

"I can hire workers through the guilds in Ayr, then."

"You can. But wait yet. Fergus Macnab will bring men. He is a man to trust."

"Is he?" he said, looking at her sharply.

"If he said he would find workers, he will keep his word. Even to a Sasunnach. He is a good man. And he and his family were kind to Michaelmas while I was ... gone."

He watched her for a moment. "You never said you had a daughter before she arrived here looking for you, my lady."

She lifted her chin. "Will you reprimand me for that? I was only protecting her."

He frowned, puzzled by her reaction. "I do not criticize you for shielding your child, lady," he said. "I only meant that I was surprised by her existence."

"I thought you might be bitter about her."

"Why?" he asked, startled.

"She is a Scottish child," she answered simply.

He was not certain what she meant, or what difference that could make to him. "A child is a child. And she is lovely. Although she does not resemble you with that blond hair and square chin. She favors the Faulkeners."

She shook her head. "Michaelmas isna Henry's and my true daughter."

He raised a brow. "Henry's by-blow?"

She shook her head again. "Henry and I adopted her the first year we were wed. His sister gave us charge of her."

"His sister Joan? But she was the prioress of a small convent in the Scottish Borderlands. My mother retired there several years ago."

Christian stared up at him. "Your mother? Was she there when King Edward closed down the Scottish nunneries? That priory was sacked and burned."

He nodded, looking away. "I know. She died that day."

She gasped. "I am sorry, Gavin. Henry never mentioned her to me."

"Did he not? He sent me word of her death when I was in France."

"I heard naught of it, but 'tis not surprising to me, knowing Henry. Would your mother have been his cousin?"

"She was wed to his first cousin, my father. Henry knew my mother and father very well. He and my father, and my uncle John, traveled to the Holy Land together. My mother had been widowed for years when she finally decided to take holy vows. I was in France then. She entered that particular religious house because Dame Joan was there. They were close friends."

"I met Joan once. 'Twas after the convent had been burned," Christian said. "She was frail—her heart wasna strong—and she was frantic to find homes for their little orphans."

"Is that how you came to have Michaelmas?"

She nodded. "Dame Joan sent word to Henry that she was ill and needed help. He brought me with him because Joan had asked him to take one of the orphans."

"He wanted the child, then."

"I was surprised that Henry agreed, but he had a good enough heart for children and horses. He just didna care for Scottish wives." She laughed flatly, but then her smile sweetened. "She was a beautiful bairn, nearly a year old, with silver-blond hair and beautiful blue eyes. I loved her as soon as I saw her," she said softly. "We returned here with Michaelmas and a wet nurse, but the woman ran off with a soldier shortly after we came back. Moira had given birth to Patrick a year earlier, so she nursed her. Michaelmas is a milk-sister to Fergus's lads."

Gavin listened, frowning, and rubbed his chin with one hand. "Henry sent me only one or two letters in ten years. I heard little of him other than that he had been granted a Scottish holding. Henry wrote to me of my mother's death, but never mentioned that he had a wife or an adopted child. He kept his thoughts and his business to himself always, as I remember."

"He was very secretive," she agreed.

"What did Joan tell you of the child's parents?"

"She told me little. Henry spoke privately with her, and later said that Michaelmas was an orphan, born in that convent. But her mother was dead and her father unknown. He never told me the mother's name. I dinna know if he even knew. The nuns named her for the feast day on which she was born."

"Ah. Saint Michael's day in September." He deepened his frown, trying to work out the curious puzzle: he did not remember Henry Faulkener as a compassionate man, likely to adopt out of kindness. And there was the fact that Michaelmas reminded him of someone he had seen, though he could not determine who; he wondered if it could be Henry, who had been a tall, heavyset, blond man like Gavin's father. "Are you certain she is not Henry's bastard daughter? His sister Joan might have taken the child, and he might have felt an obligation to take her into his own home when Joan was ill."

"I have wondered about that. I knew little of his past. Henry never said any such thing to me about the child. But then, he said little to me about any matter." She looked up at the stars. Gavin studied her uplifted profile, delicate and pale in the dim blue light.

He leaned against the doorframe, and glanced up at the arch over their heads. "I noticed that there is a stone inset about this tower door, with some carving on it. But 'twas ruined by the fire. What would that have been?" he asked.

"That was my parents' marriage stone. 'Twas cut with their entwined initials, a beautiful thing. Like their marriage. They truly loved each other."

"Where is your marriage stone?" he asked.

"Henry and I didna have a stone made. He didna want one." She lifted her chin haughtily. "Nor did I."

"Years of marriage, and so much devotion?"

Christian laughed bitterly. "So much. And only an adopted child between us." She paused, and then sighed, glancing up at him. "You have likely wondered if I am barren, since my daughter is not of my body. But that I canna tell you."

He was surprised that she mentioned the subject; her remark gave him hope suddenly that she had begun to accept him as her husband. "Why can you not say if you are barren?" he asked her gently.

"I never had much chance to discover it. Henry didna want a Scottish wife or a Scottish child," she said. "He made that clear enough." Pulling her cloak tightly around her shoulders, she turned. " 'Tis cold out here. I should go back." She began to walk away.

Gavin stepped after her. "Christian!"

HE HAD TAKEN HER ARM from behind, jarring her to a sudden stop. "Hold, my lady. I think you have more to say to me."

She sighed and turned. She was pleased, in part, that he had stopped her. Her old anger toward Henry had surfaced, causing her to flee from Gavin and from the painful reminder of her first marriage.

Talking with Gavin, these past few minutes, had actually been pleasant, and a blessed relief in part. She had not spoken so calmly with a man, a caring, intelligent man other than Fergus, for so long—at least since her brothers had died.

"Come out of the wind," he said, drawing her back into the shelter of the doorway. His tall, solid body blocked the wind and the starlight. "Will you say such things about Henry, and then run off, and leave me to puzzle out your meaning? Tell me."

She looked up at him. "Just after Henry and I were wed, King Edward issued an order that knights owning Scottish land should have English wives, and not intermarry with the Scots. Henry was very angry, after that, that he had married me."

"But you were wedded and bedded. His wife."

"Wedded," she said, "and bedded in the first few weeks only. But he would have resisted even that if he had known his king's policy earlier. He tried to get an annulment."

"But he never did."

"Nay," she said. "Though he spent good coin in the attempt, he couldna get loose of me until the day he died," she blurted, and tried to push past him.

He took her arm, pulling her against the hard mass of his body. "I am not like Henry," he said, his words clipped and certain. He stared down at her, something near anger in his gaze. "Do not seek to put Henry's feelings in my heart, or Henry's sins on my soul."

"English knights dinna desire Scottish wives," she enunciated harshly, and stepped back. "If you could find the gold, you would free yourself of the Scottish wife."

His fingers shifted on her arm, pulling her closer. "Surely you do not believe that."

She shrugged. "'Tis what I expect from an English husband."

"Ah. Henry tried that, so I will as well?" he glared down at her. "You have the temperament of an ox once you have made up your mind about a matter. When have I given you cause to think that I share Henry's opinions on marriage—or any topic at all?"

"I have fought English rule and English will since I was fourteen," she said, a slight tremor in her voice. "When I was fifteen, I was forced to pledge my oath to King Edward to keep my right to this land. But I lost that when my uncle forced me to wed Henry. I canna change so quickly because one Sasunnach has kind words for me"—Gavin reached out a finger as she spoke and traced it along her cheek, causing her breath to falter—"or gentle hands," she finished, nearly stammering.

O Dhia, she thought, he had such soothing, compelling, comforting hands. When he touched her, his Englishness slipped from her mind as if it did not exist. She forcefully pulled it back into her awareness: she could not trust a Sasunnach knight.

But her hammering heart and her surging body told her to try. Just try. When Gavin touched her, trust felt possible. She could feel a warm glow somewhere in her heart's center, like a tiny flame. Allowing that light to grow would clear the shadows that had darkened her life for far too long.

"I want to trust you." The words slipped out before she could stop them.

"Then do it." He ran his fingers along the side of her face and slipped his hand inside the hood of her cloak, his palm hot and dry against her neck, a breath of fire on an icy night. She inhaled slowly and closed her eyes, unable to resist, needing his silent, caring touch. His comfort.

He brought his face closer to hers, his breath warm over her cheek. His fingertips gently explored her jaw, her throat. He slid his fingers into her hair, stroking, soothing, creating shivers that cascaded down her spine.

She sighed, and tilted her face up to his like a lodestone drawn to iron. She laid her hands on his chest, feeling the strength of his heartbeat beneath firm muscle.

"Lady," he murmured, "you claim to despise my Englishness. But you do not shrink from my touch."

She shook her head. "Your hands make me forget you are English, though I want to remember it," she whispered.

"Forget, then," he said. "Just for now." His fingers trailed like touches of hot sun down the nape of her neck, brushing over her shoulder toward her upper chest. "Did Henry touch you like this?" His voice was husky, slipping like rough velvet over her senses.

"Never," she whispered. Her heart pounded so fiercely that she thought it must jar his fingertips.

"Henry did not love you," he murmured. She shook her head.

He touched his lips to hers then, firmly, possessively, until her head tipped back and her lips softened beneath his. The heel of his hand grazed over the golden pendant that lay against her skin, beneath two layers of wool, and moved slowly over her upper breast.

She let out a breath as a flood of feeling rushed through her body. The magnitude of that swirling force broke down dams of resistance that she had not even suspected were there. Her hands clenched at the front of his tunic, pulling him closer.

"You can be certain that had you been bedded by me, Christian," he murmured against her lips, "you would be bedded again and again, until you were mine in body"—another kiss, this one hot and deep and suddenly moist, his mouth over hers, his tongue melting over her lips until she melted, too—"and mine in heart and soul." She swayed against him, feeling his hands catch her waist firmly and his hard thighs press against hers.

Her breath heaved and her knees trembled. The urge to melt forward into his arms was strong, so strong. He kissed her again, and she moaned, a mingle of joy and protest. Part of her wanted to pull away from him, but she leaned back her head and opened her lips, beneath his. As his tongue traced inside and his hands slid up from her waist to circle her just beneath her breasts, she sighed and threw her arms around his neck.

He caught her full against him then, his hard body pressed to hers, his tongue tasting hers, his fingers slow and gentle over her breast. She sucked in her breath and caught a sweet cry in her throat. He had the most compelling, most soothing touch she could imagine. She could not get enough of it, as if she were thirsty and he offered her the clearest water.

Yet her fear of his English loyalties created a chasm she could not breach. Her thoughts tumbled on even as her senses surrendered. She wanted him to kiss her and touch her where he would; she wanted to feel his hands and lips caress the whole of her body. A pulsing, yearning demand burgeoned and grew until she craved the thrusting feel of him, deep and hot inside her.

And yet, at the same time, she wanted him to let go of her. Crying out suddenly, unable to fight the conflict any longer, she stilled against him and turned her head away.

After a moment, he lifted his head and his hands and looked down at her. His gaze was dark and unreadable in starlight. Cold wind replaced his touch on her skin. She drew in a shaking breath, and another, and looked up at him.

Gavin sighed and touched a fingertip to her chin. "You harbor so much inside of you," he said. "Anger and fear. Passion and joy. Someday you will release it. And I will be there then. I will be there." He let go and stepped back. "Meet me at first light by the great hall." He turned away.

Christian placed shaking fingers to her lips, sensitive from his kisses, and watched him stride across the courtyard. He mounted the steps to the parapet, his cloak whipping out behind him. Then he turned at the corner of the wall walk and dissolved into black shadow.

She stood in the doorway for a long time, waiting for the trembling in her knees, and in her very soul, to calm. Listening to the soft rustling sounds of the sleeping doves on their roosts behind her, she finally turned and went back to the great tower.

GAVIN TOSSED AND TURNED on the flat, ungiving pallet, made from a pile of blankets taken from the underground storage room. He had slept little since he had awoken John for his turn at watching on the parapet. Remembered echoes of his conversation with Christian had kept his thoughts actively stirring.

He glanced around the darkened chamber. Faint light from the curtained doorway defined the shapes of the others who slept in the same room, all of them on pallets just as uncomfortable as his. But they apparently slept well enough.

Christian lay a few feet away, breathing softly, her slight form curving gently beneath the blanket. During any of the nights that they had all been in here, he could have reached out to her and touched her while she slept; he could have moved his pallet next to hers. He never had, though she was his wife.

Her fervent response when he had kissed her and held her had revealed that she wanted him as much as he wanted her. Her body had spoken to him with clarity; she did not hate him.

In the abbey, when he had held her and helped her, he had felt a kind of bonding take place with her that he was certain still existed. He thought that she had felt it then, too, before she had learned who he was. He had not proved to be the saint or the Scot she had wanted him to be, but she had welcomed his kisses and the easy friendship between them when they had spoken of Henry and Michaelmas.

He stayed here at Kinglassie, despite its ruined state, because he wanted more than a castle and good land: he wanted a wife and a family. These were precious to him, more so because he had not had them yet. Jehanne had never been well after the first few months of their marriage, and her property was not truly his by French law.

He had waited a long time for this grant, and although it was in Scotland, he would do his utmost to make certain that the castle remained in his keeping. He was not eager to cooperate with Edward's plan to garrison Kinglassie, but he knew that he did not have a wide choice in the matter.

As for the wife granted to him, he intended to keep her safe as well. Gavin did not care if she was a Scottish rebel or a loyal subject of England. He had come to care about her. But she would not accept caring from anyone easily. The English had hurt her too much over the years, and Henry had done further damage with his cruel prejudices and selfish opinions.

He wanted Christian to return caring and trust to him, but he would not act the besotted fool. He would need patience and discretion. Some of her wounds lay as deep as his.

He sighed and shifted on his hard bed, and saw a movement in the shadows on the other side of the room. A small figure stood and pushed through the curtained doorway.

Wondering what caused Michaelmas to wander about in the night, he did not want to disturb Christian, who was resting peacefully. He sat up and yanked on his fur-lined boots, then grabbed his cloak and followed.

Dawn glowed through a faint mist as he walked into the courtyard. A few wild doves erupted from one of the ruined towers and flew over the yard. Gavin walked toward Michaelmas, who stood quietly, the hood of her cloak thrown back, her hair pale in the silvery light. Then he stopped, startled.

She held out her hand, and one of the doves fluttered down to rest on her shoulder. When another perched on her head, the child laughed, a sweet trill.

Gavin blinked, and looked again. She turned and saw him, and the birds lifted and flew away as she moved.

"I didna sleep much," she said. "Did you? 'Tis time to be up now."

He watched as the doves vanished into the misted dawn sky, and then he looked at her. "Are the birds trained?" he asked.

She shook her head. "But they always come to me. I willna eat cooked dove," she said, wrinkling her nose with distaste. "I think they know that."

"Ah. They sense your kindness," he said, though he was still perplexed.

"I had a dream," she said. "About you."

"Me?" He raised his brows in surprise. "What was it?"

"I dreamed my mother was dying, and you came and saved her. You were with a woman who stood beside you and told you what to do. And my mother sat up and was better again."

He stared at her. Was it the early hour, or was this child some kind of magical faery, blinking up at him with eyes like a bright summer sky? "Who was the other woman?" he asked.

She shrugged. "I didna know her. She looked like you, but older. And a bit like me. Blond, you ken. She was very kind."

He was frowning deeply. "How did I save your mother?"

"You gave her a new set of harp strings, and she said thank you." She laughed, and he did, too. "Gavin Faulkener," she said.

"Aye?"

"Thank you for saving my mother," she said. He bowed, and she held out her hand graciously.

He took her small fingers and kissed her hand. "You are surely welcome, Lady Michaelmas," he said, and smiled. She grinned and ran back toward the great tower.

Gavin stared after her for a long time. He had just realized, with a spinning of wonder and disbelief in his gut, that the child very much resembled his own mother. And his mother had lived in the very convent where Michaelmas had been born.

Shaking his head, he dismissed his next thought, not only because of its startling implications, but because he could hardly believe that it had even occurred to him.

Frowning deeply, he walked across the courtyard looking for his uncle.

CHAPTER TWELVE

CHRISTIAN WALKED SLOWLY up the narrow stone steps at the back of the bakery area. Stepping carefully over bits of fallen timbers and broken stone, she ascended to the next level and stopped at the slate landing outside the great hall, where she had promised to meet Gavin. A few moments earlier, she had heard him out in the courtyard, talking with John.

Shivering, she pulled her cloak more tightly over her shoulders. The air was so chilly up here that her breaths were pale puffs. Cool early light sliced through an arrowslit, brightening the gloom of the scorched stone walls.

Approaching the collapsed door of the great hall, she rested her hand on the stone doorjamb. She looked into the room, and sighed deeply.

Once bright and gracious, the vast chamber was now a wide hole floored with wreckage. Gray light poured through the gaping windows. Most of the timber floor beams had collapsed onto the vaulted stone ceilings of the bakery and storage rooms below.

Christian leaned a shoulder against the doorjamb, her chin quivering as she looked around the room. The shocking damage here, and throughout the castle, was her doing. She had needed stark will and courage to lay that torch to a pile of straw, that morning last summer. But she had done it. The keeper of the Kinglassie legend had caused its irrevocable destruction.

Now she had returned to Kinglassie through the workings

of fate, and needed that same courage to deal with what she had done here. She raised a shaking hand to her face. Warm tears wet her fingertips.

Her hand trailed down to touch the golden pendant that lay against her breastbone, tucked inside her gown. Leaning her forehead against cold stone, she let the tears drip down.

BREATHING OUT A PUFF OF FROSTED AIR, Gavin rested his hands on his hips and looked up at the portcullis. Jammed in position over his head, the iron grille slanted downward on one side, a precarious tilt. Reaching up, he tugged on the lowest horizontal bar, and felt no give. He jumped slightly, grabbed on with both hands, and hung from the bar. The gate held beneath his weight without even a squeak.

"Welded fast," he muttered. Using the strength of his arms, he raised up and then dropped downward heavily, but could not budge the gate. He repeated the motion, swinging outward with his feet. Still the gate did not give. A blacksmith will likely have to dismantle the thing to repair it, he thought.

"John MacKerras will scold you," said a light voice. He glanced down and saw Michaelmas looking up at him.

"Will he?" he said, and dropped down to the ground.

She nodded. "You shouldna swing from the yett. 'Tis dangerous. John said Will and I shouldna do it, for 'twill fall on our heads and smash us flat."

"This gate is not going to fall on anyone soon," he said. "But John is right to caution you. There are many dangerous places in this castle just now. If you want to play somewhere, you must first be sure 'tis safe."

"The laddies dinna care if 'tis safe. They're very brave," Michaelmas said. She watched him, her eyes wide and honest, and so fine a blue, like his mother's had been, that he felt wholly disconcerted for a moment.

"The laddies?" he asked.

"Patrick and Robbie," she said. "Fergus Macnab's laddies. Before you came here, we played at Kinglassie. Robbie can climb to the top o' the yett and down, like a squirrel."

"He's a talented lad, that Robbie," he said, suppressing a smile. "But I want you and your friends to be careful here."

She nodded. "May I swing?"

"Just for a moment, while I am here."

Her small gloved hands reached toward the gate. "Lift me, please, Gavin Faulkener," she said primly. He took her around the waist, his long fingers encompassing her slight build, and held her up so that she could grab onto the lowest bar of the portcullis. "Will's mother willna let him climb the gate," she said. "He's a Sasunnach laddie, but we like him well enough, the lads and I. He knows some sinful words," she added.

"Will you mother mind if you climb here?" he asked, as she dangled from the bar. He stood nearby in case she fell, but she showed no uncertainty.

"She willna mind if I climb as well as the lads do. Which I can." Grabbing hand over hand, she traversed the width of the bar to show him, her breaths visible puffs of mist.

"Well done," he said. "And your father—would he have let you climb the gate?" He waited expectantly.

She swung back and forth like the hammer of a bell. "He would hae said 'tisna a lady's way. But you dinna care about that, for you let me up here."

He smiled. "You will be a lady when you are ready, Michaelmas," he said. " 'Tis fine to be a child for now."

"Gavin Faulkener, are you my father now?"

"I am," he said. "But I've never been any child's father, and I am not sure how best to do it."

"Ach, 'tisna hard. 'Tis only me," she said. "Fergus Macnab has much more fathering to do. He has eight lads, and a whole flock of God's children."

"That's a task," Gavin said. "What was your father like?"

She swung for several moments. "He was muckle busy wi' his horses and his soldiers. He wasna here much, for the English king had important work for him in other parts o' Scotland." She moved deftly along the bar with her hands. "He had a deep yell, like thunder. I didna like it."

"Did he shout at you?" he asked, watching her.

"Nae me, but at my mother. I didna like him those times. Help me down, please, Gavin Faulkener," she said. He lifted her down. "John MacKerras is coming. He yells, too."

"Only a little," Gavin said, looking over his shoulder.

"Those bairnies will be hurt one day," John grumbled as he came near. Michaelmas gave him an innocent smile and ran off.

"She's a cautious girl, I think," Gavin said. He slid a glance at John. "She reminds me of my mother, somehow."

John frowned as he stared after her. "Aye, I've seen it, too. That fine pale hair, those eyes. Aye, she looks like your mother when she was a wee lass."

"Christian said that Henry adopted Michaelmas from the same priory that my mother stayed in," Gavin said.

John looked at him sharply. "When was this?"

"Just after Hastings destroyed the place," Gavin said. "Michaelmas was born there a year or so earlier."

"Was she," John said. "Was she indeed." He frowned and rubbed his blunt fingers over his bearded chin. "I remember that Dame Joan was the prioress there. Did she say who the wee bairn's mother was? Or her father?"

"Nay," Gavin answered. " 'Tis likely, I think, that Henry was her father. That alone might explain why the child has a familiar look to me. But Christian does not know if he was."

John drew a deep breath and looked at Gavin. "Well," he said, and hesitated. "I dinna mean to imply any ill thoughts, but it does come to my mind that Henry and your mother were verra close. He wanted to wed her once, before she wed your father."

"I had heard that," Gavin said. "What do you think, John?"

His uncle sighed and shook his head. "I think 'twould be a miracle if 'twere true. Hair of that pale shade is unusual, but there would have to be other proof before I would suspect my own sister of such a thing."

"True. 'Tis likely impossible," Gavin said. "The resemblance is curious, though." He thought then of the little girl's dream. She had described an older woman, kind and blond. His mother would have been at the priory when Michaelmas had been born, and may have helped care for the child. Perhaps Michaelmas had an infant's memory of her. Aye, Gavin thought; surely that was all it was.

"Likely any records of her mother's name were burned wi' the convent," John said. "*Ach,* 'tis a foolish thought, lad. We need more sleep at night, I think. Though I wouldna doubt Henry sired the lass, 'twould take much for me to believe my own sister was her mother."

Gavin nodded, and exhaled a long breath. "Aye so. Well, what then of the chimneys? You've looked at them this morn?"

"Aye," John said. "Outside the great tower, I saw only smoke vents and the one chimney for the kitchens. We could convert one 'o the privy shafts to a chimney for a new hearth."

"I will take a look when I go in," Gavin said. "Christian is likely waiting for me by now. She's promised to show me through the halls and bedchambers this morning."

"Be careful she doesna hae in mind to drop you through one o' the floors," John said. Gavin shot him a wry glance and walked away.

CHRISTIAN HEARD QUICK FOOTSTEPS as Gavin climbed the stairs leading to the landing where she stood outside the great hall. She wiped at the tears that stained her cheeks and stiffened her spine as he approached. She heard his boots scrape over the steps, and then halt just behind her. She could smell the wind about him, heard the swirl of his cloak as he stepped nearer.

"God's greetings, lady," he said. She nodded and kept turned away from him, looking into the chamber. An involuntary sniff slipped out.

"All is not well with you this morning," he said.

" 'Tis hard to look at this," she admitted, her voice trembling. She pointed toward the great hall.

Sighing deeply, he leaned a shoulder against the opposite doorjamb. He glanced around the room, at its loftily arch-vaulted stone ceiling, at the walls, charred dark, and at the double design of the pointed arch windows. "This was once a fine chamber," he said.

"It was that," she said tremulously. "Room enough for several large tables, and direct access to the kitchens and to fresh water. Glass windows, and carved ceiling bosses, and a design of thistles painted on one wall. Henry was surprised to find such civility in a cold castle in Celtic Scotland."

"What kind of hearth was here?" he asked. "I see no fireplace in the wall."

She pointed. "An iron basket, there, in the center of the room. We usually burned peats there, though Henry often complained about that and ordered a log fire. The fire basket has fallen among the floor timbers." She pointed downward.

"I see. A hooded fireplace would be best here. They heat the rooms well, with less smoke."

"Kinglassie is an older castle, parts of it built generations ago. We only had two true fireplaces, in the bakery and in the kitchen just there, that room beyond the hall. We used fire baskets and iron braziers for heat elsewhere."

"We will have wall hearths and corner hearths now, wherever you like," he said. "We can add chimneys on the outer walls."

She glanced over at him. In the cool dawn light, his hair, spilling to his shoulders, was touched with strands of gold. Framed against dark stone, his profile was finely cut, strong and lean and beautiful. Christian longed, for an instant, to trace her fingers along his jaw, to feel the texture of his beard, to feel the warmth of his face near hers once again.

She thought of his kisses last night, and of his words to her. A swirling, yearning sensation spun through her body. But she frowned at herself, still caught in the conflict between such new, tentative joys, and old, powerful fears.

"How many men did Henry have here?" Gavin asked.

His words jolted her, reminding her that his only intent was to rebuild Kinglassie and fill it with English soldiers. "Two hundred or so," she said. "They kept their quarters in the southeast and northeast towers." She slid him a glance. "Do you mean to bring that many?"

"I do not know how many men will be sent here. 'Tis not my

decision." His gaze was brilliant blue in the dimness. "And they could not be housed where Henry's men were, for those towers are almost totally destroyed. I doubt the masonry there is strong enough to support new floors. The walls could collapse."

"The walls of those two towers have always been weak, and cracked in places," she said. "My father hired masons to shore them up when I was a child. He thought there was some basic fault in the stone, or perhaps in the foundation. He intended to rebuild them someday, but we spent most of our time at his castle in the western Highlands."

"I will hire stonemasons to examine the structures and rebuild them entirely," Gavin said.

" 'Twould take years to reconstruct them," she said.

"Aye." He looked at her so directly, so intensely, that her heart bounded in her chest. "Two years at least, I think, before we see our castle complete, my lady."

Her eyes widened. He spoke as if he thought of her as his wife, his partner, as if rebuilding were a project of shared delight and not a necessity of war. As if no kings or wars existed to determine the function of the castle. As if he valued her opinion.

She was used to gruff complaining, and harsh criticism, and a cold, lonely bed every night; she was used to a husband who disliked her intensely. She found it difficult to accept that this English knight did not condemn her and reject her constantly. Henry had only softened his disagreeable manner when Michaelmas had been nearby; for that much, at least, Christian had always been grateful.

"But there are more immediate concerns than those two towers," Gavin continued. Christian cleared her throat, trying to focus her thoughts on what he said. "We need bedchambers readied as soon as possible. That little chamber we are all sharing now is rather uncomfortable. No hearth, no true beds, and too close to the stabled horses. And it has grown even more crowded of late."

She raised her chin. "I willna send my daughter back to Fergus and Moira."

"My lady, I would not ask that." He gave her a puzzled look. "Your daughter belongs here. But I will clear rooms for her and others elsewhere, and soon. That little fellow William snores louder than John."

Christian laughed, a soft burst of humor and relief. He smiled and turned slowly to examine the small corridor in which they stood. They he crossed the landing to look out the small arrow-slit window, where cold light and air knifed through the wall. Watching him, Christian noticed that he moved with a simple athletic grace. She admired the width of his shoulders and his narrow hips, the limber turn of his tall body in the black tunic and deep blue cloak.

He gestured toward the stairs. "How many bedchambers are above this level?"

"Four in all up there, two with privies," she said. "The two smaller rooms are built into the thickness of the walls. The largest bedchamber—the laird's solar—lies partly over the great hall."

"Show me," he said.

FOUR ARCHED DOORWAYS were set in the length of the upper corridor, one door placed away from the others. That door had wooden planking still intact, its gently arched doorframe a note of grace in a wall darkened and marred by smoke. Christian approached the door with Gavin just behind her. Lifting the latch, she pushed the door open.

"The laird's bedchamber," she said. "There is another entrance in that corner, with steps leading to the great hall below."

"Was this your room?"

"I shared it with my daughter," she said. "Henry slept down the hall. He always preferred a private chamber."

The last time that she had been here, she had supervised the servants, hurrying them along while they stripped embroidered hangings from the walls, carried her clothing chests down the steps, and dismantled the huge bed. Now the chamber was another empty, ugly hole, like the hall below, its floor partly ruined, its windows and raftered ceiling leaking light, open to the cold winter dawn.

Gavin sighed as he looked around. "You do surely know how

to ruin a castle," he said softly. "King Edward should have had you on his side."

She whirled. "And I would burn his great castle, with him in it!"

He held up a hand. "Hold, hold. An unfortunate remark. My apologies. Peace between us, lady?" he asked, touching her arm.

The contact sent tingling shivers down her spine. She raised her chin stubbornly, reminding herself of his Englishness. But that lever was having less and less effect on her resolve to remain cool toward him. After last night's heated, breathless kisses, she had begun to believe that he was a man of substance and kindness, virile as well as gentle. A man she was afraid that she had begun to love.

But she was also afraid to soften toward him, afraid that she would trust him to be compassionate and kind, and be proven wrong once again.

Gavin leaned into the room. "That window is set with beautiful tracery, done by a master craftsman."

"The window frames were carved at Edinburgh and brought here when I was a child," she said, glad of neutral ground. "A gift for my mother. There was colored glass set in the top section, and oak shutters below."

"A basket hearth was here as well?"

"We only used a brazier, sometimes two in winter."

"A fireplace will do better," he said. "With a long hood to keep the room free of smoke." He turned to her. "Would you like that, my lady?"

She hesitated, then nodded.

Gavin stepped forward cautiously, pushing his foot against the floorboard before he moved into the room. The blackened boards creaked beneath his weight.

"Dinna walk there!" she said, alarmed. "The floor could collapse."

He glanced back at her, then walked along the perimeter of the room, agile and careful. When he came to the window niche, he walked between its facing stone benches and looked out.

"Come here," he said, beckoning to her.

" 'Tis dangerous," she said, holding on to the doorjamb.

He shook his head. "The floor in this room is far more sound that I have seen elsewhere in the castle. Those fallen timbers, there, are from the ceiling. Look up—see where the ceiling rafters are gone, just here, and there?"

She nodded. "The roof must have caught a spark and burned through in those spots."

"Aye. Fergus told me there was a heavy rainstorm the day of the fire." He stretched out a hand to rub the wall. "These are water stains. The downpour must have come through the open roof and doused the fire in this room before the floor beams could be consumed." Christian glanced at the walls. "I have seen other signs of water damage in other parts of the castle."

"But there were heavy rains, apparently, that stopped the fire before it could destroy the entire castle. A blessing, my lady." He cocked a brow at her and beckoned again. "Come here. The floor is safe to cross. I want you to see something."

She stepped forward carefully, clinging to the wall. The floor creaked but held. Looking down, she realized that the thick oak floor beams were intact, only blackened and littered with soot and rubble from the ceiling rafters.

Gavin walked to her and held out his hand. His fingers were hard and warm over hers as he pulled her toward him and brought her into the window recess.

A cold breeze cut through the empty stone tracery as he stood behind her. "Look out there," he said softly.

The loch spread away from the castle like cold, smooth silver in the early light, surrounded by dark hills. The misty, infinite expanse of the dawn sky was a glorious, delicate blend of pink and lavender and silver. A flock of white doves soared upward like a spinning cloud.

"Beautiful," she breathed.

"Aye," he said, his fingers tightening on her shoulder. "A fine site for a castle. We will make Kinglassie strong again, for you and I."

"For your king," she said, a bitter edge to her voice.

"For us," he said.

She half turned and glanced up at him, his determined tone catching her attention. He stared out over her head toward the landscape. The dawn light gave a startling clarity to his eyes, silver threaded into indigo. He seemed a vision of power and masculine beauty, reminding her of the first day she had ever seen him.

"But your king has ordered you to rebuild here only to house his garrisons. And he wants you to find the Bruce, to—"

"I know well what Edward wants me to do. But I do not care to be master over a seat of war only. I will build here as I see fit. I have the coin for it and I will hold the charter." He glanced down at her. "And I will have your help."

"Why should I help you?" she whispered.

"You are my wife." He lifted his brows as if the idea were all so simple, without complexity.

"A poor choice for an English knight," she muttered.

Gavin swore softly. His hands tightened on her shoulders, and he spun her around. "Your bitterness and anger are proving difficult to live with."

With her back pressed against the window jamb, she stared up at him. "I willna help you rebuild if you intend to bring English soldiers here. Dinna ask it of me."

"Lady Christian, I have tried to offer peace to you. I realize that this was once your home."

"I didna ask you to wed with me and come here."

"Think you I asked King Edward for Scottish land? This is what he granted me!"

"An English sovereign has no right to grant Scottish land!" she shouted.

He blinked once, his nostrils flaring. He tightened his hands on her arms. "Ah. Here is your contention with me, then. You believe I have no right to Kinglassie."

"None at all!" she yelled. Somehow, shouting at him felt good, a release. She wanted to shout again, scream and pummel at him. Perhaps that would keep her from yearning to have his arms around her. She stared into the darkening blue of his eyes and prepared to face that storm with her own.

"No right? I am your husband!" he said fiercely. Christian

flinched, waiting for him to shout the words, but he kept control.

She fisted her hands, unwilling to hold her own temper. "You are an invader!"

"I am your husband," he said firmly, "and as such I have a right to this castle, by the laws of your king or mine."

"I didna consent."

"Consent? We all heard you answer aye in that chapel in Carlisle," he said. "We were wed in God's presence, and Kinglassie is ours together."

She looked away, breath heaving in her throat, knowing that what he said was true. Hating that truth, she also hated that she was treacherously thrilled by his words. He was her husband, and he accepted that, and did not hate her for it. She continued to draw deep breaths, striving to find a better balance for her temper. "You intend to stay here, then."

"If I returned to France just now, 'twould be an act of treason," he said.

"Dinna think to have my pity for that," she snapped.

"Lady—" He sighed heavily. "I came back to England wanting the land and the castle that was owed to me. I was weary of living in France. I did not ask for Kinglassie. And I surely did not think to take another wife when I came to Carlisle. But we are wed now, regardless of the circumstances that have brought us to it, and I will honor the vows. I am not like Henry, as I told you last night."

As he spoke, he leaned closer to her. She could feel his warm breath on her brow. Glancing at him reluctantly, her eyes dropped to his mouth, and she touched her teeth to her lip, recalling deep, fervent kisses last night.

"I will not pay for Henry's crimes toward you, or for King Edward's," he said softly. "I will not be all Englishmen to you, so that you can vent that boundless temper on me."

Her heart thumped heavily in her chest. His face drew close, his breath soft on her cheek. She wanted him to kiss her; she wanted to yell out at him again. That release had stirred something in her, like a drift of fresh air. This pushing and pulling in her thoughts and her heart was spinning her into madness.

Then something he had said echoed through her mind.

"Another wife?" she repeated, frowning.

"She died two years ago." He drew back a little, his mouth set in a grim line, a muscle quirking in his lean jaw.

"She was French?"

"Jehanne, Comtesse de Fontevras. She was but nineteen when she died." He dropped his hands from her shoulders and looked out the window. The tilt of his head, the set of his jaw, told her that he tamped down a heavy pain in that moment.

"Do you have bairns?" she asked softly. He shook his head.

Christian felt suddenly ashamed of ranting on about English knights and invaders. She had been selfish and thoughtless; she had her beautiful child with her, and her home, despite its condition, was beneath her feet, and could be whole again. She was not the only one with injuries and hurts.

Gavin harbored a deep pain; she could see its shadow in his eyes. He must have loved his French wife as she had never loved Henry. She felt a twinge of jealousy. And she felt sympathy for him as well, deep and sincere.

She laid her hand on his arm, a light touch quickly withdrawn. "I— I am sorry," she whispered.

He stared out over the loch. "You change like quicksilver, a virago one moment and a tender-heart the next," he said. "We both have our sorrows and our hurts, my lady. Mayhap now you will think to rein in your tongue and your temper." He turned away abruptly and crossed the room to the door. Then he looked back over his shoulder.

"If you are concerned about walking across this floor, keep toward the walls. 'Tis safe enough here, though you may not think it." He walked away and went quickly down the steps.

Christian left the room carefully and went down after him, her brow furrowed. At the bottom landing, she stood in the outer doorway and watched as Gavin strode across the courtyard, his blue cloak catching the first bright rays of the sun.

A deep desire stirred within her then, so fervent and strong that her knees grew weak in its onrush. She wished that the promise Gavin had made to her in the underground chamber could always be true: that he would be only a man, and no English knight, whenever they were together. Then she could be only a woman, and no Scot.

The pull she felt toward him was undeniable, increasing in power each time she was with him. He had shown her compassion and caring, had touched her soul as no one had ever done. Gavin had shown her that hearts could heal as well as bodies.

She wanted no more barriers between them. No conflicting loyalties, no hurtful pasts to feed fear, mistrust, and anger. Her anger was rightfully owed to Henry and to King Edward, but not to Gavin Faulkener.

Stepping into the courtyard, she wanted to rush after him and make an apology, but she stopped. His broad back was stiff and proud and his stride was too rapid. He never once glanced back as he crossed the yard to join John.

She sighed and glanced up at the walls of the castle in the early sun. Even damaged, Kinglassie had great strength and beauty. The castle could be repaired.

Watching Gavin, Christian feared that her anger and bitterness had irrevocably damaged this marriage. Perhaps, just as she had destroyed Kinglassie's legend, she had ruined something else ultimately more valuable than ancient gold.

She had a strange sense that, like Kinglassie, Gavin Faulkener held a kind of treasure deep within him. There was more to him than he had shown her so far, much more, the sum of the whole man. And she wanted to find it.

She sighed, unsure she had the strength to overcome and face her deepest resentments, even to reach out for what she wanted.

CHAPTER THIRTEEN

O N AN EARLY, FROSTY MORNING a few days later, Gavin
stood on the parapet with John and Will, trying to mortar
loosened stones back into the battlement wall with a mixture of
mud and straw. Hoarfrost slicked the stones and made them difficult to handle. And because the stream water they had used in
the mix was icy cold, the resultant mortar was lumpy and would
not adhere well.

Gavin's hands were chilled as he gripped a large stone. He
flexed his fingers and vowed to wear his fur-lined gloves for the
remainder of the task. Swearing in frustration as he tipped the
stone back into place once again, Gavin hardly glanced up when
William shouted.

"*Pardieu!* My lord! A host of churls advancing this way!"

"How many churls would that be?" Gavin asked
distractedly.

"Dinna jump, laddie," John muttered to Will as he stirred a
handful of straw into a kettle filled with cold mud. "You're making your pretty mother nervous down in the courtyard, there."

Gavin, tussling with the recalcitrant stone, grunted as he
slammed the block into place. Then he turned to grab Will up,
setting him on top of the stone. "Hold that down with your great
weight, boy, and show me these visitors."

"Just there, see! Hundreds of 'em!" The boy pointed.

John peered over the parapet with them. "Look at that. A

fierce enough group, God save us all," he said. "Let's hope they hae peace in mind and nae war."

Watching the large group of people who advanced toward the unprotected drawbridge, Gavin grinned and turned to John. "Fergus is good for his word," he said. "Here come our workers."

"You'll never hae enough cheese and grain to trade as daily wages for that lot," John said. "Thank God we brought a muckle load o' coin bags wi' us when we traveled north."

Gavin leaned over the parapet and called a loud shout of welcome. Fergus looked up and waved, while his two youngest sons ran looping paths around him as he walked.

Just behind them came a group of five or six women, two carrying babes, the others with cloth sacks. One of them, a tall, dark-haired woman, spoke sharply to Fergus's boys when they nearly tripped up their father. Then the boys ran ahead of the entire group to reach the drawbridge first.

Behind the boys and the women came at least forty or fifty men; Gavin tried to make a swift count. They carried tools and tugged at the reins of sturdy, shaggy, short-legged horses whose backs and saddles were loaded with an assortment of sacks and implements, among them saws, hammers, and chisels. One cart, pulled by an ox, held a blacksmith's anvil. Strolling beside the cart was a man who was nearly as broad as the ox itself, his arms like hewed oak, his wild hair furnace-red.

"I think we have our smith to fix the portcullis," Gavin said to John, and grinned.

"Aye. And the rest look eager for work and coin, and happy to find such in the dead o' winter," John said. "But not all o' them are English supporters, I'll guess."

"I'll pay good coin for good work, and no questions asked of their sympathies." Gavin turned to lift Will off the stone, then whooped, laughed loudly, and spun the boy around before he set him down and headed for the steps to greet the workers.

"MASTER TAM SAYS THE PORTCULLIS CHAINS are melted and canna be used at all," Fergus said. "Nae good, a porridgey mess of iron and stone. He willna remake the chains from contaminated iron."

Gavin nodded and watched from a doorway on the second level of the gatehouse as the blacksmith examined the chains, pulleys, and winches that had once operated the massive portcullis and the drawbridge. Beside him, the head stonemason and the head carpenter muttered as they, too, examined the mechanisms and the great gaping holes in the gatehouse floor.

Master Tam grunted, stomped heavily on the charred winch—Gavin held his breath, half expecting the rest of the floor to go—and spoke to Fergus in Gaelic. The priest nodded, replied, listened to more of the smith's mumbling, and turned to listen to what the mason and the carpenter had to say. They clearly had quite a bit to say, and all Gavin could understand was in which direction they pointed as they spoke.

He had never wanted to understand Gaelic so much as in this moment. The fate of his castle was being discussed, and he was dependent on a Celtic priest and a handful of Scots who likely did not care to see another castle go to the English.

"Master Tam says you'll need new pulleys and a winch, which can be made from a wide oak tree. He says he can remake the struts on the portcullis, and repair the drawbridge chains," Fergus said. "The carpenters will have to bring him enough wood for his forge. But he says very heavy chain links must be purchased for the portcullis. And stout hempen rope as well. He wants you to order those from the best smith and ropemaker in Ayr."

Gavin nodded. Master Tam grunted in satisfaction. "And the head carpenter will construct a new yett, a pair of heavy wooden gates to close off the castle until the portcullis is fixed," Fergus said.

"Well enough. What else are they saying?" Gavin asked. The three men behind Fergus were still muttering. Gavin thought it sounded suspiciously like complaining.

Fergus sighed. "They are saying, Gavin Faulkener, that 'tis a muckle lot o' work for the middle o' winter, and nae a sheep offered to any o' them."

"They'll have sheep, as many as they like, as soon as the spring fair begins," Gavin said. "What else?"

"The very first priority, as you ken yourself, is wood. The carpenters and laborers must go into the forests and cut enough timber for all these tasks. They need oak and pine to build new floors and ceiling rafters and doors. You've asked for fireplaces, and that requires stone and wood both. And you want a tub. They canna see the importance in that, but they'll do it, and all else that you've asked. They are willing to work for you, though you be a Sasunnach."

"I'm grateful, but why are they so willing?"

"Because you wed the Lady Christian and saved her from the cage, and because I told them you dinna care for Hastings. And because you'll pay coin. But they do ask for some livestock and grain as soon as you can manage it. Their wives dinna care as much for silver as for food."

Gavin nodded. "Thank them for their help, and tell them I will do all that I can to get what they need. Fergus, you will have to help me learn some Gaelic phrases."

"I will, but many o' the men ken English as well as you do. They just like to use the Gaelic. Being as you are a Sasunnach."

Gavin looked up in surprise. The men grinned at him, and he laughed. Master Tam mumbled again, gruff, breathy Gaelic phrases that made the others chuckle. Gavin looked at Fergus, who spoke to the men in Gaelic and smiled.

"Master Tam says he canna repair the portcullis with the wee bairnies swinging on it as if 'twas an apple tree in their grannie's croft-yard," Fergus said. "I say mayhap he would like some young apprentices. But he declined the privilege."

"ACH, THE NOISE," CHRISTIAN SAID as she walked through the yard with Dominy. "How could I have forgotten the noise of a working castle so quickly? With just the few of us here, it has been so peacefully quiet."

She looked around the courtyard at the workmen, each one making a different sort of noise with tool or voice. Some stood high on the scaffolds, using hammers and chisels, while others slapped down mortar with trowels as they repaired the damaged parts of the upper walls. Laborers climbed ladders or worked pulleys to lift heavy stones, while carpenters stood at trestles in the courtyard, hammering or sawing oak and pine to make new doors, or shaping the beams and boards to be used for the floors and ceilings. From every corner of the yard, shouted orders or remarks added to the din.

Several men, with axes slung over their shoulders or suspended through sturdy belts, walked alongside the ox-drawn cart, its two iron-trimmed wheels squealing, to exit below the still suspended portcullis. They led two of the shaggy horses with them. The men, Christian knew, would spend much of the day in the forest, and would return with full loads of pine and oak logs stacked in the cart, and the longest beams harnessed to the horses.

Christian and Dominy walked toward the great tower, the hems of their cloaks and gowns trailing in the icy mud of the courtyard. Around them swirled a rough and raucous cacophony of shouting, pounding, sawing, and scraping. Laced through it all, like a lighter beat, were conversations and laughter from both male and female voices, punctuated by the squeals and shouts of the children who ran in and out among the carts, ladders, and workmen.

"This noise? 'Tis but a small clamor," Dominy observed wryly, glancing around the courtyard. "At Carlisle, the castle was constantly filled with the noise of two thousand soldiers and—oh, I am sorry, my lady. I did not mean to mention that awful place to ye."

"I know all about the castle at Carlisle," Christian said, ignoring the swirl of dark emotion that spun in her stomach. "And I much prefer the wee clamor here at Kinglassie."

"D' ye mind, then, the repairs here? Ye were not happy with Sir Gavin when he first spoke of it, but now that the work has been going on for near a month, ye seem happier with it."

"Repairs were desperately needed, and much improvement has been made since the workmen first came here," Christian replied. " 'Tis good to see the castle coming back after the fire."

"Even with the promise of the English troops to come? Here,

Will," Dominy shouted suddenly, striding forward, "get off that gate! 'Tis no great oak tree for ye to climb! Ye'll be hurt, and then what! Get down now!"

Dangling by both arms from the lower bar of the crooked portcullis gate, William kicked his feet and leaped off, landing on his bottom in the muddy yard.

"Ah, Willikin, ye're my trial of spirit, I think," Dominy said, helping him up and smacking at the seat of his tunic and short cloak to clean them. "If Master Tam saw ye swinging there, and him set to work on that gate today, he would surely be angry. Now go find the other children and play some other game."

"Robbie and Patrick said they were going to join the Bruce. I do not know where they are. But Michaelmas said she might play swords with me. The carpenters made some wooden ones for us. I will find her."

"Do that," Dominy said. As Will ran off, she and Christian resumed walking.

"Swords!" Christian said. "She runs and climbs with Moira's sons so often, she seems more a lad that a lass at times."

"And are ye surprised? They are her only companions. 'Tis not bad for her, I say."

Christian laughed ruefully. "Scottish women have always had a tradition of handling weapons alongside their menfolk. My mother told me ancient tales of warrior princesses long ago, born in my own bloodline."

"And why not your own daughter among them? She may have need of skill with arms someday, with the English here in such numbers."

Christian nodded. "Scotswomen must defend their homes, it seems. I had to do it myself, once." She glanced away, shutting out the unwelcome memory of a day last summer, when she had barred Kinglassie's yett against her own husband.

"Ah, but with Sir Gavin as her stepfather, she will likely wed an English nobleman and have no need for such things as blades," Dominy said. "And since ye do not know her parents, she may be English blood through and through."

"There is Scottish blood in her," Christian said stoutly. "She has the look of it, somehow. And she will be a fine harper some-day. Whenever I give her a harp lesson, she seems to feel the music in her blood and her heart, as I do. Born of me or not, she is my daughter, and she will be the keeper of the Kinglassie legend after me."

Dominy sighed, glancing at her. "Scots have fine sharp tem-pers and pride," she said. "My husband, rest his soul, hated the English war against the Scots. Ye would have liked my Edwin. William is much like him in his face and in his brave heart, but the English soldiers at Carlisle filled his head with thoughts that are not fitting for a young boy. Mayhap living in Scotland will help him to understand how wrong this war is."

Christian looked at Dominy in wonder. "For an Englishwoman, you have much sympathy for the Scots. And a forgiving heart."

"Edwin and I lived in Scotland for several years, and Will was born here. Edwin talked often about King Edward's lack of chiv-alry in Scotland." Dominy sighed and shook her head. "My hus-band was but a poor knight, and had no choice but to fight in the king's host to earn his living. But he never shared the hatred that so many of the English soldiers have toward the people of Scotland. That hatred is taught by our king."

Christian huffed a short, bitter laugh. "King Edward says Scotland is but a territory of England. He thinks we are only dis-obedient rebels in need of a firm hand. So he shows us a vicious one."

Dominy stopped, frowning down at the ground, toeing its mud with her leather shoe. "My lady, what King Edward does to the Scots is not right. If a man is king, even on the tiniest hill, and stamps upon the earth and beats at the ants that live there, sooner or later those ants will bite him back. And I say that he would deserve the pain of it."

Christian smiled. "And if I were an ant, I would summon my armies to swarm and bite the invader who tramples our hill."

"Just so," Dominy said. "God gives no man, even the king, the rights that King Edward takes for himself."

"Dinna let the English hear you speak so," Christian murmured. "They regard such talk as traitorous. And they are cruel to traitors."

"If I were a man I would fight against such unfairness, no matter where I had signed my oath years before," Dominy said firmly.

Christian was silent for a moment, sidestepping a pile of stone rubble as she and Dominy walked toward the great tower. "Did you know that I signed an oath of fealty to King Edward years ago, in order to keep Kinglassie?"

Dominy stared. "Did ye?"

"Aye, and I broke that oath when I helped Robert Bruce, and the English punished me for it. But I would break it again in a moment." She lifted her chin defiantly.

Dominy nodded. "A man's oath—and a woman's—belongs where their heart is, my lady. Their fealty is best placed where they love the land, and respect the king that leads them."

Christian smiled at her friend. "You sound like a rebel, Dominy," she teased. But her glance was serious as she looked up at the soaring stone walls of Kinglassie, shining in the cold light of the morning sun. She knew without a doubt where the loyalty of her own heart resided.

She was silent as they crossed the yard toward the tower, listening to the hammering and shouting as the workers readied Kinglassie to house more English troops. She wondered when Gavin would bring those men here. Thinking of the Sasunnach knight who was now her husband, she recalled, with a flush of heat to her cheeks, his compelling touches, his tender kisses, his deep kindness toward her. She had told him, not long ago, that she wished he was other than who he was.

If he had indeed been the brave Scots knight she had once thought him to be, then the loyalty of his heart might lay closer to her own. As it was—she sighed and pulled open the narrow door in the base of the tower—she doubted that true happiness could exist between them.

That thought brought with it a deep swirl of regret.

THE NOISE WAS EVEN LOUDER in the tower, a clamor of a different sort. A steady, heavy hammering like bursts of thunder came from overhead, and a deep, uneven clanging seemed to resound beneath their feet, as if they were caught inside a great bell.

Christian and Dominy entered the ground-floor bakery chamber. Inside, the room was littered with ladders, loose stones, tools, and buckets, and crowded with workmen who clambered up and down the high ladders that leaned against the walls, providing access to the ceiling. Stacks of freshly cut pine and oak gave off a pleasant, pungent odor. A small window had been enlarged to let in more light, and a chilly blast of outside air cut through the opening.

The loudest hammering came from overhead, where workmen repaired the floors of the great hall and the uppermost level of the tower. The clanging underfoot emanated from the open well hole situated in the floor, to one side of the chamber.

Near the fireplace, Michaelmas and the two young sons of Fergus Macnab sat watching a mason restore the cracked stones in one wall of the hearth. Michaelmas's blond head gleamed beside Patrick's glossy red head, and Robbie's tangled brown curls. They glanced up as Christian and Dominy entered.

"Where's Will? We want to hunt the treasure!" Robbie said.

"We hae something fine to show him!" Patrick said. "There's a wee door beside the hearth place!"

"He knows about that," Dominy said. " 'Tis a storage place."

"But the gold might be there, hidden from the greedy Sasunnach king!" Patrick said. He and Robbie ran out of the kitchen, shouting for Will.

"Moira! Good morning!" Christian called over the din.

Bending to stir the contents of a kettle suspended over a small fire, Moira turned around and straightened. A tall woman, with a handsome, gaunt face and a fat dark braid, she grinned widely. "*Tch,* Christian," she said. "God's greetings to you. Look! The ceiling is nearly done here, and above that, the carpenters are finishing the upper floors. And below us, your husband and mine have decided to clear the well."

Christian and Dominy hurried over toward the well hole to

peer together into its depths. Inside the well, lit by a torch stuck in a crevice in the stone wall, Christian saw the gleam of tawny golden hair and strongly muscled shoulders above the water. Gavin glanced up, his face darkened with soot and grime, his eyes bright blue in the torchlight.

Beside him, she saw the pale shape of Fergus's tonsure and his round shoulders. The priest wielded a heavy iron hammer, which he was using to knock against the side of the well, trying to dislodge something.

"Throw down the bucket!" Gavin called when he saw her, his voice echoing. Christian looked around, puzzled, until Michaelmas came forward to answer.

"I will!" she called eagerly, and grabbed up a thick rope that was attached to a bucket. One end of the rope was tied to a stone block, obviously in use until the well winch could be rebuilt. The girl lowered the bucket carefully and waited, holding the rope taut until Fergus grabbed it.

"Thank you, lassie," Fergus called up. "Robbie near broke my head when he tossed it down last time."

Robbie, who had just returned with Patrick and Will, peered over the edge of the well, bending so far that Moira grabbed at the back of his tunic. "D' you want me to throw down another bucket, Da?" he yelled. "There's two or three here."

"One is all we need, lad," Gavin called back, laughing.

"Can I come down?" Robbie asked, his thin voice echoing.

"Nay, lad," Fergus answered. "We're nearly done."

Christian saw Gavin draw a deep breath and suddenly sink under the level of the water. "What are they doing?" she asked.

Moira looked down. "They've been gathering up the debris that has fallen and blocked the flow of water, and sending the loads back up in the buckets."

"How did they get down there?" Dominy asked.

"Climbed down along those iron rungs in the side of the wall there, see," Moira answered. "They've spent near the whole o' the mornin' down there, trying to open up the place where the water flows into the well."

"The water level has risen quite a bit," Christian said.

"Aye," Dominy said, looking down. "Freezing, they must be."

Moira nodded. "Fergus takes a chill too easy, and he's been down there a long time. Gavin Faulkener must be muckle chilled as well. Fergus has been up one or twa times to warm up, but Gavin hasna come out yet."

"Pull up the rope, my love!" Fergus called to Moira. She tugged at the fat rope, and with Christian's help, pulled the loaded bucket out of the well. Blackened, soggy pieces of wood filled the bucket, which Michaelmas and Patrick carried away between them, in order to dump its contents inside.

A few more loads of similar material, slimed from months of submergence in water, were caught and dumped. Fergus announced, finally, that they were done, and he climbed upward, clinging to the iron rungs embedded in the side of the well.

Grunting as he heaved himself out of the well, Fergus stood, shivering, his pale torso slick and plump as a seal. Moira threw a blanket around him and handed one to Christian to give Gavin when he came up. Then she and Fergus walked away toward the heat of the small cooking fire.

Christian, watching, noticed the tender way that Moira, who was a little taller than her sturdy husband, bent to kiss his bald brow. He murmured a remark, and they laughed, exchanging a quick, casual kiss on the lips, their eyes intent on each other. Feeling a twinge of envy, Christian glanced away.

The children ran over to talk to Fergus, interrogating him eagerly on the contents of the well, and Dominy joined them to stir the kettle and listen. Christian, standing alone by the well, looked down to see the crown of Gavin's head emerging from the hole as he climbed steadily up the rungs.

Placing his hands on the ground near her, he quickly hoisted himself up and out. Water slicked off his torso and cascaded from his black breeches to pool on the floor around his bare feet. She noticed the solid musculature of his chest and abdomen, and the water-darkened mat of brown hair that covered his chest, narrowing to a wedge that disappeared below his soggy waistband, with its leather drawstring.

He looked at her and smiled briefly, reaching up to shove

back his wet hair. Christian stared at him, holding the blanket, forgetting its weight in her arms. The sight of his half-nude body startled her somehow, stirring her heart to a fast, hard beat, fascinating her so that she could not look away. She was hardly aware of how intently she was watching him.

He was not the least like Henry, she thought, who had been a tall man, too, but wide and soft. Gavin was tautly muscled and perfectly proportioned, long and lean and strong, his belly flat, the soft brown hair over his chest and abdomen contrasting the hard, rippled muscles that moved beneath his skin. A subtle tingling rushed through her body, from her blushing throat down into her abdomen, as she stared at him.

A deep breath swelled his chest; Christian saw that his small, flat nipples were pinched with cold. Drawing a quick, deep breath of her own, she raised her eyes to his face. He was watching her, a smile tilting one side of his mouth.

"My lady," he said, reaching toward her, "is that for me?"

"Oh!" she said, and shoved the blanket toward him. He wrapped the soft multicolored plaid around his shoulders and dried his face with a corner of it. He glanced at her again, a smile still teasing his lips. She blushed and lowered her eyes, then looked up at him.

"Is the well cleared now?" she asked.

"Aye, I think so," he answered, ruffling his hair as he dried it with a corner of the plaid. "The debris had blocked off the opening through which the water runs. We pulled out quite a bit of wood before the water began to run clear through there again, and the level began to rise."

"The water was dark when I looked at it the other day," she said. "Is it safe, then, and not fouled?"

" 'Twill be fine, I think. Ash and soot had collected in the well with the fallen beams, but that will settle in the bottom now that the well is filling again. The water seems much clearer even now." He settled the plaid around his shoulders and looked down at her. A lock of hair, dark with moisture, fell into his eyes and he shook it back.

Christian was watching the long, strong column of his throat, dusted with a brown beard. She wanted, quite suddenly, to feel the texture of his beard, to trace the angles of his jaw. She wanted to comb her fingers through his tousled hair. Her blush deepened and spread, as hot as if she stood by a fire.

Gavin bent down to grab up his discarded black tunic, pulling its thick folds over his head. As she watched the elegant play of muscle along his smooth back, something elemental seemed to shift within her, a startling, heated, pleasant sensation. Her breath came quickly, and she touched her teeth to her lower lip.

"I will have to change out of these wet hosen," he said, as he bent over to pull on his leather boots.

"Else you will have a lung ailment," she said, half laughing, glad of some release of the strange tension she was feeling. Gavin chuckled. "I meant to fetch some things for you from the storage chamber," Christian said. "There is some clothing stored there that belonged to Henry, tunics and breeches and a fine fur-lined cloak. He was a large man like you, though much wider. But his tunics should fit you, if you want them."

He nodded as he fastened his boots. "If you go into the storage chamber, I want you to sort through the bed frames and feather beds there. Find whatever is needed for the bedchambers."

"Bedchambers?" she asked.

"Aye. Choose enough bed furniture for four rooms. I will have some men carry it up for you." He stood and faced her. "I asked the masons and carpenters to ready those chambers as quickly as possible. The foreman told me, just this morn, that they are complete but for some small details. We can use the rooms as soon as they are furnished. Tonight, I think."

"Sleep there tonight?" she asked, and closed her mouth, for she realized that she stared at him as if she were a dimwit. By tonight she might be alone in a bedchamber—in a bed—with her husband. Her heartbeat picked up an even faster pace, and the curious warmth that had already blossomed inside her now began to swirl in earnest. Her mouth went dry.

"Aye, Christian," he said softly. His eyes were steady on hers. "Tonight."

Chapter Fourteen

"**A**ND HERE THE KING OF THE PICTS holds his court," Patrick announced, standing on top of a wooden chest and gripping the shaft of a long, iron-tipped lance. His voice echoed in the cavernous underground chamber. "And here are his warriors"—he waved toward his brother and Will, who stood together, narrow shoulders back, chests out.

"And I am the queen who teaches all the warriors to fight," Michaelmas said. She grabbed another long lance and stood up alongside Patrick.

"What!" Will cried out in dismay.

"Ancient warrior queens always taught the lads to fight," Michaelmas said. "Ask my mother. She's a harper, and knows all the old stories and songs."

Christian, kneeling in front of an opened chest that contained Henry's old garments, glanced up. " 'Tis said that was an old Celtic practice," she replied. The boys groaned.

"I already know how to fight," William said.

Robbie lay down on the ground and began to snore loudly.

"Wha' are you doing?" Patrick asked.

"I'm a knight," Robbie said, eyes squeezed shut, "and you're King Arthur wha' sleeps under the hill wi' all his men, and will rise again and fight a battle when the enchantment ends."

"Aye!" the others cried, and lay down with Robbie, until at a signal from Patrick they leaped up and began a mock fight.

"Hold, here!" shouted Moira from across the chamber. "Dinna destroy Lady Christian's fine storage place. And put down those lances, you'll kill one another for sure."

"If you can sit quietly," Christian told the children, "I will tell you a story while I fold these things. Do you want to hear of King Arthur, who sleeps with his knights under an enchanted hill?"

"We want to hear another Arthur tale—the one about Kinglassie!" Robbie said. Christian nodded at this, and the children came over, scrambling to sit near her.

"Long ago," she began, "hundreds of years past, when the priests had just come to Scotland and the *daoine sìth*, the wee people of peace, lived side by side with the Scottish people, there lived a great king called Arthur—"

"And Merlin, his wizard!" Robbie yelled.

"Aye, now hush, Robert Macnab," she said, folding a pair of brown woolen hosen. "And Merlin, his wise adviser. King Arthur had many brave knights, who had pledged to serve him to their deaths. There came a time when Arthur called for his knights to ride north with him into the land of the Scots to do battle with the Pictish warriors. They stayed one night with the laird of Kinglassie, a friend to Arthur, in the ancient fortress that was first built upon this very rock."

"And did they sleep here, in this hidden room?" Robbie asked. The children looked around the torchlit, shadowed chamber in wonder, their mouths open and eyes wide.

"They slept in the best rooms up in the stronghold. But first, the laird of Kinglassie gave them a wonderful feast, with the finest beef to eat, and heather ale to drink, and with harp music played by the fair folk who lived in peace with the people of Kinglassie." Christian lifted out a blue tunic embroidered in gold, thought fleetingly that it would look wonderful on Gavin, then folded it and laid it aside before looking up at the waiting children. Robbie, squirming where he sat, quieted when she cast an even look at him.

"The next day, in reward for such hospitality, Merlin gave a wondrous treasure to the laird, a gift that he had created with his own magic. Merlin told the laird that this treasure had great significance for all of Scotland. But one *ban-sitheach*, a wee lady of the fair folk, had fallen in love with Arthur. She was very angry that he was leaving Kinglassie, and so she used her own magic to make another spell."

"What did she do?" Will asked.

"She hid Merlin's gift away, deep in the heart of the castle, and said it couldna be found until Scotland found its bravest king."

"She wanted King Arthur to return and get her to tell him where it was, but he was too busy fightin' the Picts," Patrick added knowingly.

"What did the laird do?" Will demanded; he had not heard the story before. "Did he take his broadsword and cut off the wee lady's head?"

Michaelmas glanced at him in disgust. "The *daoine sith* canna be treated in such a way, else bad luck will follow."

"The laird looked and looked, but couldna find the treasure," Christian continued patiently, closing the lid of the chest. "And King Arthur had troubles of his own and had no time to return to Kinglassie. So Merlin sent white doves to lead the way to the treasure. But because the bravest king of Scots had not yet come, the doves couldna find the way either. And to this day, the wild doves fly near Kinglassie, looking for its heart."

"They're roosting in the very towers now," Robbie added. "Still looking."

"Only one piece of the gold has ever been seen, and that is the pendant that Merlin himself gave to the daughter of that first laird." Christian pulled at the thong that lay inside the neck of her gown, and the golden pendant spilled into her hand, glittering in the torchlight. " 'Tis all that is left of Merlin's treasure," she said softly. The children leaned forward to look.

"One of the Scottish kings appointed a keeper to hold the pendant and guard the legend," she continued. "She was the daughter of another laird of Kinglassie, and since then, the castle has always passed along the female line whenever it could. But Merlin's full gift to the laird and to Scotland hasna been discovered."

"Why havena the Scottish kings found it?" Patrick asked.

Christian shrugged. "Mayhap 'tis truly gone," she said.

"But if we tried every day, and looked very hard, we could find it!" Will said.

" 'Tis in the well," Robbie said, nodding sagely. "All covered with slime."

Christian stood, holding the clothing that she had collected, thinking about the fiery destruction of Kinglassie so many months ago. "I dinna think the treasure will ever be found," she said.

"But if we look very, very hard," a low, mellow voice said nearby, startling her, "we can surely find it."

She spun around to see Gavin standing behind her. Clad in his black tunic and a black surcoat, he blended with the shadows in the underground chamber. As he stepped forward, his now dry hair caught a golden sheen in the torchlight.

"So that is the legend of Kinglassie," he said. "I have heard many tales of Arthur and his knights, but never that one, and so nicely told. Your voice is enchanting. You tell a tale as if 'twere a song. You are a bard as well as a harper."

Blushing so fiercely that she felt hot throughout, Christian shoved the pile of garments toward him. "These are for you. Henry's things."

"My thanks," he said, taking them from her. With the tip of a finger, he touched the rim of the pendant that lay on her breastbone, just above her breasts. "Is this Kinglassie's treasure?" he asked softly.

"All that is left," she said. Shivers danced through her at his light touch. Through the wool of the tunic, she felt the pressure of his fingers. Her breasts tingled and tightened; she blushed deeply, grateful for the dimness.

"The heart of Kinglassie," he murmured. " 'Tis a beautiful thing, this pendant, and very ancient. No wonder the English want the gold. Henry searched for it as well, I suppose. Did he look in this storage chamber?"

"Very thoroughly," she said.

He slanted a look at her, his brows pulled together in thought. "Have you told me all that you know?"

She glanced away. " 'Tisna down here. It canna be found."

"I believe that if we want to find Kinglassie's treasure, we will." He angled his body toward her as he spoke, close enough that she caught her breath.

She snapped her eyes away from his. "And why should we try? To give it to your king?"

"Gavin Faulkener!" Robbie called.

"Aye, lad?" Gavin asked, his eyes still on Christian.

Robbie bounced up from his seat on the floor. "Help us find the treasure and we'll share it with you and with King Robert!"

"Though you're but a Sasunnach," Patrick added.

"A tempting offer," Gavin said solemnly. "Allow me time to consider it. For now, your mother and Dominy have been gathering and carrying things into the tower for a while now. Mayhap you can offer them some help."

"Aye, Gavin Faulkener!" Patrick said.

"Aye, my lord," Will said, and turned to join his friends as they ran, with noisy echoes, across the large chamber.

Gavin turned back to look at Christian. "Tell me something," he said. "I have noticed that the Macnabs—and most of the workmen here—do not call me 'sir,' or 'my lord,' although I am the baron here at Kinglassie. And I have noticed that you yourself do not call me 'my lord.'"

"Should I? Does your English pride demand it?"

"Well—my curiosity demands to know," he said.

"Gavin Faulkener," she said, tilting her head, "in many parts of Gaelic Scotland we dinna recognize lords or barons as our superiors. In the Lowlands 'tis different, for some areas are very English, in their ways. But here in Galloway and Carrick, as in the Highlands, we keep many of the old Celtic ways. Men and women are thought equal to their chiefs. If you were a Scottish chief, you might use an old traditional name, or use the clan name for your title, as my uncle in the Isles is called the MacGillean. The wives of lairds and chiefs are called lady out of courtesy, but lairds are called by their own names, or by the names of their homes."

"I see. And what was Henry called here?"

She frowned. "He insisted that we call him lord, and he was often angry because many of the servants and our neighbors throughout Kinglassie didna want to do that. Such titles dinna roll easily off a Gaelic tongue."

"Nor do they come easily to stubborn Scottish pride. What did you call Henry?"

"Most of the time I didna speak to him," she said crisply. "We will call you Gavin Faulkener, or we may call you simply Kinglassie, since you have that right now. But we willna address you as lord. In Celtic Scotland, only the king and his earls have that right. Does that anger you?"

He shook his head. "Gavin, or just Kinglassie, will do."

Christian was surprised at his ready compliance. She had not thought that an English knight could accept Scottish ways so easily. "Beware, Kinglassie," she said softly. "If you take a Scot's title for your own, then you may lose a wee part of your Englishness."

"Will I?" He had turned so that his torso blocked the rest of the room from her view. She saw only his chest, his wide shoulders clothed in black wool, his face above hers as he looked at her intently. "Will I indeed?"

She nodded, watching him warily, her head tilted back. Gavin smiled and hooked a finger beneath her chin. Delicate shivers traced through her at the gentle, lingering touch.

"And does Kinglassie have a right to the treasure hidden at the heart of this place?" he asked, hushed and deep. "Will you show me what you have not shown any other man?"

She drew a quick breath against the sudden pulsing sensations that rushed through her. "The treasure is gone."

"I may find it, lady, and sooner than you think," he murmured. He reached down and took her hand, his fingers warm and strong over hers. "Come with me. I have something to show you." She hesitated, and he tugged at her hand. "Come. I think you will be pleased."

"Oh?" she answered. Something in her needed to resist the compelling force of his voice and his eyes. His warm grip on her fingers seemed to reach through her hands and arms into her soul.

Searching for words, she fished up familiar bitterness. "Have the Scots surrounded the castle to take it? Does the banner of the

Bruce fly on the battlement? That would please me."

Gavin sighed and pulled on her hand. "Kinglassie's treasure has a sour tongue," he said. "Come ahead, and keep quiet."

"HERE," HE SAID, as they reached the uppermost level of the tower. He strode to the door of the largest bedchamber. "You once showed me this room, now let me show you." He pushed open the arched door, its solid oak newly scrubbed, and stood back to allow Christian to enter first. "Your solar, my lady."

She stepped in and turned slowly around. Her startled gaze flew over every detail: the floor, newly faced with oak boards, oiled and rubbed to a shine; the refurbished windows, fitted with sets of shutters above and below; the clean, bare walls, plastered over and washed white with quicklime. Two carved storage chests had been placed against the walls, and a large wooden bed frame, fitted with a fat feather mattress and bed linens, dominated the center of the room.

Pungent and fresh, the blended smells of new wood and chalky plaster replaced the last charred traces of the fire. Gavin inhaled the clean mix of odors and walked into the room, watching Christian.

She spun in a slow circle, her eyes wide. Facing the hearth, she caught her breath. A fireplace had been built into the thick stone of the outer wall and fitted with a long, sloping hood. A small, hot peat blaze crackled there already, and Gavin silently blessed Dominy and Moira for their efforts in the upper bedchambers. Besides starting the hearth fire and directing the placement of the great oaken bed, they had piled an abundance of woolen blankets, pillows, and fur coverlets on the thick feather mattresses placed there.

Christian walked slowly to the bed and placed a hand on a thick carved post that jutted up from the footboard. She stood there silently, two pink spots in her cheeks burning as bright as the peat blaze.

"We will need to hang curtains around the bed to keep out the chill," Gavin said.

She looked at him then, her eyes as dark a green as he had ever seen them. "There is a set of curtains for the bed, packed in storage. I will find them," she said quietly.

He nodded and leaned his shoulder against the opposite bedpost. "The nights are quite cold. We will need them soon." She hesitated, then nodded and stepped away.

"My *clàrsach!*" she said putting out a hand to stroke the polished wood of her harp, which rested upright on a low stool, beside a larger stool placed on the hearthstone.

"I thought you might want it in here," he said.

"Thank you. Oh! The fireplace—how did you—"

"I had the masons construct a chimney on the outer wall. You can see it from the window. The fire hood is only wood plastered over, but I intend to order a new hood of carved stone as soon as I can."

She nodded almost absently and touched the hood, smoothing her hand along its whitened outer edge. Then she turned again to glance up at the walls and the high ceiling, raftered with oak beams and completely repaired.

He followed her gaze. "The walls of my castle at Fontevras are painted with images, bright colors and beautiful designs. The ceiling bosses are carved and painted as well. I will hire artists from York or even London to do the same in this chamber, and in the great hall as well."

She shook her head, her veil swinging softly. "Lengths of plaids can be hung on the walls, here and below. There are local women in Kinglassie who do beautiful weaving, and their plaids would be bright and lovely on the walls. And more practical than paintings for keeping out the cold drafts."

"As you will, my lady," he murmured. She glanced at him, another flash of dark green like an impenetrable forest, and turned again. She seemed subdued, yet restless and unsettled. He could not tell if her darkened eyes and the bright spots on her cheeks revealed happiness or displeasure.

"The shutters are new as well," she said, walking to the windows and drawing the lower shutters apart.

Gavin moved to stand beside her. "Aye, new cut pine, not yet oiled or painted." He reached up over her head to push open the upper pair. Pale afternoon light, filtered through fog, filled the room.

Beyond the window, the loch and the forested hills faded into the distance in muted lavender and gray. Christian stood silent and still at the window, watching the drifting mist. A chill, damp breeze lifted her veil, stirring the dark curls that showed at her temples.

"We can commission a glazier to make colored windows if you like," he said. "There was glass here before, you said?"

She seemed to stir out of some private, somber thought, and looked up at the slender empty lights. "There was," she said.

"A figure of Saint Michael, painted on glass, might look well in that upper space," he said, watching her carefully. "A fitting design, my lady?"

Her blush deepened to a dusky rose. She glanced up at him, uncertainty evident in the fold between her dark brows. "Dinna tease me."

"Not at all. Saint Michael seems a particular favorite of yours. Your daughter is named for him." And he had not forgotten that she had mistaken him for the archangel once; he valued the memory. "I thought you might like such a guardian in your bedchamber."

"I would." She gazed out the window with a subtle inner focus in her eyes, as obscure as the mist. He wondered what thoughts ran through her mind.

Certainly he had anticipated a more joyous response. He had hoped that Christian would be delighted with her newly refurbished bedchamber. He had even been prepared for a blast of her hot temper if she did not like one of the new features. But faced with this quiet, sad mood, he did not know what to do, what to say. Disappointed, wanting to please her, he felt as if he had failed somehow.

But there was one improvement he had not yet shown her. That, he hoped, would spark the delight he had been waiting to see. "Come here," he said, draping his fingers over her shoulder and guiding her away from the window toward the corner of the room, near the narrow door that led to the tiny privy chamber.

The shadowed angle of the room had been transformed by the addition of a curving wall, like an interior chimney, which enclosed the corner and formed a shaft. An opening was cut into it. Fat ropes, attached to a ceiling rafter, dangled down inside the shaft and through a hole cut in the floor.

She stuck her head inside the opening. "What is this? A well shaft, here?"

"Aye." He smiled, pleased with his surprise. "We can draw water from the well, two floors below, and up into our bedchamber." The plural came so easily to his lips—*we can, ours;* that pleased him, too, for he craved that sense of belonging, of having family, a wife, a home.

"Water all the way up here?" She looked at him in amazement, and smiled, quick as light dispels shadow.

"Aye. The masons have constructed a similar draw-well in the floor of the great hall just below. 'Tis fine to have a well in the ground floor of the tower, but 'tis even more convenient to have water brought directly to the upper rooms." He tugged on the ropes, which swung lightly, unburdened as yet, with no bucket affixed to them. "You can have fresh water warmed in the fireplace for a bath. And the carpenters made a fairly large tub. 'Tis stored in the privy corridor."

"Oh!" She straightened. "A hot bath whenever I like?"

"Aye, for both of us," he said. She flicked her gaze toward him, that curiously dark forest glance, and looked away.

"Well," he said, "what do you think?"

"About the well shaft? I like it very much."

"About the bedchamber, Christian," he said patiently.

"Oh." She turned and went to the window again, resting a hand on the stone sill. The breeze blew her white veil back from her face and shoulders, fluttering it softly. He followed her, and stood behind her, putting a hand on her shoulder. Her hair, thick and soft, spilled over his fingers; the small bones of her shoulder and arm shifted beneath his touch.

"All this is wonderful, Gavin," she said quietly.

She had rarely said his name with such gentleness. A sense

deep inside him stirred almost painfully, a wrenching demand for more from her. He wanted to spin her around into his arms and see joy on her face, he wanted to kiss her and feel her return the embrace. But she was so still, as quiet as the fog outside, her thoughts as impenetrable.

He looked down at her, and frowned when he saw the glimmer of tears in her eyes. Her sadness made him somber. He touched her shoulder. "Christian, what is it?"

"Just—" She shook her head. Raising her hand to grasp the edge of one shutter, she began to close it. With a soft cry, she pulled her hand away, wincing. She scraped at her thumb with the oval tip of her fingernail.

"You've a splinter. Let me see it," he said, taking her hand in his. A long sliver of wood was deeply embedded in the mound below her thumb. When Gavin touched it, she sucked in her breath.

Unable to coax it loose with his fingernail, he reached down and pulled his dagger from its sheath. Holding her hand still, he laid the slender edge of the blade on her skin. "A moment, now. Hold," he murmured.

A deft flick of the sharp tip, and the end of the sliver was caught. He pulled it out quickly and held it up. "Huge, my lady. Nearly a log," he teased, shoving the dagger back into its sheath.

A fat drop of blood welled on her skin. She wiped at it with a finger, and winced as she touched it. " 'Tis tender."

"Such a tiny wound can still be painful," he said, and took her hand again. Surrounding her thumb with his palm, he wanted to blot out the pain for her. He closed his eyes and felt a subtle heat where his hand covered hers. As he grew a deep breath, he heard her do the same. A peaceful, tranquil moment spun out from the shared breathing.

He felt as if a sunbeam, or a candle flame, spilled down his arms into his hands. Suddenly he imagined her pain dissolving in the light like a shadow.

Then the heat increased and spread like honeyed fire through his body to pool in his heart, sinking rapidly and luxuriantly to fill his loins. He inhaled deeply and tugged on her hand, insistently pulling her nearer. His whole body ached now, hot and hardening, with the urge to pull her into his arms.

He brought her hand to his lips to kiss the tender place at the base of her thumb, lingering at the task. Christian looked up at him, clear teardrops trembling in her eyes.

"Does it hurt so much?" he asked quietly.

She shook her head. "The pain is gone, suddenly. And look, the bleeding has stopped." She looked up at him. "You have a healing touch, I think." He heard a soft tease in her voice.

He smiled and shrugged. "My mother did. Mayhap I do, too," he said lightly.

"I didna mean to moan about such a wee injury." She half laughed, watery and soft.

"You could take a battle blow and say no word of complaint." He wiped a tear away with his fingertip. "These tears come from some other hurt, Christian."

She wrenched her hand away and spun to face the window, drawing a shuddering breath. "Gavin—this chamber—what you have done here—'tis beautiful. I know you have worked as hard as any laborer to make this castle right again. And I know you have paid the workmen good silver from your own funds." He waited silently, watching her. "Truly, I am grateful to see Kinglassie repaired. But I—" she stopped.

He took her by the shoulders and spun her then, as he had been wanting to do. "But what?" he asked, more roughly than he intended. "But you do not want to see this castle turned over to the English?"

She stared up at him, wet cheeks gleaming, and shook her head.

"Mayhap you do not want an English knight in your bed."

She sucked in her breath, and looked away. "All I see when I look around is that I destroyed this place. Because of what I did, all these repairs, all this expense and effort, were necessary." One tear glided down her cheek.

He blew out a breath, expelling anger and tension with the air. "You have too strong a spirit to give in to guilt and self-flagellation, lady. Let those memories go, Christian." His hands softened on her shoulders. "You did what you believed was right when you burned the castle. And I have done what I believe is right, and had it repaired."

"You repair it because your king orders you to do so."

"I would not spend my own coin for a project Edward wanted done. Hardly that."

"Why, then?"

"This is my home," he said quietly. She glanced up at him. "Look around the room again. Go on," he murmured. "See what is here now, rather than what is gone. This room should bring you joy, not sadness."

She glanced at the fresh walls, the bright hearth, the great bed. Then she looked back at Gavin. Shifting his hands, he pulled her gently toward him and wrapped his arms around her. She tipped her head against his chest, sniffling.

"This room hasna brought me joy since the English came here," she said, her voice muffled in the front of his tunic.

"Stubborn girl," he whispered into the side of her soft veil. "Will you not let in a little happiness and forget who is English here?" After a moment, she nodded. Gavin tipped her face up, spreading his fingertips across her damp cheek. He bent his head and pressed his lips to hers.

Her mouth gave beneath his, plaint and soft, dampened and slightly salty. Heart thudding now, he traced his fingertips down the side of her face. The fluid kiss deepened as he demanded more from her. She leaned her head back as he pulled her closer, and he felt her lips respond fully beneath his.

She sighed a little into his mouth and initiated another kiss, warm and salted and so eager that she nearly took his breath. She lifted her arm to curl around his neck. Gavin touched his tongue to her lips, groaning softly when she opened her mouth to him willingly. Pulling her closer, he pressed against the slender length of her, and tasted the inner realm of her mouth, the light sweetness of it, the faint salt of it. The depth of the kiss she returned to him took his breath away.

Fitting her slim hips to his swelling, hardening core, he swayed with her when she moved, a graceful and meaningful motion.

She had lost her breath as well, and drew back suddenly to gasp softly, leaning her head into his chest. "Gavin—"

"We are husband and wife. Will you say me nay? This has its own power now, between us. Do you not feel it?" He waited, and she nodded. "You want this to happen. As do I."

"I do," she whispered. "And it scares me."

"That fear is easily vanquished," he murmured. Heat and desire still flowed through every part of his body, and he traced his hands languorously over her spine, down the smallest part of her back to her hips, sliding up again along her ribs until he felt her draw in her breath, until she undulated against him. His thumbs, to either side of her, slipped over her breasts, and she gasped softly. His heart pounded as his fingers explored the rounded, utter softness there, and discovered her nipples growing firm beneath her gown.

Christian tilted her head back. Gavin traced his lips along her brow and down her cheek. He felt her hips press against him, and his loins swelled and hardened further as her hands slipped up his back.

He drew in a breath, moved his head—and something outside the window caught his attention. His thundering heart slammed in his chest, and his hands turned to stone. He groaned. He wished he had not glanced up when he had. He wished he had looked out earlier than this.

"Christian," he said slowly.

"What is it?" she asked, glancing up.

He set her gently away from him, and looked out between the shutters. The chill wind caught his hair and blew it back.

Emerging from the thick mist that hovered near the loch, several riders glided over the bare brown moor. Shifting, silvery, as eerie as a host of phantoms, the group of men in chain mail approached the castle. The brilliant red surcoat of the leader was a slash of color through the fog. Beside him, another rider carried a staff that displayed a bright yellow and red banner. Flapping and unfurling, its design was too evident.

"Hastings could not wait for me to ride to Loch Doon," he said. "He has decided to give us a visit."

"Gavin," she breathed, standing beside him. "He carries the dragon banner—"

"I know," he answered grimly. "King Edward's orders. No mercy will be shown to man, woman, or child." He turned to cup her face in his hands, a swift caress of her cheek. "Christian, this must wait until later, much as I regret it." Then he turned and strode to the door.

CHAPTER FIFTEEN

"**Y**OU WILL NEED TO FIX THAT PORTCULLIS immediately," Hastings said, dismounting from his horse to face Gavin, who waited inside the open gate. Twenty men followed Hastings into the courtyard, riding beneath the crooked portcullis. Icy needles of rain fell through the fog, turning the earth beneath the horses' hooves to thick mud.

"I am well aware the gate is broken," Gavin replied. Hastings had dispensed with a greeting, and there was no reason for him to express false politeness. "A smith is working on it. Until the repair is completed, a new set of wooden gates has been installed."

"Of what use is a new gate that is wide open? And the drawbridge is down," Hastings snapped. His gaze skimmed over the workmen in the courtyard, past scaffolds, pulleys, and various canvas tents set up as workshops and barracks. He scrutinized the charred stone of the gatehouse. "You are expected to hold it against the Scots, Faulkener, not open it to them."

"Should I have barred the castle against you?" Gavin asked smoothly. "Of course the gate was open—we saw your approach."

"Look at the damage here. Any fool could take this place," Hastings muttered.

Gavin cocked an eyebrow. "Any fool, Oliver?"

Hastings glared openly at Gavin. "I do not mean my own escort. What allegiance are these men? Are they Scots all?"

"Aye. Most of them have openly declared their support for King Edward. They take guard duty in shifts, since we have no garrison. They are eager to protect their own handiwork." Glancing around, Gavin noticed the sudden quiet, as if the workmen had melted away into the misted corners and doorways around the courtyard. The busy tumult of an hour earlier had been replaced by a new, quiet tension.

"At least you have begun the repairs, although the king has promised to send funds for the expenses. When will the work be completed?"

"I hired the workmen but a month ago," Gavin said. He knew the policies of Edward Longshanks well enough to know that he would not receive any funds for the work without repeated requests; and Gavin did not intend to ask. "They are making the most essential repairs first. The castle will not be completely repaired until well into next year."

"King Edward is anxious to send a garrison here. You must prepare space for three hundred men within a fortnight."

Gavin tilted a brow. "Only if they care to sleep in the courtyard with the masons and carpenters. The soldiers' barracks were in those two towers on either side of the gatehouse. The towers were structurally damaged in the fire, and must be torn down and rebuilt. That will take a year at least, even if we hire twice as many men. For now, we have space enough for ten or fifteen people on one floor of the great tower. But as I said, there is some space left in the courtyard."

"Christ's tree, man, you know the king's orders! Kinglassie is still vulnerable. Tell your laborers to speed up the work."

"The damage was extensive. Proper repairs will take time."

"We have no time to wait. King Edward wants at least two thousand men in Galloway. And Kinglassie is more important than you know. The most recent rumors place Bruce near here. The Earl of Pembroke is viceroy in Scotland now, and he has ordered the manhunt to center in this area." Hastings glanced over his shoulder as two men dismounted and approached. One wore full mail armor, but his solid build was dwarfed beside the tall, enormously heavy man in long robes who walked alongside him.

Hastings turned, gesturing toward the larger man. "Faulkener, this is Philip Ormesby, named chief justiciar of Galloway by King Edward. He is in charge of collecting taxes and rents from the Scottish people."

Ormesby held out a huge, meaty hand. "Should you need funds to complete repairs to Kinglassie, Sir Gavin, send me word at Carlisle. We can surely find just the right tax amount to see the task done." He smiled, grayed teeth glinting behind full lips, and inclined his head. Gavin saw the tonsure beneath the man's heavy woolen hood.

"You are a priest, sir," he commented. He had not missed the elaborate gilt braid on the cloak, or the expensive cut of his robes; this priest had taken no vow of poverty.

"Aye," Ormesby said. "I said vows at Oxford and taught law there for ten years before the king saw fit to use my abilities properly." He smiled, and Gavin recognized the sly quality that he had sometimes seen in high-ranking clergymen, both in Paris and in the English court. Greed and lust seemed to propel such men into powerful positions.

"And Dungal Macdouell," Hastings said, nodding toward the second man. "He is a local chieftain who has declared for the English cause. He headed the ambush at Loch Ryan that defeated Thomas and Alexander Bruce and three hundred rebels."

"Macdouell," Gavin said, inclining his head.

"We need to talk," Hastings said. "Show us to your hall."

"'Tis full of carpenters and scaffolding at the moment," Gavin said. "If you need a private space, the solar is finished. Come this way."

Hastings turned to his serjeant. "Wait with the escort until we are done," he said. "See that the men are fed. There are kettles over those open fires. Take what is in there." He gestured across the courtyard, where Dominy and Moira stood beside two huge kettles of bubbling stew.

"That food was prepared for the laborers," Gavin said. "But if you ask politely, the ladies may find enough to share with your men." He looked toward Dominy, who nodded. Beside her,

Moira scowled and turned away.

As they walked through the courtyard and into the tower, Gavin pointed out the repairs in progress. As the group pounded up the stone steps toward the upper level, Gavin found himself hoping that Christian had left the bedchamber. He intended to tell Hastings that she was still alive, but he wanted to spare Christian the man's initial and inevitable displeasure.

But even before they reached the laird's bedchamber, Gavin could hear the delicate notes of the harp. Christian was still there. Muttering a silent, swift prayer, dreading the next few moments, he pushed open the door.

STARTLED, CHRISTIAN HAD DROPPED HER HANDS from the harp and risen to her feet when the door opened. She glanced nervously at Fergus, who had come looking for her when the English knights had first arrived in the courtyard. He maintained a somber expression, folding his hands calmly as he stood near her.

Gavin entered, followed by three men whose shadows seemed to darken and swallow the space of the room. She stood by the fireplace, as yet unnoticed in the dim, shuttered room. But Gavin glanced toward her immediately, as if he knew she would be there.

Hastings stepped in just behind him. Christian's heart pounded when she saw him, and fear rose like bitter wine in her throat. She stayed still, though her legs nearly faltered beneath her. Gavin watched her steadily while the other men came into the chamber.

Hastings closed the door and turned. "Christ's blood, 'tis dark as a pit in here," he muttered. He had not seen her, and Christian clenched her fists against the black memories that flooded over her. His grating voice brought back dark flashes of the cage and of his treatment of her there. She closed her eyes and placed a hand on the harp pillar to steady herself.

"Peat fires do not provide good light, and we have documents to read," Hastings said. He shoved back his mail hood, the harsh jangle emphasizing his irritation. "Fetch some candles,

Faulkener."

"I'll fetch a torch for you," Fergus said, stepping forward.

Hastings spun in surprise. "Who the devil are you?"

"Fergus Macnab, rector of Saint Bride's church," Fergus replied. "God's greetings. I'll be back wi' lights, then," he said brusquely, and left the room.

Christian frowned, standing in the shadows, and wondered what scheme Fergus had in mind. She had never known him to behave subserviently to any Englishman.

"That man is a Celtic priest," one of the men said. "What is he doing here in Kinglassie?" Christian looked at the large man who had spoken, and saw that he had the tonsure and embroidered robes of a wealthy English priest.

"Fergus Macnab has been priest at Saint Bride's for years, and his father and grandfather before him," Gavin said. "I will not say him nay on his right to be here, Ormesby."

"Father and grandfather? I suppose he is married with brats of his own. Do you allow that man to administer your own communion? Intolerable," Ormesby said. "As baron here, you have the right to appoint another priest to the parish. I will send you a list of candidates. This Macnab is of the Scottish Church, and aside from his pagan habits, he is likely a supporter of Robert Bruce. He should be ousted from his position."

"We do not need Scots preaching to the people when we can replace them with English priests," Hastings said. "The Scottish clergy are as rebellious as their king. They teach the people that 'tis no sin to kill infidels or Englishmen. Both causes, the Scots priests say, are holy."

"Rebellious priests indeed," Ormesby said. "We sent timber to the bishop of Glasgow last summer to repair a bell tower. But he built a siege engine with it, and took back an English-held castle for the Scots." He snorted with disgust and lowered his bulk on to the top of a clothing chest, grunting heavily.

"And Bishop Wishart is now in an English dungeon, where he'll build nae more weapons against King Edward. We canna hang a bishop, but we dinna have to let him free," the third man said.

The speaker's Scottish birth was obvious to Christian. She frowned. The longer she waited, the more angry she would become at what she overheard. And sooner or later, her presence would be seen.

She stepped out of the shadows. "Bishop Wishart is an old, frail man, and deserves greater kindness than that," she said.

"Christ's tree!" Hastings said. "What are you doing here!"

Although Gavin said nothing, his sharp glance pierced hers. Head high and back straight, she could face Gavin fearlessly. But she was afraid to look at Hastings. Gavin's steady stare, though grim, offered a sense of safety. She walked over to stand by his side.

"And who is this pretty wench?" Ormesby said pleasantly. "Was it you playing the harp when we came up the steps, girl? After you fetch us wine you may play for us."

"She is no servant girl," Gavin said. "Philip Ormesby, I present my wife, Lady Christian MacGillean of Kinglassie. My lady, this is Dungal Macdouell. You know Oliver Hastings."

"I do," she said, bowing her head, though she trembled all over like a green alder branch. Gavin placed steadying fingers around her elbow.

"Faulkener!" Hastings barked out. "This girl—"

"I am supposed to be dead," she said. "But, instead, I recovered from my illness."

"Holy Jesu, 'tis the girl in the cage at Carlisle," Ormesby said. His full lips hung open as he stared at her. Macdouell, too, ogled her.

Hastings turned to glower at Gavin. "A month ago you told the king that this girl was deathly ill and would not last the week. You took her out of that cage—and took her into your custody— knowing 'twould be treason to disobey the king." Both Ormesby and Macdouell nodded and directed disapproving frowns toward Gavin and Christian.

"I trust she is here as your prisoner," Ormesby said.

"She is here as my wife," Gavin said. "King Edward himself suggested and approved the marriage. And Oliver witnessed the king's direct order to release her."

"Edward released her into your custody so that you could escort her to a convent to die," Hastings growled between his teeth. "You took her and decided what you wanted done with her."

"God decided she would live," Gavin said calmly. "Not even your priest there would dispute that authority."

Ormesby cleared his throat. "However, God allows righteous men to pronounce punishment on criminals. She was imprisoned. She should be in custody at a convent, if not back in Carlisle."

"She was never formally accused of any crime," Gavin said. "She was neither tried nor sentenced."

"Only captured and held in a savage manner," Christian said. "Just as you hold the other Scottish women captured at the same time as I was —including our queen."

"And we have let none of them go but you," Hastings said. "That was clearly a mistake. You should be returned to our custody." Christian felt Gavin's grip on her arm tighten. "They still live?" she asked.

"Aye, and in our custody still," Hastings said curtly. "Two in cage-houses, faring well, healthy and whole. Bruce's wife is held in the manor house of Burstwick, and her daughter is in a convent near London. And Lady Christian Seton, another sister of Bruce, is only detained in a convent since Edward recently executed her rebel husband. See, the king has compassion, though you Scots insist that he is an ogre. But none of these ladies will be ransomed or released until Bruce is found."

"He will not be found," she said firmly.

Hastings smiled. "Then the Scotswomen will be our prisoners forever. And you will soon join them once again."

"She is free now," Gavin said, "and will stay that way."

Hastings looked at Gavin, his eyes two black slits in his neatly bearded face. "She remains an outlaw and a rebel, and a supporter of Robert Bruce. And bringing her here to Kinglassie shows treasonous intent on your part."

"My husband only took me home," Christian said. "What crime is that? But your king expected me to die of my illness, and so it becomes treason for me to live. What folly."

"Hold your tongue!" Hastings exploded. He came toward her, glowering so intensely that Christian shrank back. "You and Faulkener have planned this together. Have you given him the gold you would not give me?"

"You mean the gold I would not give to your king?" she asked. Anger, and Gavin's hand on her arm, gave her greater strength. She glared back at Hastings.

"Leave her be, Oliver," Gavin warned. "She nearly died because of Edward's treatment of her. Now that she is the wife of an English commander, she has a right to English protection."

"We offer her none. Edward promised her a pardon only if she told you where that gold was hidden."

"Gavin knows the truth of the gold," Christian said.

"What has she told you?" Hastings asked quickly.

"Only what she knows. The gold was destroyed in the fire."

"I do not believe that."

"I have been through every part of this castle in the last month," Gavin said. "The masons have turned nearly every stone over in their repairs. You have seen the extent of the damage for yourself. Naught could have survived that fire. Naught."

Gavin's hand slid down to grasp hers as he spoke. She knew then that he would not tell Hastings about the underground room full of provisions and weapons. Straightening her shoulders, she glanced up at her husband. The lean grace of his profile was suddenly very dear to her.

Hastings looked from Gavin to Christian, narrowing his eyes. "There is some treachery here. And I will find it out."

"Do you not trust me, Oliver?" Gavin asked softly.

"Trust a man who would defend a Scot at the slightest provocation? Never. Remember that I saw you at Berwick."

"The slaughter of thousands is hardly a slight reason to defend the Scottish people," Gavin said, his voice cold and hard. "But you cannot understand that, since your sword was the bloodiest of the lot in Berwick."

"I warned King Edward against placing you here in a strategic position," Hastings said. "But you will show your true colors here, and he will see the traitor that you are. The Angel Knight will fall from sovereign grace at last, I think."

"Only the king's demon would care about that," Gavin said.

Hastings' thin lips grew white. "Where is that gold? Edward lays claim to any object that supports the kingship of Scotland."

"Whatever ancient hoard was hidden here is surely gone," Gavin replied evenly. "Melted away into the very walls. Bring that word back to Edward."

"I will," Hastings said. "And I will bring him news of you and your bride. Be certain of his interest in that matter."

The door opened then, and Fergus came into the room holding a flaming torch. The warm light brightened the room as he stood near Gavin and Christian.

"Sorry," Fergus said to Gavin. "Candles are scarce in Scotland. We usually import them from England or Flanders. When you send to the market town next, Gavin Faulkener, remember to order candles."

"Savage place," Hastings snapped. "Decent candles cannot be had, bread is unheard of outside the monasteries and the towns, log fires and tanned leather are rare as gold. Even the priests hardly know Latin."

Fergus filled his chest proudly. "I read and write Latin, English, French, and Gaelic," he said. "If you'll allow me to read those letters for you—" Fergus stopped when Hastings sneered openly at him. "*Ach,* well, I'll just hold the torch while you go on wi' your business, then."

"You will not hold it," Ormesby said. "Give the thing to Macdouell there, and be gone."

Macdouell took the torch. "You'll not listen to this conversation and carry tales back to Bruce spies. Be gone."

Fergus managed to look hurt. Christian knew he must be keenly disappointed, since his opportunity to listen to English plans had been so quickly thwarted. He bowed his head to the others and left the room.

"You have a letter from the king?" Gavin asked.

Hastings extracted a folded parchment from the pouch that hung from his belt. "King Edward has sent letters to all his commanders in Scotland," he said. "This one has your name on it." He slapped it into Gavin's open hand.

Breaking the seal, Gavin scanned the contents quickly. "This is no more than a whining complaint," he said. "Edward expresses his astonishment that none of us have captured the Bruce, and points out that I have been here a month at least. He threatens to replace me if the Bruce is not caught soon."

Macdouell, holding the torch, nodded. "We all received such letters. We're ordered to report our plans immediately. And he says our silence makes him suspect that we're all cowards. King Edward is impatient, lying in his sickbed at Lanercost, w' nae chance of riding at the head of his army in Scotland."

"So he shoots out threatening letters instead of fire arrows," Gavin said, tossing the letter onto the bed. "He winds down to his death."

"He will recover," Hastings said. "And he will see the Scots brought down. He is determined to conquer Scotland, just as he took Wales."

"Edward will never take Scotland," Christian said.

"Get out of here!" Hastings shouted at her. He turned to Gavin. "Place that treacherous woman under confinement. She is a spy nurtured in an English nest. You let your stones speak louder than your reason when you took that rebel into your bed."

A long step forward, and Gavin grabbed Hastings by a handful of mailed hauberk. "I have heard enough of your abusive tongue," he growled. "You have delivered your letter. If you have aught else to say, say it politely in the presence of my wife." He let go so abruptly that Hastings stumbled into Macdouell, who nearly dropped the torch.

Gavin turned to Christian. "Do you wish to leave, my lady?" Nodding quickly, she walked toward the door and took her cloak from a peg on the wall. Gavin opened the door for her.

"Send up some wine," Ormesby called after her.

"She might poison it," Hastings said, straightening his rumpled surcoat.

"Poison? What an interesting suggestion," Christian said as she slammed the door behind her.

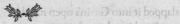

AFTER SHE HAD SENT DOMINY to the solar with a flask of French wine and clay cups, Christian went in search of Fergus. A stonemason had told her that the priest was in the great hall.

An unusual silence met her ears as she approached the hall. The hammering and chatter had stopped, though it was only midday. The vast chamber was empty but for one man.

"Fergus!" she called, crossing the room toward him. "What are you doing here? Where have the carpenters gone?"

Fergus looked up and placed a finger to his lips, beckoning to her. "Come here," he whispered in Gaelic.

"Where are the workmen?" she asked again, walking toward the corner, where Fergus stood beside the new well shaft, a twin to the one in her bedchamber.

"I sent them away," Fergus said quietly. "I told them I had to bless the well, and needed privacy to do it."

"And is the well blessed, then?"

Fergus grinned and urged her closer to the draw-hole in the stone shaft. "Blessed, and full of voices from heaven."

She leaned forward, puzzled, and tilted her head to listen.

". . . Bruce and his men have been sighted in the hills above Kinglassie," she heard Hastings say. The voice was faint but clear. ". . . a ragged group of outlaws, evading our men."

"Oh!" she gasped, and pulled back. "We should not—"

Fergus elbowed her aside. "Does it bother you? Move, then, and I'll gladly spy for King Rob." He leaned into the draw-hole.

She watched him, straining to listen, but heard nothing. The voices only seemed to carry inside the shaft. "What are they saying?" she hissed after a moment. Fergus waved a hand to silence her.

She tried to press her ear toward the opening, but Fergus's bulk blocked the way. Impatiently she hopped from one foot to the other. Finally she tapped him on the shoulder.

Fergus withdrew his head. "They are saying they want to draw Rob out of the hills and onto fighting ground favorable to the English," he whispered. He stuck his head back in the hole.

After another moment, Christian could stand it no longer. "Shove over, then," she hissed, and worked her head and shoulders in the space alongside Fergus. Adjusting his position, he had to put his arm around her waist so that they could both listen.

"We'll hope my wife and your husband do not come into the hall just now," Fergus muttered.

Christian rolled her eyes expressively and then fixed her attention to the voices drifting so clearly through the shaft.

"BRUCE'S MEN HAE THE ADVANTAGE in these craggy hills," Macdouell said. "But a few weeks ago we had them in the open at Loch Ryan. Bruce himself wasna there, but his two brothers commanded a fleet of ships and three hundred men. We had them at our mercy, trapped in the water and on the shore. Most of them died. A fair number were Highlanders and Irish *gallóglach*, or mercenaries. I had the pleasure of beheading an Irish chief myself."

Gavin listened, swirling his wine in its simple clay cup. "It must have taken Bruce months to gather up those men and ships. He lost much that day."

"Aye, a devastating blow," Hastings said, and smiled, thin-lipped and smug. "But he learned that the English are far more capable of carrying on a war than he is."

"He lives like a fugitive, with only the clothes on his back and the sword in his belt," Ormesby said. "He has a few men, and what food and shelter he can steal or borrow. He needs money, horses, men, and has little means to get them. The people are his only hope for assistance and support, and many of them are afraid to help him."

"We will have him soon, for he cannot continue long like this," Hastings said smugly.

Gavin sent him a flat look and turned back to the others. "How many men does Bruce have with him?"

"Fifty or sixty at most," Macdouell said. "An earl, some knights, several Highlanders, whatever local farmers he has been able to collect. They will need shelter if they continue to stay in Galloway through the rest of February and March. On nights when the winds blow icy and damp, he must regret his choice to hide in these hills."

"There are many caves in the Galloway hills," Gavin said.

"Caves, aye. And wolves, wild boars, and wildcats. I doubt he even feels safe enough to close his eyes and sleep," Hastings said. "He and his men strike in small parties, mostly at night. We never know where or when he will ambush our patrols."

Macdouell poured out more wine for himself, and added more to Hastings's cup. "He moves his camp daily, and fights from high in the hills, shooting arrows, or rolling boulders down on English soldiers. They fight hand to hand when they meet our men. They hide in the trees and even in the water. But we have been unable to catch them."

Gavin raised his eyebrows slightly, amazed at what he was hearing. "Bruce has a natural talent for outlawry."

"He was raised in the hills of Galloway and Carrick," Macdouell said. "He uses the land like a Highlander."

Gavin nodded. "He is a true challenge to the English." He rubbed at his chin, hiding a smile as he leaned casually against the bedpost. Robert Bruce opposed Edward Plantagenet's might and wrath with daring, intelligence, and strength of conviction. Gavin found much to admire there. "With this man to lead them, the Scots have a real chance," he mused.

"That is madness," Hastings said. "He cannot hide from us forever. We have the advantage. We will soon flush him out."

"With heavy cavalry and foot, traveling along steep inclines and over boggy ground? Bruce has the advantage over you. Do not fool yourself," Gavin said.

Hastings slid him a quick, dark glance. "He hides because he is too cowardly to face armored knights in open combat."

"If you mean to win, you will need to consider his skill and his persistence. This man is ingenious."

"He has but sixty men. He is no match for us."

"Then why have you not captured him?" Gavin asked dryly.

Hastings snarled incoherently and quaffed the rest of his wine, smacking the cup down on top of a chest.

"I hae no love for Robert Bruce, but he leads us a clever

dance," Macdouell said. "He's a worthy enemy, at the least."

"Perhaps you should adopt his techniques," Gavin said.

"We have no time to waste climbing the hills in outlaw fashion," Hastings said. "We mean to draw Bruce out onto open ground. Provoke him to fight honorably, in full combat, with horses and armor."

"Interesting plans," Gavin said. "But I have no garrison to lend you for your battle."

"Not yet. You have something else here that I need."

Gavin narrowed his eyes. "What is that?"

"Among your workmen is a laborer who has sought me out at Loch Doon," Hastings said. "He is a kinsman of Robert Bruce. And he has offered to discover Bruce's plans in exchange for several oxgangs of land."

"The man came to you, not me," Gavin said. "Who is he?"

"You will know that before we leave here," Hastings replied. "Then I will expect you to find out what this man knows, and use it to find the Bruce. Send me the information when you have it. Find the acres near Kinglassie to give to him."

"I would not give a handful of earth to such a man," Gavin said in a low voice. "Give him his oxgangs near Loch Doon if you wish to pay him for his treachery."

"You dare to speak against treachery?" Hastings asked softly.

Gavin fisted his hands at his sides and stared at Hastings. "Until Kinglassie is garrisoned, you will find little help here," he said curtly.

"Be warned, Faulkener," Hastings said. "Bruce could take this place in a moment if he chose to do so. You do not even have a decent gate on this place. And Bruce and his little group took Turnberry Castle several weeks ago, killing a garrison of three hundred men. Henry Percy was the only one left. He shut himself up in a privacy chamber while Bruce packed up the silver and the food and quit the castle."

"I have no intention of shutting myself inside the walls. And no one will take this place."

"I only came to warn you," Hastings said.

"You only came to lay your hands on Kinglassie's gold," Gavin said.

❧

FERGUS PULLED HIS HEAD AND SHOULDERS back out of the well shaft and rubbed at his bald head. *"Ach,"* he said. "I knew most of that. Spying is a tedious thing."

"But we learned of the English spy," Christian said.

"And we learned that your husband is not so set against the Scots as Hastings would have him be," Fergus said. "I find that interesting. Now go out to the courtyard, and see which of the workmen is the traitor. Hastings will surely have a word with him before he leaves."

Christian, leaning her arm in the embrasure of the well, suddenly grew alert. "Fergus," she said, "what is that? Listen, now." They stuck their heads back into the hole together. Light voices, high and wild with giggles, drifted toward them.

"If you can hear from above, you can hear from below," she whispered. "Is that Robbie? And Patrick?"

"Ach," Fergus said. "What are they doing?"

Christian frowned. "There is an odd echo—oh Fergus—"

"Saint Michael preserve our souls," Fergus muttered. "The lads are inside the very well!" He hurried out of the room with Christian close behind him.

CHAPTER SIXTEEN

"COME OUT O' THERE, Robert and Patrick Macnab!" Fergus called into the well shaft in the bakery. "And William, too!"

"They must be mad," Christian said, looking in beside him.

"Or more daring than we'd ever thought," Fergus muttered. Three small faces peered up at them from the shadowed interior of the well. Robbie and Will clung to the iron rungs along the wall, and Patrick was in the water, holding on to the lowest bar.

"But the treasure is down here!" Robbie yelled.

"Have you found it?" Fergus called back, his voice a booming echo.

"Nae yet," Robbie said. "You dinna give us time!"

"Come up here," his father growled, "before I forget I'm a priest o' God."

The boys glanced at one another and began to climb up. Halfway along, Patrick, the largest of the three, took hold of one of the iron rungs. The stone shifted and a chunk came loose as he pulled on the bar. The boy and the stone both fell into the water with heavy splashing. Will and Robbie, screaming, scrambled toward the top.

Christian stretched out her arm frantically to grab Robbie as he came higher, and reached toward Will behind him. Fergus helped her, and bent over the edge of the well calling for Patrick. In a moment, the boy called back, treading water, apparently unhurt. Once they had hauled the younger boys out of the well, Fergus clambered over the side.

Removing her cloak, Christian knelt and wrapped its fur-lined warmth around the two shivering boys. "What in the name of God were you thinking, lads?"

"We wanted to find Kinglassie's gold," Robbie said. "I had a dream 'twas in the well, behind a stone, and it spilled out, so many coins, like a king's treasure room."

"We only thought to look," Will said.

Christian frowned. " 'Twas a dangerous thing you did."

Will lifted his chin. "We were not afraid."

"I know," she said gently. "But Rob is younger than you. He needs your guidance. And you might have been hurt."

Robbie's lip wobbled. "You think us beggary wretches."

Christian rumpled Robbie's brown hair. "Dinna let your father hear you say that. Those are English soldiers' words Will has taught you. And I dinna think you are wretches," she said, "only brave lads who should have asked an adult for help."

"Adults wouldna hae listened," Robbie said.

"I would, and I would have helped you myself," she said. "Sometimes dreams must be followed."

"What dream? What was all the shouting in here?" Gavin asked. Christian, still on her knees, looked up. Gavin stepped into the bakery chamber, a deep scowl on his face.

"Patrick fell in the well," she said.

"Jesu!" Gavin leaned down and helped Fergus lift the boy out. While Fergus climbed out of the well, Gavin took off his blue cloak and cocooned Patrick inside its folds. Then Fergus and Gavin questioned the boys in somber tones.

"If that treasure was in the well, lads," Fergus said, "we would have found it when we were down there. What you did was foolish."

"And dangerous," Gavin said.

"But we werena feared," Robbie said. Beside him, Patrick nodded, teeth chattering.

"Treasure?" Hastings strode into the room with Ormesby behind him. "You found the gold in that well there?"

"You canna have it, Sasunnach!" Robbie yelled. Christian gasped and laid a hand on his shoulder to silence him.

"Scottish wildness begins in infancy," Ormesby pronounced.

"You'll have a whipping for that, boy," Hastings barked, scowling down at Robbie.

"By the saints," Fergus said, "he's but a bairn—"

"I'll whip them all and be done with it, if they know aught about gold that rightfully belongs to King Edward," Hastings said. "Boys should be whipped often by their elders."

Stepping close to the taller man, Fergus threw his shoulders wide and thrust out his broad chest. "You'll touch none o' my lads," he growled, "unless you'd relish a dirk in your belly."

"You call yourself a priest, man?" Ormesby asked in a scoffing tone. "You're as savage as your parishioners."

"Did I say 'twould be my dirk? My lads have six grown brothers, none o' them priests. And who are you?"

"Philip Ormesby, treasurer of Scotland."

"Ah, treasurer," Fergus said smoothly. "We Scots call you the treacherer." He smiled. Ormesby gasped indignantly.

"Ormesby will collect enough taxes to shrivel your damned Scottish tongues," Hastings snapped.

"Hold!" Gavin cut in sharply. "The escort is ready."

"Good. Come ahead, Philip," Hastings said. "Faulkener, we want a word with you outside."

"In a moment." Gavin turned to Fergus as the others left the chamber. "God's very bones, man, would you start a skirmish between Scots and English in my own castle?" He leaned toward Fergus angrily. "Are you a rebel only, or a priest as well, with some sense in your head? Hold your temper when you are here!" Fergus frowned and was silent. "I noticed some loose stones when we were in the well the other day," Gavin said. "Did you examine the broken stone when you went down there after Patrick?"

"I did. The rung was rusted and the stone cracked and came apart. 'Tis a wonder the block didna crush Patrick."

"The mortar in the well shaft may have been weakened by the fire," Gavin said. "I'll talk to the mason about repairing it." Nodding to Christian and ruffling Patrick's head in passing,

Gavin left the chamber.

Fergus hurried to the doorway and stood in the shadow, beckoning to Christian. "Go out," he said in Gaelic, "and see which of the workmen speaks to Hastings."

Standing beside Fergus, Christian looked out through drizzling rain. Near the gate, she saw Hastings and Gavin talking with one of the laborers. The rain was heavier now, and Gavin stood without a cloak, his hair wet and darkened.

"A carpenter, a young red-haired man, is with them," she said. "Who is he?"

"Ah, he'll be the one, then. He's been working with the men who've been going out into the forest to cut and split the oak logs. Out there he'll have some freedom to meet with the Bruce's men. I've seen him talking with my older sons, so he may well be playing a double game."

Christian looked at him, her eyes wide. "He brings Robert Bruce word of the English, and now promises to bring the English word of the Bruce?" Fergus nodded grimly. "But what should we do, Fergus?"

Frowning in keep thought, Fergus watched silently as the carpenter walked away, and as Hastings mounted his destrier and looked down to speak to Gavin. Then the priest glanced at Christian. "You've asked to see your cousin. Now is the time for it."

She tilted her head warily. "Will he meet with me?"

He nodded. "My sons Iain and Donal will see to it." He continued to frown, then nodded again to himself. "Moira has some heather ale she has been meaning to give you. Tell your husband that you will spend Friday next with Moira at our croft."

"Bruce will come there?"

He shrugged. "We shall see."

Christian nodded slowly, watching Gavin. Clearly he and Hastings were arguing, and she wondered what they said; she wondered, too, where Gavin's heart and loyalty lay in all of this. Where hers lay, now.

"Say nothing of this to your husband," Fergus said. "You must protect your king at any price."

"But, Fergus—"

"Any price, Christian," Fergus murmured. "I cannot arrange a meeting with King Robert if Gavin Faulkener will learn of it. We cannot trust his English loyalties."

She chewed at her bottom lip, and watched Gavin. She wanted so desperately, sometimes, to trust him. There were moments when she thought that he respected the Scottish cause more than most Englishmen, yet she did not know for certain. She simply did not know.

The rain fell in icy streams now. Gavin stood in it, ignoring it, although his hair and tunic were wet. "Very well, Fergus," she said, sighing. "For now, I will do what you ask, because I want to see my cousin. I need to tell him that the women of his family are still alive."

"Good." Fergus turned away to murmur to Patrick, who gave him Gavin's cloak. The priest handed it to Christian. "Go now, and bring your husband his cloak against the rain," he said. "But keep well your obligation to your king."

She looked at him, eyes wide, and nodded.

" 'Twould be a disgrace for babes to find a treasure that you cannot," Hastings said, gathering his charger's reins. Rain spattered over his red cloak as he looked down from his high saddle at Gavin, who stood in the muddied courtyard. "If there is anything of value in that well, I trust you'll have it out this very day."

"There's naught there," Gavin said flatly. "Lads' tales."

"Make certain of it." Hastings looked over his shoulder. "That carpenter will have information for you within a few days. Send word to me immediately."

"Only if he has something of worth to report."

Hastings watched him for a moment, his eyes two black slits beneath the low brow of his chain mail hood. "I intend to send a messenger to the king at Lanercost tomorrow. I will have an answer back in two days. Edward will not be pleased to learn that you have acted on your own regarding the Scotswoman. And he will expect to garrison this castle. Be ready to command your king's men, Faulkener, or ready yourself to be drawn behind a horse's arse to the gallows and hanged for treachery."

"Do not dare to call me a traitor," Gavin said in a low, graveled tone.

"I was at Berwick," Hastings said. "And so I will call you traitor until your dying day, because of what you did there."

"You have forgotten your deed that day, apparently."

"I have not forgotten what you did, Faulkener," Hastings suddenly snarled. "Or what trouble you caused for me." He wrapped the reins tightly around his left hand.

"Then we both claim debts of each other," Gavin said.

"Gladly," Hastings barked. He suddenly looked past Gavin. Turning, Gavin saw Christian coming toward them, swathed in her cloak and carrying his blue one.

"Your cloak," she said, holding it out to Gavin. "The rain grows heavy and cold." He nodded brusquely and took it from her.

"The perfect wife for the perfect knight," Hastings said acidly. "Watch your back, Faulkener. She was not exceedingly kind to her first husband. She cannot be trusted—but then, two such traitors may suit each other."

Christian glanced up at Hastings, her eyes wide and very green in the thin light. Gavin saw a flicker of true fear there, quickly covered. He circled his hand protectively around her shoulder.

"No doubt you will properly attend to the matters we have discussed," he said to Hastings. "And I will look forward to another of Edward's entertaining letters. Farewell, Oliver." Turning, he pulled Christian with him across the muddy courtyard.

Behind them, Hastings snapped an order. The full escort thundered out over the drawbridge.

OPENING THE DOOR of her bedchamber, Christian blinked in the scant light cast by the peat fire in the hearth. The rest of the room was in deep shadow, quiet but for the soft, steady beat of rain against the shutters.

She sat on a low stool, leaning her harp back against her left shoulder. Sweeping the strings with her fingernails, she released the glorious sound that always stirred her heart, an instant of sweet, private joy. The soothing sound was what she needed now. Hastings's visit, and his departure a few hours ago, had left her with an unsettled, frightened feeling.

She plucked a single string, and heard a soft splash.

"Go on," Gavin said, "music would be lovely." Startled, she spun and peered through the darkness.

He sat immersed in the barrel tub that had been placed in a shadowed corner near the hearth. She had not known he was there until he had spoken. Her heart thudded as she looked at him.

"Unless," he said, lifting his hand, holding a wet cloth, "you would care to join me in my bath." Smiling, he leaned back against the linen-draped side of the tub. His hair and beard were dark and sleek with moisture, and steam rose around him in thin whorls. He shifted in the tub, water spilling softly over the edge. She watched his chest rise and fall, noticed the dark, wet curls of hair surrounding his flat nipples. Her breath quickened oddly.

"I had my bath after supper," she said, a little stiffly. "Dominy and I filled buckets in the well shaft and heated them here, and then we all had baths, including Will and Michaelmas. We left the tub full for you. But I thought you were outside with John and would not come up here for a long while yet."

"John and some of the laborers are taking the watch tonight. I came inside while you were helping Dominy settle the children to sleep in their new rooms. My thanks, lady, for leaving a kettle of hot water on the fire. It warmed the bath very nicely. And I am glad you put the well shaft to good use so soon."

She blushed in the dim light, thinking how very useful she and Fergus had found the well shaft. "The bathwater is quite convenient this way," she said, plucking at a few of the harp strings, noticing a sour tone here and there that needed adjustment. "And I am glad to have the upper level finished at last. Dominy has put her pallet in with Michaelmas just down the hall. Will is with them, but he wanted to share with John."

"John has taken a room in the gatehouse tower, now that the

floors there have been repaired. He will keep his apartments in the gatehouse and take on the duties of the castle seneschal."

"Bailie," Christian said. "In Scotland we say bailie for seneschal." She picked up her harp key, grasping its carved handle and fitting it over one, then another of the wooden pegs that held the strings, twisting to adjust their tension. She tested a single note in the air, pure and soft. Turning the key again and again, she closed her eyes to listen to the resonating wires.

"How do you know when the sound is right?" Gavin asked curiously, watching from the shadows.

She plucked the two center strings, which rang alike, true to each other. "These two are tuned to a note like the drone of a beehive," she said. "These strings on the longer side go down in tone, like male voices, and the others, here, the shorter strings, go up like women's voices. I listen to the notes in my mind and adjust the strings to those sounds." She plucked, and twisted the harp key, and plucked again, tilting her head in deep concentration.

"Play if you like," Gavin said. The deep timbre of his voice startled her, and she glanced up. He rubbed the wet cloth over his chest, watching her. Firelight and shadow delineated his wide, muscular shoulders and powerful arms, and turned his wet hair to a color like gilded oak. She touched her teeth to her lower lip and glanced away, toward the safety of her harp.

She sensed a subtle tension in the air of their private chamber. She knew that Gavin was ready to become her husband in full truth. Her heart picked up a quickening beat as she realized that she wanted that, too.

But she had scant experience of the marriage act; after the first few weeks, Henry had managed to ignore her completely, although she knew that he had taken his release with serving girls through the years. With Henry, she had not thought the deed a pleasant one, a series of grunts and thrusts that she did not care to recall.

But Gavin's deep, compelling kisses and gentle, exciting touches had given her a curiosity and an appetite that she had never felt before. Even now slight shivers cascaded through her at the thought of what might come later.

Rain shivered against the shutters as Christian leaned into her harp and streamed her fingernails across the fine-tuned brass wires. She began to play a song she had learned from the old harper who had lived in her father's household.

Her fingers followed the complex patterns with flawless ease. And as the gusting rain grew louder, she tucked her head down and played with greater fervor, hearing only the music.

Her right hand flashed along the harp strings, creating and elaborating the melody, and her left hand formed the softly beating heart of the song. The delicate touches found haunting nuances in the music, rendering its sadness, releasing its joy.

Caught in a shimmering web of sound she forgot that Gavin was there, forgot time and place. She let go of all but the music. As the last exquisite tone faded, she looked up slowly, adjusting her eyes to the dim light as if she had awoken from a dream.

Gavin watched her steadily, his arms resting on the rim of the tub. He leaned his head back and sighed.

"Was that one of your sleeping songs?" he asked.

She shook her head. " 'Tis called a song of weeping, but not for sadness. Weeping is like a release—so this music eases away hurt. 'Tis said such songs can heal."

"I would like to hear another," he said softly.

She nodded, and played a soft air that evoked a sad, peaceful feeling. A feeling of serenity began to flow through her, a blend of music and rain, of warmth and darkness and skillfully woven enchantment.

And she knew, suddenly, while cold rain beat at the window and winter howled outside, that she was content here, safe and unthreatened, truly free. As her hands followed the song through to its end and began another, a sister song, Christian felt peace and comfort wrap around her like an embrace.

Lifting her hands when it was finished, she damped the harp strings with her palms and let the rain fill the stillness again. She felt washed clean, and vibrant.

"You should play for kings," Gavin said.

She shook her head. "The harper is at a king's mercy if the music displeases."

"Your music could not displease." His gaze did not waver.

"Thank you," she said, tracing her fingers over the wire strings, releasing delicate shimmers of sound. Hearing splashes, she glanced up. Gavin was standing in the tub, wrapping a linen towel around his waist. Leaning over, he grabbed another cloth and dried his shoulders and arms, ruffling his hair as he stepped out of the tub. His long legs were tautly sculpted, and the rippled surface of his abdomen and chest was sleek with moisture. She drew in her breath and stood.

Turning, she went to a clothing chest, lifting its heavy lid to pull out a blue tunic with a gilt-embroidered hem and collar that gleamed in the firelight. "This cool air is chilly," she said, handing him the tunic.

Gavin accepted it from her, tilting one brow. "Henry's?"

She nodded, and he pulled it over his head, the linen towel dropping from his hips to pool around his bare feet. The blue robe was of thick, soft wool, an older style, long and loose cut with close sleeves. Gavin shoved up the sleeves and went to the bed, where his own clothes were piled, and unsheathed his dagger.

From a little clay pot by the tub, he scooped up a fingerful of a soft soap mixture made from mutton fat, ash, and herbs. Lathering it into his wet beard, he sat on the low stool near the fire. "Play the harp again if you wish," he said, beginning to scrape at his beard. "Have you a shaving song?" He winced as he nicked himself.

She laughed. "You will need another healing song. Here, let me," she said, and walked over to stand behind him. He handed her the blade. "This is hardly the best kind of knife for the task," she said, gripping the ivory handle.

"John has my shaving knife packed with his things," he answered. "In the gatehouse." He tipped his head back.

"Hush now. This will go faster if you are quiet." She leaned his head against her shoulder, and began to scrape the dagger edge over his thick beard, umber touched with copper and gilt. Each stroke revealed more of his lean, firm jaw.

The soap smelled of lavender, and his damp golden brown hair smelled clean and masculine. She worked in silence for a while, feeling his hot breath over her fingers. He glanced at her, a flash of deep blue through thick lashes.

"Did you do this for Henry?" he asked.

"Never for Henry. I did this for my brothers at times. It has been a little while—*ach,* I am sorry," she said. She touched her fingertip to the tiny nick under his chin.

Gavin lifted a brow. "Go easy then, until you remember how to do it." He settled back against her. "I trust you, my lady," he murmured, eyes closed. "Remember that."

Christian smiled at his light tone, and slid the blade along his neck, scraping upward. She stopped to clean the dagger on the linen towel.

"Your brothers," he said. "How many did you have?"

"Two." She paused. "But they are dead now, and my father as well. Killed by the English."

Gavin glanced up. "What happened?"

"My father refused to give his pledge to your king. Edward declared his castle in the Highlands forfeit, and sent English troops to take it. My father was killed that day." Her voice was low and flat. But she had not broken from the pain of telling it, and she knew she could say the rest. "My mother died shortly afterward from her injuries. She had been raped by English soldiers. I wasna harmed because she hid me away in a wooden chest. I was fourteen."

"My God, Christian," he said, and sat up. His intent gaze seemed deep enough to hold her soul in its measure.

She glanced down, unable to look at him. "My uncle was an English sympathizer. He took me back to Kinglassie and forced me to pledge my oath to King Edward, so that I would have a home, and some value as an heiress. And he made me wed Henry for my own protection. My brothers often came here to visit in secret. Henry didna know, or he would have killed them, for they were rebels. My brothers always cheered me. I think I survived those days because I had them, and Michaelmas, and Fergus and Moira."

"You survived because you are strong," Gavin said quietly. "How long did you live here with Henry?"

"Eight years," she said. "Last summer, my brothers died. They fought with Robert Bruce at Methven, a disastrous defeat for Scotland. One was killed on the field, and the other was taken to Berwick and executed." She paused for several moments to master the grief that welled inside. "After I heard that word of them, I left Kinglassie. I burned it, and I left."

She touched his chin and Gavin leaned back, silent. The knife scraped softly, and rain sheeted against the window shutters. His head was a warm weight against her body, his hair damp and soft. The peacefulness of the music seemed to linger in the air. But her contentment has been ripped apart by the memories she had exposed.

Sliding the blade over the lean planes of his face, she blinked back tears. She would not allow them to be shed. Pausing, sniffing, she wiped the knife on the towel.

"You have lost much at English hands." His voice was soft and husky. "I did not know how much."

"And you wonder that I resent English." She laughed hollowly and brought the blade to his other cheek. "Be still, now. I wouldna care to cut you, though you are a Sasunnach."

"Christian," he said, "what happened to Henry?"

"Hush." She traced the steel edge along his cheek and over his well-defined chin. "I bare all of my hurts to you, but you tell me little of your past. You will listen to me and say to yourself, ah, there is a Scot for you, see, she cannot be trusted. This, that, she did to her own husband."

"I want to know what has hurt you in the past, Christian," he said softly.

She lifted the blade away and looked down at him. "Much has hurt me, all of it caused by English. I am tired of hurting."

"As I am," he said. "But I want to know yours."

She watched him for a long moment. "Then tell me yours."

"Mayhap I will." He settled his head back, and touched her hand. "Finish the task, my lady."

She drew a breath and dangled the blade over his chin, scraping slowly. "Henry told me about my brothers," she said. "He was pleased to hear of the defeat of the rebels at Methven, and of Bruce's flight into the heather. He taunted me that he would be rid of me as last." She drew a shaky breath, remembering. "The English assumed that Robert Bruce would come to a quick end last summer." She sighed, as tired of the burden as she was of the hurt. Relieving it now felt right, and she continued.

"There were many tenants and knights living near Kinglassie who supported my cousin's cause. When Henry and his garrison rode out on King Edward's orders to fight a skirmish, I sent for the rebels. I allowed them to take Kinglassie in Henry's absence."

His eyelids flew open. "You took this castle?"

"The rebels did, but I fought with them. I sent Michaelmas to Moira and stayed here to wield a weapon as best I could. When Henry and his men returned, the Scots fought them, though there were twice as many English. The Scots won—I dinna know how." She paused to close her eyes against the turbulent, awful images that she remembered. "Many men died that day. Henry was among them. He had a Scottish arrow in his heart."

Gavin pushed her hand away, sitting up and taking the cloth from her to rub his clean-shaven face. He was silent. She could not tell by his intense frown if he was angry with her or if he was simply deep within his own thoughts.

"So, Sasunnach," she said, "you canna trust me. And I canna learn to love the English."

Gavin dropped the linen and lifted her hand, which still gripped the dagger. He touched the blade tip to his own throat.

"You hold the weapon, lady," he said, low, fiercely. "If you hate me, if you cannot love any English knight, then cut my throat now, and be done with it."

She stared at him, breath heaving. Then she uttered a soft Gaelic oath and threw the knife down to clatter away on the hearthstone.

CHAPTER SEVENTEEN

"**I** KNEW I COULD TRUST YOU." He gazed at her evenly. Christian drew a long breath. "I couldna hurt you. Ever. And I didna kill Henry, though the English say I did." She laughed, a bitter huff. "I canna even shoot a bow."

Gavin nodded, knowing that she was innocent of all but rebellion. And that impulse he understood well enough. He noticed that the heavy mood, the anger and challenge of the past few moments, was changing as she relaxed. Her temperament was like lightning, striking one instant, calm the next. He saw some of that in himself when he was with her. And crossed lightning could do the most damage.

He reached out a hand, thinking, and idly touched the harp, tracing a finger along the decorative carving on the upper curve.

" 'Tis beautiful, your harp," he said. "Oak and pine?"

"Willow," she said "But oak is used here, in the forepillar, which is called the male part of the harp."

"Why willow and oak?"

"Willow wood is flexible and light, and 'tis thought to have feminine power. So willow is used for the female part of the harp, the belly—here, where the sound swells." She stroked her hand along the box of the harp. She clearly loved the instrument, and loved talking about it. And Gavin wanted to know more of what she cherished.

"And this top piece?" he asked, tracing a finger along the elaborate interlacing. "These are birds carved here?"

She nodded. "Birds usually decorate the upper curve because that piece represents spirit. Here, on the forepillar, this brass-studded carving is a double-headed eel. Water, air, earth are all present in the harp, in decoration or in meaning. Each piece has its own purpose, and its own power."

"Water, air, earth—where is the fire?" he asked.

She stroked her fingertips over the brass wires. "The fire is in the music," she said softly.

The fire is in your fine-tuned soul, he thought, watching her bowed head, her slender, strong hands. He saw how lovingly she touched the wires and the decorated wood. "That harp is special to you," he said. "You touch it like a friend."

She nodded. "A harp is a living thing to its harper, not just a tool for music. It must be respected and treated kindly. My father had this harp made for me when I was twelve. I thought of her then, and still do, as a kind of a sister of my soul."

"Twelve? Not so long ago, then," he said.

"Long enough," she said. "I have had her eleven years now. A harp will last less than its harper's lifetime. They burst," she said, touching the polished oak of the forepillar. "The wood splits, the strings pull too tightly after a while. 'Tis almost as if their hearts break with the music they make. There is great sadness in some of this music, and great, deep joy."

"I have heard you play both on this harp." His hand, on the pillar, met and covered hers. He knew, now, how deeply she had been hurt. His thumb traced a gentle caress over her slender wrist. "And we could both use some of your healing music, I think," he added wryly.

She nodded. "Gavin—what happened to your wife?"

He drew a breath and looked away, dreading the question and yet knowing he should answer. "She was ill for a long time, an ailment of the lungs. The physicians could do little for her. I even hired Saracen physicians, the most knowledgeable in the world." He shrugged; he would not tell her more than that, now.

"I think you loved her very much," she murmured.

"Aye," he said. "But I loved her like a child loves a child, like a brother loves a sister. There was little fire between us. Friendship, but little fire." He reached out and lifted the tip of her chin. "Unlike the heat and spark between us, lady." Christian glanced up at him, her eyes a deep green, intense and vibrant.

"You have endured a great deal," she said. "Your mother died in the raid on the convent, and your wife—I didna know, Gavin. But you dinna seem bitter, or angry for these tragedies."

"I have learned that hearts are too strong to break," he said, his gaze steady.

She smiled ruefully. "My heart feels like an old harp at times, ready to burst."

He shook his head, his hand gently over hers, resting on the harp. " 'Twill not break. Just trust, and be strong. You are a survivor, Christian. I have seen the fierce strength of your spirit."

She was silent, watching his thumb circle along her hand on the harp. Rain formed a steady pattern of sound overhead.

"Do you trust me?" he asked softly.

"I want to," she said slowly. "I did, once, in the abbey. There, I—" she stopped and bit her lower lip.

"What?" he asked.

"I loved you there, I think," she whispered.

His heart thudded heavily in his chest. But he stayed still and calm. "Did you?"

She nodded. "But I thought you were an angel."

"Ah," he said. "Others have made that mistake."

She glanced up. "What do you mean?"

He laughed wryly. "When I was a youthful knight, and new to the court, Queen Eleanor called me the Angel Knight. The name stayed with me for years."

She smiled. "It suits you. I thought you were Saint Michael." He smiled with her. "And then I took you for a Scottish knight. But when I found out who you were, and why you came to Kinglassie, I couldna trust you. Even when I wanted to."

"And what does your heart tell you now?"

She looked at him steadily, her eyes forest deep. "My heart isna reliable. And my mind tells me you are English." She slipped her hand out from under his.

He blew out a fast, exasperated breath. The vibration sent a hum through the sensitive harp strings. "Sweet saints in heaven," he said, folding his arms over his chest. "You are the most stubborn woman I have ever known. Do you still insist on placing all your distrust of English knights on my head?" He leaned toward her. "Aye, lady, I am English. My father was an English knight. But my mother was a Scotswoman, as Celtic as you are. I have that in me, too."

She looked up at him, eyes wide. "Gavin—I want to trust you," she said. "But you owe your fealty to King Edward. And I have broken my pledge to him, and willna make another."

"You and I are alike," he said. "More than you know."

"I am a rebel," she said. "A traitor, so say the English."

"As I am."

"She looked surprised. "You—a traitor?"

"I was accused of treason ten years ago at Berwick."

She gasped. "Berwick!"

"I spoke out against what happened there when no one else dared utter a word to King Edward. Twelve thousand Scottish people—women, children, merchants, not only soldiers—were slaughtered in the streets over three days. And I spoke out, and was named a traitor for it."

"Hastings called you such in the courtyard today," she said, frowning. "But I thought he said it in anger because you hold Kinglassie and he doesna."

"He freely calls me a traitor, no matter how much time has passed since Berwick. There is much anger between us for other reasons." He shook his head. "I paid a heavy price for the rebellious words I spoke to King Edward. I lost my inheritance, my right to live in England, all but my life. I was exiled to France."

"Then you will be very careful to do whatever your king asks of you now."

"King Edward kept me in France as long as he could. He made me ambassador to hold me there. He will never fully trust me again."

"And does he have good reason for that?" she asked.

"He does," he said. "Where the Scots are concerned, Edward

knows I may not follow his orders. That, Christian"—he looked intently at her—"is the only matter in which I choose to be untrustworthy."

"But why would the king send you here to Scotland?"

He shrugged. "In part, because his greed for Kinglassie's gold is so strong. He wants to possess it because of the legend and its tie to the Scots throne. He told me to charm you into telling the truth of the treasure."

Christian burst into a harsh laugh. "He sent you because Hastings had failed at that task." She frowned. "But I dinna know the truth of the gold."

"I believe you," he said. "But I think King Edward wants to know for certain where I stand. He has set his watchdogs Hastings and Ormesby on me. They wait to see what I will do."

"And what will that be?" she asked quietly.

He plucked at a string, listening to its pure tone. "I do not know," he said. "But I do know that Kinglassie is my home now. And I have wanted a home for longer than you can imagine."

"You have a castle in France."

He shook his head. "The property belongs to my first wife's family. Kinglassie is the only true home I have, Christian, and I mean to hold it. King Edward acted out of his own pride and anger when he gave me this place. His ambitions differ greatly from mine. And I have never been a man to obey orders blindly."

Christian looked up at him. "Your hurt for mine," she said softly. "Now I understand you far better than I did before, Gavin Faulkener of Kinglassie."

He smiled and held out his hand. She laid hers in his, palms flat together, heat stirring instantly there. "Once, when we were together in the underground chamber," he said, "you asked that I be just a man and no English knight." She nodded. "I ask the same of you now. Be a woman, and no Scot, here in this chamber. Here in my arms."

She sucked in her breath, watching him, and touched her teeth to her lower lip.

"Promise me," he said, his fingers gripping hers. "Say it."

"I promise," she whispered.

"Come here," he said gruffly, and pulled on her hand. She came into his arms. He wrapped her in his embrace, as he had been wanting to do for so long. Laying his cheek beside hers, he traced his fingers along the curve of her back. She tucked her head into the hollow of his shoulder and clung to him.

Touching the back of her neck, he lifted the silky weight of her hair and sank his fingers into its thickness. She smelled clean and soft, like wildflowers after rain. He inhaled it in, and kissed her brow, then drew back and touched his forehead to hers.

"Listen to me," he said, his voice husky. "I will not betray you. I will not leave you, or abandon you within the very home that we share. I know this was done to you before."

"You were abandoned, too," she whispered.

He nodded. "Aye," he said, and knew it was true. He had felt abandoned, years ago, by his king and country, by his mother's death, by Jehanne's passing. He had never realized it before. "And I swear to you now that I will be with you always."

With a soft cry, she circled her arms around his neck. She felt soft and giving as he held her, wholly trusting of him. Gavin closed his eyes tightly and thought he would melt in that moment, thought he would fall to his knees in gratitude that she was here, and safe in his arms, that she lived and was strong, and was his.

"I will always be with you," he said again. His mouth covered hers, lifted, covered hers again. He placed his hands on either side of her small, pale face and looked into her wide eyes, their green as deep and verdant as summer. "Will you trust me?"

A somber frown folded between her black brows. "I will," she said, her voice hushed and soft. "You willna betray me. You willna leave me when the English are done in Galloway."

"Never," he whispered, gliding the tip of his thumb over her lips. "Never."

Pausing, he lifted the leather thong at her throat, sliding the pendant over her head and setting it aside. "Naught should remind us of realm or king in this chamber." She nodded, gazing up at him.

He leaned forward and touched his lips to hers, gently, yet with an aching need. Her lips were warm and moist and insistent beneath his, and he tipped her chin and slid his hand along the side of her face.

Then he took her mouth with hungry force, parting her lips with his tongue. Moaning softly into his mouth, her small tongue warm and wet on his, she pushed her fingers through his hair. He felt the incredible softness of her breasts against his chest, felt her hips press against his swelling, filling need until he groaned and swayed with her.

He slid his hands down over her shoulders, smoothing his thumbs over warm skin and bare, hard collarbones, over the embroidered neck of the gown, toward the gentle swell of her upper breasts. He could sense her wildly beating heart beneath the woolen cloth, beneath the warm flesh. Kissing her, he opened his hands gently over her breasts, stroking his fingertips over the cushioning wool, over the peaks of her aroused nipples, feeling her soft gasp inside his mouth.

She moaned as he unfastened the little silver clasp at the front opening of her gown and laid back the flap of cloth. He pushed aside the soft inner layer of her undergown and caressed the sweet roundness of one breast. Touching his lips to hers, he felt the delicate tip of her tongue on his. A lightning charge surged through his body as his fingertips found her nipple and rolled it, ruched it, made it firm.

He lowered his head to kiss her breast, slipping his hand over the other breast, feeling that nipple peak between his fingerpads. She arched against him, clinging to his arms, offering herself to him as they stood together. He pulled aside the confining cloth of her shift to better touch his lips along one breast, taking its soft center bud between his lips, tugging at it, sensing its luscious warmth, its life as it grew firm beneath his tongue.

He drew in a trembling breath and raised his head to kiss her lips. "Oh, God," he murmured into her open mouth. "My love, my lady. I want to feel your body against mine."

She murmured assent, and helped him to remove her gown, pulling it over her head. She fumbled at the low neck of the thin woolen undertunic and slid that over her head, too, dropping it with her other gown at their feet.

She was more beautifully made, more delicate, more lush and desirable than he could have imagined. Weeks ago, when she was ill, he had seen her partly nude, had seen her fragile bones and pale skin; she had been a vulnerable, sad thing to see. Now she took his breath away.

The low firelight turned her skin to creamy gold, gave a warm blush to her firm breasts. Her slender body was gently rounded at the hips, her belly flat above dark curls. Gavin touched her reverently, tracing his fingertips over her shoulders, slowly brushing over the sides of her full breasts. Grazing over her hardening nipples, his fingers followed the curve of her ribs and waist and slid down to rest on her hips.

He cherished every part of her with his gaze, caressed her curves and smooth skin with his fingertips. She was a harmony of elegant shapes and textures, ivory and velvet and heaven beneath his hands.

Breathing out a heavy, trembling sigh, he drew her forward into his arms. Brushing back her rumpled hair, tilting her head by taking a handful of her hair and gently tugging back, he kissed her slowly, softly, sensually, until her tongue sought his and her arms circled his back eagerly.

Gliding his hands down her delicately muscled back to the smooth, rounded swell of her buttocks, he pulled her toward him, her yielding center grazing against the insistent hardening he felt. He drew in his breath sharply.

She sighed into his mouth, sighed again, and pulled at the tunic he wore. Impatiently he pulled it off and sent it swirling down to the floor. His own need was strong and obvious, and each moment that passed added to the urgency he felt.

She stepped again into the circle of his arms, her breasts brushing against his chest, warm, incredibly soft, a deep cushion against him. Her heart beat steadily, rapidly against his chest; his own thudded with fervent power.

Bending a little, he fitted his hips to hers, pressing forward until the hard length of him slid between her legs. "My God," he said, a hushed growl. He lifted her effortlessly, carrying her the few steps to the bed.

Laying her down on the fur coverlet, he knelt beside her, their combined weight sinking into the piled feather mattresses, the silky warmth of the fur beneath their bodies offering a sensuous haven.

Leaning forward, his arms on either side of her, he bent to kiss her again, tracing his tongue against her lower lip. He slipped his tongue inside, where she was hot and wet and gentle.

Tracing his tongue down her throat, between her breasts, sensing the beat of her heart, he took her nipple in his mouth, a soft, living comfort, and as it hardened so did he, further, stronger, until he thought he would burst with need.

He moved his lips over the ruched bud of her nipple, and captured her other breast beneath his hand. She moaned softly, arching, her hands circling along the length of his back, warm, gentle fingertips seeking, touching, exploring his body.

Rounding over his firm buttocks and sliding across his lower abdomen, her hands slipped upward to touch his chest, feathering through the hair there. His own small, flat nipples grew taut when her fingers found them. He stiffened and moistened and yet held back, insistently held back, wanting to give to her first.

He groaned and took her by the waist and shoulder and rolled over her, pressing her slender body to his. He tasted her earlobes, her throat, her breasts, touching and teasing and arousing with his tongue. Sliding his hands over her warm, velvety skin, he let his fingers trace lower, still lower, until he touched a fingertip to her moistened, parted cleft, startling a high gasp from her. She arched toward his hand and accepted his touch.

Sighing into her mouth, he led his fingers inward carefully, sinking into hot, yielding flesh as moist and heavy as honey. He kissed her lips as he touched her below, in her most secret heart, all the while holding back his own aching, trembling need. Lowering his head to take a nipple with his lips and tongue, he continued to stroke her heated, innermost folds, as slowly as he could manage, though his fingers nearly shook with the effort.

He savored every tremulous breath she took, every moan she made. Buttery moisture, heat, and his own breathlessness assailed him, threatening his control over his own body.

But he wanted to guide her now; he wanted to wait. She thrashed gently, a warm sweat glistening over her breasts and abdomen. As she had discovered the incandescent spark, the gift hidden within her body, he sighed and felt it move through her.

She swayed with the joy of it, undulating against him as her body called out wordlessly and eloquently. He touched his tongue to her lips and relished the airy cry she made. And then he settled his hips over hers.

Her fingers found him then, grasped around his hardness, her fingerpads smooth as silk over his aching, trembling tip. Her legs parted, her hips surged, and she guided him now, accepting his supple, turgid length into her body. He sucked in a breath and circled her hips with his hands, plunging deep, uttering a hoarse whisper, gasping her name.

Opening, yielding, her body molded over him. He moved, and she did, and he quickly taught her his rhythm, heat and blood and flesh surging. She moved in that cadence with her breath and her body, until her lambent inner heat touched off the spark that he had held back so long.

Like flame, blending into flame, creating a brighter light, his body surged into hers, his heart beat with hers, and his joy poured into hers.

HER BREATH STIRRED A WAVE of hair at Gavin's forehead, but he slept on, snoring softly. She smiled and slid her hand beneath the coverlet and linen sheet, and ran her fingers lightly over his chest. He sucked in a breath and snored on. Christian leaned over and kissed his chest, touching her tongue to his nipple.

Naught; he slept. Frowning, she laid her head on his chest and tried to drift back into sleep in the darkness, but her body remembered the lithesome, incandescent pleasure that she had felt in his arms not so long ago. She wanted to create that bliss again with him. She moved her body beside his, stretched languorously, and when he did not move, tried to rest.

His heart beat steadily beneath her cheek, his solid rib cage rose and fell beneath her hand. Rain pounded against the walls, harsh and cold, but she was protected here, warm and enclosed with Gavin.

Like sunlight through glass, her spirit felt brightened, illuminated, by love. From the first moment she had seen Gavin, when he had stood outside her cage at Carlisle, she had placed her faith in him. But she had adored a beautiful illusion, thinking him to be an archangel; she had even dreamed when she had been ill that he had an angel's wings and a healing touch.

She smiled at that, thinking it foolish, but only in part: she knew, with some deep inner sense, that his hands made her feel cherished and strong. His touch conveyed a profound love to her, just as clearly as words.

She loved him now, freely and openly. She trusted him once again, certain that he cared deeply about her, and about Kinglassie and Scotland. He had a strong conscience and a courageous heart, for he had survived loss and tragedy and found some deeper wisdom in them. He followed his convictions still, unafraid of threats. Angelic as he might look, he was no illusion. And she knew now that she completely adored him.

"Aingeal," she whispered. "Angel. I love you." The words were soft as a breath, the feeling as vital as air.

His hands moved and his fingertips traced along her jaw. Shivers danced down her body when she realized that he had heard her words. She sensed his smile through the darkness.

The first touch of his stubbled chin was harsh against her skin. His lips touched hers, and she looped her arms over his warm shoulders, turning toward him.

"Ach, Dhia," she whispered, arching against him, wanting to eagerly surrender to the power that she had once resisted in him. Now realms and kings no longer mattered between them; only touch, and joy, and merciful comfort mattered.

"My love," he said, the words a breath between their lips, "How is it said in Gaelic?"

"Mo ghràdh," she answered.

"Mo ghràdh." She had never heard it said so softly. "I do love you," he said. His lips, warm and pliant, found hers, and he spread his strong hands over her back.

"And I trust you," she whispered against his lips.

"Then show me its greatest measure," he murmured.

His hands streamed down her body like feathers, soft and gentle, arousing a shiver in her breasts that swirled into her groin. He followed down the curve of her waist and hip, caressing her, profoundly tender.

Touching her mound, his fingers traced slowly over the cleft, raising a tingle there that made her moan softly. She felt herself swell and moisten, and she opened further to him. As his fingers slipped inside, his head lowered to her breast, delicately touching her there with his tongue. She sighed, swaying her hips and sliding her hands over his shoulders and back, savoring what he did to her, above and below, with his fingertips and his mouth.

He moved his head to glide his lips down, touching his tongue to her abdomen, kissing her there until she moaned. As he moved down again, she opened even wider on a gasp of surprise. She touched her trembling fingers to the crown of his head, and shivered as she had never done before, crying out his name as an intense wave of heat and lightning shuddered through her body.

Then she shifted and drew him up insistently, settling her hips against his until his hardened arousal slipped inside her. She yielded to the first thrust he made, cocooning him in her warmth, meeting his powerful movements with her own. As if he were the harper and she the harp, he stroked a strong, beautiful rhythm and she shimmered, resonant and joyful in his arms.

CHAPTER EIGHTEEN

" 'T WILL RAIN AGAIN BEFORE EVENING. And worse
than the past two days, by the look of it. The wind has
a bite like a hungry wolf," Dominy said, casting a critical glance
at the heavy gray sky. "Why ye must travel out on such a day, my
lady, I cannot understand. Here, Will, stop pulling Michaelmas's
braid," she said irritably.

Michaelmas poked her tongue out at Will, who grimaced in
return. The shaggy pony they shared trudged on through the ice-
coated mud and old leaves that covered the forest floor.

"We would all rather be by a hot fire than out here in the
damp and cold," Christian said as she and Dominy guided their
own horses along the forest track. "But 'tis Friday, the day that
Moira expects our visit."

"This cold air will bring back yer cough," Dominy complained. "Ye'll be sick again, and need a warm posset and a tented
steam bath later."

"I willna be sick again," Christian said patiently, "but I will
have the posset and the bath if 'twill please you. But Moira is
waiting for us to arrive, and has promised us some of her stock of
heather ale. 'Tis only another mile or so to their croft."

"Sir Gavin asked ye not to leave this morn. But ye went on
about this heather ale until all of us were convinced that it must
be finer than the fair-folk could make."

Christian smiled. "The ancient Picts made this recipe, and a legend says that their last chief died rather than tell the Romans the secret of it. 'Tis made from heather bells and the water of the clearest burns. Not many can make it, and no one does it as well as Moira. She willna say what she adds to it."

"Hmmph. 'Tis still an ale, and this is a day for hot soups and spiced wines." Dominy tilted a brow at Christian. "Now, my lady, tell me the real reason we are out here today."

"What do you mean?" Christian asked sweetly.

"I've seen the way ye and Sir Gavin look at each other lately. John said to me just this morn, that a new pair of wild doves had mated and taken roost in the laird's bedchamber—and he did not mean the feathered kind. Ye'd not go anywhere without Sir Gavin just now, unless 'twere for some reason that Scots should know and English should not. Ah, my lady," Dominy said, smiling, "ye blush like a bride. I think it a lovely thing."

"Mating doves, indeed," Christian grumbled. Her cheeks grew hot at the realization that her love for Gavin, which deepened each time she saw him, heard him, or felt his intoxicating touch, had become so obvious.

Dominy laughed. "Since only the most dire matter would bring ye away from yer handsome husband on such a day, I think ye should tell me how I can help." She lifted her eyebrows meaningfully. "I think ye're going out this day to meet yer cousin the Bruce."

Christian sighed, relieved. "I did hope you would feel that way, Dominy. You are a true friend. 'Tis why I asked you to come with the children. I want the three of you to visit with Moira and the lads today."

"And where will ye be?"

"Fergus has arranged for me to meet with my cousin. I want to tell him the news of his queen and the other ladies who are in English captivity. I am sure we will be able to return to Kinglassie long before supper."

"Are ye sure this is what ye want to do?"

"My cousin needs to know what has happened to the women."

"But ye've fallen in love with an English knight, who has

responsibilities to his king. Sir Gavin would not approve."

"I know," Christian said quietly. "But my loyalty to Scotland and to my cousin did not change as soon as I wed an English knight. I told Fergus that I would meet him today, before I—" she stopped and looked away. Before she had learned the blissful freedom and comfort that came when the fire of the heart was discovered at last.

Hearing a raucous sound in the thick pine trees overhead, she glanced up. Two ravens slid silently past, wings outspread.

"Not a good omen for Scots, I think," Dominy said.

Christian frowned and turned her attention to her daughter, who yowled as her braid was yanked, and then unceremoniously dumped Will off of the pony's back.

A little while later, as they rode out of the pine forest, Christian saw the rounded thatched roof of the Macnab house, tucked behind a hill. Beyond that, on another hill, she saw the stone tower of Saint Bride's church rising through thin mist.

FERGUS WAITED FOR HER in the church, just as Moira had said. But Christian had not expected to see the thirty other men who were standing inside the nave of the simple rectangular building. A few of them glanced at her as she entered, then turned back to listen while Fergus, standing before the altar with its fine white cloth and silver dishes, led them in a Latin prayer.

Leaning against the smooth white plaster wall, Christian glanced around the little church, at the dark timber rafters of the sloped ceiling, at the whitewashed walls and unadorned arched windows. Closing her eyes, she listened to the Latin responses the men gave, but did not murmur the words herself, since she had been excommunicated by the bishops in Carlisle. Even standing inside this holy place was sinful for her just now. But she loved the familiar smell of the earthy stone, and felt blessed by the peacefulness within the little church.

Now she waited while the men prayed, and while Fergus blessed them by sprinkling holy water over their bowed heads.

She frowned slightly, perplexed that so many men were here

attending a mass without their families. 'Twas a Friday during Lent, but she wondered why they were gathered here.

Turning her head, she suddenly understood. In one corner of the little nave, weapons and armor had been stacked. Bows and quivers, long-handled axes, iron-tipped staves, and jumbled piles of leather and chain mail garments revealed the intent of these men.

Rebels, all of them, and Fergus was blessing them. She was certain that these men meant to join Robert Bruce. Fergus must be intending to guide the new rebels to the Bruce along with Christian.

The men genuflected and began to leave the church, collecting their weapons and passing by her with a nod or a murmur or a shy glance. Many of them were familiar faces, friends, a few of them workmen from within Kinglassie. Iain and Donal Macnab, Fergus's sons, were among them. She had not seen them since the day she had sat upon Gavin's charger and faced them across a wide stream. Now they smiled at her and winked, old friends as they had always been.

She looked around then and saw Fergus coming toward her.

"More men for Robert, from Kinglassie's own farms and crofts," she said in quiet Gaelic as the last of the men left, and the door shut with a dull thud. "You did not tell me."

"There are many who are ready to support King Robert's efforts now. Some of them have lately been dispossessed of their Scottish holdings. Oliver Hastings has been free with his dragon banner of late," Fergus said. "And Robert Bruce's small victories around the countryside have given these men faith in his cause. They see now that they have a courageous and worthy king who can defeat King Edward if he has the support of men and arms behind him."

"We all go into the forest to meet Robert, then?"

"We do. But first, come to the altar."

"I cannot," she said, "I am excommunicated. I should not even be in here."

Fergus smiled and held out his hand. "Come." She followed him, and knelt before the single step of the altar when he motioned for her to do so.

"The bishop of Glasgow has sent out letters to the parish priests," Fergus said. "We have been instructed to reinstate any Scot who has been excommunicated for aiding Robert Bruce. The Scottish Church will not let the souls of Bruce's friends fall into jeopardy." He raised a little silver bell in his hand and began.

As Fergus intoned in Latin, Christian bowed her head and listened to the sweet ring of the little bell. She felt that her soul was safe on earth in Gavin's care. Now she was infinitely glad that heaven would guard her and welcome her prayers once again.

"Now then," Fergus said once he had finished, "we must go. We have an audience with a king."

"PIGEONS," JOHN SAID. "I SWEAR 'twas pigeons."

"Not today, a Friday in Lent," Gavin said as they trudged through wet bracken, their shoulders brushing past dripping pine boughs. "We should try fishing if you are hungry for this night's supper. Christian and Fergus told me that the loch and the burns are always full of good catch."

"I dinna care for winter fishing in icy streams. But I swear to you, lad, Fergus told me the Scottish Church just declared pigeons good food for Lenten Friday. And Kinglassie is crammed with pigeons and wild doves. We dinna even have to leave our castle walls to hunt our supper. Thick as berries on a bush, they are, roosting in the ruined towers and walking whenever they please in the courtyard."

"I am heartily tired of pigeons and doves. We've had them stewed and boiled and roasted for weeks now," Gavin said, shifting the longbow that he had been carrying since they had left Kinglassie an hour earlier.

"Ah, but Dominy has a fine hand wi' a dove pie," John said, grinning.

Gavin chuckled. "I think you're interested in more than her fine hand of late," he said. John reddened beneath his silvery beard, and Gavin chuckled again. "But as for me, if there's any game in this forest, I'll be using this bow. Thank God Henry left longbows in storage, and not those short bows Scots favor. Good English yew, this is."

John laughed. "I've used a short bow since I was wee Robbie's age. They're muckle powerful for hunting."

"I'd like to see that—if we ever see any game. I had hoped to spot a red deer out here, but so far I've seen naught but sparrows and finches. And wolves, though they slipped away quick enough when we came near."

"Hungry they'll be, in late February," John said.

" 'Tis March now. And I have no care to mix with wolves today." Gavin pushed ahead between branches that swung wildly and sprayed him with cold drops. Pulling up the hood of his dark blue cloak, the marten lining warming his chilled ears, he stopped and turned.

" 'Tis later in the day than I had thought. And Fergus's croft is no more than a mile or so from this part of the forest," he said to John. "Christian and the others will be ready to return to Kinglassie soon."

"Aye, and I'll be eager to try that heather ale that Lady Christian has gone to fetch."

"Perhaps we should go there and offer escort," Gavin said.

"*Ach,* you canna keep away from your wee dove, eh?" John asked, smiling. "You and your bride seem to have settled matters atween you."

"We have, but 'tis not why I want to escort her home again," Gavin said, stepping over wet bracken. "Before we left Kinglassie, a rider came in from Loch Doon, sent by Hastings."

"I was in the great hall with the masons then, and I heard there was a messenger. I thought Hastings had sent an inquiry on our progress. He's eager to install that garrison here."

"Hastings has sent word to the king at Lanercost and had a letter back already, regarding Christian. King Edward still considers her an outlaw and a prisoner of England. If I do not keep her in proper custody, Hastings has permission to arrest her."

"God's wounds! And you said nae word o' this?"

Gavin shrugged. "She had already left, else I would not have let her go outside the castle. But I thought that you and I should go to Fergus's croft, and bring her home again."

"Ah, so that is why we're out hunting. Nae the Bruce, or the doves, but the English."

"If I must fight English to protect my wife and my home, then I will do that." Conviction, strong and solid, flowed through him as he uttered the words. He and John walked on in silence, scanning the forest, seeing only high, straight trunks, heavy pine branches, and flitting birds.

"We might catch sight of the Bruce while we're out here. Hastings and the king would be muckle pleased to hear it," John said. His tone was mild, but Gavin sensed the sarcasm there.

" 'Tis part of my mission to assist in Bruce's capture, according to King Edward," Gavin said. "And they say that Bruce is hiding in these hills lately."

"And what would you do if we met him here?"

Gavin shrugged. "Without being introduced, I doubt I'd recognize the man," he said easily. "I saw him once or twice in the English court, years ago. But I'll wager he's changed some."

"Aye, likely," John said, nodding firmly. "We wouldna ken the man now if we fell smack over him." Gavin chuckled softly.

Their boots crushed pine needles underfoot, a soft rust-colored expanse that spread beneath the trees. The taller pines in this part of the forest had slender, spare trunks that admitted more of the gray daylight, and wide, swinging boughs that soared toward the sky.

"Hold," Gavin said. Just ahead, the tall pines thinned out, and the forest floor seemed to suddenly fall away at their feet. Gavin walked to the edge and saw that the ground sloped acutely downward into a rocky hill. He looked up to stare out at a vast, rugged, wild scene.

Thin mist drifted over the hills, and the damp, cold air promised further rain. Beyond the pine-sheltered hilltop where Gavin stood, steep forested hills and craggy slopes rose through fog in a layered rhythm, winter-bare and forbidding.

"Bruce is here somewhere," Gavin mused as John approached. "Those hills could hide any number of men. There are countless caves out there. And the pine forests are so thick in places that a camp with a hundred men could not be found."

"I hear from the workmen at Kinglassie that the Bruce favors moving his camp each day. He's clever, is Bruce, and bold. Scotland can do well wi' such a king." He turned to Gavin. "Will you join Hastings's effort to interfere wi' that?" he asked bluntly.

Gavin frowned, staring ahead. "I think not," he said.

"A wee bit o' the rebel still in you, is it, lad?"

"Mayhap," Gavin said. "The years I spent as ambassador taught me to remain neutral in the midst of a hot dispute. But I have to say that I have gained even more respect for the Scottish cause." He looked down into the narrow valley that lay at the base of the hills, a wide space cut by a silver burn. He recognized the same burn that they had crossed weeks ago as they came near Kinglassie.

Now, through the vague mist, he saw three small figures on horses, picking their way along the rock-studded ground beside the water. At least one rider, he saw clearly, wore skirts rather than armor. "There they are," he said, pointing, "just heading home for Kinglassie."

John gazed downward. " 'Tis Dominy and Will, and wee Michaelmas," he said. "But—"

"Aye," Gavin said frowning. "Where is Lady Christian?"

THEY KNEW THEY WERE BEING WATCHED, had known it for a mile or more. The surrounding silence seemed as dense and mysterious as the ancient pines. Christian and Fergus and a few of the others rode on shaggy garron ponies between the wide, wet, out-spread branches, while the rest of the rebels walked, carrying weapons. A thick, fragrant carpet of pine needles muffled footfalls. No one spoke.

In the past hour, they had traveled over rough forest tracks and rocky slopes to reach this dark forest. She had seen, once, a wolf, lean and watchful, standing on a boulder in the distance; and she had heard the faint, haunting cry of a wildcat.

But after they had entered the pine forest, she had seen only endless depths of dark, thick evergreen branches and spare trunks, had heard only muffled hoofbeats and the constant sound of water as it rushed through burns, or burst from bare rock to form small waterfalls.

Now the sense of expectancy hung heavily in the piney air.

Christian pulled the hood of her cloak more closely about her face and shivered. The air was faintly misty and the chill had grown worse deeper into the day, a damp, wintry cold that cut through her cloak and clothing to ice her very bones. The wind was growing stronger, too. She longed to be home in front of a glowing hearth.

Frowning, she tucked one gloved hand inside her furlined coat, and wondered how Robert Bruce and his men had managed to survive these bitter winter weeks. Galloway had little snow in the winter compared to other parts of Scotland, but the damp could be bitter and uncomfortable. And the wintry gales were ferocious when they came, heavy with rain and icy winds.

She glanced at Fergus after a while. He nodded to her and angled his tonsured head; he was telling her to look. She turned to do so.

Three men stepped out from behind two enormous fir trees. They looked wild and threatening, wearing leather hauberks beneath wrapped and belted plaids, their heavily muscled legs bare. Long, unkempt hair and beards added to their savage appearance. They held lance-tipped staves crossways in front of them and stood firm, blocking the path just ahead of the party.

"Highlanders," she murmured to Fergus. "My father and brothers were like these men."

Fergus nodded. "The Bruce has several Highlandmen with him. Come ahead, lass." Christian rode forward with him, and they halted their horses several feet away.

"What do you want here?" one of the Highlanders asked in Gaelic, his voice as heavy and deep and forbidding as his surroundings.

"I am Fergus Macnab, rector of Saint Bride's near Kinglassie. My sons Iain and Donal Macnab are with me."

"And I am Christian MacGillean of Kinglassie, cousin to Robert Bruce," she said in Gaelic, her voice firm and clear. "Who are you?"

The Highlander glanced at his companions, then looked back at her. "We knew your father and brothers, lady. And we are friends of your kinsman the king."

"Then you will be glad to know we ring news for my cousin, and men with horses and armor who wish to join his cause." The man grunted, and the three of them murmured to one another. They stepped back. "Come this way, just the two of you," the spokesman said. Two of the Highlanders stood back to stay with the newly arrived men.

Christian and Fergus dismounted and followed the Highlander between the sweeping branches. They entered a small clearing, walled on all sides by tall pines, the interior as dim as a cave. When Christian turned around, the Highland rebel had gone.

Within moments, the branches parted, and a man stepped into the clearing. Christian peered at him through the shadows. He was of medium height, his shoulders broad, his body thickly muscled beneath a leather hauberk and a ragged surcoat and cloak. His auburn hair gleamed, longer than he had ever worn it.

"Robert!" she breathed. Her cousin smiled and came forward, taking her in his arms, kissing her cheeks, his beard rough against her skin. He smelled of smoke and pines. She gripped his wide arms and smiled up at him.

"Christian," he murmured. "You are safe. Thank God." He hugged her again. "What news have you? Dear God, we starve for news here, for we can obtain only so much on our own. Messages are better than food and wine, some days." He took hold of her hand, greeting Fergus with a wide grin and a clasp of hands.

"Your sons are fine men," Robert Bruce said. "I have met six of them so far, and four of them are with me now."

"I have more, my lord," Fergus said. "Iain and Donal have come wi' us. And I hae two wee laddies at home who would join you tomorrow if they could." Robert laughed and motioned for them to sit on some rocks inside the circle of pines.

"I have a friend with me whom you may know," he said to Christian. "Robert Boyd."

She nodded. "He was with us at Kildrummy—but he was captured by the English when we were."

"Aye. But weeks later, he escaped, and traveled across Scotland to find me. So I know of the capture. I know King Edward has Elizabeth and Marjorie, and my sisters and Isabel of Buchan as well. But we have not heard what has happened since then." He looked at her, his handsome face somber, his gray eyes clear. "Christian, tell me. How did you gain your freedom? And what of the others? Are they alive?

"They are alive and well, my lord, though still confined," she said. He drew in a deep breath of relief, and she told him what he did not know: cages for two of the women, confinement for the others; the sweeping excommunication of many, and King Edward's continued insistence that the Scottish women were outlaws. She told him briefly of her illness and how she came back to Kinglassie, married once again to an English knight.

"Gavin Faulkener," Robert said, nodding. "A tall blond man? I met him years ago at Edward's court. But I had heard he was exiled after Berwick, though the king made him an ambassador later. Some of our Scottish nobles traveled to France last year to seek aid from the French king, and spoke with Faulkener there. He seemed more sympathetic to the Scots than to the English. How is it he is at Kinglassie?"

"Recently Edward gave him Kinglassie, and custody of me."

"I think, from what I recall of him, you could not be in better hands, though he is English." She nodded, knowing how full and rich that truth was. "Now tell me what other news you bring."

Christian looked at Fergus. The priest glanced around the clearing and then leaned forward. "We are private here, my lord king? Good. The only word we've learned is that the English mean to lure you out into the open to fight full combat. These Highland mountain goat methods o' yours are muckle frustrating to them." Robert chuckled, and Fergus continued. "The English king is furious, and his ire makes him verra ill. Some say he'll nae live long. He pressures his commanders to drive you south, where their troops are thickest. They mean to engage you and your men in formal battle if they can, to wipe you out by sheer numbers and the strength of horse and armor."

"They would have the clear advantage over us. So we shall keep to the mountains for yet a while, and keep to our small skirmishes."

"Aye, my lord. Now then, there is a man, a carpenter from Kinglassie, who has been among your men—"

"He is a distant cousin of mine. What of him?"

Fergus lowered his voice and explained quickly what he and Christian had overheard. "So be wary o' this man," Fergus said.

"I will," Robert said, leaning forward, snapping a little twig in his hand. "I surely will. Now, tell me one other thing. Christian—what of the gold? Have the English found it? They have been persistent about that since Henry found out about it a few years ago.

She shook her head. "Henry nearly tore the castle apart looking. And with the rebuilding at Kinglassie of late, still naught has been found. I dinna know where else to look. The fire must have destroyed it."

"If we cannot make use of that gold, 'tis well the English cannot either. So be it." Robert sighed, and then smiled at her. "Have I told you how much I appreciate your loyalty to me? I know 'twas a hard task for you to burn your own home. Harder still, for you to be caged like a beast. Dear God, cousin, I am glad you are well now, as glad as I am to hear that my wife and child, and the others, are still living."

He laid his large, strong hand on her arm. She looked up and saw that his eyes were misted over. "So many of my friends and family have endured pain and come to grief because of my decision to take my place as king of Scots," he said softly. "So many have died. Christopher Seton, my sister's husband, who was like my brother. John Seton, Simon Fraser, Alex Scrymgeour, all executed. And my brothers—my own brothers, all dead now but for Edward, who is one of my most loyal men—" He paused, and Christian saw that he could not speak further. She laid her hand over his, and he bowed his head.

"Robert, my lord king. We do this because we know 'tis worth our lives and our hearts," she said. "You have earned our loyalty. You fight from the heather and the forests, and risk your life every day for Scotland and the Scots. This final agony, these last months of hardship, will surely bring us our freedom from the English. You are the truest, bravest king of Scots, my lord cousin. And many people trust you. Many more will follow you. Wait and see that 'tis true."

Robert watched her through eyes as gray and deep as mist. "You lift my heart, cousin, with your news, and your gift of men, and your loyalty."

She thought of words she had heard once before. "You are the kind of man who follows his heart, and we follow you, and trust you." Robert smiled and pressed her hand gently.

They sat together silently, all three, while the wind whistled through the sweeping, heavy branches, and a few drops of icy rain began to spatter on the stones around them. Christian pulled up her hood against the drizzle.

"Thank you both for all that you have done for me," Robert Bruce said. "You've brought me men and horses and weapons, which I sorely need. And your show of loyalty means as much to me as any number of sword-arms ready at my back."

"This icy, miserable weather must be a trial for all of you," Christian said. "How have you fared these winter months?"

He shrugged. "I may be king, but I am a poor provider for these men in the forest. We have been starving of late, and freezing in the nights, in small caves with low hearth fires because we might be seen. I only hope the winter is a short one. There are only a few small crofters near here who can give hospitality to so many of us. We have little hope of finding good shelter from the coming gale."

Fergus glanced up at the gray sky visible above the dense treetops. "A winter gale is coming soon, though, and nae doubt."

"If there is anything I can do, my lord cousin, please tell me," Christian said. "I will send Fergus's sons with some sacks of barley, and some blankets—"

"You likely have barely enough for yourselves," Robert said. Then he frowned. "There may be one way you could help us."

"Anything, my lord," Fergus said.

"Christian's father once told me years ago, of the sally port through the rock beneath Kinglassie, near the level of the loch. I believe there is a tunnel from the outside that leads to an underground room."

She nodded hesitantly. "The tunnel has been closed for many years. But we use the chamber for storage now" she said.

" 'Twould be a fine place for a group o' men to seek shelter from a winter gale," Fergus said.

"Thank you," the king said. "I appreciate it deeply."

Christian stared at Fergus, and then turned to her cousin. "But my husband is English—"

"He has no need to know this," Robert said. "There are only the few of you, and some workmen at Kinglassie. 'Twill be a safe place for us at night."

"But the English are patrolling the area," she said. " 'Tisna safe at Kinglassie. What if Hastings returns with his men?"

"Would you rather have the king and his men hiding in the forest when the patrols are searching this area?" Fergus asked.

"And what better place for us to hide than under the heels of our enemies?" Robert asked.

"They can get in and out through the loch entrance without being seen," Fergus said. "Gavin need never learn o' this. And you willna even know when they come, or when they leave."

"Christian, my life is in your hands," Robert said quietly.

She furrowed her brow in confusion. "But my lord, my husband's life could be forfeited if this were to be discovered by the English—"

"I promise you he will never know. And you have my promise that I will do my best to protect the safety of Kinglassie and everyone in it."

"But I fear for my husband's life as much as for yours," she said.

"Remember that a traitor to the English is a hero to the Scots," the king said.

"But death makes traitors and heroes equal."

"I know," Robert Bruce said sadly. "That I have learned too well."

CHAPTER NINETEEN

"**I** MUST TELL GAVIN," Christian said.

Fergus looked alarmed. "Heaven save us, he's a Sasunnach, no matter how much I like the man, or how much you have come to adore him. You cannot tell him whom you have seen this day." Fergus spoke in quick Gaelic, earnest and low, frowning as he guided his sturdy garron pony alongside hers.

She shook her head. "You and my lord cousin have coaxed me into agreeing to this. But it frightens me to think that Robert and his men might be discovered at Kinglassie. This is too much of a risk for them—and for Gavin."

Fergus sent her a somber glance. "You could hardly stop the Bruce. He could have commanded you to allow him in, but instead he asked—"

"And you told him he could," she interjected.

"He already knew how to get into the storage room. That lochside tunnel is perfect for his needs. With a small boat or two, he and his men could safely hide there, and you would never know."

"Then I wish he had not told me," she grumbled.

"Christian, you must not tell Gavin about this," Fergus said. "You owe your loyalty first to your king and cousin. This is a harmless thing, a few nights out of the storm. Bruce and his men will only sleep there. No one need ever know but us."

She sent him a sour glance, and sighed. "Well, I will at least have to tell Gavin where I have been this day."

Fergus sighed. "Think of the price, Christian. We do not know how far your husband leans to the English side."

"We do not," she admitted. "But he may suspect something. Moira said that Dominy already took the children home to Kinglassie because she did not trust the weather. They will be at the castle by now."

"And your husband will not be pleased when he sees that you are not with them," Fergus said.

"He will not." She looked ahead. "We are no more than a league or so from Kinglassie now. There is the burn that we must follow and cross."

"Pray then that Gavin Faulkener will be concerned only with your health in this cold weather, and not with where you've been."

Christian smiled. "I am not worried, Fergus. He is far more inclined to side with the Scottish cause than you know. I think he would fight with us himself, if he had not given his oath to the English king. His mother was of good Celtic blood."

"I know. John told me that he and Gavin's mother descended from Celtic princes. Saint Columba himself is part of that line, generations ago."

"And holy Columba was born to Irish royalty, founded the Scottish Church, and was a visionary and a healer," she recited, grinning at him. "You have taught your parish well."

"A man of miracles, Columba was. Your husband could not have finer blood than that."

"And any Celtic priest would quickly forgive him his English blood in light of that lineage," she said, teasing him.

"He's a good man, your Gavin of Kinglassie, and your children will be descendants of the holy Columba. I'm pleased." Fergus grinned at her. "But I do not think he should know the whole truth of what we've done."

Frowning at that, she did not answer. She had been feeling the keen tug of her differing loyalties throughout the day. The devotion she felt for Scotland and for her cousin's cause was the keen, purposeful love of heart joined with mind.

But the true fire of her soul, the flame that lit the depths of her heart, had been kindled by a man in whom mingled Celtic and Sasunnach blood.

But to which did she owe her fealty? She sighed, unable to answer that, aware of the insistent, and different, pull of both.

Scanning the moor ahead, she saw the bitter, ominous color of the darkening sky, and felt the wind slice at her like cold steel. "After we cross the burn, Kinglassie is not far," she told Fergus. "Dark is coming quickly. You ride home, then. I will be fine from here."

Fergus shook his head. "I will escort you home."

"But the gale—"

"*Ach*, I can make it home before the gale strikes. Come ahead."

Shivering, she nodded and urged her horse ahead, while Fergus rode in tandem. They guided the ponies alongside the burn. In the distance, she could see the twin pools, their surfaces roughened by the rising winds.

Hearing shouts behind her, she turned to see several men, armored and mounted on destriers, riding toward her. Christian cast an anxious glance at Fergus.

"Hastings' men," he muttered. "What do they want? They must be heading for Kinglassie, too, if they mean to cross the burn ahead. But they are not traveling companions that I would care to have."

"We will go on, then," Christian said, and clicked her tongue. Her horse moved ahead. After a moment, she turned again.

Hastings' men bore down on them, showing no signs of slowing. Christian's pony nickered softly, growing restless beneath her. She dug in her knees and the garron surged ahead, heavy, powerful, an animal accustomed to rough terrain. Beside her, Fergus's horse galloped in time with hers.

"Halt!" one of the soldiers called. She saw Fergus lean forward, urging his mount to greater speed. She did the same, her cloak beating out behind her, the icy wind biting her cheeks and hands.

But the English chargers, with their longer legs, were closing on them. Had they been in the hills, the garrons would have pulled far ahead, for English horses, weighted down by armored riders, did not fare well on boggy or rocky ground. But here, beside the wide stream, where the ground rolled on, the larger horses had the advantage.

Seeing the fording place ahead, Christian guided her garron toward the water. Both her horse and Fergus's leaped into the water at the same time, rushing side by side through the cold wash. Her pony soon cleared the opposite bank with a forceful leap, Fergus just behind her. They surged forward again, riding toward a stand of bare oaks, crushing over old bracken, creating enough noise to drown the howl of the rising wind.

Behind them, the English soldiers had crossed the burn and were heading for the wood, pursuing them relentlessly. She flashed an anxious, frightened glance at Fergus, whose face was set in grim determination as he concentrated on the path ahead.

All they had to do, she thought breathlessly, was reach Kinglassie. A mile, no more, through the oakwood and up a hill, through more trees, then down again, and Kinglassie's gates would, pray God, open quickly. Gavin would be there. They would soon be safe. Her hands fisted tightly on the reins and she stretched forward into the wind.

Shouts came again behind her, raw and threatening. Hearing the bellowing breath of the charger behind her, she dared not glance back. Leaning forward, pressing her horse onward, she heard a guttural cry and knew Fergus had been pulled fiercely from his mount.

She turned, a wild, quick glance. Fergus was gone. Several horses bore down on her. Ten, twenty, so many she could not count them. The heavily armored riders on their backs loomed huge, a terrifying spectacle in the gathering shadows of dusk.

She only needed to make it through the wood, she thought; she only had to reach the hill that would lead to Kinglassie. The garron was a good climber, and would gain ground over the English horses, and allow her to get away.

But a moment later, someone reached out a hand, huge and ironlike, and yanked her from the garron's back. She twisted savagely in the air and fell hard to the ground. She wanted to get up, wanted to run, but she needed precious moments to catch her breath.

The rain had begun, hard, icy needles that pelted her, hurt her skin, struck and soaked into the sodden earth. As she raised up from her knees, the long, muscular legs of the English chargers circled her and closed in, surrounding her like a cage.

Fear clawed at her gut, threatening to overtake her. She nearly buckled to the ground as the haunting, terrifying memory of timber and iron bars slammed through her mind.

Forcing herself to stand on unsteady legs, she glared upward at their grim, anonymous faces. Fifteen, eighteen in all, she counted. Her gaze slid around the circle they formed. There was nowhere she could run. They would snatch her if she tried, uproot her like a flower stem.

Dhia, she thought; she could not let them take her.

"What do you want?" she asked, her voice hoarse with heavy breathing, and with the weight of her fear.

"Lady Christian," a cold, deep voice said, "King Edward charges you with outlawry. You are a prisoner of England." The man who spoke dismounted and came toward her.

She tensed where she stood, fisting her hands. Freezing rain slid down her brow, down her cheeks. She brushed furiously at it to clear her vision.

The soldier came toward her and clamped his mailed fist around her arm. Christian screamed, an anguished, angry cry; and tore loose, backing away. She spit out sharp Gaelic oaths as three more men dismounted and advanced toward her.

"Hold, lady," one of them said quietly as if he were talking to a wild horse. "Hold. We have orders to take you to Oliver Hastings at Loch Doon Castle. We have no wish to hurt you. Just come."

"I willna!" she screamed in English, so that they would have no doubt. She backed away further, hair hanging loose and wild, cloak twisted, hands fisted. Weaponless, she had only her anger and fear to hold them off. The soldiers who had dismounted looked dumbfounded and uncertain. Those on horseback sat and stared at her. Stepping back, she shouted at them, wild Gaelic curses, her eyes darting quickly, looking for a way out.

She saw Fergus come to his feet, far behind the circle of English soldiers whose combined attention was centered on her. They must have thought him unconscious. He came cautiously forward, but she knew he had no weapon of his own.

Christian glanced behind her. In a gap between the horses, she saw a short stretch of rough grasses and rocks that led to the shore of one of the pools. She would jump into icy water and drown before she would let the English take her again.

Turning, she ran between the horses, and spun around as she reached the shore. Her heels sank in the boggy ground, which was spongy with recent rains. She stepped back again, into the cold sucking mud at the pool's edge.

Someone swore. "Get her, you idiots! 'Tis just one woman!"

A quick glance showed her that she was a few feet away from the narrow rocky bar that separated the twin pools. She angled toward that and moved backwards, onto a slippery ledge of rock and mud little wider than a fallen tree trunk.

One of the soldiers cursed and stomped toward her, but his heavy armor pulled him ankle-deep into the muck. He roared and pulled his foot out, cursing violently as he backed away to solid ground. "Come here, you damned Scottish whore!" he shouted.

She edged back further. She saw Fergus behind the soldiers, a little dazed, one hand to his head. Unaware that he was there, the English, mounted and on foot, came toward her.

The chargers, loaded down with leather armor and carrying men in full chain mail with weapons, sank their hooves into the oozy, icy stuff and could go no further. Whinnying and struggling, they backed away.

Those on foot fared a little better. Only one man managed to come as far as the slippery ridge, placing one mail covered foot carefully in front of the other.

She backed away, hearing the pelting rain, and beneath it the deeper rush of water. To either side of her lay the twin pools. Just behind her, she suddenly saw a gap in the bar, where water flowed through to join the pools.

She could not cross it without turning, and the soldier was

coming closer. Swearing gutturally, he tried to grab her.

Then, as if the heavens had suddenly struck out on her behalf, he fell forward, his outstretched arms grazing her cloak as he went down. An arrowshaft protruded from his neck. He rolled slowly into the water and sank into the pool's depth.

She stared after him, stunned. Then she looked up to see chaos among the soldiers left on shore. Two more fell from their horses as she watched, dead before they hit the ground, as arrows struck into the vulnerable places in their armor, at the neck and under the arm.

Standing in the center of the narrow bar, one fisted hand to her mouth, her legs trembling, Christian felt uncertain and frightened. She looked around for the archers, but the bare, forbidding tangle of oak and scrub beyond the water seemed deserted. She wondered if her cousin and his men were attacking these English knights from the cover of the trees.

As she watched, Fergus leaped forward and pulled another soldier from his horse, throwing the man so off balance that the priest was able to grab his sword and knock the man in the head. Roaring and raising his newly acquired sword, Fergus turned to fight another soldier. Though he was surrounded, he circled, sword out, fighting ferociously, managing to keep them away.

But she knew he could not do it for long.

Another knight jumped from his horse and ran toward Christian, shouting curses in English. She understood them all too well, and knew that if he caught her, she would not make it even as far as Carlisle.

Hearing another shout behind her, she turned.

Gavin and John raced across the bar from the opposite side, running in single file toward her, their booted feet sloshing through water and mud.

"Out of the way!" Gavin shouted. "Get out of the way!" He gripped a longbow in his hand; a sword angled from his low belt, and a quiver of arrows bounced at his back. With a long, sure leap, he cleared the rushing stream between the pools, and grabbed at her arm, spinning her neatly as he ran past and left her standing there, astonished.

John came just behind him, landing heavily, barely clearing the stream. She reached out to help him, grabbing his arm, nearly falling. As he raced past, she stood there for a moment, stunned, then tore along the ridge after them.

At the shore, she held back, watching as John stood at the fringes of the confusion and began to fire off sure and deadly arrows. Two more soldiers dropped as they were hit. Drawing his sword, Gavin moved like lightning among the men and the horses toward Fergus. At the edge of the clearing, John continued his succession of arrows, shielding Gavin's advance.

Picking up another sword from a dead English knight, Gavin used two as deftly as one, slicing at an opponent, turning to wound another who came up behind him. Fergus, tonsure pale in the gray rain, stood in the center of it all, looking like an enraged Celt. He now had a steel mace, and raised it high over his head. Roaring like anything but a priest, he slammed it into whatever English heads and shoulders came near him.

Christian stayed where she was, unable to look away. Horses screamed and reared, blades clashed, men shouted and struggled with the three men who defended her and each other. Rain streamed down like a filmy, silky veil, but the blood and the steel shone bright.

Gavin turned just as two soldiers converged on him. Christian cried out, unable to stand helpless any longer. Running forward, she was determined to grab a sword.

"Gavin!" she screamed. "Gavin!" A discarded battle-ax lay on the ground and she picked it up, nearly reeling under the solid weight of it.

"Christian! Get back!" Gavin shouted, glancing toward her.

"Gavin!" she screamed again, lifting the cumbersome thing, ready to swing it, planting her feet wide on the slippery grass as a soldier came toward her. Gavin shouted her name again.

She swung hard, nearly overspinning as the ax brought her around with its own force. An advancing knight jumped back in surprise. Breathing heavily, she righted the thing and aimed to swing again.

The soldier grinned and reached for her. Christian aimed for his ankles, and he went down hard as the ax knocked his feet off balance. He fell, bellowing at her as she ran past, and grabbed at her skirts. When she stumbled, he slammed her to the ground and rolled his crushing weight onto her. His heavy hands slipped around her throat.

She tried to scream but could not, her breath blocked, searing her lungs. She groped at his hands, kicking and struggling, but his weight and strength held her down.

Then the soldier arched back, his armor biting into her torso, into her hips. He fell heavily forward, limp, and his hands slid slowly from her neck.

John stood over him, breathing hard, holding out a hand to her. She took it and came to her feet.

"Get out o' here, lassie," he growled, pushing her toward the edge of the circle. He spun away as another English knight came toward him, and Christian ran toward the shelter of the trees. There, she stopped in astonishment.

Hardly visible in the dusky, rainy light, not far from where she stood, a group of men stepped silently out of the oakwood and raised their bows, releasing a stinging, clattering hail of arrows. Several more men emerged from the winter wood, swords drawn. They ran past her to enter the struggle alongside Gavin and Fergus.

One man, wearing his sword strapped to his back, turned to look at Christian and raised his hand in a salute. She blinked wide, her mouth open in surprise.

Her cousin Robert grinned at her and turned away.

"MY THANKS," Gavin called breathlessly to the bearded man in a ragged cloak and leather armor who had suddenly, inexplicably, appeared to fight at his side. Several men had joined the skirmish from somewhere, but Gavin was not about to stop and question it, or wonder at it. He was only grateful for the help.

He struck out deftly at his English opponent, striking him hard in the shoulder, and the man clattered down to the earth with a scream. Turning, Gavin assisted the ragged knight and others in beating back several English soldiers who advanced into the midst of the armed woodsmen. With the help of these strangers, Gavin, Fergus, and John soon surrounded the English, outnumbering them.

Glancing at one another, the English knights suddenly turned and ran, dragging with them their wounded. The other survivors had already scrambled up onto their mounts, and were shouting to their companions to hurry.

As the Englishmen retreated through the muck and the rain, Gavin looked around. Fifty, perhaps sixty men stood on the muddy ground where the skirmish had taken place. All of them were clearly Scotsmen.

They were as ragged as their leader, the knight who stood beside Gavin. Most of them were bearded and long-haired, with shabby cloaks and tunics; their armor, what there was of it, was tarnished and piecemeal. Plaided Highlanders stood among them, taller and more fierce in appearance than the rest, wearing quilted coats beneath their plaids and strange conical-shaped helmets that made them look even taller.

The men stared at him silently, and Gavin stared back.

He turned slowly. Christian, disheveled and pale, watched him, her eyes large and frightened. Fergus and John stood with her, and his uncle placed his hand on her shoulder.

Beside him, the knight sheathed his sword. Gavin turned again, his movements curiously slow. "Robert Bruce?" he asked.

The man looked at him, his gray eyes somber, and nodded. "Gavin Faulkener," he said. "We met once, long ago, at Edward's court in London. I know your reputation."

"As I know yours," Gavin said, smiling. "You have saved all of us here. I owe you a debt, my lord."

Bruce shrugged as if the debt were small. "I am glad to help my cousin and her husband. And I would rather have you at my back, man, than facing me with a sword. You fight like the wrath of God."

Gavin laughed ruefully. "When I saw those men threatening my wife, I surely felt that." He drew in a long breath. The battle-blood that had flowed through him had left his muscles trembling, his breath heaving, his heart pounding. Everything had an aura of unreality, like a dream played out in slow, vivid detail.

Gavin looked at Robert Bruce, the one man in Scotland he had been ordered to capture. And he held out his hand. "If ever you need help, my lord—"

"Then I will call on you." Bruce clasped his hand and smiled again, a mischievous glimmer. Then he lifted his hand to Christian in farewell, and turned to motion toward his men.

Between the rain and the darkening shadows, Bruce and the rest stepped into the tangled oakwood and disappeared.

Gavin shoved his wet, straggling hair back with his hand, and looked around. His gut turned with anguish at what he saw. He hated the aftermath of battle, had always hated it. Four Englishmen lay slain, men none of them knew, but men all the same. Of the ones who had retreated, many of those, he knew, were wounded.

Christian came toward him, and he held out his arm. She came under it, wrapping her arms around his waist as he pulled her close. She hid her face in his tunic and clung, while icy rain pelted down over their heads. He eased his hand in circles over her back, and rested his cheek on her head. Looking up, he saw Fergus and John approach, pulling hoods over their heads against the rain.

"We will surely hear from Hastings on this," Gavin said.

"Did they recognize us?" John asked.

"I have no idea," Gavin said. "Right now, I hardly care. This is just one more issue between Oliver Hastings and me. No man harms my wife and lives."

Christian looked up at him. "But we are safe," she said. "None of us were wounded, and they are gone. Dinna talk of revenge or hate. I want to go home."

"Christian," Gavin said. "Whatever were you doing out here in this poor weather, when Dominy and the others had already reached Kinglassie?"

"We were delayed," Fergus said quickly.

"What delayed you?"

"I have reinstated your wife into the Scottish Church," Fergus said. Christian nodded.

"You performed a sacred ritual, and then came out here and slayed men like a warrior?" Gavin asked. "Quite versatile. I am amazed."

"We Scots, we are an amazement," Fergus said, and grinned.

"Gavin," John said. His low tone caught Gavin's attention. "Listen. There are wolves nearby." They stood still, and soon heard a plaintive howl that mingled with the whine of the wind. Gavin thought he saw the glimmer of slitted eyes through the tangled bare forest scrub.

"Grab the horses. We'll go back," Gavin ordered. He helped Christian mount a charger left by one of the slain English knights, and mounted another himself. He spoke quietly with Fergus for a moment, who promised to send some villagers out the next morning to tend to the bodies of the slain and bring them back to Loch Doon Castle.

"Gavin," Christian said, "those men who helped us—"

"I know who they were, Christian," he said softly. "I know well who they were. Let's go home, now." He lifted the reins and urged his horse forward, riding through the sleeting rain.

Home. The simple word he had uttered to her chanted in his head like a benediction as they rode toward Kinglassie. Truly his home now. And he would do whatever was necessary to protect it, and to protect those who were dear to him.

He glanced at Christian, riding alongside of him, her hood shielding her head. For a brief moment, he reached out through the dark and the rain, and laid his hands over hers in a firm, reassuring grip.

CHAPTER TWENTY

"I DINNA NEED IT," Christian said stubbornly.

"You need it," Gavin said. "Undress, and do it."

She looked over at the tub, with its tented, dark interior. Fear, harsh and unexpected, swamped her. She thought of the tight space she had stood in today, surrounded by the English horses. And she thought of the cage. Memories of that vile place had not tormented her for weeks, but now came rushing back.

"I willna," she said. "I am tired."

He sighed. "We are all tired, lady. Exceeding tired. But you have been coughing since we got back, and need the steam."

She shook her head, feeling foolish, but feeling compelled to resist. "I willna. 'Tis too small a space."

He tilted his head in puzzlement. "What?"

"Like the cage," she whispered.

"No one will cage you again, Christian," he said softly.

"Hastings sent his men out—"

"They'll not take you again. Do you think I would allow that?" He stepped toward her. "Come, lady." His voice was gentle and deep. "I will get in with you, if you like." There was a gentle tease in his tone.

She laughed ruefully, embarrassed at her foolishness. "Then 'twould truly be cramped in there," she said. She blushed, feeling like a child frightened of the darkness inside a curtained bed. "You think me foolish. You have no fears—else you couldna have fought as you did today."

"Everyone has fears, lady," he said softly.

"What are yours?" she asked.

He watched her. "Losing you," he said finally. "Now get in the bath."

Christian heaved a long breath. "*Ach,* very well, then," she grumbled, and slid her gown up over her head, tossing it down on the floor. "I wouldna want you to think me cowardly."

He laughed softly. "I would never think that."

"I dinna need this steam bath," she said, mumbling as she lifted her white undertunic over her head. She could feel his gaze on her.

"Mayhap I shall take this bath with you after all," he said, the timbre of his voice suddenly lower. He stepped forward and swept her up into his arms.

She gasped in surprise and looped her arms around his neck, her bare breasts crushed to his chest. Then she pulled slightly away. "*Ech*, you are wet and muddy, still, in that tunic."

"Then I will take it off," he said, and lowered her, bottom first, into the water, raising a fair amount of warm splash. She sank to her shoulders as the hot, silky water enveloped her.

Glancing at the tent overhead, she breathed out her relief. Only warmth and quiet here, and no threat. The memory of the cage had frightened her, and exhaustion had enhanced that fear.

Gavin tore off his tunics, boots, and breeches, flinging them away. As he parted the tent entrance to climb into the tub, she saw the hard contour of his body, straight and tall. His muscles gleamed in the low light before he hunkered down beside her. His presence was reassuring, and rendered the small space completely harmless—and pleasantly crowded.

The round wooden tub was large enough to accommodate two people if legs were obligingly bent. A thick linen sheet was draped inside, and the hot water, its depth nearly overspilling the tub, softened the cloth until it billowed sensuously against her skin.

She turned to Gavin, her knee pressed to his leg, her foot against his hip. He leaned back, resting his arms along the tub rim, and sighed deeply. The sound sent delightful shivers through her body.

Overhead, the linen tent trapped the warmth and blocked the light. Swirling steam clouds filled the darkness, and the subtle scent of herbs tossed into the water, dried lavender and roses petals, made her senses spin. She breathed in, leaned back, and began to relax.

Rain pounded on the wooden roof overhead, and the wind shuddered heavily against the tower as the gale released its force outside. But within the steamed enclosure Christian felt a gradually increasing calm. Her fears began to disappear, lost in the lapping water and the slow count of Gavin's contented breathing.

Feeling the simple pleasure of the heated water on her tired muscles, she realized that Gavin must have a profound need for physical ease after the events just past. She leaned against the side of the tub silently, not speaking, wanting to allow him perfect quiet.

He had fought with the strength of demons against the English soldiers who had threatened her. She had seen murderous resolve in his eyes and resounding courage in his actions. He had risked his life to protect her. She felt humbled.

She had not yet had a chance to tell him of her meeting with Robert Bruce. Touching the lean, powerful muscles along his arm, she sensed both his keen strength and his deep fatigue. Perhaps this was not the time, but she wanted to be honest with him.

Fergus and Robert Bruce together had placed a burden of silence and loyalty on her shoulders that she had not asked for. She felt a deepening loyalty to her husband, but his Englishness still frightened her. She simply could not judge how he would react. But she had to try.

"Gavin," she said softly.

He leaned back his head, eyes closed. "Mmm?"

"You saved my life this day," she said. "Thank you."

"Robert Bruce saved all of our lives," he murmured.

"We owe him a true debt," she began. "And I—"

He leaned forward through the water and the sultry darkness to place a finger against her lips. "Hush," he said. "We made a promise, here in this chamber, to have no king or realm here between us."

"But, Gavin, I want to tell you—"

"Later." He slid his fingers down her arm to rest his hand on her thigh, his thumb slowly circling. "I agree that we owe your cousin a debt. I hope there will be some way that we can repay him. But for this night, I do not wish to talk or think about what happened out there."

She hesitated, then nodded, stroking his arm. "Later, then," she said.

"Later," he said, his eyes closed. "Breathe in the steam. 'Twill help your cough."

"I dinna have a cough," she said, smiling, glad for his concern, and glad to abandon her troubling thoughts. She gave in to the pleasure of his hand slowly circling on her leg. Arching back her head, she sighed.

His fingers rubbed along her thigh and traced toward the crease of her hip. She let her fingers dance along the hard length of his thigh, slipping through the warm water, sliding along the soft hairs on his leg.

"I have grown accustomed to harp music while I enjoy my bath," he said, his voice light and teasing.

"I willna play for you just now," she said, feeling the water slip around her body, heated and silky.

"Will you not?" he asked, his voice low. He slid his fingertips up her hip, grazing over her ribs, his thumb touching the underside of one breast. She drew in a long breath as he defined the buoyant shape with his fingers, and scooped its soft weight into his hand. She felt a delicious tingle rush throughout her body; against his palm, her nipple grew firm.

"I willna play for you," she said breathily. "I want to stay in here." She moved her hand. Beneath her exploring fingers, the silky, hard length of him swelled suddenly for her.

"Do you?" he whispered, a near growl. His fingertips swirled over her breasts, coaxing her nipples to react. Sucking in her breath, she tossed her head back. "Then come here," he murmured.

Reaching out, he took her around the waist and pulled her

closer. Water sloshed and waved around them, calming as she set-tled over his lap, facing him, her knees raised, her breasts cresting the water.

He circled his hands around her back and hips and leaned his head down to take one firm nipple with his mouth. She cried out softly and put her hands around his head, drawing him into the succor of her breasts, opening her legs wider over his lap.

His rigid, muscled length nudged at her, and she lifted her hips, fitting herself gently over him. He moaned low in his throat and kissed her, thrusting with his tongue as he gave a playful push with his hips. She gasped; he was hard and engorged, exquisitely silky and hot, pulsing between her legs.

He trailed his lips along her throat to one breast, circling the turgid nipple with his moist, warm tongue. She moaned and arched back, and a flush of joy, like the first tint of dawn, washed through her body. She wanted to meld fully with him; she want-ed him inside her desperately, and would not wait.

Easing over him, she pushed, and the hot, wet surge brought a husky groan from him. The wash of pleasure that cascaded through her body was sudden and intense. Heat surrounded her, filled her, soothed and caressed her. Sultry steam, hot water, his hands at her hips, his lips lingering over her breasts, blended and melted into a blissful harmony of sensation.

He pushed deeper, each thrust stoking the exhilarating heat inside of her. Rocking with him, feeling a wondrous, vital flame grow from the heat between them, she sought its brightest center with every breath, every motion of her body.

As he slipped his tongue into her willing mouth, plunging there, as he pressed her hips to his, she wanted, suddenly and desperately, to give herself to him utterly. She wanted to use this silent, beautiful way to express her love and her devotion.

Surging toward him, she offered him the pure joy that swelled through her; pulling back, she drew elemental strength from him, as the vigor of his body poured into hers. And for one soaring instant, her spirit flamed beside his and then merged, until the giver and the gift were one.

"GRANDFATHER, FATHER, SON," Christian told Michaelmas, plucking groups of harp strings as she spoke. "Those are the lower strings, the male sounds. Daughter, mother, grandmother"—she plucked the corresponding notes—"are the higher, the female sounds. Try it." She shifted the harp toward her daughter.

Michaelmas rested her small hands on the strings and plucked the groups, making tight little faces as she did so. The wires resonated faintly, some louder than others. One or two sour tones rose above the rest. Michaelmas winced and sucked on one finger, glancing up at her mother.

" 'Twas fine," Christian said. "Now remember to use your fingernails to play," she continued, as she adjusted the girl's hand position. "The sound will be much louder and richer."

"Grandfather, father, son," Michaelmas repeated carefully as she ran through the groups of strings again, lower to upper. When she was done, she plucked at the two center wires. "What are these, then? They sound alike."

"Tradition says that those two wires should be tuned to the drone of a beehive, and to each other," Christian answered. "I like to think of them as the heart of the harp, or as lovers, for they ring together." She drew a deep breath as she remembered the harmony of pleasures that she and Gavin had shared last night. "Try the pairs again, now."

While Michaelmas practiced, Christian yawned behind her hand and stretched her shoulders and neck a little. After an exhilarating, exhausting night, she had awoken late this morning to find that Gavin had already left their bed. Even now, well into the afternoon, she had not seen him yet, though she knew he had spent most of the morning in the great hall, discussing repairs with the stonemasons and the blacksmith.

Early in the day, Fergus had arrived with his two younger sons, and had sought her out to remind her to keep her silence about Robert Bruce. She had snapped, a little irritably, that she had had no chance to speak of it. Neither she nor Fergus knew if Bruce and his men had actually gone through the lochside tunnel to seek shelter in the underground room.

But against the window shutters, she could hear heavy rain. She began to hope that her cousin and his men had gone into the snug hideout. In this weather, there would be no English patrols searching for them, and none coming to Kinglassie.

A light tapping on the door startled her. She rose and opened the door to John, Fergus, and Will.

"Lady Christian," John said, nodding. "Is Gavin here?"

She shook her head. "He was with Master Tam and the masons in the hall," she said. "Perhaps they went to look at the south tower."

Michaelmas plucked the strings loudly, and stopped them with her hands. Those who stood at the door looked over at her.

" 'Twas a fine practice," Christian said.

"Aye, good," Will said. "Like cats."

"Hush, lad," John said from the corner of his mouth.

Michaelmas seemed not to have heard. "I could do better," she said, "if my smallest fingers were not so crooked." She held them up. Both fingers were delicately curved inward.

"She has crooked wee fingers?" John asked.

"Aye, see," Michaelmas said, holding them up.

"You do, lass," John said thoughtfully. "Such a thing runs in my family."

"And she'll soon have crookedy nails from harping and harping," Will said, clawing his hands and grimacing fiercely. Michaelmas wrinkled her nose at him.

"Dinna tease the lassie," Fergus said, frowning. "Go and play now. Robbie and Patrick are waiting for you in the kitchens." Will nodded and turned to go. "And dinna think to go to the underground chamber," Fergus added. "Small lads canna play there alone." He shot a swift, meaningful glance at Christian.

"Dinna go there, Will," she said. The boy nodded, looking properly obedient, and ran down the steps.

"They'll go down there," Michaelmas said sagely. "Those laddies willna listen."

"Then you go after them and make certain they listen," Christian said. Michaelmas nodded eagerly and ran through the open doorway.

"She loves to be their conscience, and they dinna like that just now," John said, looking after her. "But one day those lads will fall over each other just to get one word from her. She's a beauty, that wee lassie." He glanced at Christian. "You dinna ken her parentage, then?"

Christian shook her head. "You know the story. But it doesna matter. She is my daughter. The angels gave her to me, I think. Even her name says so."

"Aye," John said, frowning slightly, looking thoughtful. "She's an angel's gift for certain."

A deep voice shouted up the steps, and Fergus stepped across the landing. "Gavin!" he called. "We'll be right down." He turned to Christian. "Your husband wants to see us in the great hall, my lady."

"SO MUCH RAIN," GAVIN SAID, shaking his head and turning away from the window in the great hall. "The workmen can scarcely walk through the courtyard for the mud." He scratched at his stubbled chin and peered at Christian and Fergus. "I thought you said that Galloway winters are mild."

"*Ach*," Fergus said complacently. " 'Tis just some rain and wind out there. And 'twill lessen soon. Though there'll be some flooding o' the burns and lochs."

Gavin looked out the window again. The rain sheeted down through gathering darkness. So much rain had prevented the carpenters and masons from working outside, although a good stock of timber and stone rubble had made it possible for them to complete some of the inside work while the storms continued.

He leaned his hands against the trestle table that had been set up in the finished hall chamber only the day before. "The head mason intended to begin the repairs to the southeastern tower this week," he said. "And Master Tam wants me to send someone to Ayr to purchase further supplies and order the chains for the portcullis. No one has gone yet due to the weather."

"Will you send John?" Christian asked. She sat beside Fergus in front of the gleaming stone frame of the new hearth, which contained a hot peat fire.

Gavin watched his wife appreciatively; she looked gentle and lovely in the dim honey-colored light. Recalling the comfort and passion that she had shared with him, he yearned to be alone with her now in their bedchamber. But there were practical concerns that required his attention.

He shook his head. "Nay, John will stay here. A messenger came in a little while ago from Hastings," he said. "I have sent John to speak with him further, and to see that the man is fed. I offered to give him a sleeping pallet in the gatehouse, but the messenger insists that Hastings wants him to ride back in this foul gale."

"You received a message?" Fergus asked.

"Aye. Hastings expects me to join him and other commanders at Ayr Castle within two days' time."

"Two days!" Christian said. "But the weather—"

"Is foul but will improve soon, as Fergus says. I must leave tomorrow. Hastings added, too, that Lady Christian is to be kept under watch. I agree. So you will come with me, my lady. John will stay here in charge of the castle and the repairs."

"Gavin—" she began. He sensed a protest, and held up his hand. "Since Hastings's men apparently have orders to capture you once again, I will bring you with me to Ayr. 'Tis the only way to know that you are safe."

"I willna go where English garrison a Scottish castle!"

"You will not be in Ayr Castle. I intend to leave you at a monastery, safe at prayer and good behavior, while I meet with Hastings and the other English commanders. That meeting should take but a day. And then we will go the market at Ayr to order the iron chain lengths, since Master Tam lacks sufficient iron to make it himself. We will be gone for no more than three or four days."

Christian nodded reluctantly. "There are many things we could use from the market stalls. I will go, then."

Gavin withdrew a folded parchment from inside the fur lining of the surtunic he wore over his black tunic for warmth. He slapped the page onto the table. "Hastings says here that he is outraged to learn that a group of Bruce's men, including Bruce himself, attacked a patrol of Hastings' own men only a mile from Kinglassie, just yesterday."

"Does he know who was involved?" Fergus said quickly.

"He mentions some new allies of Bruce. A blond man, he says, and an older man. Both, his men claim, have to be loyal Scottish knights because they fought with the Bruce that day. One of them, though, uses a longbow like an Englishman. Oh, and a wild-tempered Celtic priest was with them." He shot a stern glance at Fergus. "I am to look for them. Hastings suspects that the priest was the Scotsman he met here. He demands his capture."

Christian gasped. "But you canna arrest Fergus!"

"Or myself and John," Gavin said.

"Well. I've heard nae word o' such a rout," Fergus said. "I was in my church most o' that day. And Lady Christian was wi' me," He smiled innocently.

"By God's own body, you are a subversive Celtic priest," Gavin muttered.

"Hastings' men didna recognize you," Christian said.

"Apparently not," Gavin said. "Just as well. I meant only to protect my wife and my friends, and surely was not declaring for the Scottish cause. And I did not expect the extra help that came out of the wood." He cocked a brow at Fergus. "But I think you might know why Bruce was so close to Kinglassie."

"He is Christian's cousin," Fergus said. "He might have thought to pay her a wee visit." Beside him, Christian gasped.

Gavin shot him a disbelieving glance. "Just a wee visit to the lady and her English husband?"

Fergus shrugged. "Bruce has been in these hills for weeks. Mayhap 'twas only luck that sent him here when we needed help. Be grateful for it, man."

"I am very grateful. I owe Robert Bruce much for that day, and so I will not speak of this to Hastings. But I want to be certain that my priest"—Gavin cast a wry look at Fergus—"is not planning a revolt within these very walls."

"*Ach*, nay," Fergus said quickly. Christian shook her head.

"Good. I am risking King Edward's disapproval as it is. I am rebuilding Kinglassie, but I am also delaying the installation of Edward's garrison as long as I can."

"Would you be thinking o' declaring for the Scots, then?" Fergus asked hopefully.

"'Tis wiser and safer for all of us not to support either side just now," Gavin said. "I learned much as an ambassador, and one of the most useful lessons was the value of neutrality. I will wait and say naught, and rebuild slowly. Bruce needs more time to gather men and arms. By spring, he will likely be ready for open battle with the English. I think he will head north into the midlands of Scotland. Edward will pursue him there, and leave Kinglassie in peace."

"Edward will leave us alone only if he accepts that we canna find Kinglassie's gold," Christian said bitterly.

"I hear that King Edward is muckle furious that we Scots are going more and more to Bruce's side," Fergus said.

"True," Gavin said. "Bruce gathers support daily, and Edward's ire grows over that. But it may take a miracle for Bruce to actually gather enough men to drive the English out. There are still many Scots who favor Edward's rule."

"Or at least fear the English enough to place their fealty in the wrong place," Fergus muttered.

"You sound as if your fealty leans more toward the Scots, Gavin Faulkener," Christian said quietly.

He looked at her. "My oath was given to Edward of England."

"But your heart is not with his cause," Christian said. Gavin shrugged as he picked up the parchment and slid it back inside the pocket in his tunic lining.

"And now you owe Bruce a debt of honor," Fergus said.

"True," Gavin said. "Christian might be captured now, and you and John and I might be dead, if not for Bruce and his men."

Fergus leaned toward Christian. "We'll make a rebel of him yet," he murmured. Gavin noticed that his wife blushed a deep pink. He smiled ruefully, watching her with her friend, and said nothing. He was keenly aware that there was at least some truth in Fergus's words.

A swift pounding of feet on the steps outside the hall, accompanied by high-pitched screams, caused Gavin to turn, startled. Christian jumped to her feet as the door banged open. The children ran in, shrieking, their faces pale, eyes huge. Will gestured wildly toward the steps. Robbie and Patrick and Michaelmas pointed, too, all of them shouting at once.

"King Arthur!" Will shrieked. "King Arthur!"

"What do you mean?" Gavin asked, coming forward. He put a hand on Will's shoulder, and felt the boy tremble.

Robbie was leaping up and down. "The enchanted king! We saw him! We saw the enchanted king with all his knights!"

"Saw who?" Christian grabbed Robbie's arm. "Who did you see? Where?"

"King Arthur!" Michaelmas said, as excited as the others. "We saw a vision of them, all sleeping in the dark cave, just as the legend says."

"A vision? What legend?" Gavin demanded. "What in God's name is going on here?"

Fergus put an arm around Patrick. "Calm down, now. Tell us what you saw, and where."

"We saw a vision," Patrick said breathlessly. "A magical vision. Of King Arthur and all his knights. And their magic swords, and armor."

"Where?" Fergus asked sharply.

"In the underground chamber," Michaelmas said. "I'm sorry, Mother. They wouldna listen to me."

"You werena to go there," Christian said sternly.

"We only peeked in the room," Patrick said. "And that's when we saw the vision. A torch burning, and knights all sleeping in armor around their king, just as the legend says."

"What legend?" Gavin demanded again.

Christian sighed. "There is an old tale that somewhere in Scotland, King Arthur and his knights lie sleeping under an enchanted hill."

"And the underground room is inside a hill, the huge rock o' Kinglassie," Patrick said, nodding. "And we saw them, the great king and his knights, asleep until the people need them again."

"We didna disturb them," Robbie said. "We made nae noise."

"Jesu," Fergus said. He was looking intently at Christian.

Gavin watched her, too, and noticed that she bit at her lower lip and fisted a white-knuckled hand at her side.

"What is going on here?" he asked sharply.

Christian glanced at him, her green eyes a deep forest of secrets. "Gavin, I wanted to tell you—"

"Come see him!" Robbie said, pulling at Gavin's hand. Looking down at the child, Gavin then glanced at Fergus and Christian. Their faces looked sober and guilty. Something distinctly odd was happening here, and he did not understand it.

"Show me your King Arthur," he said to Robbie, and turned on his heel. The children followed him like puppies, eager and clumsy and noisy.

"He might not be there!" Will said. "'Twas a vision!"

"He'll be angry do you make a noise and wake him!" Robbie yelled. "You'll suffer the curse o' Merlin!"

"Then we'll all be quiet as mice, Robert Macnab, and you with us," Gavin said. "Now show me."

FOLLOWING IN GAVIN'S SWIFT WAKE, Christian chewed at her lip as they all walked down to the underground storage level. Surrounded by clattering children, she stayed beside Fergus, who carried a torch. His silence and tension mirrored her own. A few times she cast him an anxious glance, but he only frowned, or shrugged. Neither of them could stop Gavin. And both knew well the identity of the enchanted king under the hill.

She knew, too, that while she would trust Gavin with her own life, with her heart and soul, she still did not know how far his tolerance toward Scottish matters extended. His sense of personal honor was about to meet and be challenged by his sense of duty to England.

Reaching the hidden foyer at the end of the long tunnel, Gavin shushed the children, and slowly opened the huge door. He peered inside, holding back first one child, then another, as they squirmed to peek in beside him. Then he straightened and shut the door, turning to stare at Christian. She looked away quickly.

"He's there!" Robbie whispered loudly. "He's still there! And snoring, too!"

"Merlin was surely at Kinglassie, then, long ago," Will whispered in awe. "King Arthur sleeps beneath these very walls."

"Go back up to the hall," Gavin said firmly. The children began to protest, but he pointed silently, with unquestionable power. They bowed their heads and filed away.

Gavin folded his arms and stared at Christian. "A king sleeps in there for certain," he said. "And well you know it, lady."

She lowered her eyes, gulped, and nodded.

"But there is a sentinel in there, wide awake," Gavin said, frowning. " 'Tis a wonder he did not see the children the first time. He drew his sword when I cracked open the door, but he only nodded when he saw me."

"He recognizes you from the other day," Fergus muttered.

Gavin flashed him a grim look. "Ah, so you, too, know about this sleeping king? I am not surprised, somehow." He returned his stony glance to Christian. His face was lined with such anger that she tensed at the sight of it. "You invited these guests, I presume, my lady?"

Christian nodded, looking up at him. "What will you do?"

"Do you fear that I will summon English troops to Kinglassie?" he asked, his voice soft and dangerous.

"What will you do?" she asked again.

"What choice do I have?" he asked low.

"You can alert Hastings," she said, her voice faint, "or —"

"Or I can honor a debt," he said curtly. He spun then, and walked away.

She glanced anxiously at Fergus.

"*Ach*," he said. "He'll say no word to the English. But he has a hellish look in his eyes."

"He does," she murmured. "And I put it there."

CHRISTIAN WAITED, PLAYING THE HARP until her fingers grew tired. She waited longer, until the torch flame sputtered and went out, and her eyelids began to droop in the darkness. But Gavin never came to their bedchamber.

Finally she crawled between the cold linen sheets and lay awake. She would have welcomed even the most dreadful confrontation if he had only returned. Anything but this lonely, empty silence.

She had let her cousin and Fergus coax her into allowing Robert Bruce to come to Kinglassie. Where had her judgment been? She had been foolish. Now Gavin was so infuriated with her that he avoided her completely.

Remembering that he planned to ride to Ayr the next morning, she was certain now that he would go without her. Perhaps he would not come back at all. Perhaps he had already left.

She remembered a promise that he had made to her that he would not abandon her. Now she feared that he would think that she had abandoned him by a disloyal act. She had never intended this to happen.

She turned on her side restlessly, needing his arms around her, needing his reassurance that he understood what she had done and why. But he had given her no opportunity to explain herself. She tossed and turned, uncertain what do to with her misery, until she slept at last.

Gavin shook her awake before dawn. Christian sat up, eyes bleary, and peered at him through the shadows.

"Get up," he said, handing her a linen undertunic and her dark blue gown. "Get dressed. We ride to Ayr shortly."

"I thought you wouldna take me with you," she said, yanking the shift over her head and beginning to pull on the gown. "I thought you had left me."

"Did you?" His voice was harsh. "Here are your shoes."

She fastened the clasp of her gown quickly, then drew on her woolen hose, gartered them, and bent to pull on her leather shoes. "You didna come back last night."

"I watched on the parapet with John, and slept in the gatehouse," he said flatly. "Because of our guests, more caution was needed." The last remark was laced with bitter anger.

She reached out a hand. "Gavin—"

He tossed her cloak to her. "Come. Or you will be left behind. I ride out as soon as the horses are saddled."

"Gavin, will you speak of this matter with me?"

He had turned toward the door, but stopped and blew out a long sigh. "If we speak of this now, I may likely throttle you," he said curtly. Then he yanked open the door and walked out.

CHAPTER TWENTY-ONE

"**W**AS IT HEATHER ALE you wanted when you went to Moira's house?" Gavin asked, guiding his black stallion alongside the destrier she rode. His words were mild enough, but his tone was grim. "Heather ale—or rebellion?"

Christian looked at him warily. Following the path of a wide burn, they headed northwest. Cool mist still floated around them, although the drizzling rain had finally ceased at midmorning. A tense silence, but for a few brusque necessary remarks regarding the journey, had continued between them while they rode, and when they had stopped once to rest and eat some oatcakes.

She readjusted her mount's reins. "I see you are ready to discuss this matter at last," she said coldly. His harsh silence had worn on her mood until she felt ready to shout at him, although she knew that she had been in the wrong.

"Answer the question."

She raised her chin high. "You have been drinking Moira's heather ale all week. Some would say 'tis worth any trouble."

"Do not be difficult," he growled. "That ale is fine stuff, but its price comes too high. You evade the issue. Did you plan to join the rebellion that day you went to fetch the ale? Did you mean to act as a spy?"

"I am no spy," she said, remembering with a sense of guilt how she and Fergus had listened through the well shaft. But she had been careful to say nothing to Bruce herself of what she had heard there, although Fergus had spoken of it.

"Did you invite Robert Bruce to Kinglassie?"

She felt a blush heat her throat and cheeks. "I did not. He invited himself. Or Fergus did," she amended. "They both knew about the storage chamber. Robert would have come there for shelter on his own before long. The weather has been foul."

He blew out an exasperated breath. "You endangered the lives of everyone at Kinglassie when you allowed Robert Bruce to take shelter within our walls."

"I had no choice. He is my king, and my cousin. Kin are of great importance to the Scots."

"Kin! I am your husband, lady!" he said loudly. "But that kinship was hardly important to you when you let Bruce and his men into the castle!" She raised her chin a little higher, flaring her nostrils, resisting the urge to shout back at him.

"I didna let them in," she said. "There is a sally port on the lochside, through the rock. A tunnel leads to the underground chamber. They came in that way. I never saw them until we all went down there together."

Gavin flashed her a quick glance. "A hidden entrance in the promontory?" She nodded. He swore angrily. "More secrets? What else have you not told me?"

She looked down, gripping the reins, and decided on the truth. "I did meet with Bruce in the forest that day. Fergus and his older sons took me there."

"Why?" The word was harshly spoken.

"Of the women captured last September, I am the only one free now. Robert didna know the fate of his wife and daughter, or his sisters—only that they were all taken. I wanted to tell him that they are alive. He needed to know that."

"Why did you not tell me that you were going to do this?"

"Tell my Sasunnach husband?" she asked pointedly.

"Ah. We will never get past that, I see."

Her control abandoned her. "We willna get past it as long as the English king sends you orders to take the Bruce!" she shouted. "Or as long as he plans for you to command a garrison at Kinglassie, and steal our gold if you can!"

"Steal your gold and capture the Bruce?" He turned, his

eyes a flash of deep blue in the mist. "Is that the treatment you expect from me? You once claimed to trust me. Clearly that was untrue."

Cheeks flushing hot, she looked away. She trusted him as a man, as a lover, and that brought her joy. But part of her still feared his Englishness. "I couldna trust your Sasunnach loyalties in this matter, Gavin. And I didna want to place you in danger. But Robert asked my help, and asked my silence."

"And you gave him both," he said bitterly. "You allowed him into Kinglassie. Surely you knew he and his men could have taken the castle from within. We have no garrison to fight off an attack. And not all of the workmen would willingly defend Kinglassie against the Bruce." He slid a sharp glance toward her. "Do not deal with me as you dealt with Henry, I warn you."

"I wouldna have gone against you in that way!" she shouted back at him. "Henry acted as my enemy from the day we were wed until the last. He was a cold, cruel man. I allowed Scotsmen to take the castle in Henry's absence, aye. But all my loyalty was for Scotland then." Scowling, she stared straight ahead and gripped the reins fiercely.

"All your loyalty is still for Scotland," he said flatly.

She shook her head silently. Once, loyalty had been a simple thing. But lately it had been sorely tried in her life. The opposing forces of Scotland and her king, and her English husband, all claimed her love and loyalty, tearing and pulling at her.

Summoning greater calm, she turned to him, wanting him to understand why she had done this. "I only meant to help Robert and his men. They have been starving in the forest, and living outside in the freezing rain. Some of them were sick. There was a gale coming. I didna think beyond that. I swear it."

He was silent as he rode beside her.

"Please believe me, Gavin," she said quietly.

He sighed. "Last night I went down to the underground chamber myself," he finally said.

Startled, she glanced at him. "What?"

"I owed Bruce an honorable debt for saving your life, and my own. We spoke for a long while. I agreed to allow him to hide there until we return from Ayr. And he offered to keep a secret guard over Kinglassie in my absence." Christian simply stared at him. He sent her a cold glance. "My debt to your cousin is now paid."

"Thank you," she said meekly.

"Do not think this makes a Scots rebel out of me, lady." He stared ahead as he rode, his jaw tight. Christian glanced at his profile. His hair, streaked gold over brown, floated to touch his shoulders, and his white and gold surcoat shimmered over his black tunic. But the unyielding expression on his lean, handsome face made her wary of his thoughts.

"Am I your prisoner now?" she asked, dully, after a moment. He frowned. "What?"

"Do you mean to take me to Ayr Castle as your prisoner?"

"Do not tempt me," he growled.

Misery threatened to swamp her. She drew a long, shaky breath to keep from crying. This marriage had been her salvation somehow, but she felt as if she had unknowingly destroyed it. She loved Gavin as fiercely as she knew how. But perhaps it was not enough. She could not prove her loyalty to Gavin by turning away from her king and cousin when he needed her help.

Once, she had set fire to Kinglassie and ruined a legend because her loyalty to Robert Bruce had demanded it; and now it appeared that she had sacrificed her own marriage for the same reason.

She rode on, listening to the creak of the horses' leather trappings, keenly aware of the heaviness of his silence.

"I am sorry," she said softly. "I wanted to help my cousin. But I didna mean to destroy your trust for me."

Gavin reached out then and pulled on the reins of her horse, stopping her mount beside his. She looked up at him in confusion, and he leaned over to take her face in his hand, his grip hard on her jaw. His eyes blazed an intense blue in the soft mist.

"Trust you?" he said gruffly. "I do trust you, though God knows why. I trust you to follow your heart, which you did for Robert Bruce. I know you meant no harm. 'Tis you who cannot trust me. Your heart has already decided its loyalty."

She shook her head. "My heart is torn. I love Scotland. And I love one Sasunnach," she added in a low voice. Her lip quivered violently, and a hot tear loosened to fall on his hand.

He relaxed his fingers. "No one could ask finer loyalty than what you gave so freely to Robert Bruce. I envy him."

"But I love you, Gavin. I do," she said tremulously.

He wiped at her tears with his thumb. "I know you do," he said. "As much as you can, with your fierce little Scottish heart. But I want more from you, and you will not give it to me."

"What do you mean?"

"I want from you the kind of loyalty that you show your heather king."

"You have it of me, and more," she said.

He shook his head. "I do not have it of you yet. But one day, lady, I will," he said. "And then your heart will be completely mine." He tipped her chin upward and looked intently at her. "But first it seems you must learn for yourself that I am trustworthy."

She watched him silently. The blue depths of his eyes held a cool reserve, as if he felt sadness, and yet patience. He dropped his hand from her jaw. "We are half the way to Ayr. If you fear that you will be taken prisoner there, then turn back now."

She shook her head. "I will go with you."

He watched her for a moment, then nodded and turned his horse to ride ahead.

Christian stared after him. After a moment, she snapped the reins and followed Gavin.

THEY RODE THROUGH THICK MIST, over ground that was boggy with rain, following the course of the burn. Water saturated the ground, brown and smooth in puddles and small pools, and rushing through swollen burns and streams. The mist clung in narrow glens and wreathed the rugged hillsides, but was still thin enough that they could easily find their way. To the east, the high mountaintops were blurred, pale shapes.

And each time Gavin looked around she was there, a small, stubborn figure cloaked in mulberry wool. They stopped once more to eat the last of the cheese, drinking clear water in silence. She seemed thoughtful and a little sad, but she said very little to him, as if she had decided to be cautious.

He could see the shadow of fatigue in her pale face, and saw her sometimes stretch her shoulders and back wearily. But she did not complain, had never complained that he had ever heard. He shook his head in wonder at her tenacity.

His anger toward her had vanished miles back, once he had shouted out his frustration with her, and had understood her motivation for allowing his country's enemy into his own castle. She had a sympathetic concern for the safety and comfort of the rebel Scots.

Now, on this cold, damp journey, he was heartened by her presence, and touched by the steadfastness she showed in coming with him. He wanted to take her in his arms and kiss the misery from her sweet, solemn face. But he would wait until she came to him.

He felt exposed, raw and vulnerable after what he had said to her. Reserved with his innermost feelings, he had found great difficulty in expressing his heart like that. But he had needed to let her know how much he needed her complete loyalty. He harbored a terror that she would leave him, as Jehanne had left him, bereft and alone, in spite of his efforts. He had failed with Jehanne; he had always thought that he had not loved her enough.

But he loved Christian with a passion deeper than he could comprehend. The conflict of loyalty between them frightened her more than it did him. His fear was that she would let their differences ruin what they both needed so much.

He had asked complete devotion and loyalty from her, yet knew he withheld that from her himself. He was not yet ready to reveal his own deepest, most vulnerable feelings. Trust was indeed a difficult thing.

They halted once more to rest the horses, leading them over to drink from a small trickling spring that spilled out of a rocky hillside. Gavin turned to see Christian scoop water with her cupped hands and drink, and then reach upward to stretch her arms and yawn. The sensual curves of her slender body were evident even beneath her tunic and thick cloak.

God, he loved her. The thought struck him like a fist in the center of his belly, a blow of utter truth. He watched her intently, savoring her face, her hands, her graceful movements. She sparked like a bright candle flame in his shadowed heart. He sighed and rubbed his jaw, thinking, and sat on a boulder.

She sat nearby, and they watched the deep, wide burn tumble and rush rapidly over clusters of boulders, its loud gurgle blending with the faint cry of a bird somewhere overhead.

"That's a falcon," she said, looking upward. "But I canna see it now, for the mist."

He looked up and saw a dark shadow gliding through a drift of fog. "There he goes. Gone to join his mate, perhaps. Or searching for a high place to rest," he said.

"That is true freedom," she said, her head tilted back. "See how it flies—oh, and swoops. 'Tis beautiful."

"Aye," Gavin said, looking only at her. Then he glanced northward. "We are close to Ayr here, I think."

"Another league or so that way," she said, pointing. "If the day were clearer, we could see the church tower from here. But if you mean to take me to a monastery that offers lodging, there is an abbey two leagues east. We would have to ford the burn here. Farther on the water gets too deep."

He eyed the heavy brown rush of water warily. "Deeper than this? These waters are far too swollen for crossing." He sighed. "I will have to find a place for you in the town. I did not want to do that. Perhaps you should have turned back."

She shook her head. "I would have come with you whatever happened."

He glanced at her. "Why?"

"I was afraid that you would go to Ayr and learn that you are better off without a treacherous Scotswoman for a wife."

He almost laughed. "Ah. Is that what I'd learn there?"

She shrugged, looking away. "You might."

He sighed then, sensing that she was very serious. No matter what he did, she still held back from him the full measure of her love and trust—because of Henry and his hatred of the Scots, because of Edward Plantagenet and his damned cage, because of Oliver Hastings and his greed.

She had survived the lung ailment, but the deepest hurts had not yet healed inside of her. He understood that, for he had never fully recovered from the old, painful wounds of loss that he carried in his own heart.

He looked at her. "We will go first to the town, and find an inn for you," he said. "I will be back for you by tomorrow at eventide. Promise me that you will keep to your room."

"Are promises good between us again?" she asked quietly.

"Mine always have been," he said, standing. "Are yours?"

AT SUNDOWN, SHE STOOD by the small window of a loft room in an inn on High Street in Ayr. Opening the wooden shutter to the cool darkness, she inhaled the blend of tangy sea air and the fragrant smoke of the cooking shops. She was not hungry, having finished a hot supper of fresh fish and vegetable stew, and half a loaf of bread, something she enjoyed but had rarely eaten outside of a town or a monastery. Now she relaxed her shoulders against the wooden window frame and listened to the raucous mingle of sounds.

Church bells pealed out the sundown hour of vespers, and cartwheels squeaked as families and laborers traveled home; men called out greetings to one another and women and children laughed; somewhere a dog barked incessantly. She heard the slam of shutters as the merchants closed up their shop windows at the end of the day.

Laid over it all, she heard the light, mixed chatter of birds. She saw seagulls swooping overhead, but she could hear doves, larks, falcons, even a swan's trumpet and the odd curdling note of a capercaillie. So many birds caught her curiosity, and she leaned her head out of the window to look for them.

The street was lined with buildings, their sloped wooden or thatched roofs sagging toward one another wherever the houses stood close together. Off to one side she could see the wide part of the street where the market stalls were built, near the market cross at the center of the town. The earthen street was nearly empty now in the gathering dusk. She could still hear the birdcalls, but could not see a dovecote, or any large groups of birds roosting anywhere.

She and Gavin had ridden their horses past the outlying boundary ditches and through the town gate, traveling past stone and thatch houses and small garden yards on their way toward the more crowded part of the town. Looking for an inn, they had ridden nearly the length of High Street, passing through the market square. The inn they chose was near the marketplace, surrounded by merchants' houses, the town hall, and the Greyfriars' church. From her window, Christian could see the long, narrow stone bridge that spanned the River Ayr. A little way along that wide river, the castle was set on a hill overlooking the town.

Gavin had deposited her at the inn with a generous payment in silver coin to the innkeeper. The proprietor's wife had insisted that the sheets were clean, the mattresses free of fleas, and the meals hot and fresh. Gavin had smiled his thanks, and later had slipped a few silver pennies into the hand of the little serving maid, just to ensure the truth of the claim.

He had left Christian at the door of the small upper chamber, reminding her that he would be back by the next evening.

"I have asked the maid to accompany you if you wish to go through the Saturday market tomorrow," he said. He had handed her a small pouch, heavy with coin. "I am certain there are things you wish to purchase for Kinglassie. But do not go out alone."

She had nodded, holding his leather pouch, staring up at him. After a moment, he had inclined his head. "My lady. Good night," he had said, and had turned away.

"God keep you," she had whispered as the door closed behind him. Then she had rushed to the window to watch him ride down the street toward the castle. She had stayed by the window until the black charger and blue-cloaked rider had become tiny shadows in the dusk, crossing the narrow stone bridge.

She had wanted him to put his arms around her before he left. A lonely hurt lingered because he had not touched her. Now, long after he had gone, she leaned a shoulder against the window frame and watched the distant blur of Ayr Castle, set on its mound above the wide, calm river.

Gavin was in that castle now, along with Hastings and a full array of men who were the enemies of Scotland. Ayr had tolerated the presence of the English better than some parts of Scotland. Port towns were accustomed to absorbing many cultures—Norse, Irish, Flemish, French, as well as the invading English.

But Christian's awareness was centered on the thought of one man, a Sasunnach with deep blue eyes, whose compelling presence in her life was changing her, gradually and completely. She hugged her arms around herself and felt the lack of him beside her.

But he had seemed distant and cool since their argument, and she wondered if she would ever again feel the true fire of his touch. Fearing that she would not, fearing that he had withdrawn the full measure of his love from her now, she sighed heavily and stared at the dusky twilight sky.

"Pardoned?" Gavin asked, incredulous. "She has been pardoned?"

Scowling, Hastings tossed the parchment page that he held, marked with the royal blue seal, onto the table. "Your wife has been pardoned along with all the other outlawed supporters of Robert Bruce not currently imprisoned. Edward has sent copies of this writ to his commanders."

Gavin blinked, still trying to take in the news. He thrust his fingers through his hair and laughed, a disbelieving chuckle. "What game is this? Edward must be wary of losing his stance in Scotland. He curries favors from those who openly hate him."

"He's had word that more Scots are joining Robert Bruce. My own clan willna waiver in our loyalty," Dungal Macdouell said, coming forward with Philip Ormesby from the shadowed corner of the chamber, where they had been sitting at a game of chess. "But there are supporters o' King Edward who now side wi' the Bruce. Edward has pardoned the outlawed Scots because he wants the loyalty of these other Scots back again."

"Traitors all," Hastings snapped.

"These men, I hear, have been lately dispossessed of their Scottish and English lands both, or else they expect their lands to be taken from them shortly," Gavin said. "Despite their declared fealty to Edward."

Hastings snorted derisively. "Fools all," he said. "Of course Edward must take away their Scottish lands to ensure that he controls all of Scotland. They will gain land from him later. But many do not trust him, and have declared for the Bruce."

"I wonder what any of us would do under the same circumstances," Gavin said.

"Some of us turn traitor easily," Hastings said.

Gavin longed to grind one of his tightening fists into Hastings' smirking face. But he would do nothing to jeopardize Christian's newly acquired legal freedom, however fragile that might be under Edward's fickle control.

"Still," Gavin said, "Edward must be anxious about the numbers of men who are said to be joining the Bruce's cause. Not so many in actuality, perhaps—Bruce has less than a hundred men, from what I hear—but many are now regarding him as the true King of Scots. That must make Edward quake on his sickbed at Lanercost. Else he would never have repealed his declaration that all those who aided Bruce were outlaws. He has too much spite in him for that."

"Spite? Do you say that these royal orders are not trustworthy?" Hastings asked.

"Edward's declarations often last only so long as he wants. This order will be no different, in the end."

"Regardless," Philip Ormesby said, "your little Scottish wife is free of all suspicion of outlawry. For now."

Gavin scooped up the writ. "Since you have other copies of this, I'll take this one." He tucked the page inside his tunic.

"Did you capture the men who attacked my patrol last week?" Hastings asked. "What about that Celtic priest?"

Gavin shrugged. "He was in his church that day, seen by many, performing a Lenten mass."

"What word of the Bruce?"

"He hides in a different place every few nights."

"We will find him," Hastings said. "He and his men grow more careless and bold. Last week on Sunday, his ally James Douglas—the Black Douglas—attacked an English garrison in church, while the soldiers were hearing mass. Then he and his followers sealed themselves in the empty castle and ate the holy day feast that had been prepared, before fouling the well with dead cattle and burning the place to the ground."

"I heard about it," Gavin said. Bruce and Douglas himself had told him the night that Gavin had visited Kinglassie's storage chamber. " 'Twas Douglas's own family castle that the English had taken. And that commander was careless to leave the place unguarded."

"Black Douglas took it back in Scottish style," Macdouell said. "Brave, but foolish. King Edward was so furious, they say he leaped from his sickbed screaming, and ordered more men to pour into Galloway. Bruce willna last the month, with the fury of the English on him like this."

"Bruce was seen near Kinglassie, so King Edward wants two hundred men installed there immediately," Hastings said. "I myself headed a patrol a few days ago with a hundred men and bloodhounds. We caught sight of some men in the forest, but 'twas at night, and pouring rain. The hounds lost them."

Gavin watched him evenly, giving away no emotion, no sudden thought. A few days ago, Bruce and his men had hidden in Kinglassie. "I am certain you will try again," he said.

"Aye, and this time your own garrison will form the patrol," Hastings answered. "Bruce was very near Kinglassie the day that he and his men attacked my patrol. Have Kinglassie ready by next week to house that garrison. You will lead men out to find Bruce."

"I have told you the work will not be done until well into spring at least," Gavin said. "The portcullis is proving difficult to repair. I intend to order new lengths of chain in Ayr, as long as I am here. 'Twill take time before it can be made and delivered."

"Have the bill sent to me as treasurer," Ormesby said. "King Edward has generously offered to pay part of your repair costs.

But he wants the place repaired and ready by next week."

"I would prefer that he not invest funds into my castle."

"As you wish," Hastings said. "But that will not stop him from reclaiming Kinglassie if he decides to do that." The smirk was back on his face; Gavin wanted to slam his fist into it.

"Have you made any progress on finding that gold?" Ormesby asked. "Edward wrote me a letter concerning that not long ago. This Scottish war has been very expensive. A treasure like that will be worth a great deal."

"You were supposed to convince the girl to tell you where she has hidden it," Hastings said.

"The girl," Gavin said, sliding him a glance, "is my lady wife. And I believe that the treasure, if it ever existed at all, is gone. There has been no trace of it anywhere. Such legends are not always solid truth. Whatever was there may have been taken generations ago."

Hastings snarled impatiently. "I will be at Kinglassie in one week. I expect to see that gold, and I expect the repairs to be complete by then."

Gavin leaned back against the table, eyeing Hastings lazily. "I will ready my castle in my own time, Oliver."

"You purposely delay us. That borders on treachery."

"Carpenters and masons can only work so fast given the weather and the poor availability of supplies. They are making their best effort. Do you want the barracks tower to fall down around your garrison's ears?"

"Your garrison," Hastings amended sourly.

"Carpenters," Ormesby cut in. "Did you tell him?"

Hastings shook his head and looked at Gavin. "That carpenter who had promised to inform Bruce was found dead in the forest. He was full of short arrows from Scottish bows."

"A hunting accident?" Gavin asked, one brow raised.

Hastings did not laugh. "Someone obviously told the Bruce that the man was a spy. I told only you, Faulkener. Only you."

"Certainly others knew."

Hastings shook his head. "That wife of yours is a known ally of Bruce. Did you tell her?"

"Nay." Gavin watched him evenly, his senses sharpening, as if he expected a strike from Hastings. "She knew naught of it."

"Someone did," Hastings said. "I suspect her—or her Celtic priest. Follow that man, Gavin. Or follow your own wife. With one or the other, you will find a link to Robert Bruce that will benefit us."

Gavin stared coldly at Hastings. "My wife is no spy."

Hastings blinked slowly, a dark, narrow gleam in his eyes. "She is not trustworthy, Faulkener. Watch your back."

"Even the king thought her trustworthy, Oliver. He pardoned her," Gavin said. "Or have you forgotten that already?" Inclining his head, he turned and left the chamber.

CHAPTER TWENTY-TWO

"**I** STILL HAVE CANDLES, soap, ginger, and cloves to find," Christian said, looking at Marjorie, the young servant girl. They stood together in the market square, the sun bright on their faces. "We've been to the pepper merchant's shop, the oil merchant's stall for almonds, and the weaver's stall to look at the plaids. But I'd like to visit a textile merchant to look at some sturdy linens and serges. And I need some spices from the apothecary."

"Most of those stalls and shops are here on High Street, my lady," Marjorie said, shifting the large basket that contained some of the cloth-wrapped packages that Christian had already purchased.

Christian smiled as she lifted her face to the warm sunshine. A mild breeze lifted her white veil. " 'Tis lovely today, like spring, after all that rain and wind." She heard the pealing church bells and the light blend of birds chattering. She shifted the basket she was carrying. "Where are those birds? I've been hearing them all morning."

"At the fowler's stall, down that lane there, toward the Church of Saint John," Marjorie said, pointing. "If you'd like fresh dove or pheasant for supper, we can buy them there, and the innkeeper's wife will prepare them for your evening meal."

Christian shook her head, laughing. "I wouldna care for a meal of doves. We've hundreds of them at Kinglassie. Now—where is the chandler's shop?"

"Just over here," Marjorie said. They turned, and Christian stopped, pulling at Marjorie's arm.

"English soldiers," she hissed, as several guards in chain mail rode through the marketplace on huge destriers. Their passing hardly seemed to disturb the normal level of activity.

"*Ach,* my lady, the English soldiers are everywhere in Ayr," Marjorie said. "Dinna pay them any heed." She walked on, leading Christian to a small house, where one window shutter opened horizontally to form a shelf on which various candles and soaps were displayed.

Once inside the shop, Christian greeted the chandler and proceeded to collect a few dozen candles made of practical, inexpensive tallow imported from England, and several large table candles of more expensive rolled beeswax. While the chandler wrapped her purchase in linen and parchment, she also chose four small clay pots of soft Flemish-made soap, scented with floral oils and herbs. They emerged a while later, both toting much heavier baskets.

"You've enough soaps and candles for a few months, my lady. But I hope you plan to return in June for our fair," Marjorie said. "It lasts for two weeks. You'll find the best of everything you can imagine, silks and samites, imported spices from the Holy Land, and jewels, and—"

Christian smiled. "I have little use for jewels, but my husband might want to purchase horses and cattle then," she said. "And I'm certain we'll need more candles, soaps, and spices. Are you hungry, Marjorie?"

The girl nodded. "There's a cook shop around the corner. The pies are good, and fresh."

"Let's stop at the baker's for bread," Christian said. "And I'd love some ale." They elbowed their way through the crowd, moving toward the food shop, passing the carved stone market cross that towered above the throng. The square was filled with people, carrying loaded baskets, calling and laughing, stopping to examine goods or bargaining for prices.

They went to the baker's stall, and then the brewer's for wooden cups of cool ale before stopping at the cook shop, where Marjorie insisted that the meat and fish pies were delicious. Christian gave her a sliver halfpenny to buy some food, and waited outside, the heavy baskets at her feet. She looked toward the stone bridge and the distant castle that rose above the town, thinking of Gavin.

"Are you alone, my lady?" A hand on her shoulder brought her around, startled. Gavin looked down at her, one brow lifted.

She smiled up at him in genuine delight. He returned a lopsided grin that clutched at her heart. "The lass from the inn is with me," she told him. "She's inside the cook shop just now. What are you doing here in the marketplace?"

"Looking for you," he said. "My business is done at the castle. Hastings told me of the king's latest orders, and I listened till late into the night to the commanders discussing strategies and finances, and chewing over their resentment, both toward the Scots and toward Edward's war. I left at the first chance I had." He yawned and flexed his shoulders. "And I hope you passed a more comfortable night than I did, for I slept on a cold stone floor wrapped in my cloak."

"I was comfortable enough," she said. But without Gavin, she thought, the bed had been cold and lonely. He smiled down at her, his mood obviously altered from the previous day. She was grateful that the tension between them had lifted.

She stared up at him, and thought how beautiful he appeared in that moment, tall and strong and masculine in a shaft of spring sun. His eyes shone like sapphires, his firm jaw was whiskered in flecks of gold and bronze. "Gavin—must we leave Ayr now?" she asked. "Is that why you came to look for me here?"

He chuckled softly. "We can stay another night, if you like, and leave tomorrow, though 'tis Palm Sunday. Do you want to attend mass in the cathedral?"

"Can we?" she asked, pleased.

He nodded. "But if we wait until tomorrow, we will have to travel on a holy day, and miss our feast at Kinglassie. I'm sure Dominy will be preparing scores of wild doves for the meal."

"I dinna mind missing that," Christian said, laughing. "Have you been to the blacksmith yet?"

"Aye, when I rode into town this morning. I've ordered lengths of iron chain and rope, and two thousand nails. But I will have to send a man back here with an oxcart to fetch them. And I still want to go to the tollbooth, where I hear the town council meets, to inquire about finding a glazier and a sculptor to make us some colored windows and carved mantels."

"Thank you, Gavin," she said softly.

He tilted his head. "For what, my lady?"

"For caring so much about Kinglassie."

" 'Tis my home," he said quietly. "And yours."

She blushed, and glanced down at the basket at her feet. "I bought some things with the silver that you gave me," she said. "Candles and soap, and some spices."

He bent and lifted both baskets, grunting playfully. "Enough candles for a year or two," he said.

She laughed. "Only a few months. We'll soon need more, unless you want to send another oxcart to carry all the household goods we're lacking."

"We'll come to the June fair, I think. I'll be ready to buy some livestock by then. Ah, here's your food—is there enough to share?"

"I saw you through the doorway, my lord, so I bought another pie for you," Marjorie said as she handed them two steaming beef pies wrapped in parchment.

They found a low stone wall to sit on while they ate the food and drank the rest of the ale. Gavin questioned Marjorie about various merchants, about the import trade, and about the cattle market held outside the town in the spring and summer.

"I would still like to find the cloth merchant's shop, and the spicer," Christian said, as they finished their meal. Gavin lifted the baskets and motioned for them to proceed through the crowd, following Marjorie toward the textile shop.

Inside the front room of the cloth merchant's house, which was opened for business part of each day, they looked at brightly colored lengths of silk and samite. Christian purchased some plain linen and deep blue serge for new tunics. The merchant's wife was a seamstress, but Christian refused her offer to make a gown from a lustrous, deep green silk that she had admired.

"You may have it, if you wish," Gavin said, fingering the cloth. But Christian shook her head.

" 'Tis beautiful," she said. "But I dinna have a use for such a fine gown. I would like a piece of white silk for a new veil, though."

He nodded. "And Michaelmas might like some of those silk ribbons there." As he spoke, he reached out to touch a small, fragile net, displayed with others on overturned bowls on a shelf. "These little things are worn by women in the French court more often than veils now." Christian looked at the delicate net, a glittering web of silk strands and silver beads; she reached up self-consciously to touch her plain woolen veil.

"Aye, my lady," the seamstress said. " 'Tis called a fret, or a caul. 'Tis very fashionable. You wear it over the hair just so"—she picked it up and draped it over her fingers to display it—"with a fillet of linen, stifflike, around the brow. Would you like to try one?"

Christian took off her veil and allowed the seamstress to drape the fret over her hair, catching her thick curls inside. The woman set a stiffened rim of linen around her head at her brow, and stood back. "Coil your hair beneath the fret, and 'twill show the beauty of your curls, my lady. Though you wear your hair muckle short."

" 'Tis lovely," Gavin said. "We'll take it." He smiled at Christian, a slow, secret grin that swirled sensually through her. Then he turned to pay the merchant for their purchases.

Patting her headwear, Christian followed Gavin into the spring sunshine, while Marjorie ran ahead of them toward the apothecary's shop. A light, silvery sound caught Christian's attention.

"A harper!" she said, and crossed the street.

Surrounded by people clapping their hands and tapping their feet, a man, slight and elderly, set on a stool in the middle of the street and played a fast, rapid melody on his harp.

Christian grinned up at Gavin and turned to listen to the harper, watching his skilled fingers dance over the brass wires.

When he finished the song, he bent and picked up a *bodhran* and a piece of bone, and began to beat a complicated rhythm on the stretched hide drum while he sang a song in Gaelic. He played, after that, a small wooden flute and then returned to the harp for more songs.

When he was done, and some of the crowd had drifted away, Christian stayed to speak with him in Gaelic, complimenting him on his skill. He showed her his harp, which he said had been made in Ireland, the land of his birth. She traced her fingers reverently along its interlaced carving and told him of her own harp, and they compared features of their instruments. Then she turned to smile up at Gavin.

"The harper says he will trade me some wires of new brass," she said. "I could surely use them."

Nodding, Gavin reached into the pouch of his belt. "How much will he take for them, and for his performance?"

"*Ach*, you canna offer coin to a harper!" she said, shocked, pushing at his hand. " 'Tis the greatest of insults, to give a harper coin for his music."

Gavin frowned. "What will he take, then? And how does he manage to live from town to town if he accepts no coin?"

"Harpers accept gifts of land, or goods. They willna take silver. And this man is on his way north, where he has been invited to be the harper in the household of a clan chief, who has promised him good land and a sturdy house for his services." She turned to the harper, who was hardly as tall as Christian. "I have candles, or soap, or herbs in my basket," she told him in Gaelic.

"I will trade new harp strings for a few candles," the harper said, crinkling his vivid blue eyes. "And I'll trade you my music for yours. Male and female, right and left, on the strings here, my lady."

She smiled and reached out her hands, sweeping the upper strings. "Agreed," she said. He suggested a melody, and she nodded, familiar with it. Standing on the left side of the harp while he stood on the right, she began to pluck the upper, feminine part of the melody, while he played the lower, masculine notes.

Playing, she smiled as the wonderful magic of the song lifted her spirits as high as they could be on such a glorious, lovely day, with the sun shining and the breeze blowing, and Gavin laughing while he listened.

The harper suddenly reached up and turned a tuning peg with his key, in the middle of the song, throwing a string out of tune as she plucked it. But she chuckled, knowing the game, and changed the variation to avoid the off-tune sound. Watching his clever hands as he played, striving to predict what he was going to do with his harp key, she kept up with him until they both rang off the strings, laughing in delight.

"I will give you the brass wires for free, I will, my lady," he said, grinning widely. "You're a clever harper, and I bow to your talent. You're nearly as grand a harper as I am."

"*Ach,* never as fine as you," she said, laughing, and accepted the coiled wires he handed her. And she insisted that he take some of the candles as a gift. He did, and bowed, and sat down to play a lilting melody written for an ancient Irish queen as she walked away.

FARTHER ALONG THE STREET, she turned to smile up at Gavin, her heart still filled with simple joy. She noticed that the sound of the birds, which she had been hearing throughout the day, was much louder at the end of the street.

"Marjorie said there was a fowler's shop down a side lane near here. That must be why I keep hearing—" She turned her head, and suddenly stopped where she stood.

"What is it?" Gavin asked, looking around at he. "Did you see another shop you want to visit?"

Christian said nothing. She stared at a cluster of small wooden cages, a dozen or more, stacked two and three high on a trestle table in front of the fowler's house. Some of the cages held several birds. Doves and pigeons huddled together, crowded and cooing; pheasants slept, their bright feathers shining in the sun. Larks, singing in joyful, silvery tones, clung to the struts inside two more cages. And three falcons blinked in another cage, the smallest one squeaking piteously.

The largest cages held two white swans jammed beside each other, their feathers dingy, their heads bowed, and several capercaillies, who fanned their dark tail feathers.

"Oh, God," she said, placing her fingers over her mouth. Her feet seemed anchored to the spot. "Oh, God. Gavin, the cages—" she said, shuddering.

A man stepped out from behind the trestle table, chewing on a slender stick, and patting his round stomach with a greasy hand. "Greetings," he called. "Will ye hae a pheasant for yer supper, my lord? Or a falcon for yer mews? We've muckle young larks, a fine pie they'd make for ye and yer lady."

Gavin shook his head and placed a hand on her shoulder. "Come on, Christian. Do not look if this distresses you." He led her away.

The sun poured down, the soft breeze kissed her cheeks, and the chatter and activity of the crowd moved past her in waves. But Christian no longer enjoyed the market or the spring air. The sight of the cages had disturbed her deeply. She felt as if the light and the happiness of the day had somehow gone dark and sad.

THEY ATE FRESH COD for supper. Christian had refused the offer of pigeon pie, and picked at the fish, baked in butter and herbs, swallowing only a little, although Gavin knew fresh sea catch was a treat for her. The innkeeper served red wine from Bordeaux, and the wine's heady lift put a pink glow in her cheeks. But the sadness in her eyes remained.

When Gavin pressed her to talk about her somber mood, she shook her head. "I am only tired," she said, and went up the wooden steps to the small rented room.

When he entered the chamber a while later, after returning from a walk to check on their stabled horses, she lay facedown on the bed, still dressed, her head on her folded arms. Evening light streamed over her, and the window shutters were open to the mild air.

"I can hear them," she said. "The birds."

Gavin heard them too, chirping and cooing. He hoped for

Christian's sake that the fowler would cover the cages at night to silence them. Sighing, he sat on the edge of the bed, resting a hand on her back.

"I know the sight of the cages upset you," he said softly. "But they're birds, my love. Not people. Not you." She said nothing, but after a few moments he felt her back muscles quivering beneath his hand. "Hush," he whispered, bending closer. "Do not cry. Hush now, that breaks my heart."

He pulled her into his arms, and she turned to bury her face in his tunic. He held her and rocked her. "The cage at Carlisle—I canna stop thinking of it," she said, her voice thick and hoarse.

"The cage was a cruel thing," Gavin said. "You should never have been held there." He smoothed her wet cheek and pushed strands of her hair behind her ear. The delicate fret and linen band was askew, and he slid them off gently, freeing her hair, streaming his fingers through her silky locks, silent, waiting.

"I hated it there," she whispered. "I hated it." Sobs took her, wrenching and deep. He wrapped his arms around her, tucking her against his heart.

"Hush. You are safe now," he said.

"But the English are here in Ayr. If they see me—"

"I took you out of that cage. I will not let you go back."

Her sobs grew softer, a more cleansing cry. He stroked her head and her back patiently while she cried, knowing she needed this time now to purge the fears and the anger from her heart.

After a while he spoke. "I have a parchment you might like to see, with King Edward's seal and sign on it. He has pardoned the followers of Robert Bruce. 'Tis over, Christian. You'll not be hunted again."

She raised her head. "He has pardoned me?"

He smiled. "Edward Longshanks grows nervous. He tries to woo the Scots back to his side by showing them his good nature."

"Good nature!" She laughed ruefully through her tears.

"Better that," he said. "I love your smile, and your laugh. But I have not seen enough of either." She smiled again, a wistful lift of her mouth, and he kissed her brow.

She looked up at him, her eyes deep-colored in the low light. "Gavin, why did you help me when I was in Carlisle?"

He glanced at her, a little surprised by the question. She sniffled, her nose pink, her eyes swollen, and he thought then that she was the most beautiful woman he had ever seen.

"I wanted you to live. Just that. Only that," he said. "At first, you made me think of Jehanne. 'Twas hard to see you dying of the same illness that took her."

"Tell me about her," she said softly.

"She was sweetness itself," he said. "Kind, serene, a little serious for her young age. The match was suggested by the French king. I accepted it because she was a pleasant, intelligent girl. And I was lonely, and tired of court life."

"What happened to her?" He shook his head, but Christian laid her hand on his chest. "Tell me," she said.

He sighed, realizing that he should tell her, though if he did, she would see his deepest pain. But perhaps it was time he trusted her with that.

"Jehanne had never been strong. Shortly after we were married, she caught a lung infection. Though she got well, she never fully recovered. She grew weaker, with breathing problems and a cough, and a constant fever. The illness continued for a long time. I sent for one physician after another. That is how I learned methods for treating such a condition. But naught could be done to cure her. Naught. I tried everything." He frowned deeply and opened his hand, looking at his palm.

"She was so ill, Gavin," she said softly. "God makes those judgments. We canna change them."

"You do not understand," he said. "I tried to change it." He raised his eyes to hers. "My mother was a healer, Christian. She had a gift, passed through her clan from some long-ago Celtic saint."

She nodded. "John said the holy Columba was part of your ancestry. I've heard such powers can run in the old Celtic bloodlines. In England or in France such healers are sometimes seen as saints, but more often as heretics. But in Scotland, they are respected, like those with the Sight."

"My mother could touch a person, at times, and bring something miraculous to them," Gavin said. "She kept her talent quiet, but I saw her heal small wounds and improve larger ones. I saw her cure coughs, even serious illnesses. She might have been able to save Jehanne. But my mother was dead by then. So I laid my hands on Jehanne myself." He looked at his palms. "As if I were greater than God. The Angel Knight, they called me. I think I came to believe it."

"To me you have always been like an angel," she said. "Your mother's gift is surely part of that. Your hands—"

"The gift is not in me. I tried to impose my own will, Christian. And Jehanne died." He drew a ragged breath, and uttered the words he thought never to say to anyone. "She died in my arms, at the time that I was trying to heal her."

"*O Dhia,*" she whispered.

He laughed, a flat huff. "God, indeed. A humbling experience. And a hard lesson, learned well. I swore I would not presume to effect a miracle again. But when I saw you—" He drew his fingertips along a tear track on her cheek. "Your strength, your stubbornness. And you were so very ill. I only wanted you to live, Christian. Desperately. You do not know how much."

She laid her hands on each side of his face, looking into his eyes. "Gavin," she said earnestly, "in the abbey, the night I was so ill, you laid your hands on me. I felt something then, a wondrous heat. I think you healed me then."

He shook his head. " 'Twas God decided you would live."

She shifted to cover his hands with hers. "God, aye, but you were his instrument. I swear it, Gavin. I saw an angel that night, in a dream. And he was you, with wide wings, and your face. And you and the angel both touched me with such incredible love"— she drew a breath, closing her eyes briefly—"you healed me. I would have died that night without you. I know it. I woke after that night feeling as if I had been miraculously healed, Gavin. I never told you."

"Christian," he murmured, "I wanted you to recover. But you lived because of God's will, not mine. And because of your own stubbornness."

"You have your mother's gift. You do," she said. "When I caught that splinter, you held my thumb, and the wound stopped bleeding. It stopped hurting immediately."

He shook his head. "That is a small thing. Who can say if I did that or not? But I did not have any gift for Jehanne."

She was watching him earnestly, her hands on his. "Perhaps Jehanne was always meant to die young, Gavin. What you did may have helped her move into the world of the blessed, where she was meant to go. That might be a healing touch, too."

He stared at her. A sense of truth, genuine and beautiful, washed through him at her words. He remembered how peacefully Jehanne had died, although she had been suffering greatly until then. But she had left her body gently, on a soft, sweet exhalation.

"Angels are sent to guide the dying," Christian said softly. " 'Tis why I think I took you for Saint Michael once, because I was near death. You have an angel's touch. I have felt it."

He reached out and wrapped his arms around her, laying his cheek against her hair. "God, how I love you," he whispered. "You show me such loyalty with these words."

" 'Tis what you asked from me," she said, her tone light.

"Aye." He laughed softly, knowing how true that was, and how much he valued her loyalty. "I thank you for believing so completely in me. But my mother's gift is lost, Christian. I do not have it, and John, her brother, does not have it. But if we have a child, sweet wife, perhaps the gift will be passed on." He moved his hands slowly along her shoulder and down to the front clasp of her tunic. He began to undo it. "Shall we try, then?" he murmured, slipping his hand inside.

She answered a soft agreement, her words lost as his lips touched hers. Circling her arms around his neck, she lay back on the bed, and he went with her.

Stretching out his arm, he pushed the shutter closed. The sound of the trapped birds faded, and soon Gavin heard only the gentle thunder of his heart, beating in time with hers.

AT DAWN, THEY WALKED TOGETHER to the church of Saint John amid a throng of parishioners ready for a long Palm Sunday mass. Christian wore her new fret and fillet on her hair, and walked with her hand tucked in the crook of Gavin's arm.

When they passed the fowler's shop, which lay along the same street, she turned her head away, not wanting to look. But she could not shut out the chirps and songs from the crowded cages.

After mass was done, Gavin wanted to go to the stable and fetch the horses, but Christian wanted to linger in the church and look at the stained-glass pictures. She told him she would meet him shortly, and after he left, she strolled through the nave, looking at the biblical images. She spent a long time staring up at a bright window that depicted the dove flying toward Noah, carrying a flowering branch.

The crowds had thinned considerably when she walked out to meet Gavin. But as she headed down the lane back toward High Street, she did not see him. And each step brought her closer to the fowler's shop.

The cages, horrible, sagging, confining little structures, sat untended on the trestle table, their occupants jabbering, chirping, flitting from side to side. The fowler must have gone to mass or else was inside his house, sitting down to his Sunday feast. Christian walked steadily past, looking straight ahead, watching for Gavin.

The little falcon squealed miserably as she passed. The doves cooed, low, cuddling sounds, and the larks began a high, beautiful song, so complex and wonderful that she wished, for an instant, that she could master such a melody on her harp.

She walked past without looking. And then suddenly she spun around. Running back, she stopped in front of the trestle table, reached over, and unlatched the first cage that she saw.

The larks spilled out of the cage in a flood of small brown wings, pouring upward, singing in their delight. She laughed, watching them, then reached out and pried open another door.

Doves flew out like fluttering clouds, dazzling white, soaring into the open air. Snowy feathers drifted over her shoulders as she yanked open another cage, and another. Flapping wings and joyful songs filled the air. Tears spilled down her cheeks as she looked upward. She had never seen anything so beautiful, had never felt such unbounded exhilaration.

Shouts, sudden and angry, came from all around as the fowler and his family and neighbors came out of their houses. Christian pulled open another cage—pigeons, their soft gray wings brushing past her as they left—and turned.

"God in heaven! Are ye mad?" the fowler shouted. He reached out for her, but she whirled away, bumping into another man who stepped into her path. Gavin.

He grasped her and pulled her toward him, holding her arm in a fierce grip. He did not speak to her as he faced the angry fowler. A flurry of feathers drifted down from above to dust their shoulders and heads.

"She's mad, your lady!" the fowler shouted at him. "D' ye see what she's done? I'll have the alderman arrest her!"

"No need," Gavin said. He tossed a heavy leather bag toward the man, who caught it deftly in spite of his ire. "This will more than cover your losses, I think. 'Tis enough for thrice as many birds."

The fowler hefted its solid weight and poured the coins into his hand. He grunted. "Well, then, I'll let this deed go, though yer lady is muckle crazed."

Gavin pulled, not gently, on Christian's arm. "Come with me, before the alderman and all the king's host come to see what in God's name is going on out here. I know 'tis near Easter, but did you have to resurrect every bird in Ayr?"

"I had to free them," she panted as he yanked her along with him. "I had to, Gavin."

As they passed the end of the table, the falcons, still caged, rustled their wings restlessly. The smallest one squealed. Christian, pulled along in Gavin's grip, craned her head back to look at it.

"Gavin—" she said.

"Oh, sweet saints in heaven," he muttered. He turned back with Christian still in tow.

With a quick flip of his hand, Gavin opened the falcons' cage.

One by one, the birds hopped to the door and flew out with a powerful spread of wings, brushing past him as they soared away.

Christian laughed in delight, stray feathers caught in her hair, as Gavin pulled her hastily toward their waiting horses.

Her heart had never felt quite so light, or so filled with simple joy, as in that moment.

CHAPTER TWENTY-THREE

"'TIS MAGNIFICENT. Look, Gavin," Christian said, stopping her horse to gaze toward the horizon. "Kinglassie looks as strong as it did when I was a child."

"Everything looks beautiful to you today," he said, as he halted his horse beside hers. "Ever since you freed those birds from their cages, you have been as giddy and happy as a babe." He chuckled as she grinned at him. "You released more than those birds, I think, my lady."

She nodded. "Somehow I have let go of my own unhappiness."

Still smiling, Gavin looked toward the castle, a half mile or so in the distance. Silhouetted against the sunset sky, Kinglassie's massive towers and walls, almost fully repaired, appeared flawless. The setting sun glinted off the sandstone walls and turned the castle to a rosy gold. Below the great dark mass of the promontory, the loch flowed like molten gold, reflecting the wild sky.

"Aye, 'tis beautiful," Gavin said quietly. The view was breathtaking and powerful, but something made him uneasy. He gathered his reins again, frowning. "Let's go home, my lady," he said. Christian nodded, stirring her horse forward. They rode ahead, following the edge of the forest toward the drawbridge.

Christian suddenly halted her horse. "Gavin, look. Is the castle on fire?" She pointed, and Gavin saw a long white plume rising up from the side of the promontory that faced the loch.

He shook his head. " 'Tis not smoke. Those are birds flying out of the rock. Wild doves, I think."

"Odd—'tis as if they are coming straight out of the rock. They must have nests on the promontory."

He nodded, scanning the promontory and the dominant block of the castle, with its high, soaring walls. Then he saw what had caused his earlier uneasiness. "There is a banner flying above the gatehouse," he said. "The dragon banner. Hastings is here."

She looked up and gasped. "Then those are his sentries on the parapet."

Gavin pulled on the reins to steady his black stallion, who shifted nervously beneath him. "Aye. He has obviously decided to install the garrison on his own, without waiting for my word. He must have left Ayr before we did. He probably had this planned all along, seeing his chance because I was in Ayr with you."

"But why would he take over the castle?" she asked.

"I intend to find out," Gavin said, as he spurred the horse forward and rode across the drawbridge.

"WHAT IS THE MEANING OF THIS?" Gavin shouted when he saw Hastings crossing the bailey yard toward him. A thick flock of pigeons and doves, pecking at the ground, scattered as Hastings advanced through their midst.

Dismounting, Gavin flung the reins toward a startled carpenter who stood by the gatehouse, and stomped forward. "By what right do you garrison my castle in my absence?"

"By king's right. I have not only garrisoned Kinglassie, I now command it," Hastings said.

"God's blood!" Gavin stepped forward. "I hold the charter!"

Hastings shrugged. "The king decides who holds property. I will request that he transfer the charter to me." He turned to beckon toward a group of soldiers. "Guards, take this traitor into custody. Place him with the others for now."

Two of the guards grabbed Gavin's arms, trapping them at his sides. He struggled, looking over his shoulder. Other guards had lifted Christian down from her horse and were leading her away.

She glanced back at him, her face pale and frightened. Gavin sensed how terrified she was, and that increased his anger. He turned toward Hastings, glaring, his breath heaving.

"I received a letter from the king just after you left Ayr Castle," Hastings said. "He sent word that you are charged with treason for taking the Lady Christian home to Kinglassie without his permission, and for delaying the installation of the king's troops here."

"And you wasted not a moment in coming here," Gavin said. "But Edward gave me custody of the lady. And you have no proof that I have conspired to delay the garrison of this place."

"No proof, but suspicions," Hastings returned. "I informed the king that you have been protecting spies and allies of Robert Bruce here at Kinglassie. That priest and that carpenter—"

"That man was your spy, not mine," Gavin said.

"I have no idea what you mean," Hastings said softly. "And I further suspect that you are withholding the Scottish treasure that rightfully belongs to Edward. I hoped to arrest you in Ayr, but the king's reply had not yet arrived before you left the castle."

"You have no grounds for this," Gavin said. "Your own greed drives you to take this castle. But there is naught here of value for you." The guards began to lead him away; he tore free but was forced to accompany them when two other heavily armed men approached and took his arms.

"Naught of value?" Hastings followed him. "I doubt that. My men are searching each room even now."

The guards took Gavin and Christian into the groundfloor bakery, and through the doorway that led down to the long tunnel. Hastings came with them, followed by a soldier who held a blazing torch. Their footsteps echoed loudly in the stone passageway.

"You never told me about the hidden chamber down here," Hastings said as they neared the final entry. "That was a mistake. It speaks of treason on your part. When I arrived here with my troops yesterday, I commanded a thorough search of the place. We found this underground chamber, with traces of recent meals, and stacks of blankets used not long ago. I believe that you have been hiding rebels down here—perhaps even Robert Bruce himself. Your love for the Scots has been too damned evident in the past, Faulkener. I warned Edward against placing you here in this crucial location."

Christian, standing beside Gavin in the little foyer area, looked at Hastings. "Gavin hasna done any crime," she said.

"I will find proof where I want to, my lady," Hastings said in a low voice.

"Even if 'tisna true," she snapped in reply.

He shrugged. "This would be a fine place to hide a hoard of gold, would it not?" Hastings shoved the door open, and the guards escorted Gavin and Christian inside. "But as yet we have found naught. And since Kinglassie's small dungeon will hold only two prisoners, I had no choice but to put my hostages here."

As the torchlight spilled into the room, Gavin saw several faces turned up toward them from the shadows. Fergus and the children, John and Dominy, and a few of the workmen—men who he knew were loyal Scots—were seated on the floor, their hands bound behind them.

"*Màthair!*" Michaelmas cried out. Christian lurched forward out of the guard's grip, and stumbled to her knees as she reached out to fold her daughter into her arms. As Christian moved, the golden pendant around her neck swung free, glinting.

"Here! Give that to me," Hastings said. He broke the thong roughly. "This must be the piece that Henry once described to me. He said that one ancient gold pendant proved the existence of the rest."

"That piece has been in Christian's family for generations," Gavin said. "It proves naught. Return it to her."

Clutching the thing in one hand, Hastings turned. "This belongs to the king. She too is a traitor."

"The king pardoned her of treason charges," Gavin said.

"But that order is old now," Hastings said smoothly.

"Ah. I had forgotten. Edward needs small reason to change his mind on a promise if it suits his purpose."

"And because he had reason to declare you a traitor and an outlaw, your wife naturally receives the same treatment. 'Tis

Edward's rule for Scottish women."

"What of these others?" Gavin asked, looking toward Fergus and the rest. "You cannot mean to charge children, mothers, and priests with treason. King Edward may be furious toward the Scots, but even he will not accept those accusations from you."

"Perhaps not," Hastings said. "But they will stay here for now. The priest, I suspect, supports Robert Bruce. Your uncle is a Scot, and therefore subject to arrest at any time. These children will develop into rebels unless they are taught otherwise before 'tis too late. And they have offended me."

"Offended you?" Gavin asked in surprise.

Hastings pointed toward Will. "That one there has a foul tongue in his head. He knows more curses that I have ever learned. And that loud one, over there"—he indicated Robbie—"called us tailed dogs. I was tempted to cut the tongues from both their mouths."

Despite the grave situation, Gavin smothered a sudden urge to laugh at Hastings' insistence that the children had offended him. The man sounded like a whining, malicious child.

Gavin knew of the contention, held by both French and Scots, that the English hid canine tails beneath their tunics, and therefore were no better than scavenging mongrels. Few Englishmen could take that insult with grace or humor; he had seen the remark cause violent fights. And he could well imagine Robbie, who had once accused Gavin and John of the same thing, loudly spouting out his belief to all the Englishmen here.

"When I was a child, my father beat me often to keep me humble," Hastings said. "And he was right to do it. Children are evil creatures by nature. Children and women," he added in a low, grinding voice, sliding a glance at Christian.

"You have not learned much humility," Gavin said. "Although you have learned your father's taste for punishing those who are weaker than you." He glared at Hastings. "What is it you are after, Oliver? Is it truly the gold—or is it the praise you will get from King Edward if you find it? The rewards, the prestige of providing him what he is desperate to obtain? He will not reward you for it, Oliver. He will take whatever you offer him and only please himself with it. He will not spare a thought for what you want."

Hastings shot him a sneering glance and turned away to scan the dark corners of the vast chamber. "My men have searched this room thoroughly. We will take what we need from this place"— he waved a hand toward the barrels of grain and wine and chests of household goods that were stacked around the room—"but we have yet to find anything of real value. These supplies will feed and clothe and arm English soldiers. But there is more. I know it. I can feel it." He whipped around to stare down at Christian. "Are there other underground rooms?"

"Only this one," she answered stiffly.

Hastings dangled the twinkling pendant from his fingers. "Tell me where the rest is hidden, my lady, or by God you will pay dearly for your silence." He dropped the thong around his own neck, clutching the pendant. "By the design of this, the treasure must be a sight to behold."

She stood, facing him, protecting her daughter behind her skirts. "You willna have it. 'Tis gone."

"You know something about it," he growled, leaning toward her. "Women connive and lie. Where have you put it?"

She raised her chin. "I burned it. 'Tis melted into the very walls. You willna have it. England willna have it."

"Then neither will Scotland." Hastings drew his hand back and slapped her, hard enough that she stumbled back. Gavin leaped forward with a guttural curse, straining against the guards who held him back.

"I promise you that you will die for that blow, Oliver," Gavin said between clenched teeth.

Hastings spun around, eyes narrowed. "One blow to a woman is naught. Edward himself would applaud what I do here. I have revealed a traitor, a lover of Scots, among his finest knights."

"You go too far, Hastings. You always did," Gavin said.

"Too far? Where the Scots are concerned, that cannot be."

"I should have hunted you down years ago when I heard that you had burned that nunnery in the Borderlands. Edward assured me that you had been severely punished. I could not leave France at that time. And I never thought to see you again."

Hastings shrugged. "That nunnery? 'Twas years ago, a necessary raid. But the pope ordered me to make a penance for it. And Edward took my newest holding at the time. That debt has already been paid."

"Not in full," Gavin growled.

Hastings turned and spoke to the guards. "Confine them in here. Then come into the courtyard. The southeast tower must be searched next." The guards bound Gavin's hands behind him, and turned away to bind Christian.

"I will tear down every stone in this castle if I must, to find that gold," Hastings said.

"Do that, and you will soon discover what an enemy truly is," Gavin said, his tone low and dangerous. "No confinement will keep me from you."

"You shall hang for your crimes," Hastings turned away.

"Do not think that death would stop me," Gavin said swiftly.

Hastings glanced nervously over his shoulder. Then he stepped through the doorway.

Gavin trained his unwavering gaze on Hastings. Hatred rose in him like bile, summoned up from some dark corner of his soul. He had never truly hated anyone but this one man. He felt as if he had dipped a cup into the same venomous brew from which Hastings drank. And he found the deep, black anger there surprisingly potent.

The last of the guards filed out, taking the torch with him. The chamber was suddenly plunged into profound darkness. Gavin heard the sound of a massive bar sliding into place.

"I'M HUNGRY," ROBBIE SAID. Gavin could hear him shifting around. "And my backside hurts from sitting on this stone floor."

"Mine, too," Patrick complained. "It's gone flat."

"Aye, me, too," Will said. "Hungry, I mean. Is it time for breakfast yet?"

"Not for hours yet," Christian said, seated beside Gavin. He felt the press of her shoulder against him, but could see nothing in the darkness. "There's food in those barrels over there, if we could but get to it."

"I dinna like the dark," Michaelmas said. "Patrick said that water monsters could climb in here from the loch."

There was a sliding sound, and a thump. "Here it comes," Patrick said with glee. Gavin heard Robbie and Will make the same noises. He shook his head, smiling to himself.

"Ach, stop teasing the wee lass," John grumbled through the darkness. "You laddies are enjoying this too much."

"I'm not, I'm thirsty," Will said. "There is wine over there in those barrels."

"Good French stuff, and ye'll not have a drop," Dominy said.

"I'm thirsty, too," Michaelmas said. She was beginning to sound tearful.

"We'll all have a drink when we get out of here," Gavin said. He leaned over to murmur to John. "The guards neglected to find the dagger sheathed at the back of my belt. If you could pull it loose, Uncle, I would appreciate it."

"I'll do my best," John said; Gavin heard the grin in his answer. John soon found the knife, slid it loose and began to saw away at the ropes that bound Gavin's hands.

"Are we leaving?" Robbie asked, his high-pitched voice echoing in the chamber.

"Aye, as soon as we can manage," Gavin said.

"Good. When we leave, we'll go fetch the treasure. I know where 'tis now," Robbie said.

"What!" Fergus said. "Where?"

"'Tis in the well," Robbie said blithely.

"Ach, you keep insisting on that," Fergus said. "But we pulled you out o' there once, and didna find a thing but a loose stone in the well wall."

"We went back down yesterday, Patrick and Robbie and I," Will said.

"What! Ye might have been sore hurt!" Dominy burst out.

"Hush, woman," John said, low and gentle. "Your lad has courage. Let him be. Why did you go down there, lad?"

"Because Patrick saw something in the well when he fell before, and wanted to go back," Will said.

"There was a space, where the stone was loose," Patrick added. "We saw some light there. We tried to move the stone, but we couldna. And we heard birds behind it. Like the doves in the tower, cooing."

"Doves?" Gavin frowned, trying to remember something. It tapped at the back of his mind, but he could not grasp it.

"Merlin's treasure is there," Robbie said confidently. "The birds are guarding it, like in the legend. Merlin sent doves to find the gold. 'Tis why we have them at Kinglassie."

"Did you say aught o' this to Hastings?" John asked, echoing Gavin's next thought.

"Nay. But he knows. I heard Hastings tell one of the guards to search the whoring well," Will said.

"He said to search the wretched well," Patrick corrected him. "I heard him, too. He'll look there soon."

Fergus, John, Dominy, and Christian began to talk at once.

"Hold!" Gavin called out, his voice cutting through their clamor. John had sliced through the last of his ropes, and he flexed his hands, leaning forward. "Hold and hush, all of you. We can do naught until we get out of this place." He took the knife from John and turned to Christian, beginning to cut through her bonds. "Where is the tunnel that leads out to the loch?" he asked her as he worked.

"At the back. 'Tis well hidden in a dark corner, behind trestle tables," she said. "Hastings couldna know of it, else he wouldna have put us here."

"And how will we get out?" Fergus said. "Your blade will free us from these ropes. But that tunnel leads out o' the cliffside, wi' naught but a drop to the loch. And we canna all swim to shore."

"Well, I'd like to take a look at it," Gavin said, as he sliced through John's ropes next. He handed the dagger to John, who turned immediately to Dominy. Gavin stood, holding out his hand to Christian. "Show me."

In the darkness, Gavin and Christian stumbled over barrels and sacks as they made their way toward the farthest corner. Feeling his way carefully, Gavin found the trestle tables stacked against the wall. He groped past them to find the rock wall behind it.

He felt Christian's hand on his arm. "Here, let me," she said. "I know where 'tis, and I am smaller. Follow me." She slid past him and crouched down to wriggle behind the tables.

Gavin dropped to his knees to crawl after her. At her murmur, he followed her through a narrow opening in the rough wall.

Christian stood up in the tunnel, but Gavin could not. Feeling drifts of cool, fresh, moist air, he hunched over and followed her through a passageway that was cut, like the chamber and the other tunnel, from raw rock.

After a few moments, he could see starlight flooding the narrow tunnel opening. Christian reached the end and clung to the rough-cut wall, facing outward. Straightening beside her, Gavin found that they stood in a tall, narrow crevice in the rock face, an opening that would be hidden even in sunlight among the fissures and ledges of the promontory.

Wind blew back their hair and clothing, and the dark loch below glinted and rippled. Gavin looked down and saw that the height was too great to jump safely, though a climb would be possible. The cliff face had an abundance of protrusions and ledges for hands and feet.

And he saw, too, that a small boat was moored at the base of the rock. He glanced at Christian.

"My cousin left one of the boats," she said. "There were three that he and his men used to come back and forth. I've been wondering if he means to spend another night here. But he must know that the English garrison is here now."

"He knows," Gavin said. "He is no fool. He has men watching the castle." He squatted down and saw a line of sturdy iron rungs, a hidden ladder that led down to the water. "Your ancestors provided a neat sally port here," he said.

"They did," she agreed. "They tunneled into this great rock when the first stronghold was built on the promontory. Gavin, I wonder if Robbie and Patrick are right. There could be another tunnel connected to the well."

" 'Tis possible. But for now, we must get the children and the others out of here. And this boat is just what we need." He held out a hand. "Come, my lady. We have work to do."

AS THE LAST OF THE CAPTIVES climbed down the rock to the boat, Gavin turned to Christian. "Now you," he said.

"Me? I willna go," she said.

"You will. Even John is going, to bring word that we need some help at Kinglassie. Now climb down there."

She folded her arms stubbornly; he recognized the haughty lift of that chin. "Where you go, I will go. You mean to find the treasure," she said. "And I will go with you."

"Christian," he growled low, "I mean also to find Hastings and deal with him as I should have done years ago. You are not safe here. Leave with the others."

"I willna, unless you come."

"Do not argue with me," he said. "Of course I will not come. I cannot let Hastings tear down these walls. I rebuilt this place. 'Tis my home."

"Mine as well," she said. "And I willna leave it for the English to plunder and ruin." She grabbed his arm. "Gavin, listen. I destroyed this place once, and feared that I destroyed the legend, too. If there is a chance that the treasure has survived, I must find it. I am the keeper of Kinglassie's legend. 'Tis my responsibility to claim the gold for Scotland."

He raised an eyebrow. "Ah. Do you not trust me to find your gold, then? Think you I will let the English have it?"

She laughed lightly, surprising him. "I trust you well, Gavin of Kinglassie," she said. "You know that now. But I have the right to do this."

He sighed. "You do have the right," he said. "But I will not put you in danger."

"You willna. I stay of my own will. I have lost my fear of the English, Gavin. I dinna know what happened, or where it has gone, but I dinna feel the awful fear of them that I had before. I will stay here with you."

As he listened, he remembered, quite suddenly, an image of the caged birds flying free. She seemed to have released her fears somehow, just as she had released those birds.

Just then, the thought of the caged birds brought into focus the one element that had eluded him earlier. He frowned, thinking, glancing around at the promontory, and realized that the idea that had occurred to him was quite sound.

"Go, Christian," he said. "Climb down to the boat, and go."

She tilted her head and watched him, her eyes narrowed. "What do you mean to do? You canna get out of the underground chamber. Hastings barred the door from the other side when he shut us in the chamber. How will you get to the well—you canna mean to wait for Hastings to let you out of the storage chamber!"

He looked up at the sky, which still glittered with stars. "There is another way into the castle," he said.

"Where?"

"I am not certain, but I will find it. Go, Christian. John and the others are waiting for you to climb down into the boat."

"You truly mean to find the gold," she said.

"Among other things I mean to do, aye. Now go," he said firmly, taking her arm

"I am staying here with you." She yanked away from him stubbornly and folded her arms across her chest.

He brushed at a curl that blew loose from her sparkling silvery fret, then cupped his hand along her cheek, tilting her face up to him. "Listen well to me, Christian of Kinglassie. Stay with me, and risk all. Or go with the others and keep yourself safe."

She watched him, he eyes dark, deep, trusting. "If you wanted me truly safe," she whispered, "then you would ask me to stay with you always. Always."

He drew a breath, struck by the meaning in her words, feeling the truth of them in his very soul. "Your loyalty is a true gift."

"Freely given to you," she said.

He bent his head then, but stopped to look down when he hard a low growl at his feet.

"*Ach,*" John said, looking up as he hung on to the iron rung just below where they stood. "Kiss the lassie and put her on the boat. The bairns are hungry and beginning to howl."

CHAPTER TWENTY-FOUR

GAVIN WOULD NOT TELL HER what he knew, and it aggra-vated her. She was cold, and tired, and hungry, and now she was annoyed. But Gavin hushed her, and put his arm around her, and made her sit quietly beside him, curled in the tunnel. He wrapped his cloak around them both, and they slept, finally, lean-ing together. When dawn came, with new light shining through the mist and fresh, cool breezes stirring against their faces, they awoke.

Gavin stood and went to the edge of the entrance, lean-ing there for a long while, looking out and listening carefully. Christian watched him, wondering what he was thinking. He turned his head, his golden hair, touched by sunlight, wafting in the breeze.

He looked at her. "Listen. Do you hear that?"

All Christian could hear was the *shoosh* of the loch against the promontory, the chitter of birds, and the sullen rumble of her stomach. She stood and went to him, and he put his arm around her shoulders.

"Now we may discover one of Kinglassie's secrets," he said quietly. She stood there, hearing wind, water, birdsong. "The doves," Gavin said. "Listen to them."

Then she heard the burbling, contented sound of hundreds of doves. The cooing seemed to come from overhead somewhere. "They sound so close," she said. "There must be nests on the ledges."

"I thought so, too," Gavin said. "We saw a flock of doves flying up from the rock yesterday. They roost somewhere nearby. Remember what Patrick and Robbie said about the well?"

She nodded. "They saw daylight, and heard birds behind that loose stone in the wall of the well."

"Aye. Then I realized that the birds must have found another way into the castle, through the cliffside. They have a kind of dovecote somewhere nearby, just as they have in the southeast tower. And once we find that opening, we will find our way back into Kinglassie."

"And we might find the treasure," she added.

He shrugged. "If it exists. You have always insisted that Kinglassie's gold is gone." He smiled. "But Robbie would be quite pleased if his suggestion led us to the gold."

She smiled at the thought, and glanced toward the misted shore, edged with dense forest past the stony beach. "They are far away by now, I hope. Warm and safe."

"And well fed," he said. She laughed ruefully, feeling the unhappy tremors of her own stomach; she was so hungry she felt almost ill with it. The few dried apples she and the children had eaten from the storage barrels had not gone far for her.

"Do you think Fergus will send word to my cousin?"

"Aye. Robert Bruce will surely be interested to know what has happened here at Kinglassie." Gavin turned then, and stepped down onto the top rung in the rock. Holding on with one hand, he leaned back as far as he could, looking all around the cliff face. "Once the birds stir and fly out, we'll know which one of these crevices holds their dovecote." He scanned the promontory, his hair and cloak tossed by the breeze.

Christian clung to a handhold of the rock and leaned out as far as she dared so that she could look around as well. After a few minutes, she heard the soft steady flap of wings, then again, and again, until the air was filled with a soft, rapid thunder.

High overhead, wild doves poured out of the rock face, rising toward the sun in a steady stream of dazzling white, wings tipped with brilliance in the dawn light.

"Oh! They look like angels flying up to heaven," she said in awe.

Gavin leaned back. "There is the entrance," he said, pointing. "Tucked behind that fold in the rock. We'll have to climb. Can you do it?"

"Climb up there?" She craned her head around, straining to see the tall, narrow crevice out of which some doves still flew. The sun struck a protruding wedge of rock. From where she stood, the doves' hideaway was to the left, at least a hundred feet above her head.

Far above that, on top of the promontory, the high walls of Kinglassie soared above the rock and caught the new sun like a rosy golden citadel.

"If you do not care to climb, you can wait for Hastings to let us back into the castle through the storage chamber," Gavin suggested.

"I'll climb," she said quickly.

"Kilt up your gown, then, and come on," he said.

She took off her heavy cloak and her new silver fret and put them on the tunnel floor. Then she stuffed some of her gown and linen undertunic up into her belt, lifting the hems to her knees. Gavin moved down another two rungs, so that she could climb down to cling to the first iron bar.

" 'Tis not difficult," Gavin said. "There are ledges there, see, cut almost like steps, and natural handholds all the way up. I wonder if your ancestors intended for that crevice up there to be approachable from the loch, as this tunnel is."

"It doesna look very approachable to me," she muttered.

Gavin stepped to the left and began to climb up a series of ledges, grabbing on to protrusions in the rock face. She watched his graceful, athletic advance up the cliff. Then she followed more slowly, grasping cold, rough stone, bumping her knees and grazing her legs, climbing past soft green clumps of fragrant mountain plants just beginning to flower. She went upward almost as easily as he did, as long as she did not look down toward the dark, deep loch far below.

At one point Gavin gave a little whoop of triumph, and

motioned to her that he had found an iron rung driven into the rock and another placed above that. He quickly pulled himself up, and stepped lightly on to the shallow platform of rock at the entrance.

Christian climbed more slowly and with greater caution that Gavin had used, training her eyes ahead until she finally saw Gavin's booted feet at eye level. He bent down and grabbed her wrist, helping to pull her up beside him.

Cold wind whipped at their hair and clothing, and sunlight poured down over them. Far below, the surface of the loch, rippled by winds, looked like glittering dark silver.

"This entrance was designed as deliberately as the other one," he said. "Both are hidden from sight, and yet both are accessible from the loch. The rungs were purposefully placed."

"I wonder why," she said. "There is but one underground hall, which my family has used for generations. Why this second entrance here? It doesna make good sense for it to connect to the well."

"We'll soon know," Gavin said, turning. He entered the crevice, holding her hand as she followed him. A few doves fluttered out as they entered, depositing their greetings on the rock ledge. "Watch your head, my lady, and where you walk. The birds have been here for generations. Without a broom."

"*Ech*," Christian said, stepping carefully on the crusted stone floor. They moved through a corridor, carved like the others below Kinglassie, with rounded walls scraped out of solid rock. Bright morning sunshine filled the corridor to a depth of several feet, illuminating the interior. Walking ahead, Gavin suddenly stopped.

"God's bones. It truly is a dovecote," he said. Christian looked up. On one side of the wall, small niches had been hand cut into the rock to form rows of compartments. In the nooks, a few doves still slept, while others sat calmly, cooing deeply and peacefully in their tucked throats.

"*Ach,* my wee doves," Christian said softly, approaching them. "You've been living here all this time, and we didna know it." She made a low coo in her throat, and two birds looked up, ruffling their feathers before relaxing again. Beside her, Gavin turned around, studying the space.

"I dinna understand," Christian said. "Why would my ancestors build this, if they had to climb here to pick doves for supper?"

"Mayhap they never had to climb," he said. "Look."

She turned, and saw, in the opposite wall, a massive door, similar to the one that led to the vast underground storage chamber. Its surface was scarred with bird droppings, but beneath that layer she saw the spiraling patterns of iron and brass over dark wooden planks. " 'Tis very, very old, that door," she said in a hushed voice.

"Aye, so," Gavin murmured, and turned again. Ahead of them, with the dovecote to the left and the door to the right, the tunnel continued into shadows. "That must lead into the castle," he said. "To the wall of the well." He walked slowly forward and she followed. The tunnel narrowed where rubble formed a pile on one side. Ahead, they saw a wall of dressed blocks.

Gavin crouched down and pressed against the blocks until one shifted. "Aye, look—the well!" he whispered. "The mortar has been weakened in places, most likely from the fire last summer." Gavin ran the flat of his hand over the exposed outer wall of the well. "When your ancestor built this, he must have closed off the corridor to the dovecote purposefully. I wonder why."

Christian dropped down beside him and saw that one or two of the stone blocks had cracked and slipped askew. Through a wedge of darkness, she heard the trickle of water, and the faint murmur of voices.

"The English soldiers," she whispered. "They must be up there in the bakery!"

"The lads said that Hastings intended to search the well." Gavin frowned, listening, then stood. "I do not relish bursting through the well wall just now to get into the castle," he said wryly. "We'll wait, and hope they do not remove that loosened block."

"I want to open that door," she whispered, standing.

He turned. "If we can. It looks as if it has been sealed for centuries."

They walked back toward the door, which appeared to be about eight feet tall, its top edge just below the level of the stone ceiling. Gavin tried the massive iron latch, but found it locked. He began to twist it.

Christian stood on her toes and stretched her arms up, feeling with her fingertips into every crevice beside the carved stone doorframe. Then her fingers hit cold iron. "The key!" she exclaimed, pulling it out.

Gavin laughed, shaking his head without comment, and stuck the key in the lock. After some earnest shoving on his part, the door swung wide. Behind it was a large, dark, open space.

He went through the doorway. "There are stone steps just here," he said, taking her arm and drawing her forward. "Go careful, now."

Christian stepped down to face utter blackness, relieved only the wedge of light that spilled in from the dovecote corridor. A layer of dust stirred up at their entrance, making her cough. The sound echoed as if in a cave.

As Gavin moved ahead, holding her hand, she saw something glimmering, overhead and to the sides, but could not identify it.

"Here," he said suddenly, "what is this?" He knelt, and she knelt beside him.

In the deep shadows, his hands explored a small pile of objects carefully. "A sword," he said, hefting something massive in his hands and setting it down. "A box, a small casket of some kind. 'Tis locked." He briefly jiggled the latch and laid the box aside. "And here are some smaller things—brooches, I think, and other jewelry. A few rough stones. Perhaps this is your treasure, my lady."

Christian heard the clink of lightweight metal and stretched out her hands. She felt a jumble of cool surfaces, smooth, bumpy, intricately decorated. "The treasure of Kinglassie is real, Gavin!"

"Ah," he said, reaching forward. "This object here feels like—aye, an oil lamp. And still full. Christian, I'll need a piece of your linen shift."

"What?" she asked, confused. He repeated his request, and she tore off a piece of the hem and handed it to him.

He stood and, using his dagger, quickly scraped the blade against the stone wall. Blue and white stars flew through the darkness. He scraped again, until he caught a few sparks on the dry cloth he held. Blowing quickly, he fed the spark until it smoked and caught flame. Then he touched the burning linen to the wick on the old lamp.

Holding the blazing lamp high, he looked up. Christian stood, and turned in a slow circle.

"*Dhia,*" she breathed out. "Gavin, look!"

"GOLD," HE SAID WHEN HE could speak. "All of it. Gold."

"The very walls," she said.

Gavin scanned the room, holding the lamp. They stood in a cavelike space chiseled from solid rock, a room as large as a bedchamber. And every surface—walls, floor, ceiling—was veined in gold. Sparkling, glittering, the pale quartz walls reflected the lamplight in a dazzle of sunburst yellow and ochres.

" 'Tis a gold mine," he said, stepping forward to touch his hand to the wall. The cool surface was slightly gritty beneath his fingers. "Gold ore. Silver. Iron as well. My God," he said, his voice hushed as he turned. He laughed softly as he looked at Christian. "You did say Kinglassie's gold was melted into the very walls."

"But I didna know about this," she said. "The legend only said that the gold was hidden away in the heart of Kinglassie."

"Then this room must be the very heart of the rock, rather than the storage chamber," he said. He drew his fingers along the delicate veins and arteries of gold, and the darker channels of silver and iron. "There is a vast treasure here," he said.

"Can it be mined out?" she asked.

"No doubt. 'Twas mined once, long ago. See these marks here, and there, where ore has been removed." He frowned. "This may be why the walls of the towers above have been cracked for so long. The mine would make the supporting rock unstable in places." He glanced at her. "When was the well dug?"

"Long before those stone towers were built, when Kinglassie was but a wooden fortress on top of the promontory rock," she said. "Mayhap the well was dug at the same time as the tunnels in the rock."

"This chamber was sealed off deliberately, along with the corridor," Gavin said. "The dovecote was once accessible through the stronghold, because the corridor leads toward the castle. But some laird made certain that all of this was hidden away."

"They placed the well there, and sealed this off in the well wall," Christian said.

He nodded. "They meant to protect the gold. Perhaps those who knew about the mine were killed or captured by enemies. Somehow the secret was lost, and the legend began."

"No one ever noticed that the doves were roosting here," she said. Then she gasped. "Oh! The legend says that Merlin sent wild doves to find the treasure that had been hidden by the wee lady of the fair folk. The birds found it, Gavin. They have been here all along."

Shaking his head in astonishment, Gavin went back to the little pile of objects and knelt again, setting the lamp on the floor. She joined him and reached out to pick up a brooch from the jumble of pins and pendants. "This design is similar to the pendant that I have always kept," she said. "The one that Hastings took."

"Likely all these things are made from gold mined here," he said. He lifted a small glittery stone and turned it in his hand. "These little rocks are golden nuggets. I have heard that the Celtic people were skilled at mining and working gold. Look at this sword." He pulled it loose from its secure wrappings of leather and cloth. The grip, wrapped in gold wire, looked like a spool of golden thread, topped by a pommel of gleaming polished amber set in gold. When he lifted the sword, his arm muscles tensed with the weight of the iron blade, but he found that the weapon was beautifully balanced and still sharp. He could have used it easily.

"What is in the casket?" Christian asked. She lifted the small box, its glittering golden surfaces intricately worked and inlaid with emeralds and garnets. Christian picked at the latch. " 'Tis locked."

"Mayhap the key is over the door lintel," he teased.

She shook the box. " 'Tis very light, and doesna rattle inside. It might be empty."

"This will do for a key," he said. Picking up a small silver-hilted dagger that lay beneath the jewelry, Gavin twisted its point in the latch and sprung the casket open.

"A parchment?" Christian sounded disappointed as Gavin pulled out a small piece of rolled vellum, yellowed and tied with a leather cord. "Only a bit of parchment," she said. "Likely some prayers for someone's saint's day, or a few psalms."

Gavin unrolled it very carefully. The thinly scraped vellum was old and brittle, its edges crumbling a little in his hands. There was writing on it, a few words in an unfamiliar language, and some sticklike symbols he did not recognize.

"What does it say?" she asked.

" 'Tis not Latin or any language I can read," he said, handing it to her. Christian took the translucent parchment gently and peered at it, tilting it toward the lamplight.

"These signs are ogham script, an old Druidic form of writing," she said. "I have seen it on old stones. And these words are old Gaelic. I canna read it, but there are some words I know— *rí,* which is the ancient form of *rígh,* which means king. And this phrase here"—she pointed—"means small hawk, or merlin. Merlin!" She looked up at him in excitement. "What does it mean, do you think?"

"I have no idea," he said. "We might show it to Fergus."

"We will," she said, rolling it carefully and replacing the leather tie. "He will understand the Gaelic and mayhap the ogham as well." She put the roll reverently in the little golden box and closed the lid. Then she gazed around the room. " 'Tis magical, this place, truly a treasure. The very heart of Kinglassie."

Gavin nodded. "Now what shall we do with it?"

She looked at him, startled. "It belongs to Scotland. The legend says that the treasure of Kinglassie will support the throne of Scotland. We will tell Robert Bruce, of course."

"Ah," said a voice from the doorway. "I was sure you knew where Bruce was hiding. And where the gold was kept. This is quite a find, your golden treasure room." Oliver Hastings leaned against the doorframe, his red surcoat a brilliant slash of color. His stance was deceptively casual, for his hand was on the hilt of his sword.

Gavin leaped to his feet, pushing Christian behind him. Hidden in shadow, she bent to lift and then shove the iron sword into his hand. "Oliver," he growled cautiously, grasping the hilt.

Hastings stepped down into the chamber, looking up at the glittering walls. Then he returned his sharp, nervous glance toward Gavin. "So Kinglassie truly does contain treasure. You were so absorbed in your discussion, you did not hear me come through the wall in the well. No wonder you would not tell anyone about this, Lady Christian. I, too, would have kept this secret to myself."

"We didna know about it until now," Christian said.

"My lady, I cannot believe you just discovered this place. You must have known all along. There was talk of the well when I was here last. I should have checked it then," Hastings said. "I should have known not to trust Faulkener to take care of it." His narrowed gaze flickered over the sparkling, veined wall, over the jewelry and the casket on the floor. Greed, a yearning, desperate hunger, pinched his features.

Gavin noticed that Christian's golden pendant hung around Hastings' neck, prominent against his red surcoat. Hastings lifted his sword in protection, and glanced down, touching the toe of his boot to the assortment of golden objects.

"Not much of a prize, these few things," he said. "The nuggets have immediate value, and the rest is passable enough. But this chamber is the real treasure. King Edward will be greatly pleased. He will want to set up mining immediately to extract the gold. 'Twill support our treasury nicely."

"The English king willna have it!" Christian burst out. Gavin squeezed his fingers around her arm to warn her to silence.

"My lady, you should have told me this was here months ago when you had the chance. I might be more inclined, now, to favor you, since you are shortly to be widowed again." He snapped his glance toward Gavin. "Just how did you get out of that storage chamber? And where are the others?"

"Before you confine captives to a room, I suggest you first learn the layout of the castle," Gavin said. "The others are safely gone. You will not find them."

"I will send out a search for that priest. He can lead us to the Bruce, I think." He sighed heavily. "I warned the king not to give you charge of this place, Faulkener." Hastings cast his gaze upward, unable to resist another furtive, assessing glance toward the gleaming walls.

Taking Christian's hand, Gavin moved cautiously toward the door. He wanted her out of the room, where she could escape down the cliffside. And he hoped to maneuver Hastings out into the corridor, where the other man's left-handed fighting style would be hampered. Gavin fully planned to use the ancient sword gripped in his fist. He shifted it, lamplight and shadow distorting the subtle movement.

"Kinglassie has been rebuilt at no cost to Edward, and is whole and strong," Gavin said. "He has little to complain about."

"But he was distressed to learn that one of his favored commanders is a traitor," Hastings returned. "The Angel Knight is hardly the saint the king believed him to be. I warned him. I alone knew that your treachery ran deep. I alone knew that what you did at Berwick you would do again."

"What I did at Berwick was not treason," Gavin hissed. He was tired of these accusations from Hastings. He wanted nothing more, just then, than to plunge his sword into the man's belly and be done with it. He clenched his fingers tightly around the sword. And knew, suddenly, that his hatred and disgust for Hastings could draw him to the very edge of his own humanity.

"What you did was the essence of treason," Hastings said. "You did not obey and support your king."

"Any man with a conscience would have done the same," Gavin answered in a flat voice. "There were many men who were shocked at the king's orders, but said naught out of fear. And blood lust affected the rest. Including you."

"Edward should have punished you properly for your treachery at Berwick. But he did not." Hastings sneered, shifting his sword in his hand. "He loved you too well. Christ's tree! You have been blessed with luck for some reason. But count that luck at an end."

"Do you pronounce judgments now, in place of your king?" Gavin asked softly. "I do not think your authority extends that far, Oliver." Surreptitiously, he urged Christian toward the door. They stood now in heavy shadow, so that her movements were shielded behind Gavin. Hastings glanced again at the walls, as if he could not keep his gaze from the lure of the gold ore. Then Hastings swiveled to watch him through narrowed eyes.

" 'Tis treason to insult your sovereign king," Hastings said. "You called King Edward a murdering savage to his face when you rode through Berwick that day. You told him to stop the carnage or face peril for his soul. I was there. I witnessed your disgraceful deed in front of common people and soldiers."

"Do you recall what you were doing when I stopped the king's escort and spoke my mind?"

Hastings stared at him. "I was following my king's orders. As you should have done."

"You were holding a blade to the belly of a pregnant woman," Gavin said between his teeth. Behind him, he heard Christian gasp. "I arrived in Berwick when the massacre was nearly done. Not only soldiers and men, but town merchants, their wives, their children lay in those streets." The vile memories sickened him, but he continued. "The cobblestones ran with the blood of thousands. When I rode in, the streets stank like the back of a butcher's yard. I spoke angrily to the king because I could not believe the slaughter that I saw. I lost control of my sense of reason, just as you must have lost yours. When we rode on and he saw you with that poor woman in your grip, he finally ordered the killing stopped."

"Edward punished me for your moment of conscience!" Hastings shouted. "I forfeited my inheritance that day! Because the Angel Knight, the perfect *chevalier*, could not countenance the slaying of Scots. Nor could he pay for his traitorous act!"

"I was dispossessed and exiled for what I said to the king."

"Exiled! You should have been hanged! You only lost a castle and a modest demesne." Hastings leaned forward, his eyes wild and black, his knuckles white around the sword hilt. "I lost two wealthy and important baronies! And I spent months in the tower in London. Your exile to France—hah! More reward than reprimand. King Edward made you ambassador to Paris a year later. But I have naught, Faulkener! Naught!"

"You possess Loch Doon and another castle near Edinburgh."

"Scottish castles!" Hastings spat. "I have no castle on English soil! But Edward has finally begun to listen to me. Now he knows that you are a Scots sympathizer."

"He has outlawed me. That should please you."

"Aye, it does. Because that order gives me the right to kill you here and now with no fear of punishment from Edward. You ruined me, Faulkener." Hastings, facing the door, stepped toward him. "I thought to make your family pay, but that has not given me satisfaction."

"My family?" Gavin asked.

"I knew your mother was in that nunnery. She was famed for something—miraculous healings, holiness, I know not. But I sacked the place deliberately when I found out who she was. Edward reprimanded me for that, but I pleaded ignorance and told him I only followed his orders." He shrugged. "I made a penance for killing nuns. But I knew I had made a deep strike at you."

"Jesu," Gavin growled. "Your hatred is venomous."

Behind him, Christian spoke. "Oliver Hastings," she said. "Stop now, or you willna be able to bear the weight of such great sins. You will lose your very soul."

Hastings laughed, low and viciously. "My soul craves revenge, my lady, and will not accept forgiveness, or your good advice." He glanced at Gavin. "If I had been aware how much this Scottish girl here meant to you, months ago in Carlisle, I would have made certain she did not survive that cage."

"You knew she was Henry's widow, and therefore a relative of mine. Even if I did not know it at the time you captured her."

"I treated Lady Christian with respect at first," Hastings said. "I wanted the gold. But when she would not cooperate, I suggested to the king that he construct a cage for her, as he had done for two other of Bruce's women."

"Respect! You beat me," Christian said. "You wouldna let the guards bring me food or blankets."

Hastings shrugged mildly and looked at Gavin. "I wanted her to feel the consequences of her silence. I would have done more, but her damned guards hovered like nursemaids." He scowled. "Then you came, Faulkener, and took her away. And you took Kinglassie as well. Edward knew I wanted this holding! I was sure there was gold here." He took a step forward. "When I discovered that she was here with you, alive, I swore to myself that I would expose you both as traitors."

Gavin listened, his mouth gone dry, his gut twisting with anger. Every fiber of his being strained with the urge to kill Hastings, but he resisted—not to save his own soul, but to save his wife. Her safety was paramount in his thoughts as he watched Hastings.

Advancing toward the doorway, Gavin was intent on getting her out of the room before Hastings made a move for him, and before any guards came through the well wall. He had to ensure that Christian got free.

Then he intended to release his rage at last.

Taking another careful step sideways, balancing the sword and keeping his other hand on Christian's arm, Gavin moved into the wedge of light that spilled in the doorway. The steps that led upward into the corridor were just behind them now.

"Go!" he yelled, shoving Christian. "Go!" She stumbled up the steps and fled out into the corridor.

"You will not shut me in here!" Hastings yelled, and ran forward. Gavin mounted the steps, facing Hastings, blocking the door. Behind him, Christian ran past the doves to the outer entrance.

"I have no plans to lock you in here," Gavin said, shifting his sword menacingly. "Come collect your debt full on."

"Do you threaten me, traitor?" Hastings asked softly.

"I only warn you," Gavin said, letting the heavy blade hover in the air, gracefully, dangerously. He blessed the ancient laird who had left him such a fine weapon.

"My men will come through the well at any moment," Hastings said, lifting his sword and widening his stance.

"Then you will have to fight fairly until they do," Gavin said, and lunged.

CHAPTER TWENTY-FIVE

LOUD AND RELENTLESS, the clash of swords rang out in the corridor where Christian stood. She backed against the rock wall near the entrance, feeling the wind and sunshine at her back. Glancing outside in a panic, she wondered if she should climb down to try to fetch help from somewhere.

She turned to see Gavin step out of the chamber, slicing his sword menacingly at Hastings, who advanced steadily into the narrow space of the corridor with him. Gavin glanced toward Christian and deliberately kept between her and Hastings. He angled his position until Hastings, facing him, was backed against the wall, near the dark, empty spot where the block had been removed from the well. The sloping pile of stone rubble hampered the swing of Hastings' sword. Gavin had cornered him.

Hastings could not easily turn to escape through the well in the narrow space, and he could not move forward. He swiped his sword viciously toward Gavin, spitting angry curses as he tried to sidle past him. The razored edge of Gavin's sword, still keen after so long in the hidden chamber, cut through the air, and Gavin held his widespread stance, alert and cautious.

Each time Hastings moved, Gavin forced him back again and again, but most of his blows were deflected off Hastings' armor. Without armor himself, Gavin was more agile and quicker on his feet, but in greater danger. Although none of Hastings' strikes had landed, Gavin had nicked his opponent in the vulnerable areas at the sides and neck of his armor, where the chain mesh, closed with leather strips, was more easily penetrated.

Christian soon realized that Gavin had the advantage of greater skill, more space to maneuver, and a clever mind. When Hastings made the next thrust, Gavin stepped aside almost gracefully and smashed his iron blade against Hastings' head.

Hastings faltered, nearly losing his balance. As the point of his sword dipped, Gavin kicked it out of Hastings' grip. Then he waited, assessing, swaying dangerously, a golden wildcat ready to pounce on a cornered rodent.

Christian glanced outside again, where something had caught her attention. Far below, she saw many men: fifty, seventy or more emptied out of boats silently and climbed up the cliff toward the lower tunnel entrance. She recognized Robert Bruce's followers, a ragged, heavily armed assortment of knights and nobles and farmers, carrying long staves and bows, many with broadswords sheathed at their backs. They swarmed up the handholds and ledges in the promontory and disappeared into the lower tunnel.

"John!" she screamed. She had seen him climbing toward the other tunnel. But her cries were lost in the whip of the wind. Though she called out again, no one looked up.

She heard a deafening crash, and whirled in fright. The well wall had collapsed inward. Two men, Hastings's serjeants, tumbled into the corridor, gaining their feet quickly and drawing their swords.

"The Bruce! He and his men are invading the castle!" one of them shouted to Hastings. Until their arrival, he had been cornered by Gavin. Now, as the two guards began to fight Gavin, Hastings slid past all of them and ran toward the entrance.

He reached Christian before she could react to what had happened. Grabbing her arm, he yanked her toward him and trapped her against him, tipping the edge of a dagger to her throat. They stood so close to the outer ledge that Christian feared he would throw her out into the air.

Gavin backed toward them, clashing his blade rapidly, blocking left, blocking right. Though he took a hard slicing blow to the left shoulder, he hardly faltered. Watching, Christian cried out, and arched desperately against Hastings' grip, but he held her fast.

"Now you shall watch your husband wounded to the death," Hastings growled into her ear. "And when he is unable to move, when he lays dying, I will use you however I please." His breath was hot and fast on her cheek. The hand that held her around the ribs grabbed across her breasts painfully. She wrenched, sobbing in outrage, feeling as if she were caught in a cruel cage formed by his long, sharp dagger and his steel-covered arms.

Blood soaked Gavin's arm and dripped over his hand. He kicked out at one of the guards and tripped him. In the small space, the other guard tumbled backward and fell, too. Gavin thrust quickly, wounding one, knocking the other in the head. Then he whirled to face Hastings, breathing heavily.

"Let her go," Gavin said, low and ominously.

"But I've not had a Scottish widow for a while. I am looking forward to it," Hastings rasped. He kept his hand on her breast, and his blade at her throat.

"Let her go," Gavin hissed. His eyes were cold and hard as dark ice. Christian had rarely seen such stark hatred.

But she saw an element of fear pass through that hard gaze when Gavin glanced briefly toward her; he obviously realized that Hastings could easily cut her throat or throw her over the ledge. She cried out as the razored edge bit into the tender skin beneath her jaw.

Then Gavin's eyes flashed to the tunnel entrance behind them, a flicker only, but it warned Christian. She braced her feet for what came next.

Rising up from the ledge behind them, John hit into Hastings' feet and threw him off balance, slamming him forward. As she went down with him and hit the floor with her hands and knees, Christian felt a sharp sting in her leg, from rock or chain mail, she could not tell. Hastings fell on top of her, and John shoved him aside, pinning him down with the tip of his sword blade.

"I saw you from below," John said to Hastings, breathing heavily. "That red surcoat you wear is like a banner. Did you know that Bruce has taken the castle from your men?"

Gavin reached for Christian, lifting her to her feet and pulling her away. "Are you hurt?" he asked. She shook her head. He pushed her gently toward the door of the golden chamber. As she stepped back to stand inside the doorway, Gavin turned away.

One of the guards rose up then and caught Gavin around the legs, bringing him down hard to the floor. Christian screamed out, pressing her fists to her mouth, as she saw them wrestle desperately on the floor.

At the corner of her vision, she saw Hastings grab the end of John's sword blade, grasping it with his thick leather gauntlets. Flipping John off balance, Hastings slammed the hilt end against his head. The Scotsman dropped to the floor of the tunnel like a sack of grain.

Hastings shifted the sword and leaped forward; Christian shouted out, trying to warn Gavin. Grappling with the guard, Gavin reacted when she shrieked, rolling to one side just as Hastings thrust toward him.

Thwarted, Hastings' momentum caused him to stab his own serjeant in the back. He looked up, startled, confused, as Gavin slipped away and jumped to his feet.

"You are as persistent as the devil," Hastings snarled, rebalancing his sword. "Your life has some charm over it."

Gavin, breathing heavily, flashed a grin. "Then stop trying to kill me," he said.

"Never," Hastings said, and lunged.

And as he did, the wild doves came back to their dovecote.

WINGS FLUTTERING WILDLY, their frightened cries curdling in their throats, the doves panicked as they flooded into the tunnel and encountered Hastings standing in the entrance. In a flurry of snowy feathers, they tried to turn in the midst of their flight and go back outside. But in turning, the birds slammed into Hastings' head and chest and shoulders.

He threw his arms up over his head and screamed, dropping his sword, backing away to knock into the wall. Flailing his arms wildly, he fought at the frenzied cloud of doves striving to get past him. But his balance was thrown off, and he stumbled sideways. As the birds soared out and up, away from the crevice, Hastings stepped out too far on the ledge, and fell.

Gavin had realized quickly that the panicked birds were not attacking. As he ran toward the entrance, Hastings shrieked and tumbled backward an instant before Gavin could reach him.

Halting at the edge of the rock platform, Gavin watched as Hastings plummeted, a slash of red and glinting steel, toward the loch. Weighted down by his chain mail, falling two hundred feet or more straight down, Hastings sank into the water without a struggle.

Waiting, breath heaving, Gavin pressed his hand over the stinging cut in his upper arm. As the ripples of Hastings' plunge gradually disappeared, Gavin turned to go back in.

He noticed the cluster of empty boats moored at the base of the promontory. They had not been there earlier, and he quickly realized that Robert Bruce had invaded Kinglassie Castle from within. Gavin stood there, exhausted, grimly victorious after his own battle, and knew that the inner walls of Kinglassie rang with clashing steel.

Turning away, rubbing his hand wearily over his face, Gavin leaned his sword carefully against the wall. He put his hand to his shoulder for a moment, and was surprised to find that the wound had already clotted and his tunic sleeve was stuck to the wound; he would not need to tend to it for a while.

A few white doves flew in overhead and fluttered to rest in the wall niches. Quiet filled the little sanctum of the tunnel. The soft cooing of the birds was soothing and peaceful, oddly so, Gavin thought, after a struggle that had killed Hastings and left two guards dead on the floor.

Gavin saw Christian leaning against the stone doorframe, her face pale and drawn. He gave her a rueful, exhausted smile, and stepped toward her, hands out. She pointed toward John.

On the floor, his uncle was just sitting up, moaning. He placed his hand to his head in exploration, then looked up at Gavin and grinned. "I'm fine, lad," he said hoarsely.

Gavin chuckled. "I'd expect naught less, you tough old Scot.

You are indestructible."

"If the Saracen devils in the Holy Land didna get me, then that cowardly king's demon couldna do the deed," he said as he got to his feet. "Who trained those wee birdies?"

"Just luck," Gavin said. "Though they surely came when we needed them most."

"They were sent by the angels," Christian said.

John laughed gruffly. "Aye, those doves looked like a flock o' angels sweeping the king's demon to his death. 'Tis a sight I willna forget. And I willna eat dove pie again, I can tell you that."

"I'll show you a sight you've never seen before, John," Gavin said. "Come through here." He moved toward the huge door, stopping to put an arm around Christian's shoulders as he waited for his uncle to enter the chamber. Christian leaned against him wearily, and he glanced at her in concern.

John passed them to walk down the shallow steps. The lamplight still flickered within, illuminating the glittering walls.

"The hidden gold o' Kinglassie," John said, turning slowly in amazement. " 'Tis beautiful."

"In the very heart of the stone, just as the legend says," Gavin said.

"This must be the treasure that is meant to support the throne of Scotland," John said. "Robert Bruce will be interested in this. By now he will have won Kinglassie from Hastings' men."

Christian looked up at Gavin. "Will you try to gain back the castle for England?"

"Kinglassie is my home, and I will defend it if 'tis needed. But King Edward has named me a traitor to England," Gavin answered quietly. "I have no king, now, who expects me to hold a castle for his purposes."

"My cousin burns Scottish castles when he gains them back. He will scorch Kinglassie, as he had me do once before."

Gavin gestured toward the gleaming walls. "Let him see this before he decides to scorch our home."

She nodded silently. He noticed her pallor, and how heavily she leaned against him. Rubbing her arm, he kissed the crown of her head.

John went toward the door. "I'll go up through the well and see wha' has happened inside the castle. And Robert Bruce must come down here. I'll see to it."

"John, be careful," Christian said. "Hastings' men may be waiting."

"I will be fine," he said. "You dinna need to come wi' me, Gavin. Stay here and see to your lady. She's looking muckle pale. I willna be gone long." He stepped out into the corridor and was soon wriggling through the opening in the well wall.

"Are you ill?" Gavin asked Christian. "You look like you cannot stand up any longer."

"I'm fine," Christian said. "Only let me sit." She took a step forward, but her knees seemed to buckle under her. Gavin caught her up in his arms, ignoring the stiff pain in his shoulder. Walking farther into the chamber, he set her gently on the floor, kneeling beside her.

Christian gasped and stared at a long tear in her skirt that was soaked with blood. She drew the cloth up over her knee and sucked in her breath.

Across her thigh, well above her knee, was a long gash. Blood had soaked through her hose and skirts. When she shoved down her woolen hose, exposing the wound, blood trickled freely down her leg.

She looked at Gavin, her face pale. He saw that her hands shook violently. "I felt some pain in my leg, and knew 'twas cut. But I didna think 'twas like this," she said.

"It happens like that in battle sometimes. In the turmoil, you did not notice the pain, or how badly you were cut. How did it happen?" He took her garter and twisted it tightly around her leg, just above the gash. Then he tore a strip of clean cloth from her linen undertunic, folded it, and pressed it firmly over the wound.

"I felt something sting as I fell down with Hastings," she said. "His dagger must have caught me."

"We need to stop the bleeding. And the gash is open. This pressure will help, but the cut will need stitching."

She bit her lower lip and nodded, calm and uncomplaining. Gavin wished profoundly that he could take this pain away from her. He knew her so well now; he knew that her very essence was made of finely tempered strength. She could endure any hurt, any crisis, and triumph. But he did not want her to suffer anymore, in body or in heart.

"You will be fine," he said, as he pressed on her leg.

"I know," she whispered. "You are here." She put her hand over his. "Gavin, touch me. Use your hands."

He glanced at her quickly, and felt a lightning sensation slam through his gut as the meaning of her words took hold. "My hands," he repeated.

"You can do it," she said. "I know that you can. You healed me once before."

He shook his head. "I only held you. You recovered, but I did not heal you."

"I think you did, Gavin."

He drew a deep breath, and another. Then he put the blood-soaked cloth on the ground and loosened the strip he had tied above the wound. "Lie back," he whispered.

She stretched out on the floor, straightening her legs. Gavin laid his palm over the freely flowing gash above her knee. The blood was sticky and warm against his hand. Her blood, he thought; her life. Resting his other hand over her heart, he felt its sweet thunder beneath his fingers. He closed his eyes.

Unlike Christian, he was not certain that his touch could make a difference here. But she had asked him, and he was willing to do anything for her. Even this.

Christian touched his arm, and the gentle contact sent a shiver of warmth through him. He felt the perfect breath of her love through her fingers. He wondered if she knew how deeply he loved her. He did not know if he had truly expressed it to her. Words and courtly gestures of love were not easy for him. But he wanted her to know. He wanted to convey it to her.

His mother had possessed a true gift, and he had long doubted his ability to do the same. As a child, whenever he had been sick or injured, his mother had laid her hands on him. Her touch had been a soothing comfort that had always healed.

Now he wanted to give that same sustaining love to Christian.

But he had not endeavored to use what his mother had taught him since the day that Jehanne had died in his arms.

He closed his eyes and drew a long breath. Long ago, his mother had described to him the simple method that she used in her healings: a hand on the head or over the heart, and a hand on the source of the pain. A prayer, any prayer, and breath. That was all, she had said: the gift itself, the touch itself, she had told him, was simply love, shining through the healer.

Gavin knew that the power his mother had possessed was truly rare. He had inherited her Celtic blood and her angelic features. But he had come to accept that he did not share the gift that permeated his Celtic lineage like the traces of gold in these walls.

But he was not entirely the same man as the one who had stood on a windy parapet, looking down at a sick waif trapped in a cage. He had been hardened then, from loneliness and anger and sadness. A true diplomat, neutral about all matters, he had been unwilling to involve himself wherever deep feelings were demanded from him.

And Christian had stirred very deep feelings in him. At first, she had reminded him of his lost wife, raising both sadness and sympathy in him. Then he had begun to admire her strength, her depth of feeling, even her willfulness. Loving her had opened him up to a heart and a cause outside of himself.

He knew himself better now. He knew that compassion and desire were more essential to his nature than anger and sadness. The truth of that stirred his blood, touching his very spirit.

When Christian had been near death in the abbey, Gavin had only held her. Jehanne's death had taught him a lesson in humility that the Angel Knight, adored and favored and proud, had learned well. He had not actually tried to heal Christian in the abbey, though he remembered wishing that he could.

Now, in this golden, beautiful chamber, Gavin wanted to give Christian the fullest flow of his love. And that, he realized now, was the truest essence of healing.

He held his hands serenely still over her leg and her heart. At first the warmth that gathered in his hands was subtle. He waited, letting whatever stirred there flow unimpeded by thoughts or pride.

And he suddenly understood the damage that lay beneath his hand. As if he could see it, he knew how deep into the muscle the slash had gone, how close to the bone. Though his eyes were closed, he could see, in his mind, when the blood flow diminished, then trickled, then finally seeped beneath the cover of his hand. He waited, breathing slowly.

A cloud of stars seemed to swirl over his head then, spilling down to flow through his body like liquid fire. The heat became a pulsing flood of radiance. He was drenched in beads of sweat that dampened his hair and slid down his face.

His hands trembled, not from fatigue, but from the extraordinary rush of heat and light that was like fire, and yet like flowing water. Swirling through his body, the sensation pooled in his palms like a sphere of light.

He took in the fire and the flow. Filled with it, he could not hold back its force. He let it go on a shuddering breath.

"DHIA," CHRISTIAN SAID, the merest breath. She lifted her head and stared.

Gavin's hands hovered a little above her chest and her leg. Beneath his palms, she saw tiny blue sparks glimmer, then spread like a halo around his hands. The colors changed as she watched. Blue shimmered through green into gold, and gold spun into white; shining brighter than candle flame around his hands, the delicate bands of light were there, and yet were not there.

The glow of the lamp and the glitter of the golden ore were heavy and coarse compared with the exquisite luminescence that radiated from Gavin's hands.

From his angel's hands.

The heat from his touch spilled into her like sunlight, life-giving and sweet. She felt as if her body and her soul were brimming with peace and comfort. Breathing in rhythmic harmony with him, she floated on that deep, slow cadence.

She had felt like this months ago in the abbey, wrapped in Gavin's embrace. And she knew that he had healed her then, just as he was healing her now.

In the abbey chamber, she had seen an angel in a dream. His face had seemed so familiar, his strength had been what she had needed. His arms had surrounded her with love.

Watching Gavin now, she suddenly understood: in that healing angel, she had encountered the purest essence of Gavin's spirit. When her own spirit had drifted out of her ailing body, her soul had touched the very soul of the man who had held her. And he had drawn her back.

She knew somehow that she and Gavin were meant to love each other, meant to heal each other, destined to grow and learn together. Their spirits had bonded forever in that moment in the abbey.

She looked at Gavin's strong, beautiful face lifted to the lamplight. He held his hands steady, his eyes closed, and breathed deeply and calmly. His hands were still surrounded by their own faint light.

And she knew that what flooded from him into her was the most perfect love imaginable.

Gavin exhaled and bowed his head briefly. She looked down and saw that the bleeding had stopped. In place of the open gash, there was a knitted line of clotted blood, clean and tight, as if the wound had had several days of healing time.

She stared up at him, and he smiled, a slight lift of his lip, his eyes bright. Christian loved him utterly and completely in that instant. "Thank you," she whispered, reaching out to touch his hand. He wrapped his fingers, warm and secure, around hers. "You surely have your mother's touch," she said.

He squeezed her fingers. "How do you feel?"

She smiled, feeling suddenly very happy, sailing on light, blissful joy. "I am fine and strong," she said. "And hungry."

He laughed, and glanced over his head. He stood quickly as three men came through the doorway of the chamber.

"My lord king," Gavin said, bowing his head. "We have found Kinglassie's treasure."

Robert Bruce walked down the steps. He inclined his head toward Gavin and Christian silently, and looked around the chamber with an astonished, speechless expression. John and Fergus followed him down into the room. Fergus grinned and whistled low, glancing around, then watched Robert Bruce expectantly.

The king turned, scanning the chamber. After a few moments, he went to Christian and held out his hand, helping her to her feet. She stood, her leg feeling fragile, but well. Gavin put his arm around her to support her.

"Cousin," Robert said, smiling widely. "You have been keeper of a glorious secret. This chamber is magnificent. Truly magical."

She smiled. "Indeed, my lord, true magic has happened in this place," she murmured. Glancing up at Gavin, she slipped her hand into his.

CHAPTER TWENTY-SIX

"HOLY SAINTS," Fergus said then, as he gazed upward. "The treasure o' Kinglassie is real. You did say that the gold had likely melted in the fire, Lady Christian. And here 'tis."

"This gold was melted into these walls long ago," Robert Bruce said. "And 'twill be our pleasant task to remove it."

"Now that the Scots have taken back Kinglassie, will you mine the gold, but order the castle burned to the ground?" Christian asked her cousin.

Robert half laughed. "I am no fool, my lady. I know well when an exception should be made to a rule. There is too much treasure"—he glanced at her, and at Gavin beside her—"and too much loyalty here, to destroy even a stone of this place. Kinglassie will stand, and its gold will help to support the throne of Scotland." He turned to Gavin. "I need a commander here, but I will not ask you to break a vow of honor."

"I am free to give my oath where I choose," Gavin answered. "My oath of fealty to Edward of England no longer holds, since he calls me outlaw now."

Bruce held out his hand. "Then I am pleased to call you friend and ally."

Gavin clasped the proffered hand and bowed his head. "I would be honored, my lord king, if you would accept the support and loyalty of an English-born knight."

"I would gratefully accept it of you," Robert said.

Watching, Christian felt the sweet sting of tears in her eyes. "My lord cousin," she said, "we found something else." She picked up the little golden casket and handed it to him. "There is a parchment in here that says something about a king, and about Merlin. But I canna understand all the words."

Robert Bruce opened the box and withdrew the little cylinder of vellum. Setting the box aside, he unrolled the parchment and looked at it for a few moments. Then he handed it to Fergus. "Can you make sense of this, priest?" he asked.

Fergus tilted the page toward the light and perused it carefully. "By all that's holy," he breathed, "this could hae been written by Merlin himself!"

"What?" Gavin said. "What does it say?"

Fergus tapped the page gently. "Some o' these words are in old Gaelic, and some are ogham symbols, from an ancient code used by the Druids. Both sections say near the same. Here, the ogham script—these odd scratch lines—mention that a greedy king will die, and a brave king will triumph and lead his people to peace. These marks, just here, refer to a small hawk, a merlin."

The others began to talk at once, but Fergus raised his hand. "The Gaelic says more. When the greedy king dies, the brave king o' Scots will gain victory. There will be peace throughout Scotland and Wales, too, it says, until the end of time. 'This is the prophecy of Merlin, a wise man and advisor to a brave king,' it says, just here."

"My God," Gavin said slowly. "There are other prophecies of Merlin, collected in a chronicle of the kings of Britain. I have read them myself. I had thought them invented, but this parchment has clearly been sealed here for hundreds of years."

"An undiscovered prophecy," Christian said, intrigued. "The Kinglassie legend says that when Merlin came here with Arthur, he left a great gift with the laird, fashioned by his own magic."

"Every part of that legend has proved true," Gavin said. "The gold hidden in the heart of the rock, the doves sent to find it and guard it—and now this evidence of Merlin."

"This prophecy surely must be the great gift mentioned in the legend," Robert Bruce said. The others turned to look at him.

"Merlin's words foretell victory for Scotland over England, with its covetous king. 'Tis a blessing indeed, at a time when we need such encouragement."

"When the greedy king dies," Fergus said, looking at the page that he still held, "then will the brave king o' Scots find triumph. And Edward of England is as greedy a king as ever was."

"But he is very much alive," Bruce said. "We will draw hope from this prophecy, but we must continue our resistance against England, just as we have been doing."

Fergus rolled the parchment and replaced it in the box, holding the casket reverently. "My lord king, with your permission, I will pen some copies o' the prophecy. If we send them out to every Scottish parish, the priests will spread the word in their sermons. Merlin's prophecy will give the people hope. Soon you will have all o' Scotland at your back."

Robert Bruce smiled. "I have never refused an offer of help from the Church of Scotland." He turned toward Christian. "Cousin, I must thank you for all that you and your husband have done for me, and for Scotland." She smiled and stood straight, but Robert frowned at her. "You look tired, Christian."

She nodded. "As are we all, my lord." She felt Gavin tighten his arm around her, offering his support. "My lord cousin, this chamber is the heart of Kinglassie, and I am privileged to have been its keeper. And I am grateful that 'twasna destroyed, after all, in the fire. But I confess that now I would like to return to the comforts of my home. Is that possible?"

Robert nodded. "My men have routed the English garrison by now. Most of the English soldiers have fled, and my men are transporting the bodies of those who died to the churches nearby. I think you may return now, if you wish."

"My lord," Gavin said, "we offer you and your men food and shelter for this night and for as many nights as you need."

The king grinned, a handsome, boyish smile. "We appreciate the offer, Gavin of Kinglassie. And I want you to know that I will claim only a portion of the gold and silver mined here for the treasury of Scotland. All else here is yours. The laird of Kinglassie and his lady have the greater right to what is here."

"Our thanks, sire," Gavin said. Bruce nodded, and gestured to John and Fergus to follow him out of the chamber.

Gavin touched Christian's arm. "Before we go back to the castle, lady," he said softly, "stay here for a moment." He turned away to sift through the jumble of golden things on the floor beside the low-burning oil lamp, then came back to her.

"Here," he said, sliding a glittering chain over her head. "Your other pendant is gone. This one may help to replace it."

She looked down, and caught her breath. Around her neck he had placed a necklace of small golden links. Suspended from that was a delicate golden pendant, shaped like a bird with outspread wings. The fanned wings were engraved gold, the tiny eyes were garnets, and its talons gripped a branch studded with emerald chips.

" 'Tis a dove," she said. " 'Tis beautiful."

He traced the design with the tip of his finger. "A dove of peace, worn by a beautiful lady," he said, "My own." He leaned forward and touched his lips to hers, a long, lingering kiss that took her breath, and took his. She wrapped her arms around his neck as he pulled her toward him. "Do you wish to stay here for a while longer, my lady?" he murmured languidly, snugging her hips to his. "There are other things I can do with my hands that you might enjoy." They laughed softly together.

"Your hands on me again would be heaven," she murmured against his mouth, "but that must wait until we are in a soft, warm bed. Just now, I am thoroughly tired, and very— " She stopped to utter a yearning moan as his lips took hers and his hands slid up her torso to brush the sides of her breasts.

"Very what?" he whispered, angling his mouth over hers, tracing his tongue along her upper lip. "Very eager? Very curious?"

"Mmm, those," she said. "But I meant to say, very hungry."

"Ah," he said. "We must satisfy that appetite as soon as we can. Come along, then, my lady. I think Kinglassie's treasure will keep a little longer in this place." He put his arm around her and helped her as she limped beside him to the door.

As they passed the still bodies of the guards who lay there, Christian averted her eyes, whispering a little prayer for their souls. Then she looked toward the tunnel entrance, where rich golden sunlight poured into the corridor.

Several doves flocked in through the opening. Brilliant sunlight crested their white wings and made haloes around their heads. They cooed softly and fluttered down to rest along the wall niches.

"The wild doves are truly the guardians of this place, Gavin," she said. "Will they mind, do you think, if we take their gold for Scotland?"

Gavin looked at the birds. "I think that they have been waiting for us to do just that," he said. "After all, Merlin sent them to guard it for the bravest king of Scots."

GAVIN WALKED THROUGH THE COURTYARD, cool wind rippling his hair and billowing his cloak. Late afternoon light threw long shadows across his path from the scaffolds and the high parapet. Voices, high and deep, caught his attention, and he glanced toward the sound. Michaelmas, Will, and Fergus's boys stood with John on the other side of the courtyard.

"And we held them terrified wi' our bows," John was saying as Gavin approached. The children stared up at his uncle with wide eyes. "Those English didna dare to move. We had our arrows trained fast on them—"

"Wretched dogs," Robbie interrupted.

"Aye, them, too," John said, hardly distracted. "Then, from the other side, King Rob's men attacked, fast as hawks after prey. They sliced at the English wi' broadswords and slammed them down wi' maces. Soon they were begging at our feet, and the king o' Scots took Kinglassie before he was even breathing hard."

"A fine story, though it may not make good dreams at night," Gavin said. "And I hear the mothers of these little ones are waiting to put them to sleep. Christian sent me out here to say she would play her harp for all of you if you come inside now. Fergus and Moira are sleeping the night here," he added to John.

"Go in, then, bairnies," John said, shooing them away, "and tomorrow I will tell you the tale of Merlin's gold, discovered after all these years."

"Tell us about the battle again," Patrick said.

"Later," Gavin said, turning the boy firmly in the direction of the great tower.

"I want to hear about how the wee doves saved us from the evil English commander," Robbie said.

"Not a tale for wee ears," Gavin said, giving the boy a gentle shove toward the tower.

"John, I forgot to tell you that my mother wants you to come inside and have some spiced wine," Will said. "She made it just for you, since you saved us all today by taking us to shore in the boat. She says you're very brave, and a fine man." Will looked speculatively at him. "Are you saddled with a wife? My mother has no husband, you know."

John cleared his throat, his face reddening. "Will, my lad, if you had said your pretty mother was waiting before this, I wouldna hae told such a long tale, " John said. "Now go in, and tell her I will be there soon."

" You blush like a bridegroom, Uncle," Gavin said, and chuckled. "Mayhap you've found your own wee dove."

"'Tis possible, lad." John laughed, embarrassed. Smiling, Gavin turned to see Michaelmas wandering away from the others, crossing the deserted courtyard toward the portcullis, which still hung crooked in its grooves.

Glancing up at the gate, Gavin knew that the portcullis would be fixed as soon as the massive chains he had purchased in Ayr arrived; the smith was eager to attach and align them. As for the rest of the repairs at Kinglassie, much was completed, and much was still left to do. But he would see all of it done, each detail discussed and carried out, just the way that he and Christian wanted

He turned to look at the great tower, hoping that Christian would come outside before the light faded. There was something he wanted to show her.

The sun slipped lower, casting a deep rich glow over the high walls. He glanced up, struck by the beauty and strength of his home. He would do whatever he could to keep it this way, whole and peaceful and safe.

"Gavin," John said quietly, "look." He pointed toward Michaelmas. As they watched, she knelt on the ground and scooped something into her hands. Her pale braid glinted like new gold.

Curious, Gavin walked toward her. She held a small dove, which made a weak cooing noise and fluttered helplessly as she held it.

"'Tis hurt, poor wee birdie," she said, as Gavin approached. "I saw it over here, hopping around. It canna fly. See, this wing willna come high like the other one."

Gavin nodded, watching the bird's awkward movements. He wondered if he should take it from her, and use the miraculous gift he had newly discovered in himself.

Michaelmas murmured to the bird, stroking its feathers, stilling its movements. Gavin watched, fascinated, awed by the sight of a beautiful child holding a wild thing with simple grace and perfect ease. A few steps behind him, John stood silently.

Michaelmas grew silent, too. Gavin wondered if she was praying over the wounded bird. She looked beatific and pure. Once again he was struck by the curious resemblance to his mother.

She smiled then, and opened her hands. The little dove cooed, pecked gently at her finger, and flew away in an easy, rapid flurry of wings.

Gavin stared after the bird. Still smiling, the child rose to her feet. "'Tis all healed, now," she said, and turned to walk away.

He took her arm. "Michaelmas—what did you do?"

She shrugged. Her eyes were summer blue, infinitely innocent, and wondrously familiar to him. "I helped the wee bird get better," she said.

"How did you help the bird?" he asked her. "Have you ever done that before?"

She nodded. "I've done it with birds, mostly, when the lads have knocked them down wi' stones, or tried to shoot them wi' their arrows. Once I helped Robbie's elbow when he scraped it," she added brightly. "'Twas bleeding, and stopped when I touched it."

"How?" he asked, gripping her arm. "How do you do this?"

She shrugged again. "I only close my eyes, and think how the birds look when they're beautiful, and flying. I think how much I love them, and my hands just get warm. And the other time, I thought about how Robbie's skin should look smooth. But I wasna sure I loved him," she added in wry distaste.

He blinked, taking it all in. Michaelmas reminded him so much of his mother suddenly: the wide blue eyes, the pale blond hair, the gently shaped mouth and nose. The grace of healing in her hands.

"Does Lady Christian know about this?" he asked softly.

She shook her head. "I have never told anyone," she said. "I wasna sure if 'twas a sinful thing to do this."

" 'Tis no sin to help a person or a bird or an animal heal," he said. He touched the silky crown of her small head. " 'Tis just your way of loving them. I can do it, too," he added.

She stared up at him. "You can?"

He nodded. "Someday I will tell you why we can both do this wonderful thing. But I'll keep your secret."

"And I'll keep yours," she whispered.

"Thank you," he said softly. "And thank you, dearling, for showing this to me." He was aware how silent, how still John had been throughout the last few moments.

Looking up, he saw Christian standing not far away, her cloak wrapped tightly around her, her face pale in the fading light. She was staring at Michaelmas. He knew, suddenly, that she had been there long enough to see what had happened.

Michaelmas ran toward Christian. *"Màthair!"* she called. "Will you play the harp for us now?"

"Soon, *milis,*" Christian said. "Go in, now. 'Tis getting dark." She kissed her daughter and went to Gavin.

"Did you know she could do that?" he asked her quietly.

She shook her head. "I have never seen her do that. How is it she has the gift that you have?"

"She is my mother's daughter," Gavin said.

She stared up at him. "Is that possible?" she asked in a hushed voice.

He nodded. "I believe so. I wondered about it before, but now I am certain. Although I have no real proof."

"There is enough proof, I think," John said, stepping nearer to them. "I've been wondering about the wee lass from the first. I saw my sister's face in her, just as she looked when we were children. Michaelmas has the healing gift. And she has our fingers. No document could give us greater proof of her birth."

"Fingers?" Gavin asked.

"Aye," John said, holding up his hands. His smallest fingers were curved distinctly inward. "These crooked wee fingers run in our family. Michaelmas has them. And she has the healing touch as well, that often goes with those hands."

Gavin splayed out his hands and saw the same gentle but certain inward curve. "I have them, too. I never knew it was a family trait." He frowned. "My mother must have given birth to her. And Henry must have been her father. I can think of no other explanation."

"I have always suspected that Henry was her father, though he wouldna say," Christian said. "He took her in so readily, and he was always gentle and patient with her. He treasured her as he didna seem to value anyone else."

"Years ago, just before she married Gavin's father," John said, "your mother told me that she loved Henry. But their families wouldna let them wed. Later, she was happy wi' her husband."

"But when she was a widow, Henry might have come to her," Gavin said.

John nodded. " 'Tis wha' I think. Henry was always good to her, though I canna say I liked the man well."

"Mother took a widow's vow of chastity after my father died," Gavin said. "And two years later, she went into the convent. I always wondered why she made that sudden decision."

"If she found herself a widow with child, she might have gone into a convent out of shame," Christian said.

"Aye. And she would have gone to that priory because she and Dame Joan were friends," Gavin said.

"Dame Joan must have told Henry all of this the day we came here to get Michaelmas," Christian said. She looked up at

Gavin. "Henry must have loved your mother very much. I knew he always resented that he was wed to me. Perhaps 'twas because he wanted only her, and she was gone. He must have grieved for her."

Gavin nodded. "'Tis ironic that she was Scottish." He turned to look toward the doorway of the great tower, where his half-sister had gone. "Surely my mother loved that child well. And she must have been the one who named her for Saint Michael. Mother venerated the angels particularly. She believed that her healing gift came from them."

Christian took his hand. "We have had this bond all these years, and didna know it, Gavin. My adopted daughter is your half-sister. And Henry brought us that bond."

"Someday we will go back to where Michaelmas was born," Gavin said. "Mayhap a local priest will have some document, or some memory of her birth or baptism. If there is proof, we will find it."

"Well, I, for one, am certain o' her parentage," John said. He cleared his throat. "I'll go inside now. There's some spiced wine waiting for me. And I wouldna want the sweet lass stirring it to think badly o' me for being late." Grinning briefly, he walked away through the thickening shadows.

Christian looked up at Gavin. "I truly think that you were meant to be with us here at Kinglassie," she said softly.

"Aye, so," Gavin said. He gathered her into his arms. "From the first moment I saw you, one link after another brought us together—Jehanne, Henry, my mother, and Michaelmas." He shook his head slightly in wonder.

"'Tis as if an angel has been watching over us, drawing all these threads together," she said. "Mayhap 'tis your mother."

He smiled at the thought. "I would not doubt it. She would have been well pleased with what has happened here." He looked over at the tower, where the setting sun now touched fire to the cool surface of the stone. "Months ago, when I first saw this place, I felt somehow that Kinglassie was my home."

"Even though 'twas a ruin," she said.

"Even then," he said. "And even though the lady who had

ruined it was an ill, angry little wildcat who would not accept help easily from an English knight."

"I have learned to accept it now," she said softly.

He smiled down at her, then turned and drew her along with him toward the great tower. "Come here. I have something to show you." He pointed toward the doorway. "Look up there."

She did, and gasped. The amber glow of the setting sun shone upon the new stone that had been set in place high above the doorway of the tower.

The wide, smooth slab bore the carved design of a pair of feathered wings, expertly engraved into the surface, which framed the entwined letters *G* and *C*.

"Our marriage stone," she said, grasping his hand. "When did you have it made?"

"I asked the head stonemason to do this a few weeks ago," he said. "He set it in place while we were in Ayr. But with all that happened when we returned, I had no chance to show you."

"Are the wings meant to be falcon wings for Faulkener?" she asked. "Or are they for the Angel Knight?"

He shook his head. "Others may look at this and think of Faulkener, or the Angel Knight. But you and I will know that the wings represent the angel you once thought me to be. And they will remind us of the wild doves that are so much a part of Kinglassie."

"The doves that guarded Kinglassie's treasure," she said thoughtfully. "Although you did not know that when you decided on the design. Wild doves, and angel's wings. 'Tis fitting."

She tilted her face up to him, serene and beautiful in the glow of the setting sun. Gavin loved her so much in that moment that he thought he would burst with it. He bent to kiss her. The warm, giving press of her mouth beneath his stirred a passion inside him that he could barely resist, here in the courtyard, with the swirl of the twilight wind around them.

"Let's go in, Christian," he said. "Let's go home. Play your harp for me. I have an urge to take a bath." He grinned.

"I would love a bath. But first I promised the children I would play the harp for them. And then I will play for you, if you like. I know a weeping song you may want to hear."

He lifted a brow. "I have no desire to weep, my love."

She laughed softly. "Did you forget that the weeping songs are ancient songs of healing? And I owe you some healing, I think." She frowned. "Your arm was hurt today. I saw the wound."

" 'Tis a scratch, and soon gone." He laid a hand to either side of her face and looked intently at her. "One miracle after another has come into my life since the day I found you in that cage. I have learned so much, Christian," he said. "So much. I had lost my faith in miracles long ago."

"Believe again, Gavin," she murmured. "You have a gift that brings them in. You will have more miracles in your life."

"We both will," he said. Then he opened the door to the tower, and they stepped through together.

AUTHOR'S NOTE

Sometime before May 1307, a prophecy of Merlin was said to have been discovered in Scotland, which foretold the death of *"le roi coveytous,"* and predicted peace for both Scotland and Wales thereafter. Scottish priests circulated news of this prophecy, rallying the people of Scotland with what the English called false preachings.

Nothing is known of where or how the prophecy was found. In such cases, imagination can be allowed to fill the gaps in the historical record: nearly anything might have happened.

In July 1307, King Edward, swearing to capture the Bruce himself because his commanders had failed to do so, left his sickbed at Lanercost Abbey and rode only as far as Burgh-on-Sands before he collapsed and died. The mysterious prophecy was partially fulfilled. Several years later, under King Robert Bruce, Scotland finally achieved independence from English domination.

Although I often embellish history with romantic and paranormal aspects, I always strive for accurate historical detail whenever possible. For example, Christian's dilemma in the cage was based on Edward I's imprisonment of two Scottish women, Mary Bruce and Isabel of Buchan, in timber and iron cages between 1306 and 1310. Extant documents describe the placement and measurements of the cages, and Christian's cage is very close to those.

But in searching for information on medieval Scottish harping, I found little available until I talked to two women who know and love the instrument.

Through Sue Richards, an accomplished master of the Celtic harp, I met Ann Heymann. Ann is one of the few harpers in the world who plays a wire-string Celtic harp in the old tradition, on the left shoulder. She is also a historian of the harp. The knowledge she shared with me during an enjoyable visit enabled me to write about my Scottish harper with authentic detail.

Celtic harp music is extraordinarily beautiful. If you would like to hear the kind of music that the heroine of this book might have played, I suggest these recordings: *Queen of Harps* by Ann Heymann (Temple Records, 1994); *The Harper's Land* by Ann Heymann and Alison Kinnaird (Temple Records, reissued 1992); and *The Hazel Grove* by Sue Richards (Maggie's Music, 1995).